Tremor Violet

Books by DAVID LIPPINCOTT

E PLURIBUS BANG!
THE VOICE OF ARMAGEDDON
TREMOR VIOLET

David Lippincott

Tremor Violet

G. P. Putnam's Sons
New York

For Joan

Part I

NO sign proclaims it. No graven rock or burnished brass plaque marks its beginning or end. It simply exists, a hairline fracture in the earth's crust, sometimes visible, more often not, a minor miscalculation in the massive forces which shaped the earth, and is referred to with surprising offhandedness as the San Andreas Fault.

For many years faults such as this had been considered the result of earthquake activity along a given line; more recently, scientists have decided that faults are the cause, rather than the effect. Even more recently, development of the plate theory raised the question of which San Andreas the fault should be named for: the one in northern California, the San Andrés de Giles in Argentina, or the San Andrés Tuxtla in Mexico. All lie along the edge of the same plate; all are in areas subject to earthquake activity.

To Californians eager to believe that all things evil or unpleasant originate out of state, this is somehow reassuring. In fact, one California geologist now insists the fault should actually be named after all three. To illustrate his point, he draws an arc from San Andrés de Giles up through San Andrés Tuxtla, bending it slightly to include the quake-ridden city of Managua, Nicaragua. Then he allows the arc to sweep gracefully up through Los Angeles and San Francisco and finally sends it out to sea to disappear under the polar cap, lightly touching the western coast of Alaska on the way. His explanation, while perhaps more fanciful than accurate, does account for virtually all the earthquakes from South America to the Bering Strait in one great sweep.

In any case, proof of the San Andreas Fault's ancestry is of far less significance than its effect, which is to kill people. At least five hundred perished in the San Francisco classic of 1906, an incredible fifty thousand in the Peruvian spectacular

3

of 1970, and a small but prophetic sixty-four in the tremor that struck the San Fernando Valley, just beyond Los Angeles, in 1971. For some years, psychiatrists have pondered why anyone should choose to live anywhere near it—or, even more baffling, why both private citizens as well as city, state, and federal agencies should build not only homes, but schools, hospitals, and offices directly on *top* of it—but without success. (And while pondering, some of the psychiatrists quietly build homes on top of it themselves.)

Most qualified experts now predict that a major quake in Los Angeles itself is less a matter of *if* than of *when*, but as with people who live on the edge of a volcano, the reaction of the Angelenos is uniformly low-keyed. Occasionally, a cabal of fervent officials passes a stringent new building code or announces a tentative plan for restrictive zoning, but the codes are quickly circumvented and the plans forgotten.

In short, when the San Andreas Fault, a rupture in the earth's skin of uncertain parentage but monumental potential, finally roars its way through the third largest city in the United States, no one will be able to say the inhabitants were unwarned, merely disinterested.

Chapter One

You will be visited by the LORD of hosts with thunder and with earthquake and with great noise. . . . Then deep from the earth you shall speak and your speech shall whisper out of the dust. And . . . I will appoint over you sudden terror . . . and let loose the wild beasts among you. . . . You shall eat the flesh of your sons . . . and your land shall be a desolation, and your cities shall be a waste.

— Isaiah 29:6,4 and Leviticus 26:16, 22,29,33

ON the Day, Friday, September 9, the first tremor was recorded at 4:32 in the afternoon. As noted by the seismograph at the Western Seismological Institute in Goldstone, Colorado, it was not a particularly large one—in fact, less than 1.3 on the Richter Scale. Dr. Ridgeway and his young associate, Dr. Feiner, agreed that the tremor was diffused rather than focused, appeared to be isolated rather than part of a series, and was definitely nontsaunamidic. In the records, it was formally listed as SAF (34 N-108 W), #1175. For their personal reference, they gave it the code name Ursula, in the same way weathermen use an alphabetical progression of women's names to identify hurricanes.

Many people in the greater Los Angeles area were later to say that they felt Ursula and that she gave them a premonition of dire things to come, but the truth is that Ursula was barely perceptible, caused practically no damage, and went largely unnoticed. A couple of places were exceptions.

In the estate area of Beverly Hills, north of Sunset, where

the homes are set far back from the roads up long, winding driveways, the steep contours of the land cause any tremor to become magnified. Adam Mosely, Jr.—Addie—raised his head in surprise and let go of Mishi's hand as he lifted his upper body far enough off the terrace to see what was happening. Mishi—like Addie, fifteen—had been lying on her back and had to roll over onto her stomach before she could raise herself to join him. From lying too long in the sun with only her hand to protect her eyes, at first she could see nothing. Addie's eyes adjusted more rapidly, and he watched as the water in the pool they were lying beside began rolling back and forth, almost slopping over at each end, as if it were in the bathtub of an ocean liner plowing through heavy weather.

"What is it, Addie, what is happening?" An ill-concealed note of anxiety was in Mishi's voice, a tone oddly magnified by the overly precise English she had been taught in Tokyo, each word too perfectly pronounced and immaculately enunciated. Beneath her, Mishi felt the ground tremble again and heard a loose rock from the retaining wall around the terrace tumble onto the flagstone; as her eyes slowly adjusted themselves to the afternoon sunlight, she saw the water slosh over the coping at the far end of the pool. She took a ladylike little swallow of air. "Oh, my, Addie. Oh, my."

"An earthquake. But just a little one, Mishi. They happen around here, well, you know, pretty often." Addie was surprised at how reassuring his voice sounded; he didn't remember ever feeling this protective before. The sensation was not unpleasant.

Mishi studied his face to see if he really was as calm as he sounded. She decided he was but shuddered a little anyway. "I don't believe I like your"—for a second, Mishi grappled to pluck the right word from her not-always reliable vocabulary—"your earthquakes. No, not at all." Then, her eyes, following a peculiar sound to its source, saw the enormous white rubber birthday swan bobbing solemnly at her over the edge of the pool. Mishi bowed her head to it and giggled. "It

6

doesn't feel like anybody's birthday anymore. The swan is trying to tell us. Oh, indeed, it is trying to tell us *something*."

In a way, Addie knew, the white rubber swan was physical evidence of his family's biggest problem. His mother had given the thing to him more than a month ago—at fifteen, for Christ's sake—a giant rubber bathtub toy to float in the pool. His mother was a drunk. Or, as the family doctor had more politely put it when trying to explain it to him a few years before, "A chronic alcoholic. Alcoholism, you see, is a disease, Addie. Just like the measles. Only in your mother's case, beyond the usual symptoms, there is a more than ordinarily strong, in fact, almost bizarre, sense of time displacement." To Addie, what was wrong with his mother didn't seeem like the measles at all. But the old doctor had been right about the time thing; usually, his mother didn't know what year it was. Crazy, Addie decided. To see her, you would think she was much like anybody else—oh, she acted kind of woozy and wasn't allowed to drive a car and slept an awful lot—but her lack of any sense of time was what really gave the show away. Yet he should count himself lucky, people told him, that she didn't tear off her clothes in Jurgensen's or climb palm trees on Wilshire or try to ride a horse into the Beverly Hills post office the way some of the area's more colorful lady drunks did.

Lucky? They should try to live with her. The day she bought him the rubber swan, she was convinced—and nothing anybody could say would talk her out of it—that he was eight. And a giant rubber swan, she pointed out, was a perfectly lovely present for any lucky birthday boy.

Addie had only sighed. All he could do was try to pretend not to notice it when she yelled at the housekeeper, Mrs. Herkimer, for serving dinner in the evening (at night, his mother frequently thought it was morning) or tried to telephone people who'd been dead for more than twenty years or thought that he was eight, two, or occasionally, that he hadn't even been born yet. Sometimes Addie wished she'd been right on the last point. Always, he wished he could manipulate time

7

as easily as she did and, like her, escape the grinding loneliness of his life.

Although tall for fifteen, Adam Mosely, Jr., still moved with the suppleness and grace of a young boy. The hair was tow-colored, bleached almost to whiteness by the sun, the same incessant sun that had washed his face and body the honey-gold of a Swedish skier. But Addie's eyes were the most startling thing about him. Like a child's, they seemed too large for his head, perpetually widened, as if filled with ceaseless awe and wonder.

That he was good-looking was no secret to Addie; people frequently mentioned the fact. But looks seemed a totally wasted asset in fighting the deadening loneliness he experienced living way out on Tutweiler.

His father, Adam Mosely, Sr., was of no help, and that Addie blamed on his mother, too. Adam Mosely was president of the Los Angeles Tribune Corporation and had a much more direct way of coping with the problem of Addie's mother, Georgia: he never came home. From one of the few friends Addie had, he'd heard that his father was now living with the lady who owned the newspaper. In fact, the same source allowed that this was how Addie's father had *become* the *Tribune*'s president, but Addie doubted both statements. He could not have explained why.

A largely absent father—even if one with whom he had little in common—only compounded Addie's feeling of isolation. He was too young to drive a car, and Tutweiler Drive, while beautiful, lush, and lavish in its use of land, was miles from any place where there were people of his own age. And without ever meeting her, Addie loathed the mysterious lady who might or might not have stolen his father. And the mother who'd let her.

Until Mishi. Mishi changed everything. She lived in an equally large house farther up Tutweiler, the two estates separated by a dense screen of trees, stone outcroppings, and an anemic stream, which during the Los Angeles rainy season mushroomed into a small river. Mishi was easily as lonely as

8

Addie, although for completely different reasons. Her father was the Japanese consul in Los Angeles, both a new post and a promotion for him—and the first in which he held sufficient rank to bring his family with him. With some dismay, the Yoshura family quickly discovered that outside of diplomatic circles, this part of California respected the Japanese only as gardeners or former enemies.

The blow fell particularly hard on Mishi. Correct English was a standard part of the education provided for the family of any rising young Japanese diplomat, but Mishi had gone to exceptional lengths to perfect it for all the new friends she would make in the United States.

"It's *too* perfect," an American boy from the diplomatic colony had told her in Tokyo. "Too perfect, too formal, too old-fashioned. You sound like some cat out of Henry James."

Mishi didn't have the faintest idea who Henry James was, but the gist of the message reached her. "Oh, indeed, that is serious. And what does one do, please, to avoid sounding like the cat of Mr. James?"

The friend had started to laugh, but then the serious expression on Mishi's face reached him, and he tried to be helpful. "Movies. Go see every American movie you can find in Tokyo. Then you'll hear how kids really talk."

With desperate earnestness, Mishi tried. Sadly, she discovered all the newer American movies showing in Tokyo were dubbed into Japanese and were therefore useless. Finally, she came across an art theater which showed "classic" American and British films with their original sound tracks and devoured them hungrily, day after day, week after week, sitting in an almost-deserted theater taking notes.

It was a resourceful, if exhausting, effort, and the vernacular Mishi picked up from these movies had a curiously dated ring to it, peppered with the resounding wisdom and smug cant of the middle thirties and early forties. In any case, the effort was wasted, living so far from LA proper—and with the prevailing local attitude toward the Japanese less than encouraging—she got very little chance to use it.

Until she met Addie, she found herself, like him, in elegant but virtually solitary confinement; after that, everything changed. They saw each other all day, every day—they were both on summer vacation—and talked incessantly about everything and nothing, laughing, playing, building a wall around themselves against the emptiness of the lives they had lived a few weeks before, exuberant even in their silences because each now had someone to be silent with. If love can be defined as the mutual sharing of loneliness, they were in love far beyond what their ages would seem to allow.

They felt this way from almost the moment they met, even if the meeting itself had been less than auspicious.

About a month earlier, Addie had been lying by himself in the sun beside the pool, his arms outstretched and his long legs lying wide apart. The afternoon sun, beating hard upon his bathing suit, caused an involuntary stirring; he struggled with himself for a second, caught somewhere between guilt and half desire, wondering whether to plunge into the pool and let the water cool him down or slip into the pool house and deal with himself more satisfactorily. Guilt won.

With a sigh, he took off his trunks and dived into the pool, narrowly missing the floating swan. After about ten vigorous laps, he swam to the ladder and pulled himself briskly out. Any remaining glandular drive was dispelled by twenty fast sit-ups. On his feet again, he leaned over, picked up the towel, and began drying himself. Suddenly, from the ancient avocado tree in the corner came an enchanted giggle, followed by the rustling of leaves and the sound of an overripe fruit jarred from its branch and splatting on the flagstone.

"Who's there?" demanded Addie of the tree. "I said who's up there?" Remembering his nakedness, he wrapped the towel around himself as quickly as he could. Then he returned to staring up into a tree, trying to see better, moving around and bumping one of his toes on the flagstone.

The tree giggled. There was more rustling of leaves and small branches, then: "I'm sorry—about your toe, I mean."

It was a girl's voice, a young girl's voice, but with a strangely

10

mature way of speaking and belonging to someone with an unpleasant way of spying on people from trees. Addie became outraged.

"You hid up there, dammit. You hid up there and saw me without anything on. You saw everything."

The giggle again. "Oh, yes, indeed. *Everything.*" Another giggle. "Play it again, Sam."

Addie blushed. As the injured party he felt pure indignation should be winning, yet he knew he was coming out second best. "What are you doing in our tree?" he demanded, positive he should sound aggressive.

"I live in the next house. I was lonely." The tree apparently realized the explanation wasn't entirely adequate and suddenly added, "So I was . . . I was . . . casing the premises." A small sigh indicated the tree knew the words were not quite appropriate. "I'm sorry."

But the word "lonely" had struck a receptive chord in Addie. In spite of his anger, he found his curiosity growing. "You sound funny. The way you talk." Slowly, through the leaves, he began to make out an impish face grinning at him; the skin was a yellow-golden color, but the hair was dark. Staring hard, he could see the explanation of the odd speech in the slant of the girl's eyes. There was more rustling, and enough leaves parted to reveal that the grinning face was attached to a tiny, slim body which finally swung to a lower branch and dropped lightly to the terrace.

Addie and Mishi stood staring at each other. Mishi's face became solemn, and she performed a modest Oriental bow. When she straightened up, the smile returned, accompanied now by a delicately raised eyebrow. "In my country, the way *you* speak would sound even funnier. 'Reach for the sky or I shall fill you full of daylight,' *indeed.*"

Addie laughed and Mishi laughed, although neither of them was sure why, and they sat down beside the edge of the pool and began to talk. The loneliness slowly ebbed out of them, replaced by the simple pleasure of having someone to talk to, even if some of the language didn't quite make sense.

They talked like that for hours, it seemed, and by the time a familiar voice began calling Addie's name he felt he'd known Mishi since the beginning of time.

"Addie . . . Addie . . ." called his mother in soft bewilderment, and as Addie turned toward the house, his heart sank. "I *thought* I heard voices, Addie. What are you doing out here in the middle of the night?"

Watching her come down the path toward them, Addie realized his mother must present a spectacular sight to anyone not used to her. As always, Georgia Mosely seemed completely sober at first glance, yet instinct quickly told you something was wrong; a second later you realized the something wrong was the way Georgia was dressed—in an immaculately draped long evening gown and wearing all her jewelry, convinced, in spite of the sunlight, that it was the middle of the night. Addie swore to himself. He and Mishi had talked their souls bare, but his mother was one subject that Addie had carefully avoided. Gripping Mishi hard by the elbow, he pulled her to her feet, "This is Mishi Yoshura, Mother. She lives up Tutweiler—in the old Perkins place."

Mishi's face gave no sign that she noticed anything peculiar. Murmuring slightly, she performed her proper little bow before straightening up to face Mrs. Mosely.

Ignoring the bow, Addie's mother stared at Mishi for a moment, then turned away to speak to Addie. "You don't use your head, Addie. This girl shouldn't be here."

Swinging back toward Mishi, she explained. "You people are mostly in detention camps. I don't know what you're doing out and running around." Abruptly she turned back to Addie. "You could be arrested for consorting with the enemy. I should probably call the FBI. That's what I mean about not using your head."

And without another word, Mrs. Mosely headed back toward the house, pausing only to stare anxiously at the sky.

Addie kicked himself for his stupidity; the fact of a drunken mother was both too important—and too difficult—to hide.

12

Reddening, he fumbled for words. "I'm sorry," he said miserably.

Mishi smiled and appeared not to notice. "How very remarkable!" she said. Then, seeing Addie's expression, she touched his arm. "It is not a thing to worry about, Addie. It happens now and then. Even though we look quite different, people think we're North Vietnamese or Chinese mainlanders. It is ridiculous, of course, because we Japanese have completely different facial structure and coloring." She turned toward Addie to make sure she had the words right; Mishi's vocabulary was excellent, but these were difficult and seldom-used expressions. "Still, Westerners—many people —are easily confused. And some of them, some who still feel strongly about events from the past, want to punish us even for things we are not. My father told me that once, during the Vietnam War, someone in Texas came right up to him on the street and tried to punch him in the nose." She laughed again to try to put him at ease. "Oh, well. Someone always gets it on the Dawn Patrol."

Bitterly—and beginning to feel sorry for himself—Addie turned away. "She knows you're Japanese. That's not what she's confused about. It's the time. She's confused about the time and thinks it's World War Two. Last week, on my birthday, she thought I was eight. . . ." He gestured helplessly at the white swan bobbing on the water, suddenly afraid he was close to tears and even more afraid that Mishi might laugh at him.

Mishi sensed his mood immediately and settling down cross-legged on the flagstone, reached up with her hands to indicate Addie should join her. "How very sad. How very sad for her, how very sad for you."

With disbelief, Addie stared at her. The few friends that ever made it out to Tutweiler seldom survived their first meeting with his mother.

"Perhaps," said the incredible Mishi, poking at the swan absently with her toe, "it is something we can be sad about together."

Because of Mishi, the four weeks before the Day turned out to be the happiest Addie had ever known. The days merged effortlessly, yet each one, they discovered, held something new and wonderful. For a long time, they didn't make love, although both of them, in private, had fantasies of what might happen. Addie was afraid he might not really know how or that he might in some way hurt Mishi or that, worst of all, she might be shocked that he even held such thoughts. While Mishi, captive to five thousand years of Japanese custom, was as startled by her own desires as Addie was by his. Instinctively—and more practically—she also sensed Addie's feeling of inadequacy and suspected that any suggestion of forwardness on her part might lead to disaster.

So that when the moment finally arrived—the night before the earthquake, in fact—the experience was completely unplanned and largely accidental. As a result, it seemed as easy and pure and natural as breathing. To any outside observer, Addie and Mishi might have been the last two innocents on earth.

All the old fears in both of them vanished. Even on the Day, as they saw Ursula slopping water farther over the pool's ends and heaving more rocks from the wall to the flagstone, they were calm, unconcerned, and afraid of nothing.

And when, from inside the house, they heard Addie's mother yelling at Mrs. Herkimer that the enemy must have bypassed Pearl Harbor and was starting to shell the Pacific coast—they merely smiled at each other and waited impatiently for the night to come so they could make love again and fall asleep in each other's arms.

They had no way of knowing that the San Andreas Fault, which might or might not have its beginnings in Mexico, Argentina, or just around the corner, had its own plans for the evening.

At about 4:43—the station log was never very accurate—the broadcast engineer finally reached Ken Corbit in KBDT's traffic helicopter. Corbit's job was to fly over greater Los

14

Angeles, checking the flow of traffic on the main arteries in and out of the city and reporting chattily to KBDT's listeners on which areas were clear, which were pocked with bottlenecks, and, if any given highway got into a hopeless mess, to suggest alternate routes.

Corbit was bored. Below him, he could make out individual cars inching along the freeway and could almost hear the swearing, the blowing of horns, and the crunching of fenders. (Actually, he knew, only his altitude made the traffic appear slow; in California, anyone reckless enough to travel at less than sixty invites flattening by trailer truck.)

The patterns below seemed normal, and Corbit had just banked his helicopter to turn south toward Ventura when the receiver in his ear began crackling and buzzing.

"Ken, do you read me, Ken?" The sound in his ear stopped being a buzz and began forming words.

Corbit yawned loudly enough to make sure it was heard on the other end and prepared himself for the string of petulant warnings he was about to receive. "I hear you, I hear you."

"Is there any sign of it from up there?"

"Any sign of *what* from up here?" Corbit yawned again, this time louder; the station manager bugged him.

And Corbit bugged the station manager. "For Christ's sake, Corbit, why don't you try tuning in on your own station once in a while? There's been an earthquake. A little one, but anyway, an earthquake. We didn't feel anything here, but KTLX, damn it, is already on the air with a story about it."

Corbit sniffed. Slowly, he shifted in his seat and peered down through the plexiglas bubble. If there'd been a quake below, he could see no effects. But telling this simple fact to Henry Dawes, the station manager, was far too uncomplicated. "Can't see a whole lot from up here," Corbit drawled. "Oh, there's a bridge or two down, and Mulholland finally fell into the ravine, but—"

The receiver in his ear began buzzing angrily. The language Dawes used was, for once, colorful enough to make even Corbit smile.

With a sigh, he pushed the headset away from his ear. He had wanted to be a disc jockey, and when Dawes had hired him, that was what he promised. But then they found out about his flying a chopper in 'Nam, and he'd been doing the traffic reports ever since. They'd given him a couple of nice raises—damned good ones, in fact—but Dawes always stalled when Corbit brought up moving on to the DJ assignment. Which was why Corbit hated the station manager's guts.

Dawes was only being practical. LA had plenty of aspiring DJ's but not many traffic reporters with any color at all; most of them gave their accounts in the actuarial tones of a market analyst reciting soybean futures. Because Corbit, while not quite good enough to make an outstanding DJ, was miles ahead of any other traffic reporter, KBDT's audience share was growing and sponsors were lining up to climb aboard. Corbit knew this, and the fact made him increasingly tempermental and hard to handle, which was why the station manager hated *Corbit's* guts.

From the displaced receiver, Corbit heard a new voice on the headset and pulled it back over his ear: the engineer told him the 4:45 was coming up.

Now came the only part of the job Corbit liked—talking. A wide smile crossed his face as the cue came and he went into his patter. "Hello, down there, you shook-up people. Understand you had a little quaker. Well, maybe a Richter One will shake some sense into the creeps who set the fifty-five-mile-an-hour limit. Yassir. This is Ken Corbit . . . your guy in the sky . . . with the latest guff about traffic and stuff. From all over the map, with all the"—Corbit paused just the precisely effective length of time—"latest information on road and traffic conditions. Now then, since you poor slobs are hitting the asphalt early today. . . ."

For anyone currently in the radio business around LA, it was pretty easy to see why Corbit would never make an outstanding disc jockey.

But before the night was over, KBDT's guy in the sky would make a more than adequate hero.

16

Chapter Two

Dr. McKelvey cited the major advances of the last few years in identifying earthquake precursors . . . the concern, he said, "is that a prediction itself could in some ways be worse than an earthquake . . . many would rather take their chances with no warning."

—From an article in the New York *Times*, February 28, 1974, reporting on a meeting of the American Association for the Advancement of Science.

T HE predicting of earthquakes—where and when they will occur and of what magnitude they will be—is so haphazard a science as to be no science at all. At Goldstone, Colorado, Drs. Feiner and Ridgeway of the Western Seismological Institute were trying to fill in this blind spot.

The basic piece of equipment in any seismological laboratory is the seismograph. This is a gleaming wooden box, perhaps two feet by three, and reverently covered with a dustproof glass top. Inside is a slowly moving roll of calibrated graph paper and a set of small, electronically controlled styli.

While the modern seismograph is modest in size and not particularly impressive-looking, its direct antecedent, the seismometer (developed in the late 1800's), was not only large, but mammoth to the point of being unmanageable. In essence, the early seismometer was nothing more than a giant pendulum. When the base supporting the pendulum moved, however imperceptibly, the pendulum would swing back and forth in an easily visible arc. There was only one major difficulty: picking up a distant tremor required a pendulum at least eighty-four feet long—and an impractically high ceiling. Scientists were also troubled that while the seismometer could detect, it could not record.

Rapidly, over the years, a system of levers and springs shortened the length of the pendulum (and also overcame the fact that a pendulum moves only bidirectionally and two-dimensionally). At the same time, a single mechanical stylus and moving graph paper were added, and the seismometer became the seismograph, recording as well as detecting.

Today virtually all the mechanical aspects of the device—the pendulum, the levers, and the springs—have been replaced by electronic apparatus, shrinking the seismograph in size while increasing it in accuracy. In fact, the seismograph in Ridgeway and Feiner's lab was so sensitive that—as young Feiner liked to say—"At ten miles, we know if a tractor backfires, but at two miles, well, we know if a mouse farts."

Regardless of how sensitive any seismograph may be, it can measure only two factors—the size of the tremor and the timing of the waves it produces. From this information, however, calculating the tremor's distance becomes relatively simple. The two basic wave patterns set off by an earthquake travel at different rates of speed: the primary, or pressure, waves (P-waves) move directly through the ground in a straight line from point to point at a speed of 3.5 miles per second; the secondary, or surface, waves (S-waves) snake along the earth's crust like the bump in a snapped whip, meandering along at only 2 miles per second. Using this difference—much as sailors once counted the seconds between a flash of lightning and a thunderclap to make a rough estimate of a storm's distance—scientists can fix the precise distance of the tremor's focal point, or epicenter, from the seismograph. In Dr. Ridgeway's laboratory, this figure was calculated automatically and delivered as part of the computer printout.

Finding the direction of the earthquake requires a slightly more complicated process. To accomplish it, the services of the WWSSN (World-Wide Standardized Seismograph Network) are called upon. Each seismographic station of the network knows its distance from the tremor by its own calculations on the P-waves and the S-waves. This information is relayed to Goldstone automatically, where a circle on the map representing the distance of each seismograph from the tremor is drawn. The point where all of the circles intersect is established as the epicenter of the tremor. Again, in Dr. Feiner's setup, this work was done automatically by the computer and delivered as part of the printout. By the time the printout arrived, then, it contained not only the size of the tremor (as recorded on the Richter Scale) but the exact point in the world where the tremor occurred.

The Richter Scale appears confusing at first. The difficult thing to grasp is that while the numbers on the scale advance numerically, the forces they represent advance logarithmically. Thus, a Richter 2 represents a force not twice but ten times a Richter 1. A Richter 3 is one hundred times it, while a Richter 9, largest on the scale, signals a force one million times as large as the smallest.

If all earthquakes sprang from the same source—pressure of the liquid mass beneath the earth's crust to break through it—it might be simple enough to feed all this information into a computer and come up with an accurate series of tremor predictions built on time between eruptions, locations, etc. In fact, considerable progress doing precisely this has been made on the East Coast, country unmarred by fault formations like the San Andreas. However, earthquakes along a fault have a different source. They fall into the category of sliders, a process in which one part of the earth's crust is apparently trying to catch up with the movements of the adjacent—but geologically completely different—part of the earth's crust alongside it. For a long time, no one had been able to provide a completely satisfactory explanation of how or why faults exist or why they act the way they do.

Enter the plate theory of global tectonics. This theory rejuvenates the ancient notion—but with factual substantiation—that the world originally consisted of a single giant landmass surrounded by one great ocean. Billions of years ago, this theory holds, the single landmass broke into our smaller present-day continents, which later drifted apart and became separated by a whole series of oceans.

It is not hard to see why this notion persists. If you take the two American continents and compare the outline of their eastern coasts with the outline of the western coasts of Europe and Africa, you can see that the two shapes would fit together like pieces of a mammoth jigsaw. Even the offshore odds and ends are accounted for: Ireland slips across the Irish Sea and fits neatly into England and Wales—something the Irish would never stand for—while the resulting landmass could easily be stuffed into the Baltic.

If you then move the Americas eastward across the Atlantic, the bumps in Europe fit into the hollows of North America, while the bulge of Africa slides efficiently into the curving strip of Central America. At the same time, the receding area of Africa under the bulge is conveniently filled by the breastlike swelling of Brazil. All very neat—if a little mysterious.

But the plate theory does not leave unexplained the mechanics of how one vast continent became separated into so many small ones. To put it very simply, the theory visualizes the earth's surface as a series of plates—probably no more than six or eight—each one supporting a major landmass, with an additional plate for each ocean. These plates are constantly in motion. Eons ago, the plates carrying the landmasses moved in such a way that they became separated from each other by the plates bearing the oceans.

Along the western coast of the United States, however, no ocean separates the point where the Pacific Ocean plate meets the Atlantic Ocean plate: the Pacific plate, carrying the ocean as well as the upper part of California, and the Atlantic plate, carrying the balance of California, North America, and the

Atlantic Ocean, are separated only by the San Andreas Fault—and therein lies disaster. The problem is that the Pacific plate is creeping slowly northwest at about an inch a year, while the Atlantic plate is traveling in the opposite direction—southeast—at about the same rate of speed. As these plates move, tremendous resisting forces develop, and when part of one plate shifts suddenly—overcoming the resisting forces of friction and breaking free from the other plate—the tremendous forces released result in massive tremors, totally unpredictable because the variables providing the resistance to the plate's movements are considered virtually infinite.

This last part of the plate theory is what Dr. Feiner—and to a lesser extent, Dr. Ridgeway—chose to challenge. To a computer, Dr. Feiner thought, there is no such thing as an infinite number of variables; the ITC 600 XE was installed, and he set to work reducing the variables to a logical progression.

To begin with, Feiner fed the computer all available information on each past quake along the fault, major or minor, as well as the intimate details of all tremors preceding it. This initial input established the benchmarks. To this body of facts, he added all variables which, within reason, could be expected to exert any type of force on the earth's surface: earth core and crust temperatures, tidal statistics, torque thrusts, weather conditions, the phases of the moon, positions of other planets and their approximate gravitational pushes and pulls, syzygy predictions, long-range jet-stream patterns, sunspot variations, activities of the cosmic field and the Van Allen belt, data on the outer neutron field, and an incredible array of minor statistics that might conceivably bear upon forces along the fault.

"If I thought they'd help, I'd throw in projected rates of screwings per square mile per minute," Feiner told Ridgeway, who smiled only faintly. Ridgeway was Feiner's senior, in both years and position, and knew that Feiner was convinced the computer would eventually find a set of rules, a galaxy of conditions, that would lead to a theory from which firm

21

predictions could be made. He himself was less sure but was willing to give Feiner all the leeway he needed.

Immediately, then, after each new tremor, all information collected on the tremor itself—as well as the benchmark data and the corollary fact matrix—was fed into the 600 XE and the computer asked if it could yet deliver a significant prediction on the next quake. Invariably, the printout came back a disappointing NO PREDICTION—INSUFFICIENT COROLLARY INFORMATION AVAILABLE.

The vital statistics surrounding Tremor Ursula had already been given the computer, and the 600 had obliged with its usual answer. But the computer had no answer at all to explain the uncomfortable, uneasy feeling this apparently minor tremor gave Feiner; the transistors themselves, he was later to tell people in Goldstone, seemed to be trying to articulate some message of warning, some sense of foreboding, far beyond reach of their limited speech.

Frustrated, Feiner shrugged, turned disconsolately to the blocked-off blackboard, and wrote in Ursula's name just below Tillie's; at the same time, he riffled through the book of available names and mentally chalked in an alphabetically viable one for the next tremor. It was, he thought, a whimsical name for an earthquake.

Violet.

The bell at the main entrance warned of closing time. Isaac Rosholman signaled the driver of the little electric bus to stop, and because he was a member of the staff, the driver ignored the mutterings of rebellious sightseers and detoured, letting him off near the moat which separated the animals from the animal watchers. They were in Area Five (African and Asian Wildlife), a vast tract of the Griffith Park Zoo sculptured to provide animals like lions and tigers with a natural habitat, yet equipped with moats so the animals wouldn't follow their instincts and devour the zoo's visitors. The particular section toward which Rosholman headed was also divided internally by another, less visible moat separating the carnivores from the wildebeests and bonteboks and gazelles and giraffes, allowing the latter to graze in unaccustomed safety. These animals, however, never quite grasped the principle of the moat and chewed the grass with one nervous eye well peeled for their traditional enemies. On the other hand, the lions *did* seem to understand that the moat would forever prevent them from picking off any easy snack. Possibly, they were even amused at the expense of stuffing them full of dead meat when so much living flesh was only a few dozen yards beyond their reach and would be so easy to bring down.

Quickly, Rosholman checked his watch and headed toward a corner of the moat, coming to a halt beside a small metal sign, "*Felis leo*—Africa," along with a scholarly, if telegraphic, description of lions' eating, sleeping, and mating habits. After a quick look to be sure none of the staff was nearby, Rosholman reached into his pocket, withdrew a package wrapped in plastic, and whistled softly. For a moment nothing happened. Then, slowly, his dignity marred only by a small cloud of flies clustering around his eyes, Rosholman's old friend Three Toes made his slow way through a thicket to the edge of the moat and stood there wearily, his great tail swinging listlessly back and forth, his rheumy eyes staring silently at Rosholman and blinking petulantly from the combined annoyance of the afternoon sun and the flies. This was their regular rendezvous, one which Rosholman kept faithfully, even on his days off. The plastic covering was removed, and Rosholman took the chunk of prime meat, heavily loaded with vitamin supplements, and sent it sailing through the air across the moat. Three Toes—*Felis leo* half-blind and almost toothless—accepted it as his due, immediately lying down and chewing it, although with difficulty.

"How are you, boy?" asked Rosholman in a hoarse whisper. Three Toes gave only a flick of his tail in answer, his ancient teeth still working on the chunk of meat. For a lion, the portion was pitifully small, but Rosholman suspected the rest of the pride let him have little or none during regular feedings. And even this small amount, along with the vitamin supplements and whatever else Rosholman could smuggle in to him, might help keep the curator or the zoo's vet from noticing how feeble Three Toes actually was; keeping him alive had become a mission with Rosholman.

The lion was like himself, Rosholman thought. Once both were young, both were powerful, and when they spoke, the world listened. Simple old age had reduced Three Toes to his present misery; the forces behind Rosholman's disintegration were more complex. Until three years ago, he had been staff supervisor at the Crane Memorial Zoo in Portland, the nation's foremost. Staff supervisor was not like being a curator, of course—his education was not up to the arbitrary standards for that—but the post made Rosholman the man in charge of the staff actually responsible for maintaining the zoo's animals. The job was no easy assignment, for the zoo was laid out much as this one in Griffith Park, only on a grander scale. Built without bars and with the animals roaming as freely as God had intended, Crane Memorial had the same system of moats to keep the animals under control and the public safe. Rosholman's undoing came at the hands of a twelve-year-old boy named Philip Williams, who, on a dare, slipped over the protective railing, climbed down one side of the moat and up the other, and found himself face to face with a startled cow elephant. Philip was unfazed and produced a peanut from his pocket, an idea born from years of going to the circus. But the nervous elephant, with her newly born calf standing only a few feet behind her, was equally unfazed. She picked Philip up in her trunk, dashed him to the ground, and then moved forward to step on him.

Rosholman happened to be standing only a few feet away, talking to someone, and raced over to the moat, pulling the boy out just before he was trampled. Briefly, Rosholman was a hero; pictures were taken and articles written. And outside of a broken collarbone, a damaged arm, and a badly frayed

24

set of nerves, Philip Williams should have counted himself lucky.

Instead, his father sued the zoo.

Confidently, the city prepared to defend itself. Then, in an unfortunate interview with Rosholman, a reporter was able to quote him as saying that "any kid who's crazy enough to go near a cow elephant with calf deserves anything he gets." Whether or not Rosholman was right, a legion of ordinary Portland citizens were outraged at the attitude of a man who would put an animal's rights ahead of a child's arm, and the mayor, the City Council, and the Board of Aldermen found their confidence melting. Shaken by the publicity, the attorneys suddenly recommended a quick, quiet, but sizable settlement.

Rosholman was fired.

The whole thing was unfair, of course. Rosholman was a keeper of animals, not a public relations man. For a lifetime, starting back when he was a child in Austria, he had worshiped animals and enjoyed an almost mystic communion with them. Animals could be understood; animals could be loved; animals didn't turn around and sue you for saving their lives. Philip Williams' father, a human, was not only ungrateful and untrustworthy, but grasping.

Now, like Three Toes, Rosholman had to take what he could get, and all he could get was a post as head night keeper of the Griffith Park Zoo, a sort of superjanitor's job, his work constantly being reviewed by a host of smart-aleck young curators and supervisors. There was, at night, no public to appreciate his magic with animals (and, not entirely by accident, no small boys to infuriate the elephants).

Farther down the path he was on, Rosholman could see two of the day men making their last rounds. He hissed at Three Toes to get away; he had no real idea whether the other men knew of his daily rendezvous with the animal, but Rosholman did know they disliked him—always needling him about getting to his job early, for instance.

25

"Hi, Ike," called Battock, one of his principal tormentors, after checking his watch and nudging his companion. "Bucking for curator, Ike?"

The other man from the day staff looked away, embarrassed. He liked Rosholman—or more accurately, didn't dislike him—but was too timid to fly in the face of majority opinion.

"Or maybe," continued Battock, "y 're looking for another kid to feed to the elephants." Rosholman noticed that Battock had a gold tooth which showed only when he was smiling at his own cleverness.

"Hey, Battock," said the other man, who had decided the joke was being carried too far. "We got to check the lower west gates before we punch out. Let's get it over with."

Battock hesitated—clearly, he would have liked to bait Rosholman some more—but gave in; the other man's mention of punch-out time was enough to overcome his meanness.

Sourly, Rosholman watched them leave, not bothering to return the wave from Battock's partner. He wasn't sure which kind of man was worse: a man who was deliberately cruel or a man who didn't have the guts to speak up to someone who was. Battock, he suspected, was anti-Semitic, which was reprehensible enough, but Rosholman's painful childhood had also taught him a lot about people who remained silent rather than risk trouble with people like Battock. The general dislike of the other men for him, he likewise attributed to anti-Semitism.

In Isaac Rosholman's world, the concept that the dislike could spring from a small thing like his early arrivals and late departures or even that there was an element of jealousy about his job that had nothing at all to do with his being Jewish was just too simple for him to accept.

Starting to curse Battock silently in Yiddish, Rosholman caught himself and smiled grimly. If he was such a good Jew, what was he doing working on a Friday night? With a grunt, he turned and headed toward the main office, where he would spend most of the night. From there, he would make

26

his rounds and check up on the small night staff, assuring himself they weren't trying to sneak any more naps than they usually did. The work was dull, he knew, and simply making sure that no people got into the zoo and no animals got out could make anyone sleepy.

At the office, the departing day supervisor made an effort at small talk and then proceeded to the solemn business of handing Rosholman the keys to the safe.

Nothing of much importance was inside. Keys to the reptile house (kept locked all night), stacks of special passes for school groups and community projects and the contingency plans, drawn up years before, in case of "nuclear attack, invasion, or natural disaster such as earthquake or flood." When Rosholman had first arrived at the zoo, he'd read the plans and been appalled. All of them called for the same action: destroy the animals rather than risk having them escape. After this first, required reading, the contingency plans were replaced in the safe and by now had almost disappeared under diagrams of electric alarm systems, sewage-pipe overlays, drainage layouts, and other more frequently consulted matter.

But of all the people in the world not to have in charge of an open-plan zoo during an earthquake, a man who loved animals considerably more than he did people would head the list. It was almost as if Violet herself had chosen Isaac Rosholman for the job.

27

Chapter Three

In other days a wedding was a function to be avoided. A terrible solemnity hung about the proceedings, which made it second only to a funeral in the matter of gloom . . . tears were frequently shed during the service, and also during the speeches, and the bride was supposed to depart in a flood of tears. . . .

—MRS. L. HEATON ARMSTRONG,
Etiquette & Entertaining (1903)

IF Ursula went completely unnoticed at the Griffith Park Zoo and produced only some highly unscientific forebodings at Goldstone, Colorado, at least one resident of Malibu Beach was acutely aware of her—although for all the wrong reasons. When Mrs. George Vorhees—Laura—felt the ground beneath her house tremble, she wondered for a second if it could be a sign from God. Ever since Laura had reached her decision three weeks earlier, she'd half expected some expression of His wrath for the mortal sin she planned, but none had appeared. Oh, there'd been an unpleasant struggle with the pharmacist about refilling the Tuinal prescription again so soon, but God, Laura figured, must have more direct ways of speaking than through the local druggist. Laura gave a small, sad smile of wonder that the early teachings of her stern Quaker father could still transform an earth tremor into a divine message, then dismissed the thought; the ground was shaking from a small earthquake and nothing more complicated than that.

Even the smallest tremor, though, should have caused Laura concern; her glass-walled jewel of a house, perched insolently on the high cliffs above Malibu, was cantilevered directly out over the Pacific. Only Laura's preoccupation with what lay ahead for her tonight allowed her to dismiss Ursula so lightly.

Once the trembling stopped, Laura returned immediately to the job at hand; she was sitting in her dressing room, staring intently into the mirror, searching her face to see if the years of misery had left any visible marks. Not allowing any traces of emotion to show was terribly important to Laura. "Good children never cry," her father had announced at regular intervals during her childhood. (He always made such pronouncements with a warm, almost Pickwickian twinkle in his voice, a manner that endeared him to many people. But Laura knew he meant the statements to be taken as sternly and unyieldingly as the words indicated, and she suspected the benign twinkle was only a device he used to convince both the world and himself that he was a warm and charitable man.) And in a lifetime struggle to please this long-dead father, Laura had practically lost the ability to cry. Or to smile. Or to do anything. Today would be an exception.

From somewhere below the house, Laura heard a rock crashing down the cliffside. Automatically, she looked down. Then, for the first time, she saw them.

There, over by the sliding closet doors, moving across the thick gray carpet in a pattern as precisely defined as traffic on a freeway cloverleaf were the ants. The ugly, loathsome army of small, winged ants was back.

Laura's sense of order was offended. Early tomorrow morning her bedroom would be invaded by strangers, and the ants might be noticed. Some reporter with a nose for symbolism, straining for words and phrases that would move his readers to pity, might even mention them in his newspaper account. If there was one thing Laura didn't want, it was for people to feel sorry for her; she was in agony, her existence was in ruins, she was dying by inches, but these things must be secrets between herself and God. The ants, therefore, required dispatching.

Suddenly, two problems simultaneously solved themselves. Earlier Laura had been searching for a plausible reason to demand that Gilla, her maid, come in before the usual time—Laura wanted to be discovered quickly, before too much chemistry could take place—and getting rid of the ants would provide it.

"Gilla," she called loudly. "*Gilla!*" Laura was startled to discover Gilla was so close at hand that the maid was inside the door almost before Laura's voice died away. Fighting her own surprise, Laura struggled to remain looking calm; with effort, she even managed a sweet smile.

"The ants are back," she explained, slipping off her stockings to get ready for her bath. "I've called the exterminators—they promised they'd come first thing in the morning—but I'm afraid I'll have to ask you to get here early to let the men in." From beginning to end Laura's statement was a lie; the exterminators routinely checked the house twice a year, but Laura had no idea when they might be due next. For something like an invasion of ants, they would come as soon as summoned, but Laura had not called them. Useful as it was, the lie made Laura uncomfortable. She wasn't very good at deception and wasn't sure what she'd said was entirely convincing. Uncertainly, she amplified her announcement. "I'm sorry to ask you on such short notice, but I'm going to be out late, so I'll probably still be asleep when the men come."

For a second, Laura and Gilla stared at each other. Laura was so unaccustomed to lying it never occurred to her that Gilla's answer might be a lie, too.

"Can't, missus." Gilla sighed and shook her head in a carefully executed imitation of Hattie McDaniel. "Got to put my mother in the hospital, missus, and I can't get here until noon, maybe not till two, three o'clock." She paused and pretended to ponder the problem deeply, then shook her head again at the impossibility of rearranging schedules. "Fact is, missus, instead of being able to come in early like you want, I was

30

going to tell you I'd have to come in *late*." Gilla eyed Mrs. Vorhees nervously; good jobs had been lost over such small matters. "I'm really sorry, missus, but my mother, well, she's one real sick lady."

Laura's first reaction was to cry out at the injustice of the world, to beat her hands against the wall in frustration. Almost as quickly, though, a wave of guilt swept across her; she was thinking of herself when she should be concerned about Gilla and her mother. To as desperately lonely a person as Laura, Gilla's display of devotion and love was profoundly touching.

Putting one hand to the side of her face in genuine dismay, Laura found herself blinking hard. "Oh, Gilla, I'm so terribly sorry. You never mentioned your mother before. But I'm sure everything will work out all right; doctors can do wonderful things today."

Gilla nodded in appreciation and moved quickly to nail down her job while Mrs. Vorhees was in a vulnerable position. "Your clothes is all laid out for later, missus, and I ironed the black stole. It got wrinkled coming back from the cleaners."

In the mirror, Laura went over the items neatly arranged on the bed, and the sight saddened her. Tomorrow George Vorhees would be sorry; tomorrow her son would be sorry; tomorrow everyone would be sorry. Even Gilla. The thought of Gilla abruptly reminded Laura that a response was called for. Looking away from the mirror again, she gave Gilla as warm and gratified a smile as she could manage. "I see you did, Gilla. Thank you. But you shouldn't have bothered with all you have on your mind." Listening to herself, Laura knew the response was inadequate and felt a familiar wave of shame creeping through her. For the same father who had stoppered her emotions had also educated Laura to believe that everything she did was wrong, inadequate, or immoral, and Laura wore the resulting mantle of guilt the way other women wore basic black. When she tried again, the smile was close to apologetic. "Please, Gilla, don't worry about tomorrow. And if there's anything at all I can do. . . ."

"Thank you, missus." Gilla said this with a weary little sigh, something that almost always produced a sympathetic response from Mrs. Vorhees. Because the reaction was so dependable, Gilla was stunned when, instead of suggesting she leave for home early, Mrs. Vorhees suddenly produced an additional request.

"I know it's late, Gilla, and I hate to ask, but I was wondering if you could make me some hot chocolate." The warm, apologetic smile again. "My stomach is funny." Laura hated hot chocolate—and hated even more asking Gilla to make it—but her reading and research indicated that something bland on the stomach reduced the possibility of nausea.

Gilla looked at her strangely. She knew how Mrs. Vorhees felt about hot chocolate, and the request baffled her. But then, she'd been acting funny all week.

Grunting—she was ready to go home, and this strange command would hold her up another five or ten minutes—Gilla shuffled submissively out of the room and headed obediently toward the kitchen.

Once there, she abruptly dropped her Hattie McDaniel mantle as her Stepin Fetchit shuffle was replaced by a purposeful stride that culminated in an angry kick at a leg of the kitchen table. Turning back toward the still gently swinging pantry door, Gilla raised her middle finger in the direction of Mrs. Vorhees and loosed a string of invective. She filled the kettle and slammed it on the stovetop, turning the gas to its highest, hottest setting. The cup and saucer for the cocoa were dumped noisily on the counter.

Gilla had been born and raised in First Creek, Alabama, and the stereotype black she'd been playing was a role she knew well. But it was that and nothing more: a role. In an unjust world, it proved useful in dealing with the police, petty officialdom, and the likes of Mrs. Vorhees. Much as she loathed her, the job with Mrs. Vorhees was a good one; among other things, that crazy lady paid in cash and didn't believe in

32

withholding taxes or Social Security. But ideal as the job was, it didn't mean Gilla had to *like* Mrs. Vorhees.

The sudden whistling of the teakettle started Gilla moving again. As she added the steaming water to the hot chocolate powder and watched it turn a deep, frothy brown, an idea slipped into Gilla's head. From the back shelf she withdrew a small package of Ex-Lax and melted two of its chocolaty squares in a tablespoon held over the burner. These she sniffed briefly; then she added the syrup to the cocoa in the cup, stirring vigorously until it disappeared. A small smile flickered across her face. Wherever Mrs. Vorhees was going tonight, that crazy lady would have something more urgent than her goddamned exterminators to worry about. With a flourish, Gilla added a dollop of Redi-Whip to the cocoa and, shifting to her First Creek, Alabama, shuffle, headed back toward the bedroom with the steaming mug.

White people, she conceded, probably had troubles of their own, although Gilla had great difficulty imagining any that couldn't be solved by the extraordinary circumstance of being rich or the simple fact of being white.

Laura Vorhees would not have agreed. She considered herself in agony, and the moment she heard Gilla leave the house, Laura found herself struggling hard with tears that did not want to be contained. ("If you have to *cry*, at least do your sniveling in your own room," her father had once told her when she became suddenly unable to hold back the flood any longer. "Inflicting self-pity on others is pure selfishness." Even the most Pickwickian twinkle could not soften the sternness of this statement.)

Slowly, Laura toured her bedroom, touching favorite objects she had shared a lifetime with: the Chinese porcelain figures whose heads and hands moved solemnly up and down when you tapped them; the tiny amber turtle, bought at the New York World's Fair in 1939, which had lost its right front foot on VE-Day, 1945; the ornate marquetry and marble chest of drawers inherited from her mother, its patina so smooth and polished you could sometimes catch your own reflection on its surface. Tomorrow these things would still inhabit her room; she would not.

Laura found she was close to tears again, but this time she controlled herself easily. No stern father was necessary to point out the self-pity and sheer sentimentality implicit in her short tour of the room. Her decision had been made on what she considered a purely rational basis and should stay thus. None of the conditions that had brought her to it were new, but recent events had combined with old problems in such a way no other resolution was possible. And actually, without her realizing it, the conclusion was one that probably could have been predicted many, many years before.

But to Laura, the problems had begun when she married George Vorhees. Twenty years ago friends from Philadelphia's Main Line had warned her—and they had been right. They pointed out that she would have to move to the Coast, that the Coast was different and the people who lived there even more so, that Laura would come to hate both it and them, and that George Vorhees, the flamboyant owner of a rapidly expanding chain of appliance stores spewing out television sets and trash compactors from Oregon to the Mexican border, was no prize in any part of the country.

"He's just not *you*, dear," they said, a polite way of pointing out that a man with a reputation as a swinger was an odd match for someone as prudish and sexually naïve as Laura. They did not point out that Laura seemed an equally odd choice for someone like George; it would have been unkind.

But Laura didn't listen, either to what they said or to what they were too kind to say. She was overwhelmingly—almost pathetically—in love with George Vorhees. Sometimes she was baffled that out of all the women he might have picked, he had chosen her. Gropingly, through the sense of worthlessness and guilt her family had attached to her like an extra skin, she searched for some reason. She was not ugly, but neither was she beautiful. Like George, she was tall. But while with some women, height can appear striking, hers, she knew, only made her look stretched out and awkward. The answer eluded her. For not only was George handsome, but he wore his height like a badge of authority; he was worldly where she was parochial, outgoing where she was shy, experienced in sex, where she was unknowledgeable, untried, and totally unrealistic.

One could lay the blame for this, too, on her father; he was quick to express a strong, sometimes brutal opinion on every other conceivable subject, but sex was a word Laura had never even heard him mention—with or without the twinkle. Her mother was equally silent. The result was that Laura had only her own highly inaccurate fantasies to draw upon, daydreams of an extraordinarily bland sort, with roots firmly established in the sentimentally antiseptic movies she had seen.

The advice of her friends in Philadelphia was put aside. Laura married George Vorhees in an ecstasy of happiness and anticipation and headed West with him to hammer her fantasies into reality. Their marriage was a living out of what Laura's friends had been too kind to point out to her.

"For Christ's sake, Laura, don't you *like* to screw?" George would ask, propped up on one elbow and staring in disbelief. "You just lie there like a lump of warm liver. Are you scared or frigid or queer or what?"

For Laura, the question had no answer. Day after day she struggled, trying to discover why she felt nothing but loathing. In spite of her fantasies, sex was ugly, sex was dirty, sex was painful. Typically, Laura decided the fault must be hers, unable to make up her mind whether she was simply frigid or she might even be a latent lesbian. Remembering her days at Miss Prior's School for Girls, Laura, almost with relief, opted for frigidity.

George claimed he'd never heard of anything so ridiculous, that she just didn't know what she was missing. To show her, he tried arousing her with pornographic movies from the collection he kept stashed in the basement. Outside of being

35

surprised that George had such a collection—and that his library was so extensive—Laura had no reaction whatsoever to the movies. Recklessly, George began forcing himself on her; stubbornly, Laura answered by locking her bedroom door.

Somehow a son was produced. He was dutifully named after Laura's father, Henry Severn II (classmates at grammar school would first simplify the name to Seven, while those at prep school would later corrupt it completely to Digit, a name Laura loathed).

The baby, Laura hoped, would draw her and George together, for in spite of everything she was still desperately in love with him. But Henry Severn II proved to be no help at all; George remained as distant as ever. Slowly, almost imperceptibly, their lives began to take on completely different shapes. As his chain of appliance stores grew, George said that managing the mushrooming business meant he had to spend increasing amounts of time visiting both his outlets and suppliers. And instead of using Los Angeles as his home base, he found it more and more convenient to operate out of their country house, a remodeled Spanish abbey they'd dubbed The Mission, farther up the Coast at San Luis Obispo. "More in the middle of the whole territory," George lied to her. "I can save a hell of a lot of travel time."

Reluctantly, Laura accepted the facts. The fault lay with her. She had loved George—worshiped him, in fact—but she had failed him. She supposed by now he had a permanent girlfriend tucked away in Obispo; the fact bothered her most when she considered that the girlfriend was probably living in the abbey she'd so lovingly remodeled for George. Sometimes she tortured herself trying to imagine what the girl looked like but was unable to. She was sure of only one fact: the girl would not fail George as she had.

During the last year George had come home to Malibu only once—and that in the middle of the night. He had telephoned first, so that Laura wouldn't think he was a burglar and call the police, and had stayed, Laura guessed, perhaps an hour. Laura never even saw him. Upstairs, she could hear him crashing around below, apparently searching for something, going from room to room, opening and slamming shut desk drawers and closets. In her bed, Laura lay listening. Part of her desperately wanted to go downstairs so that she could at least speak to him. But another part was too timid. Halfheartedly, she toyed with the idea of calling downstairs on some pretext or other. She wanted to see him so badly she would even have allowed him to force his painful and ugly and unmentionable sex upon her. But George apparently had no such plan in mind.

Upstairs, Laura could hear the front door slamming behind him and then—silence. Miserably, Laura lay there, wondering which of her many transgressions God was punishing her for now.

Eventually, Laura assumed, the ultimate punishment would arrive in the shape of George's lawyer; the girlfriend in Obispo, it would be explained, was not going to wait forever and the lawyer would delicately begin exploring the ground rules for dissolving a marriage of some twenty years. The idea appalled Laura, but she was resigned to it.

The thought that the failure might not be hers alone rarely occurred to her. The whispered rumors of dark goings-on in Obispo, the odd remarks about George that people in Malibu occasionally made, the persistent flow of stories concerning The Mission all were submerged in her own cloud of guilt.

"Punishment," her father had been fond of saying, "is the just lot of those who fail."

Now, on the Day, Laura's eyes moved away from the clothes neatly laid out by Gilla and wandered over to the bedroom windows. Sudden shafts of out-of-focus incandescence, blindingly bright as the sun reflected off the glistening Pacific into her eyes, were such a staggeringly beautiful sight that for a moment Laura wished she could change her mind. But the decision had been made, for better or for worse, and should not be tampered with; Laura turned her eyes from the window to shut out any further temptation.

Three weeks earlier George's long-expected lawyer had arrived. At first, Laura was stunned to discover that divorce was only a tangential subject; what George wanted of her was more complicated and painful than that. Listening to the lawyer drone on, however, Laura slowly began to realize that George was every bit as fallible as she; with some people, this fact alone would have been enough to change their minds, but with Laura, it only reinforced a decision she had more and more frequently been contemplating.

Only one alteration was made by what she gleaned from the lawyer. Now, instead of just for herself, punishment was required for both of them. She had failed George, and she must be punished for that. But George too had failed, and he also must be punished. Her fate would be quick and painless; his would be lifelong and unexpectedly agonizing. George's lawyer, that day three weeks before, had unwittingly placed the weapon for his destruction in her hands.

With a sigh, Laura checked the small desk clock: she was still ahead of her self-imposed schedule. Everything was ready; everything that had to be done had been done. Provision had even been made for a long bath, one of her favorite tranquilizers. Walking through the dressing room, she paid only passing attention to the continuing parade of ants. They, she decided, would be left for someone else to punish.

About two miles from the Sylmar Power Station, slightly to the north of the town of San Fernando but still in the Valley itself, the streets are cramped from having to follow the irregular, tiered levels of the Valley's beginnings rather than the neat patterns a city planner might draw. At its lower end the Valley spreads out to include Van Nuys and then flattens completely to become Burbank; at its other end the Valley grows increasingly narrower and deeper, finally coming to an abrupt end at the Van Norman Dams, which hold back the some seven billion gallons of water trapped in the reservoir behind them.

At the corner of Rinaldi Street and Balboa Avenue, almost in the center of the Valley, is a tiny church with a grandiloquent name: the Cathedral of St. Basil. This building is the spiritual heart of the Valley's Greek Orthodox community. A block and a half from it just before Rinaldi dives under the San Diego Freeway, sits a faded Greek restaurant and meeting hall, Georgi's, where the wedding feast of young Sporades Kristaboulos and Anna Nabukian was being celebrated. Although the Greeks and Armenians are traditional enemies, the hostilities had been put aside for the day; the Nabukians, a second-generation family of Armenians, were even holding the ceremony in this strictly Greek enclave. They themselves lived in the grape-growing area around Bakersfield, an Armenian stronghold, but Anna, who had lived and worked in Los Angeles for the last two years, insisted she be married in the city. ("None of my friends will come all the way up to a wedding in Bakersfield," Anna had told her father firmly, and under the threat of not having a traditional wedding service at all, the father gave in.)

Anna and Sporades sat now, tense and uncomfortable, at the head of the wedding table, which was laid out in a large T across the floor of Georgi's reception room, the bare walls hung with grape-leaf garlands and massed tropical greenery. With the exception of the couple, the men and the women were almost completely separated; the younger men were roaming around drinking Fix, a powerful beer imported from Greece, while their elders drank either the Greek wine resinata or the more potent ouzu or Metaxas. Anna's hip friends from Los Angeles looked strangely out of place mixed in among these white-haired men; the old ones studied the intruders coldly, staring at them through the thin smoke of their hand-rolled cigarettes, strong-smelling and acrid, hanging beneath mustaches dripping resinata. In one corner, the bazouki players had gathered and the curiously plaintive music was starting, while the old men, lilac sprays in the buttonholes of their shiny black suits, arranged themselves in a long line, joined hands, and began slowly circling Anna and Sporades, standing now in the room's center, as the traditional dance of *hasapiko* began. Their wives, still sequestered, sat solidly in their chairs, clapping to the slowly accelerating tempo of the music.

On the orders of Georgi himself, the waiters rushed to the tables at the first sound of the music and began taking away the good china and replacing it with cheap crockery; the tradition, once the dance reaches its climax, is for each guest to throw as many plates to the floor as he can to show approval, and if good china is left on the tables a minute too long, the bill can be astronomical.

Standing beside Anna and hearing her sigh with weariness, Sporades squeezed her hand; he knew that, like himself, she was only going through with this endless ceremony out of respect for her family. Earlier, in the reception line, was the only time either of them had really enjoyed themselves. To the older Greeks and Armenians, they spoke only English —and that very rapidly—so that barely a word was comprehended. What Anna and Sporades said varied from the ridiculous to the mildly insulting but was delivered with such engaging smiles that the old ones, understanding only the expression on the young couple's faces, would smile back warmly and wish them well, too, and kiss them both on each cheek. With the young Americans from Los Angeles, the process was reversed: Anna and Sporades spoke only Greek. (The expression on their friends' faces would have been something more than bafflement had they understood even a single word of what was being said about them.)

For a while it was fun, but the game paled quickly and then ended entirely as the traditional festivities took over. Looking at his watch and then at the guests, Sporades grew depressed. "My God," he whispered to Anna, "it's got to end sometime."

"They look good for hours yet," Anna noted. Then she laughed, indicating two old men in a corner, their arms interlocked in a drinking contest. "Except for Uncle Nubar. I

40

don't know the other man. But I don't think either of them will be upright by the time we go."

"I will," answered Sporades wryly, and blew her a kiss. Part of the arrangement with their families had been that they would be allowed to leave early; the party itself would continue into tomorrow.

"Aieeeeee!" a young nephew of Sporades' suddenly yelled, and then began whirling around the inner periphery of the circle as if possessed, his hands held high above his head, spinning faster and faster until his head and upraised hands and body were a reeling blur. "Aieeeee! Aieeee!" His voice had a strange sound, as if the force of the spinning were drawing it from the bottom of his soul.

Not too far from Georgi's, the great Van Norman Dams said nothing, but looked down on the scene silently. They would be heard from later.

Another place where Ursula, ambling her modest way through LA, was acutely felt was on the thirty-third floor of the Los Angeles *Tribune* building. Here, Adam Mosely —Addie's father—held forth in the *Trib*'s executive penthouse. Ursula did not pick the building out of malevolence; it was simply that any modern high-rise sways considerably from the slightest tremor, and the *Tribune* building was the tallest in town. In fact, the structure was one floor taller than the building code for the area permitted; the *Trib* had friends in city government, a privilege for which the citizens of Los Angeles were to pay dearly later that day.

Adam Mosely wore the titles of both the Tribune Publishing Company's president—besides the *Trib* itself, the company included several other communications ventures—and the paper's editor-in-chief. But he wore them emptily; the real power remained with the owner and chairman, Mrs. Dorothy Grimes. Like both the New York and the Washington *Posts*, the *Trib* based its reputation on investigative reporting, particularly in the area of national politics. Mrs. Grimes, in fact, was so involved in political reportage that she usually kept very close to the *Trib*'s Washington bureau, where the action was. Although Washington was where Adam had started, he now spent most of his time in LA—feeling helpless as he watched Mrs. Grimes turn pure investigative reporting more and more into advocacy journalism. He was, he thought, every bit as much of a liberal as she, but disagreed violently with journalism which smacked in any way, either through commission or omission, of political bias. Disagreed, and therefore felt trapped.

Tomorrow would be different. Tomorrow would be the end of his bondage and the beginning of his freedom. Tomorrow he would become whole again. The front page of the next issue of the *Tribune* would not look different to anyone—unless he worked for Dorothy Grimes. Those who did would recognize it for what it was: Adam's declaration of war.

The article that did this—personally by-lined by Adam —seemed forthright enough. In it, no mention was made of unfavorable investigative reports squelched because the people involved were political allies or friends of Dorothy Grimes; there was no voicing of Adam's suspicion that the "usually reliable sources" frequently used to discredit her political enemies might exist only in her imagination (but immune to identification because of the First Amendment); no comparison was made between the choice space showered on her friends and the back-page treatment given those out of favor. In fact, no national political names were mentioned at all, although Adam's investigative files bulged with suppressed revelations about people in high places whom Dorothy Grimes was protecting.

On the surface, the article appeared to be of no more than local interest. LA's mayor, Manuel Ortiz, had, Adam's investigative team reported, once again been caught with his hand in the till. It was an elaborately documented, first-class job, one the *Trib* should have been proud to run. But Manuel Ortiz, the first Chicano mayor of any major city, was a personal cause with Dorothy Grimes and someone she supported without reservation ("Ortiz only *seems* local," she once told Adam. "Actually, the national implications of the man are tremendous"). And if Dorothy Grimes had known about the article, she would have killed it, just as she had the one on Ortiz four years before.

Running tomorrow's story, therefore, was a gamble, and Adam knew it. He was not even sure he'd survive the moment when Dorothy Grimes discovered it had been printed on her first page.

Because of this, elaborate precautions had been taken to keep her—or anyone—from knowing about the article until press time. So far Adam didn't think Dorothy Grimes had heard anything, but earlier in the day he'd been shaken to discover she'd arrived unexpectedly in Los Angeles. In spite of all his precautions, Adam knew how reliable her grapevine was.

"Jesus," exclaimed Sylvia Carpenter, a secretary stationed outside Adam's office, as she watched Ursula shaking file drawers out of their built-in wall recesses to the full limit of their tracks. Wide-eyed, Sylvia turned for reassurance toward a cool, handsome-looking woman who'd just come out of Adam's office.

"Jesus," Sylvia repeated. "What's happening, Lottie?"

With a calm bred of years of dealing with nervous secretaries, Lottie, Adam's executive assistant, threw back her head with an artificially loud, if reassuring, laugh. "The end of the world, Sylvia." Carefully, she pretended to check her wristwatch. "And it's late."

The remark caused several of the other secretaries to giggle. But the Eastern-bred Sylvia neither laughed nor smiled; she just kept staring at Lottie.

Lottie Nettleton took pity. "An earthquake," she explained. "Just a little one, Sylvia. Nothing to worry about." The words were remarkably close to the ones Adam Mosely's son, Addie, had used to calm Mishi beside the pool out on Tutweiler.

43

Now that someone else was seen to be more nervous than they, the other girls grew braver. "Unless, of course," one said with a giggle, "the building falls down."

"We're all supposed to be standing in doorways, I think," added the one sitting directly behind Sylvia. "The metal frames keep bricks from falling on your head."

Lottie's broad smile conflicted shårply with the look in her eyes. "A building with Mr. Mosely in it wouldn't *dare* fall down," she said firmly, putting an emphasis in her words that clearly ended the subject. The girl behind Sylvia seemed prepared to carry the joke further, but a giant shadow in a suddenly opened door silenced her.

Adam Mosely—he was a huge man, graced with a quick smile and an even quicker temper—filled the doorway. Like his son, he was very tall, but with him the frame had filled out to match his height. The hair that on Addie was bleached white by the sun on his father was prematurely grayed. This gentle aging process, however, had not robbed Adam of his crackling dynamism. He appeared to be constantly leaning forward, as if impatient with a world that revolved too slowly. What both father and son shared down to the last genetic tittle were the oversized, ever-curious brown eyes.

"Thanks for the compliment, Lottie." He turned the smile toward the secretaries, focusing it so it seemed personally beamed at each of them. "Everything all right out here?"

He was answered by a quick murmur of agreement, although Sylvia, in spite of the smile, continued to look skeptical. Lottie searched the strong face and the oversized eyes for any sign of concern, but could find none. Besides Adam, she alone of them knew there should be. Tomorrow the *Trib's* readers would share the secret. For the article on Manuel Ortiz included, among other things, one fact unearthed by Adam's investigative team four years before: that, for reasons known only to himself, Ortiz was allowing contractors and architects to broach the city's earthquake-resistant building code almost at will. But Adam's face showed nothing.

Studying the secretaries, he appeared only to hear the

44

sounds of agreement. "Good. As for this building, it'll be here long after we're gone." It was a brave statement, but one Adam very much doubted was true.

With a final reassuring smile, Adam strode back into his office, followed by Lottie, who closed the door carefully behind her. Adam stared at her a second. "Any word from—" His hands beat the air as he searched for some colorful phrase to use in place of Dorothy's name, yet, because he was unwilling to be unkind to her, he was unable to find one. In the Ortiz matter he and Dorothy Grimes might be adversaries, but over the years she had treated him well. More than well. The question hung in space, unfinished.

Lottie smiled grimly, sensing the struggle. "Yes, Mrs. Grimes called. You're having dinner with her." She paused to study Adam. Then: "She's made it a command performance, I'm afraid."

"Oh, Christ." Wearily, Adam massaged his left temple. "Do you think she knows?"

"I don't see how she could. There's a phony front-page dummy downstairs in makeup in case anyone gets nosy. And the mats of the real stuff aren't even in San Francisco yet."

The type had been set and the mats made out of town to avoid any internal leaks. And manuscripts for later articles in the series—previously killed stories on everything from a President of the United States to an alderman from Van Nuys—were locked in Adam's office safe, to which even Lottie didn't know the combination. Still, Adam was worried. Losing his job to strike a blow for freedom of the press was one thing; losing it for a front page Dorothy Grimes could still kill before press time was something else. Trying to exorcise her presence, Adam spun his chair around so that he faced the glass wall of his office; all he could see was his own reflection, dim and wraithlike, in the glass. But he could *feel* Dorothy there, taunting him, shadowing him, setting his nerves on edge. Her sudden appearance in LA could be coincidence and nothing more. Still.

45

"I don't know," said Adam slowly. "Maybe we should have had the type set in Canada or abroad. She probably has confreres we don't even know about."

"Well, unless one of them is a linotypist at the Tri-Arts Printing Service in San Francisco, they won't do her much good." Lottie tried not to look at Adam; his worry was infectious.

Adam sighed. His feelings about Dorothy Grimes were so mixed as to defy analysis, but he did know that doing anything—like the Ortiz story—behind her back upset him even more than it frightened him. With a shrug, trying to shake off the intangible, he brought himself back to a practical question. "This dinner. When and where?"

"Early. Cocktails at five thirty. And you're not going to like where."

Adam smiled. "The early is fine. I can check the front-page mat myself when it comes in." Curious, he looked at Lottie. "The where. . . ."

"The Penthouse Terrace of the Park Plaza."

"Oh, for Christ sake," Adam exploded. Then he paused, seized by a new worry.

"You don't think she's trying to let me know she *knows*, do you?" (The Park Plaza, built only two years before, was cited in tomorrow's article as a prime example of what was happening to LA's building standards under Ortiz.) Dorothy Grimes was entirely capable of insisting on dinner at the Park Plaza—nobody in L.A. went to the place if they could possibly avoid it—and then playing with him, torturing him with uncertainty, pretending to know more than she did but letting him know she indeed *did* know—and then firing him. Or did they call it "terminating his contract"? Adam couldn't remember. The hell with it. He'd made his decision.

Lottie burst into laughter. "You're becoming paranoid. She just hates to be seen in public; you know that."

Sheepishly, Adam shrugged. Walking over to the window, he looked out over the city, studying the cloud of light-brown

46

smog that was settling across the nearby low buildings. His eyes smarted from just looking at the pollution, and in spite of knowing better, he rubbed his eyes to try to clear his vision.

As might well turn out to be the fact with tomorrow's edition of the *Trib*, the cure was considerably worse than the disease.

Chapter Four

And how about this guy who says after the next earthquake, most of Southern California will sink into the ocean? A lot of people got nervous, but I didn't start to worry myself until I heard the real reason Howard Hughes bought Las Vegas was so he could have waterfront property.

—WAYNE LESTER, *Sunset Strip Varieties*

AT Goldstone, Colorado, Drs. Feiner and Ridgeway were about to call it a day. Feiner's feeling of general frustration was newly sharpened by the 600 XE's failure to digest the material on Ursula and respond with a prediction. As he was well aware, he had no reason to think this particular minor tremor should accomplish a feat no other tremor yet had. But Feiner was a superstitious man—not a healthy trait in a scientist, he knew—and Ursula was a mere two states away, not the usual minor quake their seismograph showed happening in Japan or the Kuriles or on some unheard-of South American mountainside. *Very* unscientific thinking, Feiner muttered, staring disconsolately at the gleaming equipment ranged along the far wall of the lab.

With a resigned sigh, he lit a new cigarette and began stuffing papers into his briefcase, wondering if his annoyance with his wife was as unjust as his petulance at the lab equipment. Sometimes he found Rachel's sense of humor subject to bad timing; always he found her requests to "pick up a few things at the store on your way home" infuriating. In

48

her last call, a few minutes after Ursula, she had managed to combine both.

"I heard about it on the radio," she had explained. "Did you know it was coming?"

"No, dammit. I didn't."

"Some expert," Rachel laughed and then waited for a response. There was none. "Mike?" she asked, her voice showing the hurt. "*Mike?*"

"I'm sorry. I'm mad at the goddam Six Hundred. And that crazy little quake. It's stupid." He kicked himself, knowing he shouldn't be taking out his frustration on her; Rachel wasn't to blame.

She had laughed again, reassured now that she knew he was mad at something other than her. Actually, she had no way of realizing that his anger was rapidly taking on a life of its own, fury in search of a target. "Mike," Rachel said, "the reason I called—if you can stop kicking your computer long enough to listen—is that, well, on the way home, I was wondering—I know you hate to—but what I mean is, if you could stop at the A&P—I forgot some things when I was shopping, and you go right by the place. Some unsalted butter, maybe a pound of it. . . ."

The reaction she got from Dr. Michael Feiner stunned her. He was irritated, disappointed, and disturbed by unexplainable forebodings. Yet the tenor of his response was completely out of proportion: "Goddammit, Rachel. Get off my back. I've got better things to worry about than the stuff that didn't make it to the check-out counter. I don't know what you think I do down here, but—oh, shit."

He hung up and immediately regretted the whole thing. He had been unfair and knew it.

Remembering the conversation made Feiner swear to himself again and caused Dr. Ridgeway to look at him oddly. Feiner said nothing but continued stuffing the papers into the case, wishing he'd had the guts to call Rachel back and apologize. But he hadn't, and couldn't now. Doing it in person was better, anyway—later, when he got home. The two scientists were almost at the door, Feiner a few steps behind Ridgeway, when the phone in the lab rang. Possibly, Feiner thought, Rachel with some contrived conversation to give him an excuse to apologize. He couldn't do that with Ridgeway standing beside him and for a second he thought of not answering at all. But he saw Ridgeway hesitating and staring at the phone and knew the man would come back and answer it himself if Feiner didn't.

Glumly, Feiner picked up the receiver. "Hello," he grunted, already struggling with what he would say to Rachel.

"Dr. Feiner? This is Matt Bremen at Paragon Oil, Field Number Six, in LA."

"Yes."

"Well—we made that arrangement a couple of months back—what I mean is—you asked me to monitor the wellhead and casing pressures for anything unusual, remember? And something funny's going on."

"Something funny, Mr. Bremen?" repeated Feiner, suddenly interested and pulling a chair up to the table; his free hand motioned to Ridgeway not to leave. "Like what?"

"Casing pressure's up, way up again."

"*Again?*" asked Feiner incredulously. "I didn't know it had gone up at all."

"Well, couple of hours before that small quake—did you know we had one here, Dr. Feiner?"

"Yes, I know."

"Anyway, for a couple hours before it, the casing pressure went up, maybe two, three times normal. I guess I should have called you, but we got busy. Then, right after, the pressure dropped off. In the casing, at the wellhead, everywhere we could measure it. Now, it's going way back up."

Feiner struggled to remain calm. Oil casing pressures —anything in fact, that indicated a change of forces beneath the earth's surface—were an important but highly fallible predictive source. Many subcrust forces totally unrelated to an earthquake could cause the phenomenon. But taken together with other factors and fed into the 600, the data from

50

Paragon Number Six might help break the cause-and-effect logjam. And the rise in pressures before Ursula, then a drop and a new rise, particularly intrigued him. He wasn't sure why. When Feiner spoke into the phone again, he sounded almost disinterested. "I see. Pressure up. How far up?"

"In hole number seventy-three it's five times normal. Jesus, the oil's beginning to seep out of the ground in a couple of places."

"Just that one hole?"

"No, I checked three others. No oil seepage, but the pressure is way high in them too. It's crazy."

Feiner carried the receiver with him as he walked over to the chart wall, trailing the long, twisted extenson line behind him. He pulled down a detailed map of the Los Angeles area. By now Ridgeway was standing beside him. "Mr. Bremen," Feiner said, "exactly where are you reporting from? I don't have my list of map coordinates handy."

"Field Number Six runs right along Sepulveda, on the way to Los Angeles International. You know the place."

Feiner did. On the map the area looked tiny, but he could remember driving to the airport past oil well after oil well, separated from the road by Anchor fence, their booms dipping endlessly in eccentric plunges like giant birds searching the earth for food. "I've got it," he said into the phone, and stuck a push-pin into a shaded area beside Sepulveda on the chart.

Bremen's voice sounded distant, almost worried. "Does it mean anything? I mean, anything important?"

"I don't know yet, Mr. Bremen, I don't know. But thanks a lot. Keep checking the pressures for us, will you, and let me know if any more sudden increases or drops take place."

"OK. Sure, Dr. Feiner."

"And call collect, will you? There's no point your getting into trouble with Paragon," added Feiner, either feeling or imagining a slight hesitation in the man's answer. The lab paid the engineer a small fee for his monitoring work, but Bremen's real employers wouldn't appreciate a stiff set of long-distance charges for something they probably knew nothing about.

Ridgeway, seeing the look on Feiner's face, was already slipping out of his raincoat. "What's up?"

"Wellhead and casing pressures near LA is what's up. In one place, so high the stuff's seeping through the ground."

Dr. Ridgeway sighed. Feiner, he thought, was too easily carried away, yet continuingly dampening his enthusiasm might discourage him permanently. "Well, Michael, you know underground oil and gas pressures have misled a lot of good seismologists before."

Feiner was already seated at the programming console, feeding the new information from Paragon Field Number Six into the tape. "I know, I know," snapped Feiner. "But it's one more piece of information. And it all might add up to something." He couldn't shake the ominous sensation he'd felt ever since the first reports of Ursula.

Ridgeway stood there, not quite sure whether to go or stay. His raincoat, half off, was slipped back on. In a mood like this, Feiner could be very difficult to cope with; the price of brilliance, Ridgeway supposed, a single-mindedness of purpose that was at the same time both valuable in its intensity and destructive in its blindness.

Almost brusquely, Feiner pushed past him to get another cigarette, then pressed the button that fed the tape into the 600 XE.

The computer didn't take long; it never did. Watching the reels of taped memory spin back and forth, the lights on the console behind them flashing brilliant, erratic patterns, Feiner always got the impression he and Ridgeway were actors in a science-fiction drama, grown men playing with mammoth toys. Abruptly, the teleprinter chattered into life, typing like some secretary with an incredibly even-measured touch, the only break in the rhythmic sound coming when the teleprinter carriage crashed back to begin a new line.

Feiner leaned over the machine, watching. He was stunned.

For the first time since they had been working on the project, the 600 was grudgingly willing to commit itself to a prediction.

The printout—although riddled with computer hedge phrases like "NONDEFINITIVE" and "PROBABILITY HAS LARGE RELIABILITY TOLERANCES"—indicated a major earthquake, "OF THE RICHTER SEVEN TO NINE MAGNITUDE," in an area described as "APPROXIMATELY THIRTY-FOUR DEGREES NORTH, ONE HUNDRED EIGHTEEN DEGREES WEST." These were almost the precise map-coordinates of Los Angeles.

"God damn!" whispered Feiner hoarsely, caught somewhere between the triumph of a scientific breakthrough and horror at what his breakthrough indicated was in store for the people of Los Angeles. The printout machine chattered relentlessly on. "ON BASIS OF PRESENT DATA, DATE FIXED AS OF TODAY. ESTIMATE OF EXACT TIME SUBJECT TO LESS RELIABILITY BUT AS OF PRESENT INPUT STATUS IS FIXED AT APPROXIMATELY NINETEEN HUNDRED HOURS PLUS OR MINUS ONE."

Wordlessly, Feiner turned toward Ridgeway, who was now staring at the printout as if hypnotized by it. Ridgeway tore off the long roll of computer typing and sank into a chair, his eyes traveling back and forth across the lines as if he might find some secret error which would prove the printout wrong.

His hands shoved deep into his pockets, Feiner studied him a second, then said softly, "We've got to let them know; we have to tell somebody. Fast."

Ridgeway took a deep breath and exhaled it forlornly. Sitting there, holding the wide strip of partly curled-up paper, he looked suddenly small and defeated. "The three hours it gives them is no lead time at all. And that's the outside figure. Nobody can do anything in three hours."

"It's better than nothing."

Ridgeway's eyes rose from the printout. "We don't even know how reliable the prediction is. The computer—well, it seems to me the computer's hedging."

Taking the printout from Ridgeway's hands, Feiner studied it a minute and after shaking his head, looked at him in bafflement. "Beautiful. What's the use of being able to predict a quake if you don't use the information? Reliable or not, it's better than nothing."

When Ridgeway spoke again, his voice had a little more edge to it; Feiner's persistence, at first only irritating, was beginning to awaken a detached, scientific resistance. "If we cause an unnecessary panic, then we haven't helped anybody. In fact, quite the opposite."

"Isn't that for somebody in LA to decide, not us?"

"The responsibility's too great. Particularly in a case like this—where we're not really sure—we have to keep ourselves completely open and objective."

Strangely, it was Feiner who finally exploded. "For God's sake. 'Objective,' you say. We're being so damned objective, so clinically responsible, so tied up in pure science, we're forgetting what's at stake here. People. Not neutrons shooting around a Fermi chamber or points counted up on the modified Mercalli, but people. And the day you get completely objective about *them*, you might as well cash in your PhD and take up selling soda pop." Feiner's voice had risen sharply, a fact that surprised him as he heard the words bounce off the tile walls of the lab. Equally surprised, Ridgeway was on his feet, his eyes blinking.

Feiner looked away in embarrassment and quickly brought himself under control. "I'm sorry," he said softly. "I didn't mean to come on so strong."

"No, no, you're quite right to point that out, Michael. Too much objectivity is as dangerous as too little." Ridgeway paused for a second, then: "But I just don't see—even assuming the predictive computations are one hundred percent correct—how anybody could do much with just three hours' lead time."

In spite of his effort at self-control, Feiner felt his anger returning and could not keep the ugly sound of it out of his voice. "In three hours they could clear everybody out of all high rises. In three hours they could alert the Valley areas where the dams might go. In three hours, they could close off underpasses, empty bridges, shut all gas mains, seal up atomic power stations, and put the fire department and police on an emergency footing. And in three hours they could evacuate housing, hospitals, and assembly points that are built, God help them, right on top of the fault itself. That's what they could do in three hours."

To Ridgeway, whose mind saw tremors as stylus tracings on moving graph paper or as logarithmic extrapolations of precisely calculated equations, the awesomeness of what the 600 XE was saying was difficult to accept. Finally, he threw up his hands, a man of abstracts in a world of flesh and blood. "Who do we call?"

The defeat was accepted without comment. "The OCD, I guess."

"I have a friend at the LA County Earthquake Commission."

"Too damned political," said Feiner, and then softened the remark. "What I mean is, calling Civil Defense people would be more logical because they can move faster."

Reluctantly, Dr. Ridgeway picked up the phone and asked for the operator. There was to be nothing either logical about the reaction he got or fast about the action taken, but these variables were beyond his control. Watching him, Feiner reached into his pocket for another cigarette and then thought of Rachel. He shook his head. She would be waiting a long time for his apology—and waiting was something Rachel was not good at.

Neither was Violet.

Half-submerged in the hot tub, Laura Vorhees struggled not to think about what she was going to do and concentrated instead on what had brought her to the doing of it. Her whole life was a preparation for it, she supposed, from the distant Quaker father to the now even more distant husband, George, to the son, Digit, who was rapidly becoming as distant as the rest of them. (At the age of eighteen, his grandfather's trust opened up to Digit; so did the world. Suddenly, Digit

55

had told his mother he was moving to an apartment of his own, and had. All of her pleadings against his departure had been in vain; the only promise he made was that he would call every day, a promise, oddly, which he kept.)

Digit, then, was part of it. But not as much as George was.

The water suddenly felt chilly, and Laura added more, almost entirely from the hot tap. The steaming warmth soaked into her so thoroughly she quickly had to add some cold.

George. George and his highly unlikable lawyer. Laura shifted herself in the tub, using her hand to swirl the water around so that the hot and the newly added cold would become a more comfortable mixture. Blaming the lawyer wasn't entirely fair; he was only doing what his job required, what George insisted he do. Three weeks ago, when the lawyer had come to see her, he'd confused her at first, seeming to speak in riddles and not getting near the point Laura assumed had brought him: divorce.

In his own way, the man appeared as uncomfortable as Laura felt and kept shifting in his chair as though embarrassed. Laura decided he was playing a legal game, skillfully working his way around to his subject, laying the groundwork for property settlements and the nightmare of other details that would surround the matter. But to Laura, the subject of divorce was far too painful to be treated as a legal cat-and-mouse game; the careful training of her father began to desert her as her face collapsed into a twisting rubber mask of despair, the struggle not to cry showing in every contortion.

"You're here—you're here about the divorce," Laura blurted, imminent loss of control hiding just beneath the surface of her words.

For a moment the lawyer looked stunned. Then he recovered quickly, becoming almost snappish. "Under the circumstances, if that's what you want, of course a divorce can be arranged." He paused a second to stare at Laura, carefully pulling a handkerchief from his pocket so he could be ready to offer it when needed. "But that's not why I'm here, Mrs. Vorhees—as I suspect you know. We can get around to the question of divorce some other day."

It was Laura's turn to look stunned. With effort, she composed herself, resetting her face into the mask she had been trained since childhood to wear. By the time she looked at the lawyer again there was no evidence her façade had ever cracked. "I'm sorry," she said calmly, "but I don't understand."

In court, the lawyer had bad experiences with women who could alternately appear highly emotional or completely self-possessed; every time he'd tried to assess their probable reactions as potential jurors he'd gambled and lost. Faced with Laura's unpredictable highs and lows—George, the bastard, had described her as "about as emotional as a tree snail, a real ice-water lady"—the lawyer decided his only course was to be direct. "The tapes," he announced flatly. "I'm here about the tapes."

"The tapes?"

"The videotapes taken at the motel. George said"—the lawyer paused, suddenly remembering the lawyer-client relationship—"what I mean is, I assume you know about them."

Laura knew about the motel, of course; George had built it practically next to The Mission, claiming it would prove a good investment. But the tapes baffled her. The lawyer, sensing her confusion, approached her from a new tack. "The tapes could mean real trouble for George. You see, George is in considerable difficulty—some of the people involved were, technically, at least, minors—but the district attorney doesn't have much of a case. Anyway, without the tapes he doesn't. And the reason I came down here today was to see if you would release them to me."

"I really don't know anything about any tapes," answered Laura, although somewhere in the back of her mind a dim bell was beginning to ring. "Technically at least, minors," videotapes, the motel—all these things had come together in

57

Laura's mind in a sudden, ugly fashion, while the wound inside her, newly opened by the picture of George that was now emerging, made her want to scream out in pain.

Leaning forward, the lawyer decided it was time to take the gloves off. "Mrs. Vorhees, I don't quite understand what you hope to accomplish. I'm not suggesting the willful destruction of evidence or anything like that; it's simply that it would be better if we, not the district attorney, had possession of the tapes. Of course, I realize how you must feel about them. But George—my client—assures me that he placed the tapes in the wall safe of the library here, directly after the 'raid'—if you choose to consider it that—at Obispo. That was about six months ago. Then, he states, he returned about three months later—that would be perhaps three months ago—and discovered you had had the library remodeled and the safe was no longer there. He further states he didn't see you on that visit—he arrived quite late at night and stayed only about an hour—and that he looked everywhere but couldn't find them." For a moment the lawyer hesitated, then fixed her with the eye of hanging judge. "Earlier you mentioned divorce. I can only conclude you intend to keep the tapes as a threat—to insure yourself of a better settlement. I assure you, Mrs. Vorhees, that no such tactics will be necessary."

"I know absolutely nothing about any tapes. I have never seen them." For the first time, Laura found herself lying. She was not sure why. "The library *was* remodeled and the wall safe moved to my bedroom, but I went through the contents myself, and no tapes were in it. I have never laid eyes on them."

"Lying is the refuge of the weak." Laura could almost hear her father say it, twinkling merrily. Well, all right then, she was weak. When the safe was moved and its contents examined, she remembered the two thick boxes of 3M videotapes very clearly. They were something, she assumed, for the portable videotape machine George had brought home from one of his stores and kept tucked away in a closet downstairs. The tapes took up a lot of room in the safe, and she'd finally put them in her own closet, pushed way back out of sight on the top shelf. The sudden noisy visit in the middle of the night was now explained: George was looking for the 3M boxes—to "protect" the tapes for the district attorney—and had turned the whole first floor upside down trying to find them. The mystery of what could be on the tapes still puzzled her, but the dim shape of the sort of trouble George had got himself into was clear. She shook her head as the full impact dawned on her, partly in wonderment, partly because in spite of all that had happened, some secret inner fraction of her could still be hurt by anything about George.

The lawyer obviously did not believe Laura had never seen what was on the tapes, and at the same time he sensed Laura was still capable of being hurt by George. "I'm sure you realize, Mrs. Vorhees, that George has to be a pretty sick man to tape the sort of material he did, but there's a big difference between being sick and being guilty of what the State is trying to prove. That's why the tapes are so critical to our case."

That George was sick, Laura couldn't dispute. But the growing resentment at his making her feel guilty all these years—for making her feel it was *she* who was sick—began taking hold of Laura completely. With effort, she clung to her façade of calmness. "I don't know what it will take to convince you, but I've never laid eyes on the tapes. Oh, there were some odd articles in the safe when I cleaned it out—papers and things—but I sent them on to George." (This much was true; Laura never considered sending on the tapes because she had no idea they were important.)

"He received the papers," agreed the lawyer, "but the tapes must still be in your possession. If I may reiterate my point about the settlement. . . ."

Laura ignored him; the subject of divorce and settlement was still too painful to face. "Well, I'll search the house again, if it's that important, but I'm absolutely sure they're not here."

In the face of this final lie, the lawyer had no choice but to

59

leave as gracefully as he could. His card was pressed on Laura, who promised that she would call him in a couple of days, as soon as the search was completed.

Watching him leave, Laura felt as if some other being were beginning to control the movements of her arms and legs, not herself. For no reason, the other being picked up the ashtray full of cigarette stubs, turned it upside down, and caused her heel to grind the ashes into the thick gray carpet.

For thirty-six of her forty-two years, Laura had remained as tightly stoppered as an unopened bottle of champagne; now the other being took full possession. Sobbing with rage, she allowed the picture of her father, the twinkle captured for posterity on film, to be flung across the room against the wall; George's picture quickly followed. In the bedroom, scissors were placed in her hand to attack the few clothes George still kept in the house, cutting them into patterns as jagged as her hate; a cold cream jar was wrenched open, its contents smeared over one of the floor-length mirrors, and her finger forced to write George's name over and over again in the white, greasy mess. Then, from halfway across the room, the other being completed its job by heaving the empty jar at the mirror, shattering it into a thousand, splintering pieces. With a wail of defeat, Laura threw herself on the bed and, for the first time she could remember, wept uncontrollably.

For reasons she would never understand, it made her feel better.

Still soaking in the tub, Laura felt uncomfortable recalling those moments; they were the workings not of her, but of someone else, a someone else whom even thinking about George could still rouse to fury. Laura turned on the water again, as hot as she could stand it, and stared into the light cloud of steam that rose from its surface. This helped soften the memory of the lawyer's visit and its aftermath, but not much.

Turning the water off with her toe, Laura again tried forcing herself to think about things that had nothing to do with George.

The effort was not entirely successful.

The house on Tutweiler was suddenly swept by a wave of noise and confusion. Addie and Mishi, still beside the pool, looked toward the house, startled. One of the large sliding glass doors opening onto the upper terrace was roughly shoved open, and the houseboy backed out, dragging a heavily smoking mattress behind him. A roll of smoke billowed out the open door. Dropping the mattress and coughing terribly, the houseboy disappeared back inside and returned, pulling the box spring behind him. Through the smoke, Addie could see his mother hauled out the door and dumped heavily onto a patio chaise. She looked almost as lifeless as the mattress.

Both he and Mishi raced toward the terrace. Looking inside the smoking room, all he could see was more smoke and some sickly yellow flames which the chauffeur was struggling to control with a dry chemical extinguisher. He would spray for a few seconds, then come gasping onto the terrace and cough wretchedly, then disappear again into the room.

Mishi, who had started rubbing Mrs. Mosely's wrists, was brushed aside by Mrs. Herkimer, the housekeeper, who began slapping the woman's face. When Mishi protested, Mrs. Herkimer gave her a withering look. "Don't worry about the slapping, miss. She doesn't feel a thing and it usually brings her around." She surveyed her charge for an instant. "That woman's going to burn the whole house down around our heads someday."

The chauffeur, Harry, announced the fire was out. "Nothing left in there now but a lot of smoke. The box spring was still smoldering a little, but I doused it real good. The mattress is where the real trouble was." He looked at the extinguisher in his hand almost forlornly. "Lucky I was here," he added, turning around and waiting for someone to compliment him.

"Thank you, Harry. Thank you a lot," said Addie, who

61

knew what was expected of him. "The whole house could have gone." He turned toward Mrs. Herkimer who was now alternating slapping with rubbing. "Is she all right?"

"Coming around."

On cue, Mrs. Mosely opened one eye and began coughing loudly. The other eye followed the first, and she looked about her, apparently startled at the ring of faces. "What are you all doing in my bedroom in the middle of the night?" she demanded.

Mrs. Herkimer ignored the question. "There was a fire, ma'am. In your bedroom. You're out on the terrace now." The houseboy, Pepe, sitting on the edge of the terrace wall gave a cough that sounded as though he were throwing his insides up. Without warning, the wind changed direction and blew more smoke from the doorway into their faces, causing Addie's eyes to smart painfully and the chauffeur to look inside the room again to make sure the fire was really out.

"A fire? In my bedroom? Impossible." Mrs. Mosely's pale-blue eyes searched their faces for an explanation.

Mrs. Herkimer was blunt. "A cigarette, Mrs. Mosely. It's very dangerous to smoke in bed when you're—you're—you're not wide awake."

"Nonsense. I never smoke in bed. The electric blanket probably. I never liked the idea of them anyway." Her eyes wandered down toward her hand to check that the lie was not contradictable, finally stopping, unable to force themselves past a series of small but unmistakable cigarette holes burned in the edge of her light-blue peignoir. Suddenly, without any warning, her face collapsed, and she began to cry as if electric blankets were the cause of all the misery in her life. The help began drifting away in embarrassment, Mrs. Herkimer already giving orders that the guest room downstairs be made ready for her.

Addie, usually hostile to his mother, found himself shaken; it was not right that a grown-up should cry like this. Quickly, he moved to her and picked up her limp, moist hand. "Everything's okay . . . just a lot of smoke . . . a little fire, and a mattress burned. . . . There's nothing to cry about, honest."

His mother reached out and touched his face, then pulled him to her desperately. "The fire *wasn't* much, was it, sweetheart? And I'll bet you would have liked one where all the fire engines came and went clang! clang! clang!" Addie stared at her, fascinated. Her eyes had taken on the distant look that signaled she'd lost all contact with reality again; time had ceased to exist. Both her hands rose, and she moved him back a little to give him a radiant smile. "Oh, I know how little boys' minds work, and you mustn't cry, darling; I know what to do. Next week we'll go the village and I'll take you to see the fire station and we can ask the fireman if you can sit on the seat of the big engine and pretend you're driving, and maybe if you're good, really good, they'll let you ring the bell and blow the horn and play with the levers. Won't that be fun, sweetheart, won't that be fun?"

Addie reddened to the roots of his hair and drew back roughly, the surge of sympathy completely vanished. Mishi looked across the terrace and then walked away and coughed, but not from the still-lingering smoke.

There was, she thought, no apt phrase from the movies she'd seen in Tokyo to cover a situation like this.

Chapter Five

ISAAC ROSHOLMAN leaned against the zoo's administration building, his eyes squinting into the slowly lowering sun. As always, these were the pleasantest moments of the day. The visitors were gone now, leaving him and the animals at peace; the vendors had packed away their wares, and he was in charge.

Almost aimlessly, he began wandering down the concrete path. Eventually, he knew, he would have to make sure someone had checked the gates and then log the fact in the book kept inside the admin building. He would have liked to have walked down and seen Old Three Toes again, but he wanted to be sure Battock was really gone before he did that.

Instead, he turned and walked toward the reptile house, a small brick structure with a copper pagoda-style roof that squatted menacingly on a low hill. The log required he personally check that the reptile house was locked and the protective devices operational. The building was one Rosholman hated, its inner walls lined with glass cases stretching from floor to ceiling. Inside, he could see the cobras, the pythons, and the rattlers; slithering around on their rocks and sand; the coral snakes, copperheads, cottonmouths, and massasaugas; the bulls, the boas, and the indigos. Under the dim light that was all they kept on after hours, the snakes looked to Rosholman more evil than ever, their slit eyes constantly staring through the glass in silent rage because they could not reach out and strike.

Rosholman walked quickly from the place, carefully checking the door lock behind him. Outside the building, he tried the protective cover to the cyanide valve to be sure it was securely locked. In case of emergency, the contingency plan called for the opening of the valve to gas the snakes before they could escape from their cases; an automatic sensor turned off the ventilating system when the valve was open, ensuring that the cyanide wouldn't be sucked out of the building and drift lethally across the zoo grounds. All the creatures inside the reptile house—and a few humans outside it—would be improved by a jolt of cyanide, Rosholman thought, but the idea suddenly brought back childhood nightmares of Cyclon B and he shuddered.

Turning back toward the admin building, he could see someone waiting by the door for him and assumed it was his newly hired attendant—the man was on the master schedule as due to report today—showing up for his first night of work. Slipping the valve key back on the ring with the others, Rosholman sauntered back toward the building to brief the man on his duties.

He hoped Battock was gone by now. New attendants had to be impressed with the importance of their responsibilities right at the beginning, and any sniping by Battock would only make this more difficult.

Fortunately, it looked like an otherwise slow night.

On the Day George Vorhees arrived in Los Angeles from San Luis Obispo at about four o'clock, alone and without letting his lawyer know. This was not by accident. After the attorney's trip down three weeks before had turned out a failure, George, fed up with the man, began muttering about going to see Laura himself. The lawyer pleaded with George not to attempt anything that risky and, in fact, virtually demanded that George not interfere at all.

"For Christ's sake, George," he had implored him. "You're in big enough trouble as it is without opening yourself to charges of intimidating a witness or suborning to perjury or willful destruction of evidence. There *are* ways of raising these possibilities with Laura, but they are lawyers' ways, couched in very indirect language, so that no one can accuse you of anything more than they already have. Jesus! Leave Laura to me."

George looked at him sourly. "That's what we tried three weeks ago. You went down there, and *you* did the talking, and *you* came back with exactly nothing."

"Well, it's not easy, George." The lawyer, who always looked miserable, had assumed an even grimmer mien than usual, and George could see him weighing the high fees brought in by George's corporate self against the extreme discomfort of having to deal with George's personal legal problems. This weighing process produced a halfhearted conclusion. "Of course, George, if you want to retain other counsel . . ." the lawyer had said without conviction.

Giving in to this implied blackmail, George pretended to agree and promised he would leave Laura to the lawyer. The lawyer was a good one, he supposed, but he didn't know Laura and couldn't possibly understand George.

In fact, nobody understood George, including himself. And if he'd been the type to believe in psychiatry, he would, in his usual blunt way, have been quick to lay this fact on the line.

"The picture thing. I don't know how or why it worked out this way," he would have told the doctor. "I always liked to watch—even when I was a kid. I don't mean I didn't do things myself, of course, but well, there was a special kick to it that I still don't understand.

"And when they introduced the Polaroid Land Camera

—about forty-nine, I guess it was—instead of just watching, I started in with pictures.

"And I'm telling you, Doctor, I bought enough film to keep that company in business. Pictures of myself. Pictures of kids at high school. Pictures through glass windows into shower rooms, through venetian blinds into bedrooms, infrared pictures into the back seat of cars at drive-ins. Thousands of them. Then came videotape, and the pictures could move.

"Like I said, I can't explain it. But it's sort of like voodoo. You know—if you've got somebody's picture, you own their souls."

And George would have paused, wondering if he should keep going or if the doctor was ever going to say something. "Sometimes," George would finally have volunteered, "I sort of wonder if maybe the pictures don't own *me* instead of the other way around. Sometimes I think they own me and are punishing me for being such a bastard. Does that make any sense to you at all, Doctor?"

The psychiatrist might only have nodded, but George would have unwittingly hit the bottom line. His sexual acrobatics, his picture taking, while degrading to others, were most of all degrading to George, and it had struck him more than once, usually on the thin edge of sleep, that the reckless way he went after his kicks was an open invitation to disaster and subsequent punishment. Certainly, that was what happened with the tapes.

"You want cameras *where?*" the engineer who was doing the electrical work for the new motel had asked.

"You heard me say where," George had answered, making sure there wasn't going to be any more nonsense about it by staring at the engineer grimly. The man shrugged and let the matter pass. When George had asked for remote television cameras in the motel lobby, the setup made sense as an antirobbery device. Putting them in the bar was marginal, but with George in the electronic business, you could make a case for it. But when he wanted cameras—carefully concealed

67

ones—in every bedroom of the motel, all connected to a master control set up in his den at The Mission, there was only one explanation. But George wasn't the sort of guy you pointed this out to.

When the system was first hooked up, George was disappointed. A lot of the people apparently would arrive at the motel too tired to do much but sleep. He would punch up the various buttons, letting the camera roam from room to room, a sort of electronic Peeping Tom, and see them: the men smelling their socks to see if they'd last one more day, the women wearily sticking curlers in their hair in the hope that tomorrow would be better, and then, after a ritual peck on the forehead from their husbands, quietly turning off the lights and falling asleep. What little sex his cameras picked up was perfunctory, awkward, and self-conscious, almost as if the people in the rooms sensed George's cameras.

Changes were made to attract a livelier clientele. The decor was redesigned to add some erotic overtones; the bar's name was switched to The Leather Boot; B-girls sat conspicuously on the barstools. And little by little, the changes began to pay off. Regulars started appearing in the rooms, George noticed—and of a more interesting variety: there was a well-dressed middle-aged Southern lady, much too heavy to be attractive, who materialized every few nights, a different young man in tow. From conversations picked up by the hidden microphones, the men were well paid for their time. Probably, George thought, working their way through nearby Delbert College.

Later on a couple of hookers, a hefty bleached blonde and a small Mexican-American girl, began showing up every night—and sometimes twice. A pair of college-age boys, nice enough looking but painfully furtive and self-conscious, became regulars, as did a trio of two men and a girl, invariably drunk. From the very beginning, George had been meticulously recording all these activities on one of the new videotape machines his stores were now pushing. As sellers they hadn't done well; as entertainment for George, at first at least, they were perfect. He would spend hours in his den crouching over the monitors, his face lit only by the strange half-light coming from the picture tubes, and play the tapes back to himself endlessly. Every now and then he would press a series of buttons and run an instant replay of something that particularly interested him, urging the unwitting actors on by slapping the control panel with his hands.

If he'd just stopped there, George wouldn't have been in trouble and the tapes no legal millstone. The most any enterprising young DA could have raised was invasion of privacy and, perhaps, allowing his motel to be used for immoral purposes or lascivious carriage.

But something was missing from the tapes as George studied them, sitting in The Mission and running them over and over; the arguments, the ecstasies, the rapprochements all were duly recorded, but some terribly important element was absent. The violence. The hate. The punishment. The something George needed to feed his endless fantasies. To correct this, George decided reluctantly, he would have to expand his cast, something that would not be easy to do safely.

Shortly after he began showing up at the motel's bar himself. He sought out the regulars—almost all of them stopped in either after or before their stint in the rooms—with particular attention to the two hookers and the lady with the constantly changing array of hired young men. A few others were drawn into this circle. All of them had further contacts that would provide additional interesting people. A deal was struck. And George sealed his own fate.

Thinking of the tapes, George swore loudly enough so that the taxi driver taking him from the Los Angeles Airport to the Beverly Hills Hotel turned around and stared. Mumbling something to the driver, George continued to reproach himself. How could he ever have been so stupid as to try to hide them at Laura's when the trouble broke? She probably didn't even know what they were or what they were worth, but he sure as hell couldn't explain it to her. Why hadn't he left well enough alone and burned the tapes of the performances when the trouble began?

No answer presented itself. George groaned slightly, and the driver turned again, this time wearing an alarmed expression. "I was just thinking of a bad night ahead," George explained, and hid behind a newspaper to escape the driver's stare.

He would go see Laura after dinner. The meal itself would be with his son, Digit, to see if he knew whether Laura had seen what was on the tapes, and if she had, if Digit knew where they were hidden. Thinking about dinner with Digit made George want to groan again, but this time he controlled himself. As usual, Digit and he would have trouble making conversation. They had practically nothing in common and both preferred to keep things that way. Talking to him on the phone from Obispo, George had sensed only curiosity —certainly not anticipation—in Digit's voice when he told him they had something important to discuss. Even had he known Digit well, explaining about the tapes would have been an uncomfortable process. Sometime—the boy was his son after all—he should probably get to know him better, but this wasn't the time. Not when he himself was on the brink of a possible prison sentence.

The cab came to a halt, and George found himself staring at the pink stucco of the Beverly Hills Hotel. A terrible color, he decided, but better than the grim gray of San Quentin. A lot better.

Beth Czemki was feeling very good. She was Isaac Rosholman's niece—his only living relative in this country—but their paths rarely crossed anymore. Uncle Isaac had never seen too much of her anyway, but when Beth had married a goy—and a Polish Catholic at that—instead of a nice Jewish boy, he saw even less of her. At first, Matt Czemki and she had made a considerable effort, but while Uncle Isaac reportedly enjoyed an almost mystic communion with animals, he enjoyed none whatsoever with the rugged animal spirits of Matt Czemki. Even the proud explanation that Matt was a computer programmer in the aerospace program cut no ice. "Run by that Nazi lover, Von Braun," snapped Rosholman, and firmly put an end to any further discussions on the matter.

"Face it, baby," Matt explained. "Your precious Uncle Isaac is a bigot. If you're not Jewish, almost extinct, or a protected species, he doesn't want anything to do with you."

Eventually, Beth knew, she would have to tell Uncle Isaac about the new baby growing inside her and face the usual argument about what religion he would be raised in, but not for a while yet. First she had to tell Matt, and that already was presenting her with a small problem. Earlier today, this morning, was the first she'd known for sure herself; the doctor had walked back into the examining room with a big smile and announced that yes, the test was positive and, no, the rabbit hadn't felt a thing.

The problem was that she wanted to tell Matt as soon as possible, but giving him the news over the phone was too impersonal. Later would also present difficulties; they were having dinner at the Iveliterris', and the sitter wasn't due until just before Beth would leave to meet Matt there. With a slight pursing of her lips, Beth concluded that the Iveliterris just weren't good enough friends to hear this news at the same time Matt did. Looking at her two children playing in the small living room—Gregory, nine, and Sarah, six—Beth reached her decision. She had to tell Matt before dinner or she'd explode. He'd wanted another child desperately—he was one of six himself—and now a baby was coming, a couple of years late, perhaps, but definitely on the way. The kids could fend for themselves for an hour. Just an hour. Quickly, before she could change her mind, Beth called Matt at the company and asked him to meet her at the little cocktail lounge just around the corner from the Iveliterris'.

The decision was not a popular one with Gregory. He would only be alone with Sarah for an hour, Beth reassured him, and then the sitter would arrive. And it would still be light and she knew he would be a good boy and take care of Sarah and they could watch *Mister Rogers* and the *Electric Company* and she would leave a note for the sitter saying they could, as a special treat for being good, even stay up long enough to see *Truth or Consequences*, a special, if inexplicable, favorite of Gregory's.

But Gregory had a one-track mind, and his face became suddenly solemn with worry. "But when will *you* be back?"

Sarah, catching the infection of worry from Gregory, screwed up her face and stopped doing somersaults on the floor long enough to look anxious, too. "Yes, Mommy, when will *you* be back?"

"After dinner."

"Why can't we go with you?" demanded Gregory, already knowing the answer; the same question was always asked whenever she went anywhere.

Patiently, knowing he was making a fuss mostly just to make a fuss, Beth went through the ritual explanation that this party was for grown-ups and so he and Sarah wouldn't have any fun there.

Gregory studied her; grown-ups always gave excuses for things they wanted to do that made it sound like they were doing them for your benefit. He resorted to the ultimate weapon. "I don't like being left alone; neither does Sarah. Something might happen. I'll be scared."

Being scared hadn't occurred to Sarah before; now she started crying.

Here they had scored a point. Beth didn't like leaving them alone, even for an hour, and seldom did. As a result, she was unusually severe in answering, slipping into her coat as she did. "That's ridiculous, Gregory. You're too big to be scared. And the sitter will be here at six."

From her reaction, Gregory could sense the ploy was effective. "I don't care. Something will happen, and I'll be scared."

"Nothing will happen, Gregory. I promise you. Now just

stop whining about it or I won't leave the note for the sitter about *Truth or Consequences.*"

Gregory caved in and, sulking, followed his mother to the door. In the exchange of ultimate weapons, he had lost. He was too young to know anything about the plate theory of global tectonics, but long before the hour was up, validation of the hypothesis would make a liar out of his mother.

Chapter Six

In an emergency, it is best to call the police or operator for coordinated aid, particularly in this area, where confusion can arise as to State, county and city jurisdictions.

> —*Citibook, Los Angeles*, issued by the National Travel Department of the American Automobile Association.

NEATLY framed and bordered by a funereal black mat, a faded newspaper clipping from the New York *Times* hung on the office wall of Henry Kraypool, director of the Federal Office of Emergency Preparedness in Los Angeles, a spin-off from the Office of Civil Defense:

> LOS ANGELES, Jan 9 (UPI)—The city council's public health committee said yesterday that the second most common cause of accidental death here was drowning in a private swimming pool. The committee then drafted a law requiring owners of private pools to keep the water clear enough to see a corpse on the bottom.

The clipping had been presented to Kraypool by his staff because it pretty well summed up the Los Angeles attitude toward any emergency; the example was bizarre, but illustrated why Kraypool felt constantly frustrated in dealing with Los Angeles officialdom. Other communities might pass laws demanding the fencing in of such hazards, but in Los Angeles the approach was cosmetic. His staff—although suspicious of all Easterners—liked Kraypool and understood what he was trying to do.

With him, they had drawn up and had on file contingency plans, meticulously researched and worked out, for nuclear attack, sudden and total drought, complete power failure, smog attacks—of both the nuisance and the lethal variety—earthquake, tidal wave, riot, civil insurrection, and various types of explosions, both man-made and natural. The only trouble, once the plans were drawn up, was getting anyone to read them. From Mayor Ortiz on down, Californians acted as though nothing bad could ever happen to them. For the three years he'd been there, Kraypool had tried mightily but was rapidly despairing of ever mobilizing city officials to the possibilities of the disasters he could see everywhere.

On the Day, a little after four o'clock, most of the staff had already left when his secretary came into his office and said there was a Dr. Feiner, from the Western Seismological Institute on the telephone; the doctor, she said, had described it as a "matter of tremendous urgency." After a quick glance at the office clock behind Kraypool, the secretary asked whether she should have Feiner phone back Monday morning.

Kraypool took the call. The secretary, handbag clasped in front of her to show she was about to leave for the weekend, stopped at the door as she saw Kraypool's face go ashen. "Are you *sure?*" she heard him ask, and then, responding to his urgent waving, came slowly back into the office.

Dazed, Kraypool listened to the thin, anxious voice on the other end of the line. "We can't be sure," Feiner said. "Not completely, anyway. But it's what our computer predicts."

After a glance at his watch, Kraypool began making notes in a frantic scribble as Feiner spoke, outlining the prediction in detail. The picture which emerged was so bleak Kraypool sagged, putting his pencil down with a sigh of defeat. "If there

75

was only more time . . ." he said. "These guys down here don't exactly jump through hoops when I tell them something, and I don't have the authority to evacuate a single person on my own say-so. I'm federal, but they're city. And in these things, only the city has legal authority to act."

Feiner sounded glum. First Ridgeway, now this man. "Well, somebody has to do *something*."

"Agreed. But all I can do is advise. And in this case, I'll couch my advice in the strongest possible terms. We have a contingency plan drawn up specifically for this kind of disaster, but the problem is going to be to get anyone to buy your prediction."

A thin, whispering sound came over the phone, someone in an aside to Feiner; Kraypool could hear a hand being placed over the receiver and then being removed. Feiner's voice sounded subdued and angry when it came back on the line. "I have to point out, of course, that it *is* only a prediction."

At first Kraypool was baffled. Initially, the Goldstone earthquake prediction had been couched in very urgent terms, a firm and unequivocal warning. Then, suddenly, the seismologists on the other end of the phone had begun backtracking, pointing out it was, after all, only a prediction. Dimly, the whispering and the hand placed over the phone suddenly came back to Kraypool, and he smiled grimly; that science too had its own set of men as reluctant to stick out their necks as any in city government made him feel better.

"Look," Kraypool said, realizing that he had a great deal of talking to do and very little time to do it in, "I'll have to check on my own, and then I'll tackle the mayor. Prediction or fact, it's nothing we can just sit on. I'll be back to you. Is there anything—more facts, local statistics, information from UCLA or the Geodetic Station at Drago Park—that would help harden your prediction?"

"No. We have the computer working now on the possibility of aftershocks. As you know, they can sometimes be worse than the initial tremor."

"OK, then. I'll be back to you."

76

Feiner's voice stopped him as he was removing the receiver from his ear. "Mr. Kraypool? May I ask what floor you're on?"

"Third."

"It would be better if you could establish a command post somewhere on the first. And you have radio as well as telephone communications? What I mean is, underground telephone lines are particularly susceptible to tremor activity."

"Yes, we're fully equipped for radio transmission. It's part of the CONLRAD setup."

"Good. I'll call, of course, as soon as we get any predictions on the aftershock." There was a pause, during which Kraypool could hear only Feiner's breathing over the phone. Then: "Good luck."

Slowly, Kraypool put down the receiver. For the first time, an ominous feeling touched him. He had been so absorbed worrying about the city that any thought that his own life and that of his family's might be in danger had, until this moment, not occurred to him.

Along with the rest of Los Angeles, Kraypool had almost come to believe disasters were something that happened to somebody else.

Adam Mosely strode out of the *Tribune* building feeling unfairly put upon by the world—and with only further injustices in sight. This feeling had been growing in him all day. With a grunt, he yanked the car door open and climbed behind the wheel, heading toward the Park Plaza and his meeting with Dorothy Grimes. Worrying that she already knew something about tomorrow's edition was stupid; Adam could think of no conceivable way she could have learned of it. But Dorothy Grimes prided herself on her shrewdness and had an unpleasant habit of doing precisely what other people thought was inconceivable.

Pulling into traffic on Wilshire, he was so absorbed in Dorothy Grimes and what she might be up to that he nearly collided with a trailer truck. The driver leaned out his window and bellowed at him; Adam lowered his window and yelled

77

back just as loudly, which at least made him feel a little better. But incident by incident, the day was turning into a disaster.

Just before he'd left to come downstairs, Mrs. Herkimer, the housekeeper on Tutweiler, had called. Mrs. Mosely, she said, had set the place on fire again. No, nothing serious, just a lot of smoke. Started by a cigarette.

"Is she all right?"

"Mean, Mr. Mosely. Very mean. She fired me. All of us."

The brusque way Mrs. Herkimer was speaking told Adam he had to handle the woman very carefully at this point; Georgia fired her at more or less regular intervals, but as a practical nurse who specialized in alcoholics (while doubling as housekeeper) she ought to be used to that. An unusual note of self-pity and frustration in Mrs. Herkimer's voice, however, said she needed both sympathy and reassurance.

"Well, *I* pay the bills, not Mrs. Mosely, so she couldn't fire you even if she wanted to. As far as I'm concerned, you're doing a great job. And, frankly, sometimes I don't know how you stand it."

A murmur came from the other end of the phone, then an appeal for additional sympathy. "I don't know, Mr. Mosely. She was really vicious this time. Told me—Harry and Pepe and Mary, too—to pack our things and get out of the house. I don't know."

Adam swore under his breath. "Is she there? Let me talk to her."

"Sound asleep, Mr. Mosely."

Her words illustrated a facet of the handling of alcoholics that Adam always found particularly irritating. Even people like Mrs. Herkimer—who dealt with them every day—insisted on using euphemisms instead of plain talk. And the plain talk for "sound asleep" was "passed out." The hell with it; he would be blunt. A glance at his watch and at a frantically waving Lottie told him he was going to be late for Dorothy Grimes—in her world an indictable offense. "Look. You're used to drunks. And you know as well as I do, Mrs. Herkimer,

78

that tomorrow she'll be all sweet words and promises. Just don't let her get to you. If any more problems come up tonight—I've got an appointment out of the building—call my assistant here. You've talked to Lottie before. She'll know how to reach me. You're doing a fabulous job, and I don't know what we'd do without you."

Mrs. Herkimer was appeased. Abruptly, she changed the subject. "Mr. Addie is all right, too. A little upset maybe, but all right."

Adam mumbled something, ashamed he hadn't thought to ask about Addie himself.

But between Georgia and Dorothy Grimes, he sometimes wondered how he even survived, much less succeeded.

When Adam Mosely joined the *Tribune* and first met Dorothy Grimes—shortly before Addie was born and back when Georgia still knew what day it was—he was awe-stricken. This reaction was no accident; Dorothy Grimes struck awe the way Getty strikes oil. To a young reporter, she seemed everything a newspaper owner ought to be or ever could be. Like Kay Graham and Dorothy Schiff, she was a lady with a great deal of money but dedicated (as was Adam) to a fiery brand of outraged liberalism. She was not pretty—in fact, almost ugly—but managed to dress and carry herself in a way that made her look almost glamorous; she had taken command of a *Tribune* floundering in the rising tide of television, salvaged it, and then relaunched the paper brilliantly, quickly earning it a reputation as one of the three most influential dailies in the country.

In spite of the difference in their ages—Dorothy Grimes was a good twenty years older than Adam—their personal chemistries were attuned. She found in him a rare combination of brilliance, curiosity, and memory-bank brain, all these qualities harnessed to the dogged drive and refusal to be intimidated that separates the merely good investigative reporters from the great. For her part, she provided Adam with her personal backing, the resources of the *Tribune*, and what appeared to be an almost unlimited program of raises and promotions. In those early days they became so close Georgia grew jealous of both Adam's job and his employer, suggesting Dorothy Grimes might have more than Adam's brain in mind; Adam only laughed, but it was honest laughter. Working relationships with women in business have never been easy to explain to insecure wives.

At first, almost everything written by Adam and the team of gifted young reporters he hired was not only well accepted but actively promoted by Dorothy Grimes. Soon he had pushed far beyond news of regional interest into areas of national importance: his investigative study of Eisenhower's Presidential assistant Simon Goss led to an IRS audit and Goss' forced resignation; his series on Senator Welbeel's use of highway funds to block black registration in Alabama became a journalistic classic; his uncovering of how the aerospace industry and several Pentagon general officers shared not only a common love of military hardware but also large amounts of unaccounted funds, high cost overruns, and occasionally even their wives led to the Senate investigations that collapsed the arrangement.

But some months after those triumphs, as Adam's reach expanded, he began running into a curious resistance. Over a period of time he noticed that some of his team's reports were soft-pedaled, appeared far back in the paper, or were never run at all. The most heartbreaking of these—and the one that caused his first confrontation with Dorothy Grimes—involved a series of articles on Lyndon B. Johnson, then Majority Leader of the Senate. At first, Adam himself had trouble believing what was uncovered, but the documentation made the facts inescapable. Johnson, the information alleged, was growing rich by buying up franchises of as yet unbuilt television stations. Because of his former position as chairman of the Senate committee that oversaw the FCC, he had known where these franchises would be well in advance and then would corner every station in the proposed areas. Adam's team had all the documentation which, if true, even showed how the stations were to be listed under bogus names to avoid being traced back to him. It was a brilliant piece of reporting—bold, crisp, and hard-hitting. But the series, he heard from one of his team, was going to be killed. For Adam, the series was far too important—both for the *Trib* and for the country—to have anybody try to stop it. He faced the outraged members of his staff: nervous rumors like that, he told them, inevitably circulated about any story as controversial as theirs. Almost without exception, they amounted to absolutely nothing. The staff appeared mollified and Adam only wished he could be as sure as he sounded.

Less than a week later he was standing in Dorothy Grimes' office working delicately around to exploring the question. "Someone—of course, I realize it's so ridiculous I shouldn't even bring it up—someone's saying that there's a move afoot to kill the series on Johnson."

"There's no move afoot." Dorothy Grimes sat behind her tiny French antique desk and confronted Adam with a faint smile. The desk always sas oddly out of place in her slab-modern office, and he suddenly felt as out of place as the desk. Dorothy stuck another cigarette into her elaborately inlaid ivory cigarette holder and let the smile die. "There's 'no move afoot,' Adam; you know I don't work that way. My action was very direct: the story is dead. Killed. Personally. By me." She was waiting for a reaction from him and, when none came, decided further explanation was needed. "I *was* indirect in only one area, and that was a mistake: I should have told you myself earlier instead of having you pick it up on the jungle drums. I know that. But frankly, Adam, I dreaded having to tell you, so I kept finding excuses to put the moment off." Dorothy was growing nervous and laughed to relieve the tension. "All right, Adam. I'm a coward."

Most of what she had just finished saying did not register with Adam; his mind was still on the story. "You can't have

81

seen the documentation, Dorothy. Poor Johnson. The stuff really nails him."

"I've seen it. And you're very right; the documentation *does* nail him. In fact, so thoroughly that I killed the story."

Adam felt a coldness creeping into his stomach. "I don't get you then. I must be dense today or something, but I plain just don't understand."

"We like Senator Johnson."

Adam's mouth fell open. "He's a crook, and we can prove it. We've got the documentary evidence, the statements of the people who were involved with him, even, for Christ's sake, copies of some of the correspondence. The whole thing is pretty sordid."

Dorothy Grimes looked away and stared out the window. "Oh, Adam. Adam, Adam, Adam." She let the words trail off as if mourning a lost lover before turning back to him. "Adam, you always try to paint everything so black or white. Naïve. All right, Johnson's a crook. But all politicians are crooks of one sort or another. And when this one's not busy making himself money, most of what Johnson stands for is good. He's a liberal in the FDR tradition. There are not too many of them around anymore."

"His record on civil rights stinks."

With a small laugh, Dorothy Grimes put out one cigarette and lit another. "In Texas you don't get elected more than once unless it does. And besides, Johnson works a lot on civil rights behind the scenes, back where nobody sees him, doing things nobody ever knows about. He's a good man, Adam."

Adam exploded. "I can't believe what I'm hearing. Goddammit, I can't. What you're saying is the end justifies the means. And to hell with the truth."

"When the truth gets in the way of what I believe—and I know you think and believe in the same things I do, Adam—that's it precisely. If we blow Johnson out of the water now, all the essential good he stands for goes up the tubes with him. That's stupid."

For a long time, Adam stood and stared at her. The

moment reminded him of the first time he'd realized his own existence was the product of his mother and father's screwing. He couldn't believe that then; he couldn't believe Dorothy Grimes now.

She broke the silence. "I know you've done a lot of work on the series, Adam, and I know it's never much fun to see good work go up in smoke. But I'm glad you came to talk to me, because there's something I've been wanting to talk to you about—only I've been hiding from you because of that Johnson story thing." Dorothy Grimes came around from behind her desk to lean against it, staring intently at Adam. "I don't know whether we ought to break out the champagne or what. But last week the executive committee and I were talking about you. And we felt that you're being limited—tied down—by the investigative reporting team." She could see an awful doubt beginning to grow in Adam's eyes and hastened to clarify the proposition. "Look, Adam, this is no bribe to keep your mouth shut, believe me. If you want to, you can walk right out of here and go to any paper anywhere with your Johnson story. We just felt you're wasted where you are now. . . ."

Adam's first reaction was to quit on the spot. But when he opened his mouth, he found he couldn't speak. His voice was completely paralyzed. It was a little like autohypnosis: if you tell yourself you can't move your hand and keep telling yourself you can't long enough, pretty soon you begin to realize you couldn't move your hand no matter how much you might want to.

Numbly, Adam Mosely accepted the post of senior vice-president of the Tribune Publishing Company. Without a fight, he agreed to divorce himself from direct control of his investigative team, something he knew inside himself he would never do. In return, Dorothy Grimes promised Adam complete editorial freedom and that she would never again interfere with his decisions, something she knew inside herself *she* would never do.

When it was all over, she walked over to her bar. "I don't

83

have any champagne, Adam, but just about everything else. The moment calls for a celebration. At least, I think it does."

Adam didn't feel in the least like celebrating, but going along with her was less painful than thanking her. Dorothy sensed his mood and looked thoughtfully at him over the top of her glass. "You realize, Adam, I'm a little disappointed. You wouldn't have given in like that a year ago. You'd have yelled or quit or socked me or something. Possibly the phenomenon is called maturity. I don't know. Anyway, you've changed."

And he knew he had but was totally unable to fix the reason. Over a period of months the former assurance, the self-confidence, the resistance to intimidation of the old Adam had dissolved into a new self given to indecision, vacillation, or, worst of all, compromise. Pondering it, over and over in the middle of the night, the nearest he could come to an explanation was that the change was connected to Georgia's drinking in some way. Probing any further produced only a blank wall, one that confused him, troubled him, sometimes infuriated him.

In a daze, he left Dorothy Grimes' office. To the people, the secretaries and members of the staff outside, Adam Mosely's promotion had just made him one of the *Wunderkinder* of the newspaper world. Inside himself, Adam could glimpse the haunted beginnings of a defeated man.

A year later Adam became editor-in-chief, and a year after that, president of the Tribune Publishing Company. These new promotions didn't happen by chance; he played ball with Dorothy Grimes. She was not, he knew, a bad or corrupt or evil woman, but with age, she had hardened her positions. Unlike Adam, who believed the media's responsibility was to present the facts and let the public draw its own conclusions from them, Dorothy Grimes more and more believed the *Tribune*'s job was not only to tell the readers what the facts meant but to *keep* from them any facts that might weaken her argument. She was completely sincere in this; her belief in the liberal position never wavered. She simply refused to acknowledge any other position might have merit; it was, as Adam had pointed out in their discussion about Senator Johnson, a sincere case of believing the end justifies the means.

Still, he played ball. Every now and then the old Adam in him would rebel, but the changes were so deeply ingrained that the insurrection would be quickly and firmly put down.

And when, in 1960, his investigative team turned up a strong possibility that the Presidential election might have been stolen, it was Adam who killed the story, not Dorothy Grimes.

He didn't reach the decision without an agonizing struggle. At first he had found his own investigative team's changes almost impossible to accept, particularly since he himself had worked so hard for Kennedy's election. For a while Adam not only didn't want to believe the story, but couldn't and *wouldn't* believe it. But the allegations were all there, sitting on his desk like a time bomb; tombstones voted in Cook County, massive irregularities in Missouri, and, in many Texas counties, more votes cast for Kennedy than the total of voters registered in both parties. In a hairline-tight election, these votes could have made all the difference.

But the idea of Nixon was anathema to Adam. Even more compelling, an investigation and recount would take weeks; the country would be in desperate confusion; the world would look at the new President, whoever he finally turned out to be, with high suspicion. Adam killed the story. The end justified the means.

It wasn't until almost a year later that he even told Dorothy Grimes what he'd learned. The facts and questions about the election still preyed on his mind. Had Kennedy known about the irregularities? If he had, did he know about them before or only after? Even if he had only known about them after, had he allowed them to be covered up? All these questions intrigued and tortured him, and he told Dorothy Grimes so.

With a small smile, she leaned far back in her desk chair, let her head lean back even farther, and studied the cloud of smoke rising from her inevitable cigarette. The smile was her way of telling him she had known all along. Suddenly, she snapped forward in her chair and stared at Adam across her desk. "Did you *want* Nixon to be President?"

"Good God, no. But if the country voted him in and then didn't get him, what I want doesn't matter."

"It does, if the country was misled—pressured—into voting the wrong way."

Adam ignored her last statement; he saw no point in going into the complex means and end question with her again. "All right, but somehow the facts have to be gotten out. Sometime, anyway. Possibly it's still too soon. But later, maybe. The public has a right to know—if only so they can protect themselves next time."

Dorothy Grimes smiled again, her face showing that she now knew how to resolve the question. "I agree, of course. But it *is* still too early, too much damage to the country would be done. I think you used the key words when you said 'Later, maybe.' There, I think, is the way to handle it. When the time is right—later—the public sees how an election can be stolen, but the country doesn't receive a mortal wound. That's important. And the people see how to protect themselves from the same thing ever happening again. That's important, too. Yes, Adam, you've hit on the way. Later."

But Adam knew, just as Dorothy Grimes knew, that later would never happen. First, the time wasn't right because of the Bay of Pigs. Then, the time wasn't right because of the Cuban missile crisis. Adam still fooled himself into thinking he would eventually publish the story; his need to become whole again, his own self-loathing at the change that had taken place inside him, demanded that the story be published. And it *would* be published. The sole remaining requisite was the right time.

But the right time never came. Because one day, the screens of every television set in the country, the headlines of every paper, the thoughts of an entire world, were suddenly focused on Dallas. The story was now—and forever —unthinkable. Adam's last battle with himself was lost.

Later was never.

With a sigh, he pulled the car off Wilshire and down the broad concrete way that led to the Park Plaza complex. The man at the front of the hotel opened his door and waited for him to get out. Adam was staring fixedly at the button you press to wash the windshield, smiling a little and ruefully wishing the human body had a button that could cleanse your soul as easily. Push, squirt, and wipe.

The man holding the door cleared his throat and, when he still got no reaction from Adam, stuck his head partway into the car and tried not to sound irritated. "Sir? Can I help you, sir? *Sir?*"

Blankly, Adam turned and looked at him, then grinned sheepishly and climbed out. The man handed him the valet-parking stub and climbed into the car as Adam walked slowly toward the entrance of the pretentious, bastard-modern building. Almost at the door, Adam remembered that the Penthouse Terrace had its own express elevator, a small car which raced up and down an external glass shaft stuck on the outside of the building like an afterthought. Although these external elevators were very popular in Los Angeles, Adam usually tried to avoid them; they made him nervous. However, taking it would avoid waiting in line at the Park Plaza's regular elevators, and Adam strolled around the outside of the building to the entrance of the Penthouse express.

Looking up, he watched fascinated as the tiny elevator shot down the glass shaft toward the ground level. Part of him wished it would never arrive. For if Dorothy Grimes hadn't learned of tomorrow's edition yet, she soon would. The waiting was over. She would have to be faced, if not now, later.

Tomorrow's front page spoke for itself; his declaration of war on advocacy journalism. Admittedly, a blast at the mayor of Los Angeles, Manuel Ortiz, might not seem all that important, but for those in the newspaper business it would be a ' clear signal; they knew about Dorothy Grimes. More important, beyond the article itself, the front page carried a listing of future articles, articles that reached into places far higher than any mayor's office. Adam wasn't sure where he'd got the courage to revert once again to his old self, but he knew that God somehow had given him another chance. His last chance, probably, to be a free man.

The bus, too full of people, gas fumes, and futile hostility, slowly swung around the corner of Firestone and Avalon avenues and stopped. The passenger door sighed open and shut, the engine rattled uneasily as the motor accelerated, and then the bus, with a groan of resentment, plunged into Watts. Gilla, Laura Vorhees' maid, grabbed at the hanging strap as the movement yanked her suddenly backward; she had to struggle with the brown paper bag in her arms before she could regain her footing. For no reason, the violent lurching made Gilla begin grumbling aloud about Mrs. Vorhees; an old man seated in front of her, his eyes glazed and white stubble showing starkly against his skin, looked up briefly to find the source of this new voice and then shook his head in wonder.

Gilla fought with the package again and turned away from him. The battle with Mrs. Vorhees had been a draw, she decided. As usual, the lady had been contrary but then had tried to buy her forgiveness by acting sweet. Shit. For herself, she, Gilla, had been stupid about the lie; it was a transparent one, and she should have been able to dream up something more convincing.

She would have to do better tomorrow. Tomorrow ineffective lying could keep Oskie in jail for a lot longer than she liked to think about. Tomorrow she was due to appear at nine A.M. in Part IV, Criminal Court, County of Los Angeles, and swear that she had been with Oskie Davenport, her common-law husband, on or about the night of last October 12, and that no, Oskie Davenport indeed had not stabbed the bartender at Lefrak's Soul Palace. No, *sir*. He wouldn't kill nobody. Not him. One Coverdale Kelly had stabbed the bartender at

Lefrak's Soul Palace, and she, Gilla, had seen him. And because in court, as in other places outside her home ground, she would be playing Hattie McDaniel, she'd maybe sniffle a little into her handkerchief to show she still hadn't got over watching Coverdale Kelly commit murder.

And Coverdale Kelly's lawyer would jump to his feet with an objection—Kelly was just a witness, but Gilla had been warned he would have a lawyer there anyway, "to protect his rights"—and the lawyer would ask the court to remind Gilla that she was under oath, and the judge would pretend to brush him aside at first and then lean down from his great bench and remind Gilla of the penalties for perjury. And the lawyer prosecuting Oskie would get to her on the stand later and scream at her about bearing false witness against her neighbor, and Gilla would shake her head to show that she wasn't lying, although that small, very small, part of Gilla that had been left behind in First Creek, Alabama, would remember all those Baptist preachers leaning down from pulpits as high as the judge's bench, and she would shake a little inside.

But the lie tomorrow had to be told, just as the lie today to Mrs. Vorhees had to be told, and Gilla hoped she would do better with her made-up testimony against Coverdale Kelly than she had with the hospitalized mother invented for Mrs. Vorhees.

Mrs. Vorhees didn't know she had a husband—common-law or otherwise. And since she couldn't very well tell Mrs. Vorhees about him now—it was much too late for that—the hospitalized mother had materialized out of necessity. Inside herself, moreover, Gilla wasn't sure Mrs. Vorhees' story about the exterminators was any truer than her own about Coverdale Kelly. That crazy Laura Vorhees had just happened to pick a lousy day to demand she come in early.

She was lonely, that lady, what with a creepy husband smart enough to spend all his time someplace else, and she just wanted Gilla around so she'd have someone to talk to.

Almost automatically, Gilla pulled the cord for the bus to

89

stop at her corner. Tomorrow, anyway, she'd get a chance to see Oskie, even if only at a distance. And maybe they'd let her visit him before they took him back to the prison in the Valley where they were holding him.

Clutching the bag, Gilla stepped off the bus into the heat and the sounds and the smell of the street. She walked across the sidewalk quickly and leaned against the wall of the building, opening her purse and pretending to check her makeup in the mirror. She'd seen the two-bit buck that was always after her waiting down the street, and today she was going to fix him. Carefully, Gilla reached inside the purse and unscrewed the protective top from her perfume atomizer; the atomizer was about the size of a large cigarette lighter and worked like an aerosol spray, designed to throw off a cloud of perfumed mist when the button was pushed. With Gilla's, there was one significant difference: the atomizer was very definitely not filled with perfume. Straightening up, she started ambling down the street toward home.

As she expected, the buck made a couple of dirty cracks and then barred her way with his body, leering at her, waiting to see if she'd try to get past. With a weak smile, Gilla pretended she was going to go around him; as she got alongside and the buck began edging over to block her way again, Gilla aimed the atomizer directly at his face and pressed the valve.

The Mace hit him squarely and unexpectedly. For a second, he looked confused. Then the pain reached him and he screamed, pawing at his eyes with his hands. A moment later the Mace reached his lungs and the screams turned into a coughing, gasping rasp as he fought for breath, half-stunned, reeling, tears streaming down his face.

When his voice returned, he started alternately screaming and yelling as Gilla slowly climbed the uneven steps of the converted old house that contained her apartment.

What she said back to him, Hattie McDaniel wouldn't even have understood.

Speeding toward LA at about the same time as Gilla's bus

was inching toward Watts, Oskie Davenport stared out the window of the Los Angeles county sheriff's car and sighed. He was sitting beside Simon Pokress, a white who was due in court about the same day he was. The charges against Pokress were awesome: rape, murder two, two counts of attempted assault, and, as an afterthought, illegal flight to avoid arrest.

To look at Pokress, the man hardly appeared aggressive enough to commit the crimes he was accused of, yet his wary fellow prisoners had declared him deceptively powerful and cunning. Oskie studied him, trying to solve the riddle.

Simon Pokress was a short, slight man with eyes far too big for his head and a head, in turn, frighteningly oversized for his body. Instead of having the ordinary prison pallor, his skin lacked any pigment whatsoever, giving his complexion the dead, colorless look of watery cement. If Pokress had curled up on the floor, the inescapable effect would have been of a gray fetus too soon torn from the womb. To hear Pokress speak only heightened this impression; for reasons unknown, his vocal cords had never fully developed, and Pokress could utter little more than a hoarse, croaking whisper. Ordinarily, any prison community would have been brutal to someone as grotesque as Pokress, but he exuded such an unhealthy aura of pure evil the other prisoners left him very much alone.

Oskie himself had moved as far from Pokress as the width of the car seat allowed. Both Oskie and Pokress were seated in the back of the sheriff's car, separated from the deputies in front by a grillwork of heavy steel mesh. A similar grillwork covered both the side and rear windows, making the back seat a portable jail. Gilla better give a good performance in court tomorrow, Oskie told himself, or he'd be in a highly unportable jail for too long to even think about. Remembering that the lawyer had told her exactly what to say—over and over until she could repeat it from memory—he felt a little better.

Oskie raised his free hand and rubbed an itching nose. Pokress was watching him, his mammoth eyes squinting but moving away from the deputies for only a second. Pokress,

Oskie could guess, was trying to figure the chances for a break; once they got that guy into court, he was dead. But escape, Oskie figured, was a wan hope.

Up front the deputy riding shotgun—literally, the man seated on the right had a shotgun propped between his knees—picked up the radio transmitter and asked about traffic conditions on the San Diego Freeway; delays at the prison were going to put them squarely in the middle of the five o'clock jam.

The radio crackled and a voice told shotgun that, according to KBDT's traffic helicopter, a trailer truck had overturned just below the Mulholland turnoff; no traffic beyond that point could move. Alternate route into LA suggested, but decision up to them. Keep HQ advised.

The driver swore. Ordinarily, he and shotgun didn't like transporting prisoners on anything but well-traveled roads, but neither did they want to sit on the freeway all night.

"Turn off at Mulholland," ordered shotgun. "We can cut through Beverly Hills—down Beverly Drive to Wilshire and into LA that way."

The driver started inching the car over toward the right and the turnoff. He cast an uncomfortable look over his shoulder toward Oskie and Pokress. "Those bimbos in back . . . ."

"Ain't going nowhere," reassured shotgun. He turned around and pushed up his steel-rimmed dark glasses. "*Are* you, fellas? Of course not. So we're taking you on a little tour. Through Beverly Hills. Enjoy the scenery."

The driver laughed and reminded shotgun about advising headquarters. Shotgun snorted and made no move toward the radio. In back, a new look of hope had come into Pokress' eyes: any change from routine always made your chances better. Oskie only sighed; his own best chance, he'd decided, was in court.

Taking the Mulholland turnoff, the driver, a little nervously this time, again reminded shotgun about radioing in their change of route.

"Turn on the screamer," snapped shotgun. "We can make

up time easy. But not if headquarters knows where we are and can clock us."

Slowly, the siren rose from a groan to a wail as the car sped down through the steep hills to the area of the big estates, each set at the end of a long driveway, each driveway flanked by a set of stone gates, each set of stone gates more formidable than the last.

To the outsider, this section of Beverly Hills is both awesome and puzzling; there is no way to be certain whether the gates are meant to keep strangers out or the people who live behind them in.

Chapter Seven

One misconception—perhaps a left-over from its days as the movie capital of the world—is that Los Angeles is a "wild" city, filled with irreverent, unconventional, bizarre people. This, of course, is not true.

The majority of the citizens of Los Angeles aren't much different from those of any other town: quiet, honest, normal people going about their business. One only has to look, for instance, at the number and diversity of houses of worship that dot the telephone directory. . . .

—Moody's Guide to Travel:
Western United States Edition

STEPPING out of the tub, Laura listened to the mournful gurgle of the water being sucked down the drain. She could sympathize with it—doomed and being pulled under like herself. Making up her mind not to think about George and the tapes was easier to say than do; additional recollections of his unfairness kept creeping into her brain, torturing her, and making her angry all over again. For one of the few times in her life, Laura was allowing herself the luxury of feeling real anger.

With a yank, she pulled her bathrobe off its hook and marched into the bedroom. She still had things to do, and maybe they'd keep her mind off George. But her eyes were drawn to the package on the marble-topped commode as relentlessly as the water in the tub had been pulled toward the drain.

For a long time Laura stared at the parcel. Neatly wrapped

and tied, the label was addressed to George at San Luis Obispo. Inside, written in Laura's precise, almost old-fashioned hand, was a short note. In keeping with Laura's usual way of blaming herself for anything that happened, the note was low-key, almost apologetic, only this time the *mea culpa* was designed for effect.

The note said merely that since the lawyer attached so much importance to the two reels of tape the package contained, she felt it only right that George should have them. No overt attempt was made to attach her own misery to either George or his peculiarities, only a thoughtful suggestion that, having looked at the tapes now herself, she felt he was more in need of help than she.

By Laura's figuring, the package—already weighed and stamped with the correct postage to make sure it would be mailed without arousing more than passing curiosity—should be delivered at Obispo no more than a couple of days after it was found among her belongings. By then George would be well aware of what she had done, and the arrival of the tapes and the note was to be the beginning of his punishment. (Laura had no background in psychology to tell her that one of the asic motives behind suicide is actually a form of murder; the survivors are supposed to hold themselves responsible for the suicide and become so stricken with guilt over their past actions and indifferences that they literally destroy themselves. She needed no psychological expertise; her instincts were more than sufficient.)

At first, Laura knew, George would be relieved to have the tapes so they could not be used against him in court. Then, slowly, his responsibility for her death would begin to eat away at him—even George could not be wholly free of sensitivity—saddle him with guilt, and eventually ruin him. And the more selfless she was in her note, the faster this destructive cloud of guilt would settle on him.

In spite of herself, she picked up the package they were in, turning it over and over in her hands, pondering it, weighing it, trying to decide whether the punishment she planned for

George was too subtle. Fleeting glimpses of the tapes she'd seen on the videotape machine downstairs raced in front of her eyes and made her shudder.

The early sequences from the motel Laura found disgusting. Disgusting but also dull. It was difficult to understand why George had even bothered to record them. Then the tenor of the tapes began to change. A repeating cast of characters—a sort of pornographic repertory group—began appearing in most of the scenes, and the activity grew less casual and more inventive. For someone as naïve as Laura, what she was seeing became increasingly bewildering.

But it was the last few scenes on the tape that really shook her. George had apparently recruited even more depraved participants; the cast was all new, and their performances were difficult for Laura to understand. There was the man in his late fifties who sat on the edge of his bed while another, younger man dressed himself as a policeman; then, one by one, the older man cut the buttons off the uniform. When the last shiny brass fastener came off, the button cutter gave an intense sigh of pleasure and ejaculated over the floor.

To Laura, who found normal intercourse baffling, the gratification the pair got from this was beyond comprehension.

There were the four middle-aged ladies who—with a little unseen help from a burly man who quickly disappeared—raped a drunken or drugged marine corporal, apparently working on the theory that the marine's masculine pride would keep him from ever telling anyone about the incident. What the four women got out of it, totally mystified Laura.

And finally there was the kid—he couldn't have been much more than fourteen or fifteen—who arrived in a room where three men waited for him; calmly he told them he was willing, as the boy put it, to "give them a party" for twenty dollars apiece. Without warning, the three men fell on him, and what had started for the youth as an easy way to pick up a few dollars abruptly turned into a fatal nightmare. Laura stared at the screen in disbelief; she had led too sheltered a life to understand what they were doing to him, but she could tell from the boy's agonized screams that the "party" had got badly out of control.

For once, George must have been equally stunned, for he suddenly burst into the room yelling at the men for Christ's sake to stop, they were going to kill the kid. Then he paused, the unspoken question on his face as to whether he might already be too late. Simultaneously, his eyes rose directly toward the camera as if he'd just remembered it was there to witness the event. "Jesus!" George whispered, and rushed from the room. A few seconds later the screen went black.

Still holding the package in her hand, moving it gently up and down, Laura again considered whether George's punishment might not be too subtle, too lenient. She could not tell whether the question arose—she hadn't really worried about it before—because running the tapes through her mind this way made them seem so vivid or because her own time was growing so short.

The sudden, painful recollection of the boy's screams made the decision easy. Putting the package down, she took a fresh label from her desk drawer and wrote a new name and address in the blank space, wetting her lips and grimacing from the taste of the glue as she pasted the label in place.

And for the first time she could remember, Laura Vorhees had made a major decision which left her with absolutely nothing to feel guilty about.

As a Catholic church, St. Bridget's falls into no known category of church architecture. Set in the run-down section of Wilshire Boulevard that lies between the Miracle Mile to the west and the financial district to the east, it is, like its neighbors, nothing more than a dilapidated two-story storefront,

The Archdiocese of Southern California did not locate St. Bridget's there by accident. On either side, as far as the eye can see, is a collection of similar buildings, tenanted mostly by

97

hypnotists, yoga schools, mind readers, a few small, un-profitable businesses, and a flurry of splinter religions: the Children of God, the Seventh-Day Buddhists, the Divine Temple of Living Light, and the True Abyssinian Synod. At a diocesan meeting six months earlier, the bishop coadjutor had raised the point that some of these, with their heavy appeal to the young, might represent a wave of the future—or if nothing else, be attended by any number of lapsed Catholics. Reluctantly, the diocese decided the Mother Church should be represented there as well.

This decision solved a second problem at the same time: what to do with Father Reed. Reed was a young activist priest, a Jesuit, who had concluded that ritualistic religion in the world of today was an anachronism. With all the wealth and machinery of the Church in place, however, he did see one very important role for religion—as a means to an end. The end he visualized was total economic equality and the means was to be massive social protest—with the Church and her priests squarely in the middle of the battle. To virtually all in the diocese's moderate and right wings, Father Reed's views represented both blasphemy and rank socialism, if not some-thing far worse.

Father Reed was appointed pastor of St. Bridget's. There, the bishop figured, his casual ways, his disturbing shock of bright-red hair, and his social activism would be safely out of the way. And he might, added the bishop, even do some good.

On the Day, Derek Usher let himself quietly out of his mother's antique store, about two blocks from St. Bridget's, and closed the door softly behind him. To Derek, this covert way of acting was an outrage: thirty-five and he still had to sneak around like a kid so his mother wouldn't hear him and demand to know where he was going. Actually, she'd probably have approved of his going to St. Bridget's, even if she'd have been appalled by the reason he was going there.

Derek and his mother had shared the small apartment above the antique store for four years now, but the mission Derek was setting out on would, if successful, mean they would share it no longer. Starting to walk down Wilshire, Derek mentally crossed his fingers and reminded himself not to become overconfident. Three years earlier he'd thought he was finally rid of her, only to discover he'd been cheated. For in spite of dire predictions from all the doctors, her heart attack had not been fatal, and Derek found he was still saddled with her incessant nagging and suffocating, smothering hold on him. If possible, things were worse than before. "You must remember, Derek," his mother pointed out, looking at him over the top of her crumpled handkerchief, "that your mother is living on borrowed time. You heard the doctors. And you mustn't get Mother worried or upset or nervous the way you used to; my heart can't take it anymore."

Shaking his head at the recollection, Derek continued down Wilshire, turning off onto a side street a block away from St. Bridget's. His mother's health seemed robust as ever, heart attack or not. All she had to show for the coronary was a moderately irregular heartbeat—and this was taken care of by the pacemaker they'd implanted. He had been outmaneuvered.

Still, the irregular heartbeat and the pacemaker delivered to him the means for getting rid of her for good, so he shouldn't count the attack as a complete loss. His would be the crime of the century, a masterpiece, the seldom-perfect perfect murder, and Derek felt almost sad that no one but he could ever know about it. Only two things were still needed to complete preparations—Derek had been working on the idea for a couple of months—and the small electrical store off Wilshire he'd just entered would provide the first of these: an electrical timer. The kind you can preset that turns appliances on and off while you're busy elsewhere. The store had one, as Derek knew they would; he'd called earlier in the day to make sure but did not now identify himself as that caller.

Back on Wilshire, Derek clutched the small brown parcel and whistled softly. Every few steps he reached up and brushed the long, shaggy hair away from his eyes, which darted furtively from side to side like a small animal's. With Derek, the nervous eye movements—they'd been worse when he was a child—were nothing unusual; they became particularly noticeable whenever one of his schemes looked as if it might work, and this one already exuded the sweet smell of triumph.

St. Bridget's would provide the other essential element: an alibi for immediately before and then during the actual happening. His plan was to seek out Father Reed—he'd heard that the new cleric was highly unconventional, but even the police wouldn't dare question the word of a Catholic priest—and say his confession. The confession Derek had in mind would be of a kind the priest would not be likely to forget, and Father Reed would be able to testify that yes, one Derek Usher had indeed been right there in his church at the time of his mother's death, giving his confessions, and that, yes, it was also true he had returned a little later for vespers. Although Derek had not been inside a church since he was fifteen, he could still remember the ritual of the confession well enough to carry it off, and a priest as an alibi was as perfect as the crime itself. Derek's uneven teeth showed slightly as he marveled at how smart he was.

Through the plate glass window of the church, Father Reed eyed him curiously as Derek started toward the door. It occurred to the priest that Derek Usher was a pretty odd-looking man, even for this neighborhood. About thirty-five or forty, Father Reed guessed, although the man tried to appear younger; his eyes, narrow, slitted, and constantly moving, were what gave him such a sinister aura.

"Father Reed?" asked Derek, sticking his head inside the door.

"You got it," said the Father leaning against one wall to show that formality was not called for in St. Bridget's.

Derek was unsettled by this offhand approach. Scuttling crabwise across the short distance, he held out his long, limp hand. "Derek Usher, Father." He paused a second as Father Reed mangled his hand like a longshoreman; then he repeated his name, spelling it out carefully: "U-S-H-E-R. Derek Usher. A lot of people get that wrong." He studied the priest's face, wanting to be sure the name sank in.

"I'm Father Reed," the priest said, then, remembering that Derek had called him by name as he came in, felt suddenly embarrassed. "But you already know that."

Derek was delighted; Father Reed was an easy man to rattle. "I'd like you to hear my confession, Father."

The Jesuit looked about him anxiously, searching for something. "Sure, Mr. Usher. Just pull up a chair." Father Reed paused. "There's one here somewhere."

Derek let his eyes travel around the stark little room, thinking of the Byzantine opulence of Our Lady of Valencia, where he'd had his first communion, and the elaborate confessionals with their curtained entrances and grillwork openings separating priest from penitent. "A *chair?*" he asked in bewilderment.

Father Reed smiled broadly, trying to relax this strange man. "Well, we don't go in much for formal confessions—we don't even have a confessional here at St. Bridget's, Mr. Usher—we just sit in chairs and you talk about what's bothering you, what you feel guilty about. It's like therapy."

Uncomfortably, Derek settled himself into the chair Father Reed had finally found him; the confession he had planned for the priest's benefit was going to be much harder staring the man in the eye. Swallowing hard, Derek began. "Bless me, Father, for I have sinned."

The priest nodded but did not reply with the traditional response. Instead: "Why don't you just put whatever's bothering you into your own words, Mr. Usher? What I mean is, the *pro forma* confession, litany and response is fine—I'm not criticizing it. But to me, I think it stands between the priest and penitent. Just talk it out in your own way."

Derek's eyes kept slipping around the room. "I have not been to mass for a long time, Father. Twenty years, to be precise."

Father Reed nodded solemnly, but quickly added an un-

101

derstanding smile; this uncomfortable, nervous man with the eyes that never looked at you had to be put at ease. "Well, I've had people with lapses of a year or two, but I've got to tell you, Mr. Usher, that you're the first to come in with a twenty-year hiatus to confess."

"Don't you want to know why?"

"If it will help you to tell me."

Derek's slitlike eyes for the first time fixed themselves on the priest's. "Because the Church, Father, has abandoned religion. Instead, it's become a political movement. Taking part in political and social controversies—look at the Berrigan brothers; criticizing foreign policy—consider the Church's stand on South Africa; interfering in social, racial, and economic problems. Even sending its priests into Congress."

Father Reed had been struck on a sore point and felt the irritation make his skin prickle; this was precisely the sort of reaction Derek both anticipated and wanted. "No church can divorce itself from the social problems around it," the priest snapped.

"Then it's not a religion."

Father Reed stood up, walked around his chair, and rested his hands on the chair's back. Something was drastically wrong with Derek Usher's thinking. He made the diocese's right wing sound liberal, but the something wrong went deeper than that. An intensity that was frightening. To the priest, this intensity suggested that Derek Usher might even have had some far more sinister reason for being here than merely giving his confession. This was a flash of insight on Reed's part, but a fleeting one; when he tried to focus on it, tried to make sense of it, the insight evaporated. Leaning slightly forward across the chairback, he angled his head so that he could look Derek in the eye again, but Usher's pupils were moving so rapidly the effort was wasted.

"You haven't answered me," said Derek, a self-satisfied little sneer slipping across his mouth.

Father Reed raised his hands helplessly. "Well, it's a big issue you're getting into. And I'm not sure what's really bothering you has as much to do with the Church as it does with yourself. I *am* sure we haven't got the time to go into anything that complex right now. And I am also sure you need help. Help of some kind. Whether from me or from someone else."

If Derek had planned the priest's speech himself, he couldn't have laid the groundwork for his alibi better than by the priest's casual mention of the time. Derek leaped at the opportunity. "What time *is* it, Father?"

Automatically, Reed checked his watch. "Five oh five."

"Five oh five," repeated Derek, pretending to set his own watch. "There. Five oh five." Repeated three times, Derek thought to himself. Well done. The important moment of his first visit was established—to the minute.

Coming around from behind the chair, Father Reed studied Usher, trying to think what he could say that might be useful; in his own mind, he suspected the kind of help this man needed would have to come from a psychiatrist, not himself. Arrangements would have to be explored. "You might want to come back some other day, when there's more time, and we can try discussing this further," he suggested.

"You even *talk* like a politician," Derek said with a smirk. And without another word, he walked out of the church, leaving Father Reed staring at the door, deliberately left unclosed behind him. The priest walked over and shut it, hanging the small hand-painted sign in the window. "Vespers: 5:15."

Out on the street, Derek felt good. Clutching the paper bag from the electric store, he began walking toward his mother's antique shop. The first stage of his alibi had been a total success. The priest would remember him.

Without argument, Father Reed would have agreed that Derek Usher was a hard man to forget.

Dr. Michael Feiner sat fingering the number given him by the man on the other end of the phone. Henry Kraypool of the Los Angeles County OEP. Since Colorado's time was an hour earlier than the Coast's, there'd already been some confusion on precisely what the 600 XE was talking about in terms of the two- to three-hour lead time.

"Well," Feiner told Kraypool, "we're on Central Time. The computer corrects for that. So the readout giving nineteen hundred hours plus or minus one in your time zone really means *eighteen* hundred hours plus or minus one."

"Christ." Kraypool had a basically deep voice, but the combination of the telephone receiver and his disturbed state of mind made it sound high-pitched, almost petulant. "That's one hour less than I thought."

"I should have been more specific," apologized Feiner, the telephone tucked between his chin and shoulder while he folded and unfolded the slip of paper with his hands. Given the circumstances, this polite conversation suddenly struck him as inane.

"Anyway it was the only good question that the deputy mayor asked," Kraypool continued. "The rest was nonsense. You know, how can I be sure, what will people say if the prediction turns out to be a false alarm, why doesn't anyone else know a quake's coming if it's that easy to predict. He thinks I'm some sort of nut, babbling on about an earthquake nobody else believes will happen."

Feiner thought for a second. "There's a seismological lab—a good one—in Drago Park right there in Los Angeles. A Dr. Christianson. Someone there ought to be able to scare the hell out of him."

"Already talked to them. In fact, somebody from Drago will probably be calling you. But they don't have the computer or know too much about your system, so all they could say was that you might well be right, but that they didn't know."

"I'll call Christianson myself, he knows more than that about the work we're doing here."

"Well, that number I gave you. It's Burt Aptner's, and I wondered if you'd try talking to him. He's deputy mayor and is usually more receptive than most of them at City Hall. I

104

didn't get very far when I tried, but maybe you can convince him."

Feiner felt uncomfortable. Talking with the deputy mayor of a city a thousand miles away and trying to accomplish what a federal official just down the street from him couldn't seemed an impossible assignment. "Nobody will do *anything?*"

"Don't believe it's going to hit. Simple as that. Scared of the repercussions if they raise a big fuss and nothing happens."

"All right, I'll call him." He looked at the slip of paper with the telephone number on it. Badgering officialdom was not his favorite kind of work, but somebody had to do something.

"Mention the Van Norman Reservoir and Dams," suggested Kraypool. "They almost went in the seventy-one quake. The reservoir holds seven billion gallons of water, and eighty thousand people live just below it. Even thinking about the Van Norman Dams scares me."

Feiner found himself becoming irritated; there were a lot of unanswered questions about aftershock possibilities he should be looking into rather than spending his time trying to persuade distant authorities, which seemed someone else's job. "Were *you* able to do anything?" he asked. "I mean, even without the mayor's office."

"A little." Kraypool's voice sounded discouraged. "I got permission from the city at least to put the police and fire departments on alert—but without being allowed to tell them why. On my own, I alerted all Civil Defense units, but, at the request of Washington, I wasn't able to tell *them* why either. The Army bases, Navy, and Air Force are on alert; their brass, I assume, *was* told why. In other words, everything within federal jurisdiction, but nothing local. Oh, Interior called the governor, but he hasn't been heard from yet." He paused. "Politics."

"I don't know anything about politics."

Kraypool laughed. "Count yourself lucky." The laugh vanished as fast as it had appeared. "You will call Aptner, won't you?"

"Yes. It's not my business, but yes, I will call Aptner."

"Let me know."

There was a click and Kraypool's end of the line went silent. Feiner picked up the phone again and dialed the number Kraypool had given him for Aptner. He could already guess what Aptner's reaction would be.

For an instant, Feiner toyed with the idea that all these people might be right, that he was letting his own prediction carry him away, that he would be proved wrong, but dismissed the thought. He *was* right. And that anyone should, at this point, have to be persuaded into believing Violet was real struck him as completely ridiculous.

Aptner's phone seemed to ring forever before someone answered.

Chapter Eight

---

a suicide is a person who has considered his own case and who acts as his own judge and executioner and he probably knows better than anyone else whether there is justice in the verdict

—DON MARQUIS,
archy does his part

FROM the bedroom, Laura Vorhees walked through her dressing room and into the bathroom. On the way she dropped the package on top of her bed, where it would be at hand later. She checked her watch; she was still on schedule, but barely, and fought to keep her feelings about George from mushrooming into something that could further delay her.

From her medicine cabinet, Laura withdrew the eye liner and carefully began brushing it on. Hard, exacting work. Usually she was good at it, but Laura was surprised to find her normally steady hand had a slight tremor. That son of a bitch, George; he deserved everything he would get. Thinking about George caused her to botch the eyeliner and only made her madder at him. Laura snatched up a folded bath towel and wiped all the eye makeup off. She always looked better without the stuff anyway, she told herself, pretending not to see the ugly dark smear the liner left on the towel.

Weighing the towel in her hand a moment, Laura suddenly stuffed it roughly over the towel rack; years of training had taught her that towels should be folded and hung neatly, but she ignored them. Let someone else fold and hang the

107

towel—or put it in the hamper or send it to the laundry or burn the damned thing, if they wanted to. They would be sorry, all of them. George. Digit. All the people in Malibu who had stayed so securely distant. Gilla. The friends in Philadelphia.

In the dressing room, she slipped into her underclothes, making a determined effort to think only of objects and things around her. In three long strides, she passed through the dressing room, crossed to the bed and then pulled the evening dress over her head, pausing to smooth the gown straight in the floor-length mirror. To the dress, she added her evening jewelry and the neatly pressed stole. The effect was not displeasing. From her desk she took out the five letters, written some days earlier, and carefully lined them up alongside one another on her bedside table. Each was addressed to a different person, each told its recipient that he (or she) was in no way responsible—thereby making sure each knew he (or she) was. A sixth letter was propped up on a table near the back door where it was sure to be discovered by the late-arriving Gilla.

Then she checked to make sure the living room would look right for tomorrow morning; it was, without question, a pretty room. An arrangement of silver-framed photographs on a small drum table bothered her, and Laura changed their positions, standing back a few feet to assess the affect before returning to her bedroom. With her, from the kitchen, she brought a wine cooler with two bottles of champagne chilling inside. She didn't really like champagne but had read it was effective in situations like this; champagne opened the valve of the stomach and depressed the nervous system without any danger of making you sick. No expert, she had quite a struggle with the spider's web of wire encircling the cork before she could pour herself a glass. As always, the taste caused her to wrinkle her nose with displeasure. She studied the label again: Roederer. No one could argue with that.

In the splendor of her favorite evening dress, she lay carefully down on her bed and propped herself up against the mound of pillows. From the marquetry nightstand, she brought out the bottle of Tuinal and placed it carefully beside the neatly stacked letters, staring at the bright green and black pills with awe.

For a moment, small doubts flickered across her mind. She had sudden recollections of herself as a child, surrounded by a well-mannered mass of brothers and sisters. Briefly, she wondered what had happened to them, scattered, as they were, around the world, living lives so distant and different from hers. They had not liked her very much, she supposed, but they had felt sorry for their youngest sister and been kind to her; Laura wondered what they would have thought if they could have seen her at this moment. She started to wonder what George would have thought but remembered he was forbidden territory and forced him out of her mind.

Leaning over from the bed, she began to unplug the telephone. If someone happened to call her, she might lose her resolve. For her part, there was one call she was almost obliged to make, and leaning over even farther, she dialed meticulously.

After several rings, no one had answered, and Laura grew annoyed. This was no time for people not to be at home. Finally, she could hear the phone being picked up. "Hello?" said the voice tentatively, a tinge of impatience laced through it.

"Digit." Laura Vorhees gave a nervous laugh. "I'm going to be out later, and I didn't want you to call and not get any answer."

But the trace of impatience in Digit's tone seemed to grow more noticeable. Laura thought she could hear someone else in the background and wanted to know who was with him, but was afraid of seeming nosy. With reluctance, she allowed her curiosity to wither. "Well, dear, I just didn't want you to worry. Usually, when you call, I'm here."

A grunt came from Digit. He either had no intention of worrying or was very preoccupied. "I'll call tomorrow," he said, speaking much faster than usual. "There's a friend here now," he added, verifying what Laura had already guessed.

"Of course, dear. I didn't mean to interfere."

A second grunt from Digit was almost buried beneath Laura's nervous laugh. "OK, then, so long." Digit said this almost desperately, as if his life depended on getting off the phone quickly.

"Good night, dear."

Sadly, Laura returned the phone to its cradle, then leaned over the edge of the bed again, pushed the lever that turned off the bell, and pulled the jack from the wall. She studied the phone with its wire going nowhere and decided it looked messy. With an impatient sigh, she walked across the room, put the phone on the desk, and made a careful coil of the wire. Then she returned to her bed.

More Roederer was consumed and the Tuinal bottle opened; fourteen capsules were counted into the palm of her hand. With a detached, almost clinical interest, she noted that when she looked at the pills, her hand trembled slightly. As it had trembled applying the eyeliner. She raised the capsules toward her mouth, but washing them down with champagne suddenly struck Laura as not right. She strode into the bathroom and swallowed them quickly, one after the other, with plain water.

It was done.

Pausing on her way back to the bed, Laura discovered she was waiting for something important to happen, although what she wasn't sure. But nothing at all happened. In fact, she felt exactly the same as she had before taking the capsules, the only possible difference being a slight feeling of relief at having survived the hard part.

Back on the bed, she propped herself up against the pillows, carefully arranging her evening dress so that it lay smoothly across her legs, and then brushed an imaginery speck of lint from the black velvet. Because her hands felt awkward and folding them across her chest would look ridiculous, she picked up the package and held it firmly to her; besides the overtones of symbolism, it gave her hands something to do.

110

The package would take care of her hands, as it would take care of George. Because now, instead of being addressed to him, it was addressed to the district attorney of San Luis Obispo County. He would know what to do.

Possibly it was her imagination—could a reaction come so quickly?—but Laura began to feel a drowsiness creep through her, a numbness that started in her legs and was moving slowly upward. She felt an itching on her face close to her nose, but while she wanted to scratch it, the torpor inching through her made any movement seem like too much work. This, she supposed, was how death came.

Trying to look at herself from across the room, she wondered if she ought to feel afraid, then dismissed the thought. After death, there would only be a nothingness, and how could anyone be afraid of a nothingness? A distant sound—children playing on the beach far below her cliff probably—again produced the recollection of her brothers and sisters, and this time, along with it, a half-forgotten scrap of childhood trauma. Her father, his fury for once not concealed behind the twinkle, was roaring about something Laura had clumsily broken. "Careless," he bellowed, "means exactly what the word says. *'One who doesn't care!'* "

The recollection caused Laura to squirm. It seemed she had spent the first twenty years of her life made to feel guilty by her father, and the second twenty made to feel guilty by George. And unfairly, God, how unfairly.

She felt her eyelids slowly drooping and automatically fought to keep them open. Little by little her vision, she realized, was becoming blurry, as if someone had placed a very thin gauze between her and the rest of the room. Looking down, she was surprised to see how far away her feet looked. Her mouth felt uncomfortably dry, and she considered reaching for the Roederer, but like scratching her nose, stretching her arm toward the wine cooler seemed too much work.

Now even the struggle to keep her eyes open was becoming too great an effort. Something inside her fought to wrestle free, to move off the bed, to call for help, but she was no

111

longer sure she could move even if she really wanted to. Slowly, the eyelids closed. One finger of her right hand gave an involuntary twitch and slipped off her stomach onto the bed beside her. As if possessed of a mind of its own, the hand began to creep slowly toward the package. Laura made no effort to stop it. And wearing a brave, unevocative expression her father would have been proud of, Laura Vorhees sank into a deep and presumably endless sleep.

Although she had spent a lifetime almost eager to assume guilt for just about anything, even Laura would have had trouble blaming herself for what was about to happen to her meticulous plan; the timing of Violet's arrival, after all, was an accident of nature.

Falling back on the pillow, Digit Vorhees replaced the phone on the hook. The girl in bed beside him had lain there quietly, smoking a cigarette and trying to pretend she couldn't hear the conversation; now she turned toward him and let one hand move across his chest and slide down his stomach. Almost brusquely, he pushed it away. The call from his mother—he should have guessed she'd call him if he didn't call her—had robbed him temporarily of all desire. When he had moved into an apartment of his own, Digit had done it not so much to escape from his mother as to escape to a new kind of life. The girl beside him was part of that new life, and now his mother, although unintentionally, was interfering with it. He'd been after this girl for almost three weeks, he had her in bed, and wham! that sudden call in the middle of things left him impotent.

"Something wrong, Digit?" she asked. Digit wasn't sure whether she meant with him or with his mother.

"No, it was my mother. She just gets lonely, I guess." He flashed her his most confident grin and stole her cigarette long enough to take a deep drag before returning it. "She doesn't have nice kind of company like you."

The girl appeared satisfied, perhaps distracted by the compliment, and they both lay still, reflecting, listening only to each other's breathing.

Like his mother, Digit Vorhees just missed being good-looking; on a man, however, the near good looks were more acceptable, almost handsome, and what his face lacked in classic line it made up in its constantly changing, highly animated expressiveness.

Unlike his mother, Digit Vorhees was not weighed down by any pervasive sense of guilt; he was realistic about the world and trusted no one other than himself. How much of this philosophy was the product of his generation's attitude and how much sprang from having George and Laura Vorhees as parents, no one knew. But the result was that Digit was a consciously unpleasant "loner"—self-reliant, self-sufficient, and, considering his age, remarkably self-confident.

The phone call might bother him, but only because it intruded on his independence; his mother had interfered with work in progress. The work in progress began to snuggle closer.

Another phone call earlier that day had bothered him far more—and still did. It had been his father, calling from San Luis Obispo and urgently petitioning him to have dinner with him tonight. Digit couldn't stand his father. Still, he called Digit so rarely and saw him so seldom that he couldn't very well avoid the summons.

"Where do you want to eat?" his father had asked in his salesman's voice, too hearty, too loud, too jovial.

Digit paused for a second, trying to think of someplace where he wouldn't run into anyone he knew. "The Park Plaza. It's not far from here."

"That awful place? Christ, Digit, it's a morgue. I thought you might like Le Bistro or the Tap Room at the Beverly Wilshire. The food's better and they've got more people."

"My car's in the shop, so either one would be a drag for me to get to," lied Digit. "The Park Plaza, I can make on foot." More people was the last thing Digit wanted. His father was

113

something to be kept out of sight, not put on display. For eighteen, Digit was remarkably self-confident, but not *that* self-confident.

It had been that kind of day. Maybe he should have read his horoscope more carefully. The girl, a child-psych major at UCLA, moved her hand again, this time lightly dragging her fingertips up the inside of his legs.

Irritating calls from his mother and father vanished; Digit was ready. He heaved himself roughly upon her and stared directly into her eyes. "Today seems to be parents' day," he apologized with a smile, and then, without warning, thrust himself inside her so hard that she cried out from the suddenness of it. "But I always keep a little time open for my own peer group."

Digit was disappointed. The child-psych major didn't even smile.

As he went down the street from St. Bridget's toward the antique store, Derek Usher knew the plan was going to work. He had said this to himself several times before he realized he actually was speaking out loud. Derek shrugged. Let people stare. *The plan was going to work.*

Derek shifted his package and reached for his key; the antique store had a dingy sign hanging in its glass front door that announced the store was closed, and when Derek went inside, he didn't bother to turn the sign around to "Open." It would make little difference; the kind of junk he and his mother sold attracted very few customers.

"Is that you, darling?" His mother's voice came down the narrow staircase, a mixture of anxiety and querulousness.

"Yes, it's me," Derek shouted back, muttering to himself as he picked his way through the phony early Americana, dusty and disreputable, that crowded the store's floor. He snorted to himself. Did she really think she'd get an answer if it was Jack the Ripper?

Her voice, relieved now of worry, concentrated on the injustice of her being left alone. "You didn't tell me you were

114

going anywhere, Derek. You know I worry. And the sign was left 'Open' so Lord knows who might have come barging in."

"I'm sorry. I had to buy something, and finding it took me longer than I thought."

"Well, you should tell me when you're going someplace. I was half beside myself, Derek. And the doctor told you that worrying isn't good for my—well, you know what it isn't good for."

Indeed, Derek knew precisely what it wasn't good for. Arriving at the bottom of the narrow staircase, he could see her standing at the top, dressed in her faded flowered kimono. "And you knew it was time for my bath and the *Fabulous Forties* program," she scolded shrilly. "I don't know how you can be so thoughtless, Derek."

"I'm sorry," he repeated, looking up at her contritely. She turned away and disappeared into the bath, carrying her transistor radio and muttering something about having done his socks while she was waiting. He not only knew it was time for her bath, but was counting on the fact; her regularity in these matters was one of the things that made the plan possible. Every afternoon, precisely at five, she would disappear to soak herself in the tub, listening to some disc jockey play recordings of the forties. The forties, Derek decided, must have been the only time she was fully alive. Today's program would be the last.

Bounding up the stairs, he unwrapped the small package. Inside was the timer. Plugging a table lamp into it, he checked to be sure that the timer worked, seeing if the device turned the lamp on and off at the correct moment. It did. Anxiously, he listened to make sure the water was running in the bathroom—the tub backed up against one of the thin walls of the dingy kitchen—and plugged the timer into a wall socket nearer the kitchen wall. Extra carefully, so he would make no noise, Derek took the microwave oven from its shelf, placed it on the floor, and then plugged the oven into the timer. The oven was his key piece of equipment, and Derek touched it almost lovingly; he'd bought it about a month earlier, when the plan first began to take shape, guessing correctly his mother would pronounce the oven "newfangled" and stick to her old gas broiler on the stove. Sniffing scornfully at its gleaming chromium exterior—the thing had cost Derek almost four hundred dollars—she'd scolded him for wasting his—actually she used the word "my"—hard-earned money on such an overpriced piece of junk. "Irresponsible, Derek," she'd complained. "Always buying gadgets. Just like when you were a child."

The microwave oven was no piece of junk to Derek. It was a ticket to freedom. When he was at high school, he'd been fascinated with electronics; the fascination grew, and Derek had dreamed of being an electrical engineer. The dream had vanished when his father's death sentenced him to a lifetime of waiting on his mother.

With his background, then, a small item in the Los Angeles *Times* warning that people with pacemakers could be dangerously affected by microwave ovens made easy sense to him. The ovens and the pacers apparently operated on nearly the same electrical frequency; if someone with a pacer was exposed for any length of time to a microwave oven, the oven, with its similar but stronger frequency output, not the pacer, would control the heartbeat. Too late the wearer would discover his heart rhythm was changed completely—and fatally.

Only a week after he read the newspaper item, Derek bought the microwave oven; with growing excitement, Derek discovered that the instruction book that came with it repeated the same thing as the *Times* article, carrying a bold-faced warning to people with pacemakers.

The thin wallboarding between the kitchen and the bathtub would provide no protection at all from the oven's high-frequency electrical waves. *Convenient.* The oven was on the floor so that its electrical field was almost opposite his mother's chest. *Smart.* The timer was set to turn on the current in five minutes, then off after an additional ten. *Crafty.* He would return after a second, perhaps even more memorable visit to Father Reed, to discover his mother dead in the tub.

116

Timer to be removed. Oven to be replaced on shelf. *Simple*. No permanent change in pacemaker so the doctors would assume the heart had simply quit of its own accord. Age. *Very sad*. And if there were any questions—Derek didn't see how there could be—he had an airtight alibi: two carefully noted visits to St. Bridget's. Why, he wasn't even around when it happened. *Brilliant!*

Derek waved a happy good-bye to the kitchen wall and patted the timer for good luck. From the bathroom, he could hear a record on the *Fabulous Forties* program blaring "You Made Me Love You," sung by Helen O'Connell. Very appropriate. His mother owned the store, several tenements, and a considerable quantity of securities and had almost come to own him. But she hadn't made him love her.

With a glance at his watch, he turned around and left the store, about to carry out the perfect murder.

And it would have been except for one small thing: Violet.

Chapter Nine

Petty men possessing modest power can only bring defeat;

Petty men possessing great power can bring disaster.

—MARSHAL GEORGES LA ROCHE
1812 Diaries

DR. Feiner's telephone conversation with Deputy Mayor Burt Aptner disintegrated into invective within three minutes of getting his call through to Los Angeles. "Goddammit," Feiner yelled into the phone. "I don't know anything about city-federal lines of responsibility, rights reserved to the states, or the superseding of local county ordinances. What I do want to know is: is anybody going to get moving while there's still a little time left or not? You've got eight million people out there, with their lives literally in your hands, and all you guys seem to think about is organizational charts."

Burt Aptner's voice was soothing, with the reassuring resonance of a man used to calming the frantic. Possibly, Feiner found himself thinking, Aptner's job was to listen to nuts like himself and keep them off the mayor's back. "Please understand, Dr. Feiner," said Aptner's soft, deep voice, "that we are not indulging in self-protective buck-passing at all. But you have to realize that you have put Mayor Ortiz in an extremely difficult position. Consider. You and your colleagues have predicted an earthquake of major proportions, with a corollary prediction that it will strike at an awesomely

118

early moment, yet no other seismologist—or you yourself, for that matter—can tell us how reliable that prediction is. A wrong reaction on our part could cause a devastating panic in this city. You are quite right in pointing out that we hold a great many lives in our hands, but an unnecessary panic could endanger the very lives you, Dr. Feiner, are so anxious to save."

Feiner struggled with himself. He felt a curious sense of *déjà vu*, a sensation that baffled him until he realized that what Aptner was saying was not very different from what Ridgeway had said earlier—could it only have been thirty minutes ago?—only Aptner was saying it better. He turned to look at Ridgeway. The man, his face gray with worry, was sitting at a desk across the room, still wearing his raincoat. He was telephoning one seismologist after another around the country, checking their own and other readings and trying to get some sort of consensus on how reliable Feiner's prediction might be. One of the programmers, called at his home, had already returned and was feeding more information into the 600 XE, searching for indications of aftershock probabilities. Over the receiver, Feiner could hear Aptner's deep and throaty breathing; with a grunt, he came at him from a new tack.

"The dams," he said urgently. "The Van Norman Dams. Certainly you can at least start getting the people out from below them."

"That sounds much easier than it really is, Dr. Feiner. To evacuate the people from there without having the rest of the city immediately know about it would be impossible. Then we'd have everybody in town climbing into their cars and trying to get out themselves. Five is the hour of highest traffic density. The freeways would be murder—and I use the term advisedly."

Feiner exploded. "For God's sake. You just plan to sit there and do absolutely *nothing?*"

Aptner's ability to shrug off urgency continued to amaze Feiner. "We have put both the police and fire departments on full alert, Dr. Feiner. Beyond that, for the moment, barring

119

some more tangible corroboration of what you predict, I don't see that there is anything we *can* do."

"For one thing," snapped Feiner, "you could turn off the gas mains and shut off electrical power. Earth movements will shatter those mains like they were made of paper, and then you'll have fire and explosions all over the place. If you're scared that would cause panic, just put out some other story—a grid overload or a regional line failure or anything else that gives you an excuse."

Aptner sighed heavily. "Doctor, let me ask you a question. Suppose—just suppose—we *did* turn off electricity and gas and then absolutely nothing came of your earthquake or that it was so minor as to cause none of the things you're worrying about. And suppose just one person died in an iron lung from lack of electricity or that just one person died in an automobile accident because the traffic lights weren't working or that just one person was asphyxiated because his pilot light was out when the gas came back on. Would you want to take the responsibility for that, Doctor? would you? I wouldn't—in fact, I won't—take that responsibility, and neither will I let Mayor Ortiz."

For a moment, Feiner was silent. He had no answer to Aptner's question and suspected it was a question that *had* no answer. Almost unconsciously he swore at himself for his helplessness, then: "May I talk to the mayor myself?"

For the first time, the smooth voice suddenly sounded a bit ruffled. "There would be no point, Dr. Feiner. Mayor Ortiz has been kept fully apprised of your prediction and is deeply concerned by it. You see, if you could just give us something a little more concrete. . . ."

"OK, dammit I will." Angrily, Feiner slammed down the phone. The noise was so violent Dr. Ridgeway looked up from his own call in surprise. Feiner shrugged and gave him a weak grin, then picked up the phone and asked to be connected with Dr. Christianson at Drago Park in LA.

At the moment, he didn't have the faintest idea of how to

120

give them something more concrete, short of causing an earthquake himself.

And right now that was precisely what he felt like doing.

In the hot late-afternoon sun, Mishi was trying to explain to Addie the painstaking Japanese art of bonsai. "You see, Addie, every year they take the tree out of its pot—every year from the time it's just a tiny seedling—and trim the roots back severely. Oh, my, but *very* severely. This stunts the tree's growth, if you see. So a tree may be—oh, twenty or thirty years old but stand no more than six inches high. The art lies in knowing just which roots to prune, and when, which is a very difficult thing, so the expert bonsai man is an extremely venerated person in my country."

Addie looked at her in bewilderment, half-real, half-affected. "But why would anybody want a shrunken tree? You know, who *needs* a thirty-year-old oak that will fit in your pocket?"

Mishi was about to answer how pretty these twisted little trees looked growing in windowsills when she realized Addie was kidding. With a giggle, she gave him a small shove. "It is because Japan is such a small island. We need the room." Then she looked at him reproachfully. "Sometimes I don't think you're a serious person at all, Addie; we are very proud of our bonsai experts."

Addie lay back, stretched himself in the light shade they had moved into earlier, and rolled up his eyes as if struggling to get his Joyce Kilmer right. "I hope that I shall never see"—he paused for a second, groping for the words—"a Jap transistorize *my* tree."

Pulling his head down between his shoulders, he turned over quickly, put his hands over his head, and waited for the expected blow from Mishi.

She studied him silently. Then, reaching over, she picked up a small watering can from beside the wall. "It was beauty killed the beast," she murmured, and dumped water over him

121

from head to foot. As he jerked upright, gasping and sputtering, she saw the look in his eyes and with a small squeal dived into the pool, followed quickly by Addie, who roared until the water silenced him.

He was in the process of giving her a good—and to his mind well deserved—ducking when a shadow fell across the pool and he heard Mrs. Herkimer clearing her throat.

Addie brushed the blonde hair, made darker by the water, out of his eyes and struggled to clear his vision; there was something strange about Mrs. Herkimer, but it took Addie a second to make out what was wrong. She was dressed for the street, wearing a hat and carrying a small black purse, looking, Addie thought, suddenly small and fragile. He wondered if all her strength and power lay in the white uniform, and if without it, she might not be totally helpless. Behind him, he could hear Mishi swimming softly up to join him at the coping.

"Excuse me, Mr. Addie, but I just wanted to be sure you understood." Mrs. Herkimer's voice sounded strained, but firm. "I'm leaving this house, Mr. Addie, and this time for good. Your mother fired me, Mr. Addie—along with Harry and Pepe and Mary, mind you—and not that she hasn't done it before, but this time I'm shut of it for once and all."

Addie stood in the pool, staring at her, still shaking the water out of his eyes, and said nothing, not being sure he knew what was supposed to be said. "Oh, my," said Mishi, who knew that somebody had to say something.

"Now, I liked it here in this house, Mr. Addie; you're a nice boy and I'm sure Mr. Mosely's a fine man"—here Mrs. Herkimer was unable to resist editorializing—"not that I've clapped an eye on the gentleman in the three years I've had my position—but I've talked to him now and again, and he seems a very decent man. But your mother discharged me, just like that, and then she said she was going to call the police and tell them I'd stolen her jewelry if I didn't leave the house immediately, and God knows she probably hid it somewhere years ago, poor creature, and can't remember where now, but enough's enough, so like I said, I'm shut of it for good."

122

Addie struggled to think what words his father would use; housekeepers who are also trained as practical nurses and equipped with infinite patience, he could guess, were not easy to come by. "Oh, well, Mrs. Herkimer, you know my mother says things like that and doesn't mean them. And the fire probably upset her a lot and made her mad at herself. . . ."

Mrs. Herkimer shook her head firmly. "No, Mr. Addie. Twenty years working in this country, and no one's ever accused me of stealing so much as a lump of sugar. And maybe we, your mother and I, we were getting on each other's nerves. I feel sorry for that poor lady, I really do. But my mind's made up." She blew her nose causing Addie to wonder if she might not start to cry.

He was about to speak but felt awkward standing in the pool. He started to climb out when she suddenly straightened herself and became all business again. "Now, then. I talked to Lottie whatever-her-name-is at your father's office, and she called back to say that the agency is sending a temporary out right away, so there's no need for you to worry. Just keep an eye on your mother, and I left sandwiches in the icebox for dinner, and anyway the temporary should be along by seven o'clock. And now my taxi must be here, so if you don't mind, Mr. Addie, I'll be moving along." She walked a few steps, paused, and looked back toward Addie and Mishi. "Good luck, both."

Then, with a sad little wave of her right hand, Mrs. Herkimer walked slowly toward the house, where Addie could now see Harry and Pepe and Mary, also dressed in their civvies, waiting near the door into the house. Harry picked up Mrs. Herkimer's suitcase from beside the French doors, and the trio disappeared inside. A few seconds later he could hear the taxi door slamming twice and the sound of wheels on the driveway, and it was as if Mrs. Herkimer and Harry and Mary and Pepe had never existed.

"Jesus." Addie's voice had an uncertain sound to it, already suspecting his father would think there was something more he could have done to stop Mrs. Herkimer. This worry was replaced by a sudden wistfulness as the finality of their departure fully reached him. For as long as he could remember, little chunks of his life, things and people he'd grown used to, were abruptly climbing into taxis and dropping out of his world. Panicked by the thought, he looked up and stared helplessly at Mishi.

She seemed to read his mind. "It's all right, Addie. I'm here." With one hand, she shooed away a fly resting on his shoulder.

"Goddamn," Addie said, trying to cover his confusion with a respectable gruffness. Pulling himself up on the coping, he reached back and helped Mishi out. "What a mess."

"We should dry off," Mishi pointed out, "and make sure your mother is all right." Addie grunted and let Mishi keep on talking. "Then we can come back out, and later I shall cook us dinner. Eggs Benedict, perhaps." There was a note of growing excitement to Mishi's voice. "Oh, indeed, yes. Eggs Benedict."

"I don't know," Addie answered, and looked around for the towels. "She said there were sandwiches."

"Don't be silly. I'm quite a good cook, Addie. Really."

"Sure." He had to move quickly as she flicked a towel to pay him back for his sarcasm.

"That is," she added, "if you're not afraid of the Yellow Peril."

Addie stopped drying himself to stare at her in confusion. "I don't follow." He watched as she turned and grinned at him like a golden nymph.

"My hollandaise."

Chapter Ten

Behind these facts lie the most important element of all: that the broad boulevards, palm-planted parks and gleaming new buildings of Los Angeles are the distillations of a thousand dreams . . . a place unclogged by tradition . . . where the imaginative come to forge his own El Dorado . . . .

—A publication of the American
Automobile Association

SOME days, looking down through the Plexiglas floor of his traffic helicopter, Ken Corbit would develop a strange feeling that everything on the checkerboard surface of the earth below was a personal plaything made solely for his benefit. Without much effort, he could imagine he controlled this miniaturized toy world, that it was he who made the cars trace their complicated patterns, racing, turning, zigzagging, as though he were advancing them from one square to another on some mammoth gameboard.

Loftily, he would study his other playthings. Tiny houses, stamped out in neat rows of development tracts, struggled to preserve some shred of individuality, in spite of the fact that they were all attached to identical backyard pools glowing aquamarine in the late-afternoon sun. Each of them, Corbit knew, was someone's anchor, the place he came home to, his castle, the receptacle of his hopes and dreams. But at Corbit's altitude, they appeared as fragile and impermanent as cereal-package plastic toys.

When the chopper dropped lower, Corbit could even make

out the toy people: people walking, people riding bicycles, people playing softball, mowing lawns, making love, lying in lawn chairs, drying raisinlike in the sun, hanging laundry, delivering packages, being born, getting old, dying, rushing to meet new husbands, and running to avoid old enemies, each of them doing something which must, to them, be of importance, yet which to Corbit, suspended in the blue sky above them, seemed a pointless waste of energy.

Yet, unlike toys, the people-dots had minds, minds that Corbit couldn't see into. He did not know, for instance, what thoughts were passing through the head of Isaac Rosholman at the Griffith Park Zoo, where, at that precise moment, Rosholman was silently invoking God, calling on Him to give him patience. The briefing of the new man had been going well, but then Battock, a little drunk from the beers he'd had while changing out of his uniform, showed up and started heckling. "Hey, Ike," he called. "Tell the new boy how you got fired in Portland for annoying the animals. Or was it for feeding the kids? Or maybe it was for feeding the kids to the animals, I'm damned if I can remember which."

The new man had looked at Battock and then at Rosholman, not sure whether he was expected to laugh. Rosholman's face was the answer. Battock continued his jeering with its pointed references to Portland until Rosholman finally walked back and told him to get the hell back to the locker room if he wanted to booze it up. Surprisingly, Battock got up off his bench and ambled away without saying anything, just a wide wink to the new man to show him that Rosholman was bats.

Across town, in Westwood, Beth Czemki, Rosholman's niece, had just told Matt about the new baby, and Matt had spilled his drink all over the table of the little bar in excitement. "Jesus," Matt said, and grabbed her hand. "We did it. We did it, Beth."

And Beth laughed. "How could it *not* happen, the way you went at it?" Matt ordered another drink for them, and they celebrated the conception of the third Czemki they had contributed to Los Angeles.

Back at the Czemki house, nine-year-old Gregory had shucked off his sulk and was watching *Mister Rogers* with Sarah. They were eating uncooked frozen french fries from the freezer; being left alone had its advantages. But there was still a small knot of fear in Gregory's stomach; his mother's assurances that nothing would happen hadn't quite made the knot go away, although he couldn't be sure now because the uncooked french fries were making a knot in his stomach all their own. Gregory had a feeling eating them might have been a mistake.

Anybody can make one.

In Malibu Laura Vorhees lay regally on her giant Venetian bed. Her head had slipped sideways on the pillow, and her mouth was open in a gentle snore. At first, she had slipped peacefully into a deep sleep as the Tuinal took effect; during the last few minutes, however, Laura began tossing fitfully, still asleep but uncomfortable in it, as with someone who has eaten too well before going to bed. The Ex-Lax fed to her by Gilla was beginning to make her stomach cramp, and even the Tuinal could not fight the peristaltic discomfort. Laura's right hand, still lying beside the package of tapes, twice had raised itself as if to fend off some unseen object; her sleep pattern was becoming more and more disturbed; her breathing was as heavy as before, but as the laxative fed itself into her digestive system in greater quantities, the measured pattern of the snoring became more irregular. Inside her brain, wild and uncomfortable dreams were flashing past her, and she moaned, a mumbled "George" being the only word anyone could have made out.

Or the word could have been "father"; the nightmare would have been the same.

Across town, her husband, George Vorhees, was pushing his rented car as fast as he dared. He was not heading for the

127

Park Plaza, where he was supposed to meet his son, Digit. This idea was abandoned when, sitting alone in his room at the Beverly Hills, he had called Laura. There had been no answer. A second call fifteen minutes later had also got no response. Laura, he decided, had gone out, possibly for the whole evening.

Straightening himself from the phone by the bed, George Vorhees reached a decision: the opportunity was too good to miss. Somewhere in the house—probably her bedroom, where he hadn't been able to look the night of his visit—were the tapes. Laura seldom went out, and his chances of learning much about the whereabouts of the tapes from Digit were marginal. He still had a key to the house, and even if, for some reason, the lock had been changed he knew a way in through the cellar window.

Thumbing through the phone book, George found the number of the Park Plaza and left a message for his son with the headwaiter of the Penthouse Terrace. The note, full of apologies, explained that something so urgent had occurred that he would not be able to make dinner. Halfheartedly, it suggested that Digit might enjoy calling up friends and having them join him for dinner; he, George, had told the headwaiter to send any bill to the Beverly Hills. And he would call, he would definitely call, in the morning so they could set up a date for the next day. In a pig's ass, he would. If he could find the tapes, he'd be on the next plane he could catch to Obispo.

As it turned out, Digit didn't need any suggestion from his father to invite a friend for dinner; he'd come to that conclusion all by himself. The psych major had been asked along before he left his apartment; she would provide a buffer. The old man wouldn't be too happy about that if, as he said, he really had something to talk about, but screw him. Dinner alone with him was too painful even to think about. "Oh, he'll love you, baby, believe me he will," Digit had told the psych major when she'd protested she would be interfering in a father-son conference. "He's a horny old goat, and you'll

128

probably make him drool all over his alligator shoes."

The note from his father, handed to Digit by the headwaiter, was received with sadness. Except, as Digit pointed out, if he'd known his father wasn't coming, he'd have chosen some place really expensive—or any place but the Park Plaza.

As George hurtled along the Ventura Freeway toward Laura's house in Malibu, Digit was far from his mind. He was preoccupied with considering how quickly his problems would disappear if he could get his hands on the tapes and destroy them. What a moment that would be! His lawyer would have a heart attack when he told him—along with Laura and the district attorney for San Luis Obispo. Maybe they should form a club and get in line for the privilege.

In Watts, Gilla had put Mrs. Vorhees out of her mind. Instead, she was concentrating on her story for court tomorrow. Pacing the living room of her tiny apartment, she went over, word by word, the details of what Oskie's lawyer had told her to say, exactly how to phrase the lie, the lie which must be better than the oat-burner told Mrs. Vorhees about her pathetically sick mother. Tomorrow was critical to Oskie, and what was critical to Oskie was critical to Gilla.

To Corbit, hovering close over the Sepulveda Freeway, the Los Angeles county sheriff's car was no more than a small black-and-white dot with a blinking red light. Inside, Oskie watched as the "portable prison" threaded its way around the traffic jam by taking a short cut along Beverly Drive. Shotgun, ordering a detour from the detour, had directed the driver to turn off Beverly Drive at the next northward crossroad; his map showed taking Tutweiler would save even more time. Simon Pokress had swiveled his oversized head to exchange a furtive glance with Oskie; with every change in route there came a new kindling of hope, waiting to be fanned into life by some incident that would make escape more than a chilly, outside possibility.

The circle of people surrounding the sleeping Laura

Vorhees in Malibu was complete, each going in his own direction, each unaware of the other, all of them heading inexorably toward an unexpected and unwelcome rendezvous with Violet.

Looking forward through the bubble, Corbit swore and stepped hard on the pedal that changed the rotor's pitch. He had come upon downtown LA faster than he'd expected and had to climb quickly to get above the taller buildings which dotted the area. From Corbit's new altitude, only the top of the *Tribune* building was visible along Wilshire; Adam Mosely was not in it, but already facing Dorothy Grimes in the Penthouse Terrace, a place as stark and tasteless as the customers it attracted. From its windows, the hotel advertised, you could see the "entire breathtaking skyline of beautiful Los Angeles"; actually, what you saw was a patchwork of one- and two-story squat, bleak buildings of concrete block and chromium, punctuated at random intervals by faceless, biscuit-box high rises. At this hour of the day, however, with the light bouncing off the thousand-windowed building fronts and the skyline washed a soft, warm gold by the lengthening rays of the sun, and all of it silhouetted against the still-snowcapped peaks of Mount Baldy, even a biscuit box can look pretty glamorous.

The Park Plaza's main restaurant consisted of two levels: an upper tier that ran along the outside edge beside the windows and a circular main dining room, set some feet below and surrounded by the tier. As Lottie had predicted, the room was virtually empty; it was too early for dinner, and the place had never caught on with the cocktail crowd. Along the upper tier, by the windows, Digit Vorhees and the psych major were deep in conversation. Digit, freed now from the responsibility of meeting his father, wanted to leave as soon as the headwaiter had delivered his message, but the girl was determined to stay.

"Oh, come on, Digit," she teased him. "When you're into psychology, it's fun studying people."

"*What* people?"

"They'll come. *Somebody* must come here."

"Sure," answered Digit, indicating two new arrivals with his head. "The ones that get thrown out of MacDonald's."

Turning in his chair, Digit studied Sporades and Anna Kristaboulos, who had just been seated farther along the same tier. The wedding feast was still going on at Georgi's, but Sporades and Anna had finally ducked out a side door. The ceremony itself had been celebrated shortly before noon, according to tradition, but the wedding feast would still be going strong tomorrow. Even chickening out early, both of them showed signs of wear. Sporades' blue suit was sprinkled with rice, which, from a distance, looked like oversized dandruff; the knot in his necktie had become loosened during their exit from the reception, and he struggled to retighten it before anyone noticed; gratefully, Anna slipped off the unaccustomed hat—it made her feel and look slightly drunk, something not too far from fact. Neither of them was saying anything. The agony of the endless party at Georgi's was still too fresh in their minds. After a moment or two of catching their breaths, Anna heaved a great sigh of relief and reached over to squeeze Sporades' hand; in the process, she upset a water glass over the white tablecloth and flushed with embarrassment. With the waiter who rushed over to mop up the water, Sporades returned to the game which had provided the one bright moment at the reception. "Thank you," he said, and then added—in Greek—a string of unflattering comments about the Park Plaza, its glasses (which tipped over too easily) and the waiter's inefficiency in coping with the spillage. However, the smile with which Sporades accompanied this was so dazzling that the waiter mentally added an extra dollar to his tip. And for the first time since they got there, Anna relaxed enough to let herself laugh.

With a condescending smirk, Digit conceded his first impression might have been wrong. "No," he announced. "I missed the crucial point. That couple didn't get thrown out of MacDonald's; MacDonald's wouldn't let them *in*."

He was not in an agreeable frame of mind, and the psych major was feeling increasingly uncomfortable.

But far less uncomfortable than Adam Mosely. He was still farther along the same upper tier, struggling to guess what Dorothy Grimes was getting at. Never given to pleasantries or idle conversation, tonight she'd come quickly to the point.

"The newspaper business is a funny thing, Adam. I don't have to tell you that." She pulled a cigarette out of a silver case and slipped it into her long ivory holder with the precision of a surgeon doing a brain implant. The elaborateness of the operation was her way of telling him she felt she *did* have to tell him that.

"Two days ago, for instance, I got a call from Raleigh Cooper. We used to go on shoots together in Kenya—back before the British folded up the Empire. What I'm trying to say, Adam, is that Raleigh is a very old friend of mine."

"I see." Adam was lying; he didn't see at all. The name, Raleigh Cooper, had been said in a way that indicated Dorothy Grimes expected it to mean something to him, but it didn't. The name had also been spoken in a tone rich with undercurrents of unpleasantness. Slowly the twinge of concern first raised when he'd heard Dorothy Grimes was in town began making itself felt again—and this time more acutely; Adam realized he had no choice but to march up to the issue squarely. "Raleigh Cooper," he repeated, turning the name over loudly for Dorothy's benefit. "Am I supposed to know him?"

"He's from San Francisco."

The twinge of concern expanded into a full-scale ache of fear, like the dull pain of a dormant toothache whose time has come. In spite of it, Adam allowed no feeling to show; if anything, he permitted a tinge of belligerence to break through his surface calm. "OK, he's from San Francisco. But I still don't think I know who he is."

"You should. He's been doing some work for you." Dorothy Grimes let a puff of smoke curl lazily from her almost completely closed mouth, studying Adam through it for his reaction.

Someone had the pliers on Adam's aching molar now and was pulling it as hard as it could be pulled. Pieces of enamel, bone, and root filled his mouth. She knew. Something impossible, something that couldn't happen, something against which every precaution in the world had been taken, but the old bitch knew. "I see," Adam repeated. This time the statement sprang not out of blindness, but from being able to see too well.

Dorothy Grimes smiled. "As I said, Raleigh and I go back, way back. He owns all sorts of odd but highly lucrative supplier companies. You know the sort of thing: repro labs, offset processors, mat shops, typesetters. Among them is an outfit called"—she fished for a small slip of paper in her handbag and produced it—"the Tri-Arts Printing Service. Nothing big. Quite small, in fact. That's why he called me in D.C. He was very flattered, he said, but as one old friend to another, he couldn't understand why the *Trib* should be going all the way to San Francisco for typesetting and mat work. I was as confused as he was until . . . until I saw it."

Dorothy Grimes' eyes never left Adam's as she pulled a four-column mat from her bag and laid it carefully on the table, right side up; it was the mat for tomorrow's *Trib* story on Manuel Ortiz.

Adam shrugged. There was no other gesture that was possible. Poking at the mat with her cigarette, Dorothy Grimes spoke very softly, almost gently. "Why, Adam? Why?"

It was a good question and one Adam knew he had to answer. And, if possible, without sounding pompous. "Because the story had to be told. The way we *didn't* tell a lot of the others. Although, one way or another, those suppressions have to be made up for, too. I'm sorry if tomorrow's article eats at you, but I can't pretend I didn't know it would. Obviously I knew; witness the secrecy. And all the elaborate nonsense of getting the typesetting and mats done in San Francisco. I didn't like that part—going behind your back made me feel sort of unclean—but I knew unless I kept what I was doing undercover, you'd hear about it somehow, and the story would be killed."

Turning the mat around and around in her hands, Dorothy Grimes looked up. "That only tells me why the *secrecy*, Adam. That much I guessed anyway. What I'm getting at is why should this particular story be so damned important you'd stomp all over our years together to print it?"

"Because the story had to be told." Adam was a little shocked to hear himself repeating this line again so soon, but that simple statement was more than at the heart of the matter; it *was* the heart of the matter.

With the kind of defeated shrug you give an exasperating child, Dorothy Grimes put down the mat. "Because the story has to be told," she mimicked. "Well, you were right in knowing that I'd kill it, but you knew *that* when you took to skulking around Tri-Arts so I wouldn't find out what you were up to." She paused a second. "This terrible thing of yours. What have you got against Manuel Ortiz? Do you realize he's the only Mexican-American who's ever really made it in this whole damned country? That he's all that keeps hope alive in millions of Chicanos? And because of that, he's an inspiration, not only to his own people, but to Puerto Ricans, blacks, Indians, Orientals—all people of all minorities anywhere? Why do you want to destroy him, Adam? I know you're no bigot, no racist. Why do you want to destroy him?"

"Precisely because he *is* an inspiration to all those people. And because he's let them down. And because, tragic as it is, they have to be told the story before he lets them down any further. What Manuel Ortiz has done is nothing short of out-and-out betrayal." Adam exhaled a long, deep breath. In spite of his attempts not to, he couldn't help sounding pompous; Dorothy Grimes always brought that out in him.

She didn't sound in the least pompous. "Balls. A few necessary shortcuts in administrative procedures, a handful of technical expediencies to accomplish highly desirable results. No betrayals. No lettings down. Expediencies."

134

Adam exploded. Dorothy Grimes could justify Judas. "Expediencies, my ass. Three, four years ago, Dorothy, I let you kill the story on how he was letting contractors slip around the earthquake building code. I don't know why Ortiz was doing it; that was the one facet of the thing we could never get our hands on. But with the amount of money involved, we could only assume he was being paid off by the contractors. Your hope and inspiration of the country's minorities was being bribed and bought off—like any small-town alderman. You know it now, and you knew it then. And I only hope to Christ that someday—well, that little quake earlier today sent shivers clear through *my* guts—it doesn't come back to haunt you."

Dorothy Grimes prepared herself to speak. Holding up his hand, Adam silenced her; he was not ready for rebuttal yet.

"OK, so you killed that one. One story that should have been told wasn't, one important piece of evidence buried. I'm to blame for it, I suppose. To blame for letting you do it. But now the same thing's happening again. Or a variation of it anyway. You read the new stuff"—he inched the mat over toward her with his fingertips—"and Ortiz is back playing the same game, only this time with city paving contracts, city lighting installations, city-financed sewer lines, water mains, and traffic controls systems. No real open bidding, and contracts let at figures far above what seems normal. Again, we can't trace it back *directly* to payoffs to Ortiz, but the implications are pretty obvious to anybody who can count higher than ten. Your man Ortiz is a simple out-and-out thief. And *that's* a story that has to be told because people have a right to know that their mayor is geting rich on their tax payments."

A sudden burst of genuine laughter from Dorothy Grimes stopped Adam in his tracks. He had expected cajolery, anger, pressure, threats, anything but laughter. Adam stared at her.

Dorothy Grimes took a swallow of water and brought the laughter under control. "You're naïve, Adam. So naïve it's hard even to stay mad at you. Do you know why you couldn't trace where the money was going? Can you really imagine a

135

man like Ortiz pocketing bribes? Can you imagine? Can you guess?"

She wiped her mouth with a napkin, and Adam watched, fascinated, as her expression hardened. "Well, I'll tell you exactly where it was going. Precisely. Dollar for dollar. The difference between normal or average cost and actual expenditure—both four years ago and today—was used by Ortiz to break the contractors' anti-Chicano barrier. Theirs and the unions. Ortiz paid—overpaid, to be more precise—the contractors so they could overpay the unions. In return for that, the union's labor force had as high as a fifty percent Mexican-American breakdown. That contractors and unions should have to be paid to do that is stupid, but there it is. And now that the contractors have gotten over the idea that the Chicanos spend all their time sitting around under straw hats taking siestas and the unions are beginning to get their membership to realize Chicanos can pull their own weight and aren't a bunch of deadbeats, aren't trying to steal their jobs by working for less, and don't particularly want to run off with the bwana white man's woman, the maneuver has paid off. It's set an example for the building trades—for antiblack union men across the country—that no one can argue with. To do it, Ortiz at first had to pay a white union man to stand beside every Chicano the union would let work; that's a thing of the past. Now that they've learned, the whole picture for minority workers is changing. That's what your 'thief' Ortiz did. That's what the 'petty swindler' was up to. That's why you couldn't trace the funds back to him; he didn't have them."

Adam sat stunned. On the one hand, he felt as strongly about the antiminority policies of employers and unions as Dorothy did. On the other, Ortiz's actions, however well intended, were blatantly illegal. Adam was right back struggling with the means-and-end paradox again. Adam made his decision. "I can't accept that, Dorothy. I admit I'm surprised—happily—that Ortiz is no common crook. But what he did still smells to high heaven. If racial balance was his aim—and it's admittedly a good one—he should have gone to

136

the people of Los Angeles and *told* them what he was doing. And why. As it stands now, he can go to prison for the game he played.

"Because maybe everybody wouldn't have agreed with him that that was a good way for their tax money to be spent. And maybe they'd be right. Who's to say that the next Ortiz won't channel the same kind of money to—well, say, to *block* equal hiring of minorities? No man has the right to make that decision. Only the people can. That's why the story has to be told. And will be told. If not with the *Trib*, well, some place else. I feel that strongly about this story and all the others that have been killed in the name of the end's justifying the means."

Dorothy Grimes sighed. "I'm sure you can take it to any West Coast paper. I'm sure the other stories—LBJ, Kennedy, the media gang-up on Watergate—can find a home in any paper. A little out of date, perhaps, but explosive enough anyway. However, I don't think you'll be taking them anywhere."

Somewhere in Adam's brain a small bell rang. Dorothy Grimes had expected his reaction and was totally prepared for it. "I don't understand. If they're to be out of the *Trib*, *I'm* out of the *Trib*. And the stories go with me."

Dorothy sighed again. "You talk, Adam, so scornfully of using the end to justify the means. God knows, we've yelled at each other enough about it. But are *you* so innocent?" She fished into her handbag and came out with another small slip of paper. "For instance, you remember one Charles Traynor?"

The bell rang louder, but the source was obscure. The name meant something, but nothing Adam could fasten his fingers around. Because of this—he was well accustomed to the curious workings of his nearly total recall—he knew the name must be related to something extraordinarily unpleasant, something so painful his brain was blocking it. In confusion, Adam shook his head.

"All right," Dorothy consulted the slip of paper again. "How about Richie del Gado, Adam?"

Adam felt he might be sick. It was impossible. Georgia's secret from years back. Back before they had taken to locking the car keys away, back before they knew the permanent loss of her license for earlier crack-ups would only be a challenge to Georgia to drive. They'd hired a chauffeur so she wouldn't have to, so she wouldn't feel imprisoned on Tutweiler, but that wasn't enough for her. She liked to drive, she said. And Georgia had driven on that day, swiping the car keys off the hook in the kitchen and heading pell-mell down the long driveway before anyone could stop her. Richie del Gado was ten, riding his bicycle past the gates. He never even saw what hit him; the doctor said he was dead by the time the ambulance arrived.

There was no witness to the accident except Charles Traynor. Back then Traynor was the chauffeur and had been a witness because he was racing down the driveway, hoping Georgia would hit something soft before she got to the road. Instead, she hit Richie del Gado. And over the phone, before the police arrived, Adam had talked Traynor into saying he, not Georgia, had been driving. That the accident was unavoidable. That no, the slightly drunken lady, Mrs. Mosely, had been in the back seat. Yes, Officer, in the back seat. No, of course she wasn't driving.

Adam squirmed. The payments to Traynor to keep his mouth shut. The payments to the del Gado family as an out-of-court settlement for the loss of their son. Out of his own pocket, because Adam was too honest to let the insurance company become involved. And too frightened that Traynor, under oath in a civil court, might not hold together. For no reason, he wondered where Traynor was now; the payments to him continued, but were made to a post office box. His eyes rose to meet Dorothy's.

"I don't know how you found out. The whole mess was a terrible tragedy. One that I took steps to keep from ever happening again. As you know—"

Dorothy Grimes' handbag seemed to hold endless surprises. Out came Xerox copies of all the checks to Traynor, as well as the ones to the del Gado family. "This is how I found out. These and a little snooping around by the insurance company. They were understandably baffled why you were paying the claims of the del Gados without either legal contest or without shoving it off on them for settlement. In the end, finding out didn't take too much figuring. Particularly because, like Ortiz, your intentions were good."

"For Christ's sake, Dorothy, sending Georgia to jail wouldn't accomplish anything. And that's where she'd have gone. Driving without a license and vehicular homicide while drunk made her a sitting duck. Who would gain? *I* paid the family. It was sad—that little boy, my God, it was sad—but putting Georgia in jail—maybe it's where she belongs, I don't know—wouldn't have accomplished anything. God knows, keeping her out wasn't for my own sake; I don't even go home anymore. But prison, well, prison wouldn't have helped *anybody.*" Adam took a long swallow of his drink and found he was shivering. "And if you try to draw a comparison between that and what Ortiz did, well. . . ." Adam sighed. There *was* a comparison. Fucking Dorothy Grimes and her justified means. He was no better, no worse than Ortiz. He turned partly away, rubbing one hand against his temple. Surprised, Adam realized the hand was trembling.

When she finally spoke, Dorothy's voice had an unusual trace of emotion. "I'm sorry, Adam, very sorry, that this miserable hunk of papier-mâché"—she picked up the mat again—"forced my hand. Making a person face himself is always a painful business. Painful, but sometimes necessary."

Adam nodded. His eyes rose to meet hers, the too-large eyes usually so filled with curiosity now brimming with defeat. "What are you going to do, Dorothy? Where do we go from here?"

"Do? Nothing. Absolutely nothing. The Ortiz story, if you want to run it, well, that's your business. I hope, of course, that you won't. The reason I brought all this crap"—she waved the Xeroxed checks forlornly and dropped them neatly into her handbag—"wasn't to blackmail you. I had to make you look inside yourself. To realize that it isn't just the Ortizes of this world who cut corners to serve a higher purpose, but people like you. And me. Anybody with a social conscience. So the fate of Ortiz—and all the things, both good and bad, he stands for—is yours and yours alone. You make the decision, Adam."

Suddenly Dorothy Grimes laughed that laugh that had originally won Adam to her. "And, in the meantime, for Christ's sake, Adam, buy the mean old lady another drink, will you?"

Without any enthusiasm, Adam weakly raised one hand and signaled a waiter.

It took all the strength he had left.

Out at the house on Tutweiler, Adam Mosely's son, Addie, was as short on enthusiasm as his father. He could not put his finger on the reason behind the reason; he knew only that he was experiencing a passing discomfort with Mishi.

Earlier they had both looked into the guest room, where Georgia lay, surrounded by a cloud of stale cigarette smoke and the odor of half-digested vodka. Addie tried not to see the face as he remembered it as a child; it was ravaged now by an angry road map of tiny red veins, punctuated irregularly by swollen pores that would no longer close. The lips had an oddly colorless look covered by a thin white film from antacids too frequently taken and never completely rinsed off.

In the kitchen, Addie had found Mishi excitedly lining things up for the Eggs Benedict, and the fact further upset him. When he told her they would wait for the temporary, Mishi flared up for a second, and then, seeing his face, sensed something of what was going on inside him and abandoned the eggs for the moment.

They compromised on a game of Ping-Pong and the stereo turned up full blast. "Never," said Mishi with a giggle, "underestimate the potency of cheap music."

For the first time Mishi could remember, Addie had not smiled.

140

At Georgi's, in the shadow of the Van Norman Dams, the wedding feast for Sporades Kristaboulos and Anna Nabukian was reaching a fever pitch; that the couple had deserted the hall in favor of their bridal room at the Park Plaza was barely noticed. As long as the resinata, the Fix, the ouzu and the Metaxas held out—and the Nabukians had laid in a supply that would long outlast any of the guests—all other details were unimportant. The dancing grew progressively wilder, new supplies of dishes for the guests to smash on the floor were brought in, and the laurel hanging from the walls was being turned into wreaths and placed on heads, looking oddly out of place attached to necks rising from shiny black suits.

And somewhere slightly to the southwest of the Valley, the last guest was slowly making her way to the party:

Violet.

On Wilshire Boulevard, Derek Usher stood outside the glass door of St. Bridget's and knocked. When no one answered, he knocked again, as loudly as he dared.

Finally, from somewhere in the back, Father Reed appeared, looking puzzled, and walked toward the sound of Derek's pounding. When he saw who it was, his step faltered. Ever since Derek left the first time, a slow resentment had been building inside the Jesuit. The California right wing was invading his sacristy, threadbare as it was, and the priest had even wondered if this strange man, Usher, might not have been sent by the diocesan conservatives to see how he, Reed, handled the touchy question of intermingled radical politics and religion.

Derek Usher watched Father Reed advance, pleased by the expression of displeasure he saw on the priest's face. The more upset he could get him, the more he would be remembered. Father Reed struggled with the lock and opened the door—although only a crack and blocking the entrance with his body.

"Vespers," noted Derek, pointing to the small sign on the

141

door. "Vespers at five fifteen. And it's five seventeen by my watch, Father." Derek fixed the priest with a stare, his constantly moving, narrow eyes for once focusing in one direction and staying there.

"Oh, Mr. Usher. It's you," said Father Reed, pretending he hadn't noticed until now. "I'm afraid, Mr. Usher, we won't be holding vespers tonight." His arm indicated the empty interior of St. Bridget's. "Nobody's here."

"*I'm* here."

"You are indeed, Mr. Usher. But holding vespers for one person—well, what I mean is, without a congregation, vespers would seem a little forlorn. If not ridiculous."

Derek was delighted. Not only was the time fixed, but Father Reed even remembered his name. The alibi was complete; he could leave now, he supposed, but it would be better if he spent more time in the church to make sure his coming and going overlapped the actual moment of his mother's death.

"If you're too busy, of course . . ." Derek taunted.

"I'm not busy at all," snapped Father Reed, feeling his hostility rising. "But a congregation of one. . . ."

"Is better than a congregation of none," Derek completed for him. "Actually, I suppose you're all tied up writing activist tirades against the oil companies and the sales tax and the profit motive."

Reed controlled himself with difficulty. This man, Usher, was a pain in the apse; unconsciously, he grinned at his own crude humor. Without hesitation, Derek leaped at the priest's smile as an easy way to buy a wider timespread for his alibi. "You're laughing at me, Father. I came to you for help, and you're laughing."

In spite of himself, the priest felt a surge of sympathy. This psychopath needed help and he, as a priest, should be more than willing to give it—even if both Derek's manner and his politics infuriated him. *Especially* if they infuriated him; this was the essence of Christianity. Stepping aside, he threw the door open for Usher to come in.

142

"I'm sorry, Mr. Usher, genuinely sorry. I wasn't laughing at you, please believe me; the smile came from a bad joke that crossed my mind—one all the way back in seminary. And if you need help, I always have more than enough time to try and give it. Please come in."

Derek Usher walked humbly into the church. Coming through the door, he had glanced at his watch; the timer, if everything was working right, had turned on the microwave oven some three minutes before.

Following Father Reed toward the back of St. Bridget's, Derek hoped his mother's pacemaker hadn't gone haywire while the water in the tub was running.

It would make a terrible mess.

But Ken Corbit surveying his toy world, could see none of this. He banked his helicopter eastward and began his chatter over the radio. There was little new to report, except to repeat the information about the overturned trailer truck on the San Diego Freeway and to point out that a new jam was building just short of the La Cienaga underpass. Automatically, he checked his chronometer and noted that there were thirty seconds left before time announce.

It was 5:17 and thirty seconds.

Part II

Chapter Eleven

On the Date of March 26, 1872, an earthquake of major proportions shook Owens Valley, and nearly destroyed the entire population.

Twenty-seven persons were killed.

—A tombstone
in Lone Pine, California

AT Goldstone, Colorado, Michael Feiner was feeling a little better. He had called Rachel, explained what was going on, and apologized for his reaction to the A&P. No, he doubted that he would get home until late—very late. The aftershock probabilities still had to be checked out. And obviously, they would want to monitor the seismograph to see if the 600's prediction came through.

But beside his settling accounts with Rachel, other things had been happening, too, and a new mood of confidence, a sudden feeling of relief that Los Angeles was finally taking their prognosis seriously, had buoyed Feiner's spirits.

This change of attitude had begun about twenty minutes before when Kraypool called and explained why the city had until now—in spite of Feiner's personal plea to Burt Aptner, the deputy mayor—remained indifferent to Goldstone's warnings. "Jesus, I'm sorry," Kraypool had apologized. "Sorry and mad. Burt Aptner was precisely the wrong guy to have you call. My fault. But after you talked to Dr. Christianson at Drago, Christianson got hold of the governor and the governor got hold of the mayor." Kraypool had paused, as if still unable to believe what he was going to say next, then: "The mayor, believe it or not, didn't know a damned thing about the prediction. . . ."

Feiner had exploded. "But Aptner said the mayor knew all about it. In fact, Aptner said the mayor was deeply concerned, but felt he couldn't act without more concrete evidence."

Kraypool had remained calm. "Until the governor called him himself, Ortiz was totally in the dark. Aptner said he was just trying to protect the mayor. Well, Ortiz bounced him on the spot; the mayor's on his way to a television studio now to personally issue the alert. The announcement will be hedged to minimize panic, of course, but at least it's a beginning. In about five minutes, the police will get the message and start clearing the freeways. Also the Valley beneath the dams. If your computer could just be a little bit early on the time thing and give us an extra hour or so. . . ."

That phone call and realization that LA was finally waking up explained the new mood at Goldstone. In the middle of Feiner's reverie, the programmer working on aftershock input walked over and handed Feiner a printout. Like the earlier printouts on tremors, it was nonconclusive. "Keep trying," Feiner told him. "Call that guy at Paragon Oil and see what's up out there; that worked last time."

The phone rang: Kraypool in LA again. "Dr. Feiner —Mike, I mean—the engineer here wants to test out the radio tie-up. We'll need anything you can give us on the aftershock situation as fast as you get it. He says to set your band for eleven hundred megacycles and turn the. . . ."

"I'm sorry, I can't hear you," said Feiner. "Kraypool? I can't hear you. Are you there, Kraypool?" The phone had chosen an awkward time to go dead on him.

Ridgeway's voice startled Feiner. It came from behind him, where Ridgeway had been standing watching the printout. "Mike!" Ridgeway's voice had a sound to it Feiner could never remember hearing before.

148

Turning, Feiner saw the blue light on the seismometer that indicated a new recording was blinking on and off. In two long steps he was beside Ridgeway, who had moved quickly over from the teleprinter when he saw the light begin to flash.

Feiner looked at the lines the stylus was drawing on the moving graph paper and sucked in his breath in a single, sudden gasp. Slowly, Feiner raised both hands to his face, squeezing it hard, and began to rock back and forth in shock. The stylus was stuttering eccentrically to its farthest limits, forced both by the magnitude of the tremor and by its own momentum far beyond the Richter 10 it was calibrated for.

"Jesus Christ." It was the ultimate expression Michael Irving Feiner could find.

The words used by KBDT's Ken Corbit were shorter, sharper, and completely nonsectarian. They were also of a kind definitely not suitable for broadcast. High in his traffic helicopter, Corbit was reporting on traffic on the cloverleaf where the San Diego and Santa Monica freeways overlapped; the interchange was a complex, raised construction, a network of overpasses and underpasses where local roads were interlaced with the two freeways. The cloverleaf was also a notorious traffic-flow hazard, particularly at this, the rush hour on Friday.

Below him, Corbit could see the slow-moving black lines on the roads beginning to grow darker as the cars and trucks backed up; he started his usual banter warning motorists to avoid the area. Earlier, Henry Dawes, the station manager, had acidly reminded him to keep giving the time signals; drivers liked that, Dawes said. With a sigh, Corbit shaped his sentences so that he could lead into the time signal naturally; his eyes searched the roads below, looking for one small point of color to dress up the fact that traffic still wasn't moving.

The traffic wasn't, but the roads *were*. It was hard to make out exactly, because a great cloud of whitish dust was rising from below; whole sections of both freeways appeared to have dropped down and disintegrated; the cloverleaf itself had almost disappeared, but the network of roads leading into it remained intact, as if the hand of an angry God had torn a sinning spider from the center of its web. Directly to the north of the cloverleaf, he could see what seemed to be a giant fissure in the ground; from this, there rose another cloud of dust, only darker and smokier than that billowing up from the collapsed roads themselves. Corbit was too high to make out what was happening to individual cars, but the neat, slowly moving pattern of a few minutes earlier had been shattered into a jagged series of broken lines; even at his height he could see the body of a bright-red trailer truck slip slowly over the edge of the La Cienaga underpass and roll ponderously into the fissure.

For a few moments Corbit said nothing. He was unable to. Then, he recovered his voice and loosed a string of expletives familiar enough over Vietnam but never before heard over the La Cienaga underpass.

Tight-lipped, the daytime producer of station KBDT nodded to the engineer and watched him yank the cable patching Corbit into the board out of the monitor panel and cut him off the air. Frantically, he signaled through the slanting, tinted glass separating him from the studio and cued Mel Rawlings, his late afternoon DJ, that he was on.

"Corbit's on the juice again," the producer grunted, and reached for an inside phone hanging from the control panel to call the station manager. He'd had Ken Corbit once and for all.

But today everything seemed against him; the phone was as irascible as Corbit and appeared to float away as he reached for it. He heard a cry of surprise from the engineer as the other cables patched into the board began popping out of their sockets like slices of toast. From below the board came a sudden series of crackling sparks and a thick cloud of pale-blue smoke as the maze of wires beneath the control panel fused together.

Abruptly, the glass wall between him and the studio collapsed in a cascading wall of tiny shards. Through it he could see his DJ, Mel Rawlings, struggling to stay upright. The whole thing was Corbit's fault, the producer told himself, and began getting to his feet, but the floor was sinking as fast as he was rising. He tried to call out to Rawlings, but his voice was lost in a terrible shuddering noise as pieces of the studio began falling inward. He was baffled at how much more clearly he could see Rawlings now, until he realized that this was probably the first time in three years he'd not been separated from him by the tinted glass. My God, but he looked old.

The last curious thought, one that flashed through his brain just before the walls of the small two-story building collapsed entirely, was that Rawlings wore a hairpiece.

And that he had it on all crooked.

Laura Vorhees slept through the actual moments of Violet's fury. But a conspiracy of happenings caused her to become drowsily aware she was still alive a few minutes later. Her first sensation was of feeling cold; her second was of irritation that she should be feeling anything at all. With her eyes squeezed shut, she fought to return to the safety of nothingness. She couldn't. The bed beneath her felt as though it was spinning, at the same time rising and sinking erratically, as if she were on some insane ride at an amusement park. The effect was reinforced by a growing feeling that she was going to be sick.

A few seconds later she became conscious of another problem. A sudden signal from her stomach told her that not only was she going to be sick, but that getting to a bathroom had just become desperately important. That her stomach should choose this moment to develop diarrhea struck Laura as unnecessarily cruel.

For a few moments, she stayed lying with her eyes closed, hoping that both her suspicions were wrong, that the feeling would go away. It didn't. She also became aware of a great deal of noisy rumbling in the distance and of a mysterious breeze that was flowing directly across her. Reluctantly, she accepted that she could no longer avoid the truth; she was going to throw up, and she had to go to the bathroom and you just didn't lie back on your bed and let that happen. Slowly, she allowed her eyes to open, but discovered her vision was extremely foggy. The brightness above her seemed strangely powerful, and for a second Laura wondered if she'd been discovered prematurely and was staring up into the operating lights of a hospital emergency room. Impossible.

She struggled to a half-sitting position and swung her legs over the edge of the bed. The floor was as uncooperative as her stomach. It had always been there before when needed; now, even when she stretched her legs to their fullest, the soft shag rug that should have met her foot evaded her. Laura blinked hard and struggled to focus her eyes so she could discover what the matter was. The sight made her gasp in disbelief. The floor wasn't there; her bed was standing on a platform of empty space, and, far below, she could dimly make out the sea beating against the rocks at the base of the cliff.

Terrified, Laura found her body frozen in its position. Raising her head, she turned to see if the rest of the room made so little sense. Actually, the rest of the room made even less. The three other walls and the roof had disappeared as completely as the floor; the fourth wall, to which the headboard of the mammoth bed was fastened, was all that remained of the room.

Swaying back and forth, Laura was so shocked she almost let herself slip off the bed into the void below, but the urgent messages from her stomach forced her into action. With a sharp movement, Laura yanked her legs back up on the bed and then turned on her stomach with her head sticking out over the edge, her hands clutching the covers and the mattress to make sure she didn't lose her balance.

Laura couldn't remember being this sick in years. Her entire insides seemed determined to make their way out, racking her body again and again with heavings and convulsions that left her totally spent. Even after nothing was left

152

inside her, the spasms and heavings continued, subsiding only slowly.

Drenched in perspiration, Laura carefully rolled over on her back and lowered her head to the pillows. Ordinarily the first thing she would have done would be to wash her face and brush her teeth, but the equipment for these had vanished along with the bathroom. Laura compromised by ripping the pillow slip off one of the mound of pillows and wiping her face as clean as she could with that. She could think of no way to take care of the awful taste in her mouth.

She was allowed the luxury of lying there for only a few moments; the other signal from her stomach—it had more or less disappeared while she was being sick—now returned with redoubled intensity, demanding to be taken care of.

With a yank, she pulled the drawer out of the night-stand—like the bed, it was firmly attached to the wall behind her—and moved it to the foot of the bed. Maneuvering carefully, she crawled the length of the bed and lowered herself onto the drawer. A sea gull, returning to the remains of its perch on the cliff below, peered at her as it flew past; Laura knew her reaction was stupid, but the bird's presence embarrassed her. As she squatted there, the ridiculousness of her position, her plight, her suicide attempt, her whole life, hit her. With a vehemence unusual for her, she began berating George, her father, Digit, Gilla, and the architect who had designed her house and put it in such an unsafe place. Unreasonable, she knew, but Laura had abandoned all reason.

As if from a great distance, she heard herself screaming. Struggling to her feet, she leaned against the one remaining wall at the head of the bed and beat the cracked plaster surface with both fists. "Why?" she screamed at the blank, silent surface. "Why, why, *why?*"

Above her own cries, she could hear her father answer, stern and foreboding, all pretense of the Pickwickian twinkle stripped away. "Evil *is* its own punishment," he announced in his most ponderous, sepulchral voice.

153

Turning around, her back and arms flattened against the wall, Laura rocked sideways dangerously and pointed an accusing finger at the scudding clouds above her. "Damn you, Father. Damn you! For God's sake, leave me alone. You've punished me enough. More than enough. Tell me, what you want of me and leave me alone!"

No voice answered, only the hostile scream of the sea gull as it continued circling Laura, scolding her for having showered its nesting place in the cliff with tons of rock and fallen timber. Exhausted, she sank from her standing position to a safer one on the bed itself. And then, because she was both cold and tired, Laura lifted one corner of the bedcovers and slipped inside. She did not make this move solely for warmth; being under the covers automatically makes anyone feel safer.

From the distance, she could hear what seemed to be air-raid sirens; the sound was intermixed with the roar of the sea beneath her and the breathy sigh of the rising wind. She should, she knew, be trying to think of ways to get off this terrible bed and onto the safety of the land that lay beyond the bed-wall. But even thinking was too great an effort. She lay back, staring blankly at the empty sky and damning the people who had put her in this agonizing position.

She had no way of knowing that the architect's careful reinforcement of a single wall—to make sure it would bear the weight of the giant headboard as well as the bed—was all that had saved her from plunging, along with the rest of the house, to the rocks far below.

Or that Gilla's thoughtful addition of Ex-Lax to her hot chocolate was what had unwittingly rendered her overdose of Tuinal ineffective.

And it is extremely doubtful if Laura Vorhees would have thanked them if she had.

Unlike Laura Vorhees, Isaac Rosholman was not asleep when Violet hit. He was leaning against the director's small red-brick building, watching the sky darken as the sun slipped below the rolling grounds of Griffith Park. At first, the meaning of what he was feeling didn't strike him; he noticed a series of small rapid movements beneath his feet, somewhat as if an electric vibrator were being pressed against the soles of his shoes. Then the surface of the ground around him began rising and falling like waves on an ocean. He found it difficult to stay upright and clutched the window frame of the building behind him for support, but the building seemed to be moving on its own set of waves, rising as he was sinking, and Rosholman had to let go and get down on all fours. Almost at eye level to him, the gently curving, neat concrete pavement that led to the building's door at first appeared to undulate gracefully with the motion of the ground, a thick ribbon being waved underwater. Then the strain became too much, and huge pieces of cement abruptly flew up from the pavement, some landing alongside the original pathway, others moving backward or forward and settling heavily on those parts of the concrete walk still remaining.

To his left, Rosholman strained to find the source of a sudden groaning followed by a rapid series of splintering crashes; he watched as a giant avocado tree, gnarled and venerable, was wrenched out of the ground. It landed heavily on its side, its ancient roots tearing great clods of subsoil out of the earth with them. The shock of the fall snapped limbs the size of a man's waist and scattered the ground with a premature harvest of unripe fruit; some of the avocados rolled erratically down the gentle slope and stopped just short of Rosholman's hands.

From below the hill, Rosholman could hear the sounds of terrified animals—the tortured trumpeting of the elephants, the screams of the monkeys and birds, the ominous grumbling of the lions, and the breathy screech of the cheetahs—and suddenly wondered about the moats. Like the pavement, they were made of concrete; if, like the pavement, the concrete had collapsed and the earth behind it fallen in, the animals would easily cross out of the zoo into the park itself. Slowly, Rosholman began to get to his feet—the ground seemed steady now—and looked around behind him at the director's building. A large crack ran down the brickwork from top to bottom, and all of the windows were gone, the glass in them reduced to a fine powder when the window frames were forced into trapezoidal shapes by some shift in the building's foundation. Curiously, the structure itself still appeared basically sound.

But when Rosholman tried to enter to phone the guardpost nearest the moats, he discovered the door tightly jammed; as with the windows, the doorframe now formed a trapezoid, while the solid oak door remained a rectangle. He put his shoulder against it and heaved as hard as he could, but quickly gave up and moved over to one of the gutted windows, brushing away the broken glass and splintered frames with the sleeve of his uniform.

If Rosholman had known anything about the behavior of earthquakes, he would not have been surprised at what happened next. Just as he put both hands on the window frame to pull himself through, taking care to avoid the jagged pieces of glass still sticking to the frame, the ground beneath him again began trembling in a succession of erratic spasms, the earth in orgasm. The surface was twisting and writhing and a large boulder or piece of ledge rock ripped itself out of the ground and rolled spastically down the sloping lawn. A sharp pain in his right hand made Rosholman realize the hand had slid up the wood into the glass and been cut; he let go of the frame and once again had to drop to all fours. Standing without anything to hang onto was impossible. In the distance, he watched fascinated as the brick square of the reptile house disintegrated; the building was about a hundred yards away, and it looked as if someone simply yanked the walls out from under the roof, which settled on the pile of rubble beneath with great dignity, its copper-green pagoda shape still in one piece.

Wrapping the cut hand in his handkerchief, Rosholman tried once more to get at the phone; he would need all possible guards to help him, not only in checking the entire circumference of the moat system, but in releasing the cyanide gas in the reptile house before any of the snakes made their way out of the rubble. He hoped the gas system had survived the second wave of tremors.

"Rosholman, Rosholman!" The voice sounded breathless and came from behind him. Rosholman turned and saw one of the guards, his face ashen, running toward him, stumbling and tripping over the fallen branches and heaved-up stones. "Rosholman," the man said, pointing behind him, "Jesus—the moats caved in. The guns. We need the guns."

Rosholman ignored the demand and stared at the guard. "Are you all right? Good. Then, listen. The reptile house. It's a rubble. Get down there and see if the cyanide system will still work. If it will, turn it on—quick."

"The guns—" began the guard again.

"The snakes, first the snakes. Get going, get on down there." Shaking his head, the man accepted the key from Rosholman and headed toward the reptile house. Rosholman called after him. "And once it's turned on, get away fast. That stuff's going to be blowing all over the place." The guard, who had paused to hear what Rosholman was saying, shook his head and began running again.

Rosholman leaned against the building and put his hands to his face, wondering what he should do. Or could do. The phones, obviously, were out or that guard wouldn't have run all the way back. Inside the director's building the shotguns were locked in the gun racks on the far wall, lined up one beside the other with their barrels gleaming dully, surprisingly graceful for instruments of death. Rosholman stared at them through the window and then climbed inside. The contingency plan called for them to be issued to the guards; with no way of keeping the animals from crossing into the park itself, the guards were to station themselves along the moat and destroy any animals they saw. But Rosholman issued only one shotgun—and that one was to himself; then he locked the rack.

The contingency plans were drawn up by men who did not understand animals as he did. He had his own idea for keeping the animals inside the moats and Rosholman yanked a long drawer open to get what he needed to make his plan work.

The shotgun was part of his own contingency plan—in case the other guards didn't agree that his was the right way.

Beth Czemki checked her watch and suddenly realized they were going to be late for the Iveliterris'. But the little bar they were in wasn't too far from the Iveliterris' home, and if she could get Matt moving, they could still arrive there without suffering anything more than minor embarrassment. Her problem was Matt. As soon as she mentioned leaving, he began grumbling, and Beth could guess he wanted to stay right where he was and maybe get a little drunk and keep on talking about the wonder of a baby and the hell with the Ivelitteris'. Firmly but gently, Beth was as insistent about leaving as Matt was about staying, and finally, after a little more complaining and some only partially serious grousing, Matt looked around to find their waiter, and couldn't, and began to complain loudly.

Beth, spotting the waiter, made a scribbling motion on her hand to signal for the check. The waiter was a very old man and stared at them resentfully before beginning to move across the room toward them.

"Jesus," Matt snorted, studying the waiter's maddeningly slow progress toward them. "That old guy must have worked the party at Donner Pass."

Beth laughed, but only because she knew she was supposed to. After a few drinks, Matt frequently turned indifferent to the problems of others. Today of all days, however, she wanted no argument to spoil her happiness. Because of this, Beth didn't point out that it was pretty sad a man as old as the waiter had to work at all.

"*Now* what?" Beth heard Matt say at the same time she felt an odd motion beneath her feet. She turned to follow Matt's stare to see if the question and the sensation were somehow related. The waiter had stopped dead in his tracks, perhaps fifteen feet from them, and was spinning slowly around where he stood; for no apparent reason, the tray of drinks he was carrying in his right hand went flying off in one direction while the pad with Matt's check sailed off in the other. Beth's first reaction was that she'd had more to drink than she thought. She watched as the waiter appeared to rise a couple of feet off the floor and float upward; an instant later she realized Matt and she were doing the same, rising gracefully up from their table toward the acoustical tiles in the ceiling. At first the sensation was deceptively pleasant, a sort of double slow motion, and she watched without surprise as she saw Matt's mouth open to comment on it. Automatically, she grabbed at her purse as if it contained something of great value; this made no sense at all because her purse had only ten dollars and change, but then none of this made sense. Then her feeling of wonder was translated into one of fear, but by the time she could find her voice and yell at Matt to do something she found she and the table and the chair had stopped floating and she was on the floor screaming as loudly as she could, trying to protect her face from the pieces of broken glass that were flying everywhere.

Matt had one arm around her by now—Beth could sense rather than feel it—and with his free hand was pushing up hard on the table, struggling to keep it from falling over on top of them. From what seemed a great distance a series of small explosions sounded; a quick glance told Beth the noise came from the bottles behind the bar bursting as they hit the floor. At first, the bartender had tried to hold them back, but soon became too busy protecting his face from the pieces of flying glass. The lights in the room flickered for a second and then went out completely, their soft barroom glow replaced by harsh daylight pouring in through the shattered plate-glass windows that looked out onto the street. For no reason she could understand, Beth felt reassured by being able to blame all the glass flying around the room on the fractured windows; it was the first thing that had made sense to her in several minutes, and this fact alone helped bring her back to reality.

Over all the noise—the shards of glass gave a particularly highly pitched whine, like bullets, as they flew past her—she heard Matt's voice. At first she could not make out what he was saying, but his voice was firm and calm and was intended, Beth knew, to reassure her. But as she began to understand, his words had the opposite effect. Matt was saying "earthquake" over and over to her, telling her that everything was all right, that the worst was already done with, and that in a few minutes they would both be laughing at what had happened. But Beth had told herself—had *had* to tell herself—that this was no earthquake, it was an explosion, a gas main bursting, a fuel truck exploding—even a bomb going off—because things such as these were localized and confined to a small area. But an earthquake, well, an earthquake could have effects anywhere and everywhere across the city—even at their own house, the house where Gregory and Sarah were, the house where there was no sitter. Yanking herself free of Matt's protecting arm, Beth sat up and began rocking back and forth, her head cradled in her hands, moaning.

Matt was sitting up too, now, looking around him. The building had stopped shaking, all the glass that could break had broken, and the customers were struggling to their feet, shaking the dust and plaster and broken glass from their clothes. Only one person seemed to be really hurt: the bartender. A pair of decorative crossed beams above his head had fallen and pinned him, facedown, to the bar. Two men were struggling to lift the heavy pieces of wood off him, but when they finally raised the beams, the bartender appeared attached to the wood, his neck, his trunk, and one outstretched arm nailed to the timbers by the same spikes which had originally attached them to the ceiling. The bartender hung there for a moment, as if half of him had been crucified, before the men lowered him and his cross gently onto the floor.

Beth could feel rather than see Matt getting to his feet; she couldn't bring herself to look at him. Her face covered with her hands, she remained sitting where she was, still rocking and moaning. At first, Matt thought Beth was reacting to the sight of the bartender, but when nothing he said seemed to help, he became confused and almost impatient-sounding. "Come on, Beth. It's over. You're OK, you're OK. Everybody is OK." Slowly and carefully, he pulled her hands away from her face to see if she'd been cut or gashed in some way. "Hey, Beth. Snap out of it, darling. We've got to find some way to get home." He gave her shoulder a little shake and laughed reassuringly. "That sitter will be scared out of her mind."

For a second, Beth stared straight at him. She wanted to scream or laugh or throw up or fall back dead—*anything* that would spare her from having to tell him the truth. But she managed to control herself and face him with the truth. "There isn't any sitter," she said flatly. "I left before she got there. I left the kids alone. Oh, Matt. . . ."

He didn't say a word, just grabbed her hand, yanked her to her feet, and pushed her toward the shattered front door, shoving his way through people, broken furniture, and fallen beams without making any distinction at all.

At the Czemki house, the television screen had gone black at Violet's first quiver. (And with good reason: the main cables into the area had fused into a glowing, smoking mass of molten copper wire some five miles away, just outside the power relay station.) In front of the television set, beginning to thaw greasily, were the uncooked french fries, some still in the dish Gregory had put them in, some spilled on the rug beneath.

The spillage could not all be blamed on Violet; a lot of the mess was Gregory and Sarah's doing. For although this part of Westwood was in a state of confusion just now—people standing outside their houses, scanning the brickwork and feeling the foundations for cracks, pointing to downed tree limbs and broken windows—the area had come through the quake pretty much intact. From the occasional transistor radio glued to someone's ear, the people there knew by now that they had been lucky—but the rest of the city had not. There was growing talk among some of the men about trying to go help friends and relatives, but the local Civil Defense volunteer—he had access to the first radio reports coming from Kraypool's headquarters—was being firm to the point of rudeness in telling them to forget the idea. Any travel into the city itself, he said, was for the moment forbidden, dangerous, and impossible.

No one thought to look inside the Czemki house to see how the children were because no one thought the children were there. And the assumption was correct. Almost ten minutes before Mr. Rogers was halted in mid-sentence by the power failure, Gregory and Sarah, for reasons having nothing at all to do with Violet, had left the house and headed due east.

Straight for the heart of the city.

Chapter Twelve

It is computed that eleven thousand persons, have, at several times, suffered death, rather than submit to break their eggs at the smaller end.

—JONATHAN SWIFT, *Gulliver's Travels,*
Voyage to Lilliput

As George Vorhees drove down the private road that led to Laura's home in Malibu, first the road was there, then it wasn't. He blinked hard, unable to accept what was happening, and fought the wheel for control. Spinning the wheel hard right did nothing; the road was moving in the opposite direction, and the car skidded wildly across the blacktop, finally coming to a halt in the shallow ditch that ran alongside the left-hand side of the road.

Then for the first time—the car door open and radio silenced—George heard it: a sickening, roaring, thundering sound as parts of the cliff edge broke off and plunged into the sea far below. Automatically, his eyes searched for and found Laura's house, splendid and alone; he watched, motionless, as the cantilevered part of the structure facing the ocean began to crumble. The house shuddered once or twice and then, like a torpedoed troopship, slipped slowly and gracefully over the cliff and disappeared below its rim. When the shaking stopped, only one wall remained standing: the inland wall, built with small, high windows to ensure privacy from the driveway. This lone wall looked absurd, George thought, like one of those antique Italian prints Laura collected, with everything fallen down except a single Corinthian column.

After a struggle, George was able to get his left-hand door closed again—the car was leaning over so far to the left that the bottom edge of the door had half buried itself in the dirt when it sprang open—but when he tried to drive the car out of the ditch, racing the motor as hard as he could, he got nowhere. Until he could find some large stones or pieces of wood to put under the wheels, the car would have to stay where it was. Climbing out, George looked around and decided against even trying; instead, he started down the road toward the house on foot.

The closer he got, the surer he was. With the exception of the inland wall, the whole house was gone. Demolished. Dropped into the ocean. Disappeared. The sight shook him, two conflicting emotions affecting him at the same time: on the one hand, a feeling of awe at the forces that had destroyed the house and, on the other, a sense of relief that, along with the house, the tapes were gone. Forever. He was free.

The sensation was an exhilarating one, but because the reasons behind it were almost too good to be true, a dim bell of warning rang somewhere in the back of George's brain. Carefully, he looked around him to make sure there was no place *outside* the house where the tapes might have been stored by Laura. All he could find was an isolated pile of rubble to the left side of the standing wall. The top of a clothes dryer poking above the heap of masonry reminded George that this had once been the service area with laundry, linen and utility rooms. Conceivably, the tapes could have been hidden in one of these, although it would be a crazy place for Laura to choose.

For a second, thinking of Laura caused George to wonder if she could possibly have returned home while he was on his way here and plunged over the cliff with the house; but the thought made him uncomfortable, and he quickly dismissed it. George might loathe Laura, but he was still not ready to wish her dead. Besides, he assured himself, twice on the way here he had stopped and telephoned to make sure she was still

164

out; the last time had been less than five minutes before the earthquake struck. No, Laura was, as he had first thought, out for an early dinner somewhere.

As he looked again at the single standing wall and the pile of stones with the dryer top thrusting above it, strangely white against the gray stone and crushed plaster, a nagging uneasiness returned to trouble him. A chink in his feeling of relief about the tapes. Granted, the only absolutely positive way to know that the tapes had been destroyed would be to have held the reels in his hands, set a match to them, and then watched them burn, but that was now impossible. And he could acknowledge that knowing they were safely at the bottom of the Pacific was almost as good. Yet a feeling of disquiet, a vague uncertainty, still clouded his new sense of safety. The laundry and storage area would be a crazy place to hide the tapes, but then Laura was crazy. To come this close to knowing he was free and then not to explore every possibility would be stupid.

With a sigh, George walked toward the washer and began lifting the stones away, one by one, checking every foot of the ground beneath them. It was hot and dirty work, and even after half an hour of effort, all George had discovered was a lone bottle of bourbon that had somehow escaped destruction when the liquor storage closet collapsed. With a smile, George put the bourbon to one side.

The celebration would come later.

When he was sure.

In Watts, Violet hit with such devastating fury one could almost think she was racist. Gilla, Laura Vorhees' maid, was thrown halfway across her second-story living room by the first shock wave, then found herself careening back to where she had started. Leaning for support against one of the shattered windows, Gilla looked out; unlike most of Los Angeles, a good many of the houses in Watts were built of wood. Oddly, this made them more structurally resistant to

165

earth tremors than brick or concrete, since wood will "give" under stress, while brick and concrete block fracture and collapse.

There was, however, one fatal difference. Concrete may shatter, but wood—particularly of the dried-out, ancient variety found in Watts—will burn. Fiercely. From her window, Gilla could already see bright flames and dense smoke begin to dot the windows across the street almost while Violet was still shaking the ground beneath them; homemade cookstoves, overturned gas rings, and improvised hot-water heaters fell against curtains and walls riddled with dry rot, exploding into full flame. From behind her, Gilla could hear the dishes stacked on the sink slide off and break and was surprised to find she was smiling, glad now she hadn't bothered to wash them.

A new sound caught her ear, and Gilla turned back to look out the window again. People were beginning to pour out of the rickety houses, shoving, scrambling, pushing and cursing at each other, in a frantic rush to get into the street. They streamed down the outside stairs of the old buildings, carrying bundles stuffed full of the things that counted most in their lives. The choice of valuables was curious and varied from person to person: some carried armfuls of dishes and an occasional piece of battered silver; others lugged heavy television sets; one old lady staggered under the weight of a faded framed print—a clipper ship in full sail—while a man and woman virtually blocked the steps of one building trying to carry down a fully made up brass bed—mattress, blankets, sheets, and all. In less than five minutes after the first tremor, the entire street was taken over by a seething mass of people, a blackish sea that eddied back and forth, while the buildings on either side of them belched ominous gray smoke and sullen red flame.

At the intersection, Gilla could see the neighborhood's lone concrete-block building was having troubles of its own. The structure housed Leverman's, a discount clothing-appliance-dry-goods store. As she studied the place, Gilla couldn't tell whether its plate-glass windows had been the victims of the earthquake or the crowd; the glass was gone, and Gilla's friends and neighbors were gingerly climbing through the jagged openings to help themselves to Louis J. Leverman's inventory.

Gilla pulled back from the window and decided it was time to get out of her own building. So far she could detect no sign indicating the makeshift apartment house was on fire, but with so many of the structures around it spewing sparks and flames, this was only a matter of time.

She walked toward the door without even a backward look at the apartment that had been her home for over three years. In the back of Leverman's, Gilla remembered, was a black cloth coat with a little fur collar. The store would be well stripped of anything worthwhile by the time she got there, but the coat had been hanging on a rear rack, out of the way, and was partly hidden by other items more popular this time of year. There was a good chance, then, that the coat hadn't even been noticed yet. The atomizer in her purse would get her through the crowd quickly enough.

On her way down the stairs, she saw old lady Butkins, the fat grandmother who owned the building, rocking back and forth, moaning and praying God to please spare her home and her livelihood.

The mention of God reminded Gilla of the oath she had been supposed to take tomorrow.

And for the first time since the earthquake, of Oskie.

Oskie would like the black coat with the little fur collar.

The eggs hit the boiling water in the saucepan with a satisfying plop, took on amoebalike shapes of white and orange in the swirling water, and then, without warning, began to congeal before their eyes, an unhealthy white film covering the partially hardened yolks.

"Oh, my," cried Mishi, putting down *Fannie Farmer* and looking at the eggs uncertainly. "How peculiar. How *very* peculiar. I have made them before"— she turned to Addie and sought words to remove the skeptical expression from his face—"truly, Addie, I have done the poaching part before and the eggs never came out like this." She studied his pursed lips and quizzical eyebrows and grew somewhat desperate. "Please don't look at me like that. Honestly, Addie, this never happened before."

As she turned back to the eggs, peering at them hard as if her eyes could transform the unappetizing blobs into the elegantly crested white mounds Eggs Benedict demand, Addie lifted his hand and began massaging the back of her neck. "If you say so, Mishi." From the stiffening of her shoulders, Addie knew she was genuinely upset and felt it time to transform his tone from one of sarcasm into one of understanding good humor. With his finger, he gently turned her face around so she faced him. "Perhaps the water in Japan is different."

"Dammit," she exploded. The expression was one she'd heard Addie use so often she now felt quite natural saying it herself; spoken in her immaculate, overly precise way, however, the word seemed less expletory than quaint.

"The sandwiches," Addie reminded her, smiling softly. "Mrs. Herkimer put sandwiches in the refrigerator."

Mishi shook her head with determination and started across the kitchen to dump the egg blobs down the sink and begin again from the beginning. She had said they would have Eggs Benedict, and Eggs Benedict is what they would have. If it killed her. If it killed both of them.

"*Addie!*" The scream was sudden and genuine. At first, Mishi had felt only the slightest trembling as she walked; now the floor first seemed to sink beneath her—like an express elevator going down so fast that your stomach can't keep up with the descent—and then, just as suddenly, the floor slammed up so hard she could feel a stinging on the soles of her bare feet. As she pitched forward, Addie grabbed her by one arm. This threw Mishi so completely off-balance that the other hand lost its hold on the saucepan and let it fly off toward the sink. One of the eggs hit the Formica splashboard and began slipping slowly downward, leaving a wet, shiny path behind itself like a giant snail's. Some glassware that was standing on the countertop slid off and crashed to the floor; the fluorescent lighting—recessed behind frosted plastic panels in the ceiling and always overly bright—turned suddenly black; from the pegged oak beam that ran the length of the kitchen ceiling a dusting of white powdered plaster drifted lazily down.

Seeing Mishi go pale with fright, Addie grabbed her and held her to him tightly; her black eyes were widened to full roundness, and the expression on her face was that of a terrified child's. Helplessly, Addie struggled to find the right words to calm her. "That crazy earthquake again, Mishi. Nothing to be scared about. *Really.*" He spoke reassuringly and soothingly; the house was well built, and they were safe enough, he supposed. Still, Addie felt little of the confidence he displayed for Mishi's benefit.

And when, from outside, they heard trees being wrenched out of the ground and rocks bouncing heavily off the terraced hillside and great slabs of flagstone snapping from the heaving of the earth beneath them, Addie himself became as visibly terrified as Mishi. Wordlessly, they clung to each other, clutching tightly, desperately.

Finally it ended. The sudden silence was shattering.

"Oh, wow." The words were nowhere near adequate, and Addie knew they weren't, but possibly nothing he could say would have been. He looked at Mishi and realized that she too was shivering, although the earthquake had brought with it strangely oppressive heat. Like Addie, Mishi was still in her bathing suit, and he could see the network of small muscles beneath the skin of her whole body quivering.

Mishi shook her head once or twice, trying to bring herself back to reality. When clinging to Addie during the actual moments of terror, she had been surprised to hear herself whispering in Japanese, invoking ancient gods to spare her. As she remembered this now, the thought was acutely embarrassing, and when she finally spoke, the language was both casual and determinedly American. "Wow, Addie! Wham." Mishi paused, listening to the curious sound of the words she had just spoken, and, to reassure herself, retreated to more familiar ground. "Well, it goes with the territory."

Anxiously, she looked up at Addie. "Your earthquake is—I mean, is it over?"

"I hope so."

In a glance, Mishi appraised the damage in the kitchen. It was not great. Watching the remains of the egg take its final slide down the splashboard into the sink, she reached for a sponge to clean up the mess. But when she turned on the faucet, nothing came out but a lone drop of water and a sigh of escaping air. After she thought a second, she wasn't entirely surprised. "No water, Addie. Like the lights, I suppose."

Addie's answer, when it came, was from a slight distance; he had walked to the picture window in the dining room. "Mishi! Look, Mishi. Come here."

When she got to the window, she stared out and felt her stomach give a little turn. The concrete shell of the pool had been fractured and the water was disappearing rapidly into the ground through the cracks. Mishi gave a small cry that only Addie could have fully understood: it was from the great avocado tree at one end of the pool that Mishi had climbed down to begin the merging of their lives; it was beside the pool that they had spent day after day together, talking endlessly; it was in the poolhouse that they had made love—could that really only have happened the night before? The pool had become part of them, an integral facet of their joined lives; now the pool was broken and bleeding, the white rubber birthday swan rocking forlornly on top of the fast-receding surface of the water.

"Oh, Addie." Mishi's voice trailed off, mourning the passage of an old friend.

He took her hand and stared at the wrecked pool with her, searching for something he could say that would cheer her up. Finally: "I bet they can fix those cracks. They probably look worse than they are. Then the pool will be like always." Turning, Addie looked around the inside of the room. "Actually," he added, "what's really lucky is the whole house didn't fall down around us. Poof! Gone in a cloud of smoke."

Mishi picked up his light tone. "Oh, my, yes. Very lucky. A house should never go poof. Indeed, no; Tara shall be rebuilt." Suddenly, a stricken look crossed her face as Mishi remembered. "My family, Addie, my family. Do you think they are all right?"

But the allusion to smoke had raised a more immediate fear in Addie than houses that went poof or pools that leaked or Mishi's family; he looked as if he didn't even hear Mishi's question. "Mother. My God, *Mother*. There hasn't been a sound out of her." In his mind, Addie briefly pictured a room in flames, result of an ashtray full of half-extinguished cigarettes sliding unnoticed off the table onto the bed. "C'mon," Addie ordered, and running down the hall, he and Mishi headed for the guest bedroom where his mother was.

They both were stunned to discover the room completely empty.

In the attendant's locker room at Griffith Park Zoo, Battock had watched the two remaining guards from his shift leave. Over the top of his Lucky Lager can, he stared at their departing backs. Unlike Battock, they had families to go home to and looked upon the nightly beers in the locker room as a pleasant diversion before calling it a day; to Battock, the longer he could get the men to linger over their beers, the less of the night stretched out ahead of him futile and lonely. Tonight he had been unsuccessful in delaying them at all.

With a resigned shrug, Battock reached into his locker to pull out the rolled-up newspaper that he kept on the top shelf. Perhaps a good movie—or at any rate, an acceptable movie—was playing downtown. But the newspaper was as uncooperative as the two guards who had just left. When he reached toward it, the paper seemed to move away from his hand as fast as the hand moved toward the paper. For a second, he was baffled. Then he became aware that the room and everything in it—the battered wooden benches, the grim concrete floors, the paint-chipped green lockers—was shaking and quivering, the metalwork of the locker doors beating a frantic tattoo against each other as they swung open and closed.

Battock was more annoyed than frightened; he'd been through earthquakes before. But when some of the lockers, slowly and at random, began falling over, he could sense fear rising inside him. This one was big. From outside, he could hear trees splitting, bricks cracking, glass breaking. For a second, he debated whether to stay where he was—the building was soundly constructed—but he decided, after feeling the floor beneath him start to heave convulsively, he would play safe and go out into the open. There was no way of guessing how bad things might become, but the zoo grounds, mostly flat and open, were probably as safe a place as you could find in Los Angeles. Steadying himself—the room seemed to be pitching and yawing like a ship in rough water—Battock made his way up the half-flight of stairs and out into the grounds.

The first thing he saw was that the moats were now half filled with dirt and shattered concrete—and therefore no longer effective in keeping the animals where they belonged.

Battock whistled at the implications. As soon as the shaking and trembling stopped, the animals—from the harmless bonteboks to the always-hungry cheetahs—would pick their way across the remains of the moats and roam at will. A shudder passed through him. Beneath his feet, Battock felt the ground heave again and, turning toward the source of a sudden sound, saw the collapse of the reptile house. Someone, he could see, was running from the admin building toward the flattened structure, trying, he supposed, to activate the cyanide system. Battock headed toward the admin building, accelerating his pace to a trot, an indication of concern which surprised him. As he ran he thought he could see his old enemy Rosholman either climbing into or out of the admin building through a window.

By the time he got to the building there was no sign of Rosholman. Somehow, this fact surprised him; Rosholman, as the man in charge, should have stayed put and taken command of things. Perhaps he was inside on the phone. A shadow crossed Battock's mind as he realized that by being here he more or less put himself under Rosholman's jurisdiction. Well, the hell with the pecking order. Rosholman might be in charge of the night shift, but he, Battock, was a day shift man; he'd go along with Rosholman if he agreed with him, but as far as taking any direct orders, fuck *him*.

When he looked through the window of the building, Battock was surprised again: Rosholman wasn't inside either. And the shotguns hadn't been issued. He could see them, neatly lined up and shining dully in the gunrack. Stupid. Rosholman had forgotten to hand out the shotguns to the other guards, and the animals would soon be pouring over the moats. Quickly, Battock pulled himself in through the window and walked over to the gunrack; the metal bar that secured the guns in place wasn't even unlocked. Bracing himself, Battock gave it a hard yank, but the bar was of heavy steel, a heavy unassailable rod running through the trigger guard of each shotgun. At both ends of the bar there was a double safety hasp of three-inch brass; without a key, you couldn't get anywhere.

Backing away in frustration, Battock noticed one of the shotguns was missing. So Rosholman *had* been here, unlocked the rack, removed one shotgun, and then relocked the steel guard. It made no sense.

Still baffled, Battock looked around the room to find a tool to force open the steel locking bar; in a corner, he discovered a rugged brass rod used to secure the door of the small retaining cages employed when the vet wanted an animal isolated or confined for treatment. Battock slid the brass rod under the steel locking bar, raised it to an acute angle—counting on the wall to act as fulcrum—and pushed the rod down heavily, as you might a crowbar. There was a groaning and creaking as the brass rod dug into the wall behind the rack, but

173

the locking bar wouldn't give; instead, the brass rod itself began to bend. Fuming, Battock abandoned the attempt. Without Rosholman's keys, the guns would stay where they were.

Heaving himself over the windowsill out into the zoo grounds, Battock could hear the animals slowly wind down their trumpeting and screaming. As their fear diminished, their curiosity, Battock knew, would grow. The collapsed moats would first be sniffed suspiciously, then explored more closely, then gingerly and tentatively crossed. After that, the exodus would become both generalized and torrential. Time. It was only a matter of time.

Picking his way along the fractured cement path, Battock began yelling Rosholman's name. Much as he might dislike him, Rosholman and his keys were very important just now, and Battock couldn't figure where he had got to. Probably praying somewhere. Chanting in Hebrew and calling on Jehovah to save his ass.

Well, somebody had better.

Chapter Thirteen

First the man takes a drink,
Then the drink takes a drink,
Then the drink takes the man.

—Japanese proverb

AT City Hall, Mayor Manuel Ortiz strode down the long ornate gallery between his office and the elevators. His expression was grim, as cold and hard as the Spanish-bastard architecture some much earlier mayor had burdened the city with (its yellow stucco, ornate iron grillwork, and massive vaulted ceilings had been described by one critic as "early Balaban and Katz").

Traveling in a buzzing swarm around the mayor were the usual aides, their expressions carefully patterned after Ortiz's and therefore looking, if possible, even grimmer. Today the mayor was also surrounded by a specially augmented group of press secretaries and PR men. This latter group had just finished putting together the bluntly worded announcement on Feiner's prediction which the mayor was on his way to deliver over Station KNCB-TV. The PR men felt the statement was *too* blunt, and one of them, Larry O'Brien, clutched a sheaf of notes with some proposed last-minute changes. Trying to get agreement from Ortiz to dilute and soften the statement a little, O'Brien kept brandishing the papers under Ortiz's nose, but already knew he would fail. The answer now—as it had been earlier—was a determined,

175

vigorous shaking of the mayor's head. What had to be said, Ortiz noted, had to be said.

The group, moving in a long, narrow wedge with the mayor at its apex, was about twenty yards short of the elevators when Violet hit; the iron grillwork of the outer elevator doors fell into the hall with a thunderous crash; the stucco walls cracked almost immediately, sending a shower of broken plaster down the length of the hall; the vaulted ceiling began pelting the group with ornate Spanish tiles. In spite of the hands that reached out to steady him, Ortiz lost his feet and fell to all fours on the tile floor; the papers O'Brien was carrying flew up into the air and drifted slowly back down like unsuccessful paper airplanes; cries of fright and surprise mixed with muttered imprecations to God.

The lights went out immediately, but a moment or two later began to flicker dimly back on as the City Hall emergency power system, designed to cut in automatically, sprang to life; from elsewhere in the building came the crashing sounds of falling masonry and the terrified cries of receptionists and secretaries; all down the hall, doors were thrown open as city employees poured into the hall.

For a second, Mayor Ortiz sat on the floor, blinking at the muted lighting. "Son of a bitch," he said, and got to his feet. He was startled to find the speech still clutched in his left hand and used it to dust the plaster off his clothes. Ortiz stared at the sheaf of papers. "Thanks to Burt Aptner, this"—he crumpled the speech and hurled it to the floor in disgust—"this announcement is now after the fact."

Barking orders—to get hold of Sacramento, to get hold of Kraypool, to get hold of police and fire headquarters—Ortiz stalked down the littered hall and back toward his office.

Burt Aptner had the bad luck to pry his door open and come into the hall just as Ortiz reached it. Without a word, Ortiz grabbed Aptner by the necktie and delivered a roundhouse punch that flattened him.

Looking up from the floor, one hand pressed appraisingly against his bleeding mouth, Aptner tried to explain. But the

176

expression on the mayor's face quickly made Aptner abandon the attempt.

Ortiz stepped carefully over Aptner's sprawled legs; for one brief instant he considered delivering a hard kick to Aptner's balls but decided he had more important things to do. "Get this jerk out of my sight; I might kill him," he snapped to one of his aides. Ortiz was being unfair, and he knew it; even if Aptner had told him of Feiner's prediction the moment he had heard it, not much could really have been accomplished in the brief period of time given them. But Ortiz was already beginning to feel responsible for the disaster. To him, the earthquake had become a living, breathing thing that had sought him out, sneaked into his city, and was now personally out to destroy him. And Burt Aptner was its agent.

Ortiz knew the notion was ridiculous; the earthquake would have happened whether he was mayor or still just a councilman from La Puente.

Besides, the thought was too painful even to consider further. With a final instinctive slap at his trousers to remove the last of the plaster dust, Mayor Manuel Ortiz entered his office; from there, he would learn what he could about the city he loved. And from there, he would find out how much could be salvaged—of the city and himself.

About two blocks from City Hall, in the Woolverton Building, Kraypool's Civil Defense spin-off was already getting scattered damage reports by radio: Kraypool had considered Feiner's suggestion that he move his command post to the ground floor but ended by rejecting it; the Woolverton Building was only six stories high, was practically brand-new, and had been built—at Kraypool's insistence—to the most exacting of quake-resistant specifications. Nobody else in LA might be following the rules, but Kraypool, in trying to force builders and architects to stick to the official specs, had made sure his building was a prototype of everything a quake-resistant structure should be. (Even its supporting piers "floated" on a layer of Teflon, so the structure could literally

177

move forward or backward, or from one side to the other, without putting any strain on the basic building shell.) At the time, some people—even the contractor who charged a fortune to put it up—had smiled patronizingly at all this, but now the design was paying off. The building had swayed a little, a handful of windows had shattered, but the structure was otherwise totally unaffected.

It was difficult for Kraypool to get a clear picture from the sketchy reports; many of the local CD men who should have been calling in were not. At first, this gave Kraypool a sense of false well-being, for the men who did radio in indicated no great degree of destruction. However, when his radio operator reported continued failure in raising the majority of the local CD stringers, Kraypool realized this either had to be because the damage in their areas was so great they couldn't get to their transmitters, or because, simply, they were dead. No other explanations were possible; that many men couldn't all have gone out for a beer at the same time.

Trying to reach the precinct fire and police stations produced the same pattern; Kraypool's radioman could raise stations only where damage was reported as light; the rest didn't respond. A check with LA police headquarters confirmed Kraypool's worst suspicions. Because the police had so many men on the street, and most of them were equipped with highly portable equipment—even down to the walkie-talkie level—the police were getting a far more frightening picture of the situation than Kraypool, who had to depend on fixed transmitters and limited personnel. Beyond that, the police told Kraypool, they'd been able to contact at least two of their helicopters and already had them in the air. But when Kraypool requested the helicopters be used to give him an overall picture of the city's situation, he was refused. The choppers, a headquarter's lieutenant told him curtly, were already assigned to urgent rescue work in precinct areas, and no amount of reasoning would change the man's mind.

When the break came, it happened largely by chance. Kraypool's radioman was "reading the frequencies" when he

178

first picked up the signals from KBDT's "guy in the sky," Ken Corbit. Over the static, the operator could hear Corbit frantically trying to raise someone at his home station. With a questioning look, the radioman turned toward Kraypool to see whether he wanted the calls acknowledged.

Kraypool listened for a second to Corbit's repeated "KBDT. KBDT. Come in. KBDT, come in. This is Corbit. Repeat, Corbit. Come in, KBDT. Can you read me, KBDT?" There was a lot of noise in the background, the man's name was unfamiliar to him, and Kraypool looked confused.

"It's KBDT's traffic helicopter. But the station must be knocked out," the operator explained.

The word "helicopter" moved Kraypool into action. "Let me have it," he said, grabbing the desk-top mike. "Can we reach him?"

Over the speaker, they could hear Corbit trying again: "Come in KBDT, this is Corbit. Come in anybody, please." Corbit's tone sounded somewhere between confused and desperate.

The operator fine-tuned a transmitter dial, listened a second, and nodded. "Try him now."

Kraypool stared at the mike; suddenly he wasn't sure what he wanted to say. Finally: "Corbit. Corbit, I can hear you. Can you hear me? Acknowledge if you can hear me."

"Roger. I can read you." There was a significant pause, then: "Who the hell is *you?*"

The Air Corps jargon he remembered from boyhood had always struck Kraypool as pretentious. But combined with Corbit's sudden down-to-earth question, the effect struck him as bizarre. As a result, Kraypool's answer sounded annoyed and pompous at the same time. "This is Commissioner Kraypool. Office of Emergency Preparedness."

"Well, Commish, I hope you guys were more prepared than me. I can't even find a place to put this jalopy down." There was a new pause from Corbit, during which you could hear his tongue clicking against the roof of his mouth, followed by a soft sigh; Corbit was having second thoughts. "I don't mean to

179

sound funny or anything. I mean, you know, Christ, it's *not* funny. It's just that, well, you know what I mean."

Kraypool's annoyance dissolved. Like everyone else, this distant voice in the chopper was having a hard time accepting what had happened. Quickly, Kraypool turned to a question of hard fact. "How much gas have you got, Corbit?"

"Half a tank. Maybe more. But my pad's a wipeout so I can't go back there for more. Fact is, I can't even see where it used to be."

"How long's half a tank good for?"

Corbit thought for a second. "In most choppers, usually half an hour. Maybe a little more. But this job's got extra big tanks plus a reserve unit so I don't have to come in during the rush-hour reports for refuel. I've never pushed her all the way, but I guess maybe she'll stay up about an hour longer."

Kraypool's decision was made. "OK now, Corbit. Look. We need an overview of the whole area. From one end of LA to the other. And we need it fast. Most communications are out, a lot of the radio points that are supposed to be checking in aren't, and you've got the one way in the whole city of getting around. As I'm sure you already know, all thoroughfares and freeways are blocked; anyway, that's what LAPD tells *us*. Covering the whole area, Corbit, is going to take more than any hour, but we'll find a refueling spot for you somewhere. Now get yourself out a map and let's start marking off zones. . . ."

In the chopper, Corbit was still in a state of half stupor from what he'd seen below him—the collapsed buildings, the fallen bridges, the fires, the floods, the exploding gas mains, and, by implication, all the people he knew must be somewhere down there in the midst of it—but the everyday action of putting the map into the chart holder cut through the drone of the chopper blades and began slowly bringing him back to reality.

And, for the first time since he'd hit LA more than a year ago, Corbit felt alive.

Huddled in the corner, Georgia Mosely pulled the blue and

180

white peignoir tighter around her, trying to convince herself her shaking was due to the cold. The effort failed. Out of one of the deep pockets, she carefully drew the bottle of Smirnoff's she'd grabbed on her way out of the house. For a long time she stared at it, as if just looking at the bottle might somehow stop the shaking. She knew better. Georgia looked around the dusty interior of the shed, searching for something to drink the vodka from; in all her years of trouble, in all the desperate situations she'd found herself, Georgia had been meticulous about one thing: she had never once taken so much as one swallow straight out of the bottle. *That*, she told herself, was something drunks did.

But the garden shed, perhaps twenty yards behind the main house on Tutweiler, didn't seem to hold a glass anywhere. In the dim light Georgia could make out flowerpots, both empty and full, insecticide containers, aerosol bombs, hoses, tools, and stacked sprinklers, but not a single glass. Unconsciously, one hand stroked the Smirnoff's nervously as if to draw strength from it. Finally she saw a cheap, fluted glass—the kind that comes as a premium with jams or jellies—rakishly stuck upside down on a shovel handle. As she moved over to it, she carefully lifted her peignoir robe off the shed's cement floor. An inspection of the glass was far from reassuring—the inside was coated with dust and bore ring marks where different levels of fluid had stood at different times—but Georgia could detect nothing like the smell of insecticide or Paris green and decided the glass would have to do.

The Smirnoff's stopped the shaking almost immediately.

With one hand, she cleared away a small area of dirty window to see how far the enemy had progressed. She could hear voices, but they were indistinct. For a second, it sounded as if they were even calling her name, but that was impossible; she was as unknown to them as they to her. But the voices confirmed her feeling that she must stay hidden at all costs. Everybody knew what they did to women, even middle-aged ones. Softly, very softly, she cursed them from the depths of her soul. There. She heard the voice again. And this time she was sure. Someone was definitely calling her name, a girl's voice, calling, "Mrs. Mosely, Mrs. Mosely! Where are you, Mrs. Mosely?" Georgia raised her head carefully and peeked out again through the cleared-off spot on the window. She might have guessed; the voice belonged to the girl she'd seen with Addie. Georgia sighed. She had tried to tell Addie then, but boys never listen to their mothers. Tried to tell him the girl belonged in an internment camp, but he'd paid no attention. Now the girl was back, spying for her army's forward elements, telling them where the antiaircraft batteries were, outlining which houses would make good strong points and which would be indefensible, filling them in on highways, power plants, everything. For being so pigheaded, Addie was probably dead by now.

The girl's voice, still calling her name, sounded closer, and Georgia looked around the small shed for a place to hide. Over in one corner were some tarpaulins and the folded-up pool cover. Holding the Smirnoff's and the disreputable glass in one hand, Georgia lifted one corner of the tarp and slid between the layers of plastic cloth.

They would never find her there.

And by the time the shed door was pushed open and a head stuck inside to look for her Georgia Mosely was already fast asleep.

The Los Angeles county sheriff's car had barely started on its "detour from the detour"—off Beverly Drive up Tutweiler—when the police radio crackled with a frantic all-frequencies message. "Urgent Bulletin—All Personnel. Urgent Bulletin—All Personnel. Los Angeles area is—" The voice was abruptly silenced. The driver and "shotgun" had time only to exchange a quizzical glance before the subject of the interrupted headquarters bulletin made itself known to them—personally and violently. A sudden heaving of the road sent the car tacking from one side to the other, tires screeching; before the driver could regain control, the vehicle was heading helplessly toward a tall tree. "Jesus!"

shotgun screamed. But the imprecation came too late. While the driver missed sideswiping the first tree, one of the trees on the other side of the road, a giant eucalyptus, began to lean heavily and, with incongruous grace, fell over onto the front end of the careening car, stopping it like a scurrying bug crushed under someone's toe. The driver and shotgun were flattened under the roof; for a second or two you could hear the driver moaning, but then he too was quiet.

In the rear of the car, separated from the front by the wire mesh, Oskie Davenport and Simon Pokress, being farther back, had been able to see the coming of the tree and had thrown themselves to the floor. After the initial impact, Oskie warily opened one eye; he had expected the whole car to be crushed instead of just the front end. Looking forward, he could see the remains of the steel mesh screen; to one side, there was a small gap near its bottom where three fingers of shotgun's hand still clutched the seat back tightly. Slowly, the hand relaxed its grip and opened; for a second, the fingers seemed to claw at the air; then a spasm ran through them, and they fell limp.

Oskie had to cough loudly before he could clear his throat enough to speak. "Mother of God, that was close. But them poor guys up front has had it."

Simon Pokress' eyes were bright with excitement and hope, a thin smile across his gray skin. "Very sad," he hissed in his croaking whisper. "However, them dead is us free, cousin." Pokress stared at Oskie, unable to grasp why the black didn't seem to see what he did. "Davenport, you don't understand, do you? We're free now. Free, if I may use the prison vernacular, as broad-assed birds."

It was the first time Pokress had spoken during the entire trip and Oskie was startled by Pokress' odd mixture of sometimes earthy, sometimes elegant, schoolteacher language. He understood what Pokress meant well enough but was bothered by his suggestion of escape. Not the morality of it, of course; that was for people who could afford it. But the practicality. Oskie still clung to the belief he could beat his rap in court (especially if Gilla came through on the witness stand as he expected her to). This would make him really free, not hiding in alleys the rest of his life as Pokress, fancy language and all, would be. A sudden shadow crossed his face. What if Gilla had been killed by the quake? There would go his alibi, the one piece of evidence, albeit contrived, that would keep him out of the slammer. Oskie struggled with the problem, pondering his chances in court without Gilla. Anyway, *maybe* without Gilla.

Pokress was struggling with something else. Impatiently, he turned around toward Oskie. The message was urgent; the voice remained a sibilant croak. "*Help*, will you?" Pokress was trying to bend the wire-mesh screen forward, wrestling with the opening where shotgun's hand had been. If he could bend the screen back far enough, he could reach the small, thick lever that locked the rear doors and they would be out. The mesh, however, was made of surprisingly heavy-gauge wire; it took both of them pulling their hardest to make the hole big enough for Pokress to get his hand and arm through. Finally, wheezing and stretching, Pokress was able to trip the lever and was rewarded with the gratifying "click" of the rear doors unlocking.

Outside, the two of them stood beside the car, its spinning red light still blinking on and off through the branches of the eucalyptus tree. Pokress was afraid someone might come barreling down Tutweiler, see the wrecked police car, and go for help; he underestimated Violet's fury. For although the area would later be described in official reports as "only lightly affected," fallen trees and rock slides had effectively closed off the road in both directions.

Without explanation, Pokress dropped to all fours and began crawling through the tree branches toward the right front door. "Hold 'em back, hold 'em back, dammit," he gasped at Oskie, pointing to the branches that by now almost hid him. "If I can get to the front door, I can reach their guns. We need them."

Oskie moved slowly and reluctantly. He knew Pokress

would go all out for escape, and Oskie still wasn't sure which way to play his meager hand. But Pokress scared him—there was something about Pokress that would scare anybody—and so Oskie obediently, if unenthusiastically, did his best to hold the springlike eucalyptus branches away from where Pokress was working. After a lot more grunting and swearing and cracking sounds, Pokress finally reemerged from the branches carrying the sawed-off shotgun.

Balancing it in his hands, Pokress lightly tossed the gun up and down to accustom himself to the feeling of its weight. "It was all I could get," he wheezed thickly. "Their thirty-eights would have been better, because you can carry them in your pocket, you know? But the bastards are slumped over so far—pushed down by the roof, I expect—I can't reach their holsters. Anyway, this packs a lot more firepower." He pulled some extra shells from his pocket. "And I found these in one of their breast pockets. We're in business." Pokress studied Oskie's solemn face for a second and pronounced a verdict. "Mr. Gloom." Pokress' laugh was a dry, choking rattle. "We're free, and you stand there as if you'd just been handed ten to twenty. Come on, let's get going."

With that, the decision was made for Oskie. His lanky frame moving disjointedly behind Pokress, the intense black of his skin in sharp contrast with Pokress's colorless gray, Oskie Davenport reluctantly followed until they turned in through the gates of the first driveway they reached.

Because Pokress kept urging him along faster than was comfortable, the sawed-off shotgun waving him forward with unspoken menace, Oskie barely had time to read the small polished brass sign on the gatepost that identified the home's address and name for convenience of guests, delivery men, and the post office.

"1350 Tutweiler," it read. "1350 Tutweiler Drive—A. Mosely."

At Georgi's, in the Valley, the wedding feast for Sporades and Anna Kristaboulos had got its second wind and was run-

185

ning full tilt again—in spite of the absence of its guests of honor. Georgi himself was in the cellar, pulling two more large plastic bags of ice cubes out of the walk-in meat locker; he always kept his ice supply there for long parties like this one. (Georgi was never sure where all the ice went at these parties—Greeks take all their drinks except Fix, at room temperature—but they appeared to use up cubes by the ton anyway.)

The second Violet hit, Georgi could identify precisely what had happened; he'd been through the San Fernando quake in '71. He looked up as the single light bulb in the freezer flickered and went out; the electricity had gone in '71 too. Georgi grumbled to himself. Why did these things always have to happen on days he was making money? He wasn't particularly worried, even when the meat locker began to shake as the ground beneath it groaned and moved; the walls of the freezer were three-inch steel, the whole thing was supported in each corner by heavy I beams, and if you had to pick a safe place to spend an earthquake, his freezer was about as good a spot as you could find.

Georgi leaned confidently against the heavy safety lock; it looked like a flat, chromium door knob stuck on the end of a long steel rod. To unlock the door, all that was ordinarily required was a light push on the knob and the lock would spring open. But Georgi, pushing hard, suddenly discovered the lock had no give at all. For the first time, a trace of worry crossed his mind, one that grew bigger and darker as he considered what must have happened. Something, on the outside apparently, had fallen across the door, blocking the other end of the knob so that he could no longer push it to release the lock.

From his pocket, Georgi pulled a package of book matches and lit one. In the eerie light of the single match—the flickering glow made him look as if he were cracking a safe—he struggled again with the safety lock's shiny knob, leaning close to see if it might somehow be blocked on the inside. The knob was clear. Clear but inoperable. The trouble was on the outer

186

side of the door. With a sudden flapping movement of his right hand, Georgi cried out as the match burned him. A second match was used to see if there was a spare coat or jacket hanging forgotten on one of the hooks lining the walls. Some days there was, but today there was nothing but the split carcasses of beef and lamb, row after row of them, rigid and reproachful. Again, the heat from the match singed Georgi's fingertips.

Turning up his coat collar—the cold of the meat locker crept quickly into your bones—Georgi began pacing the room to keep his circulation up, automatically counting off the number of steps in each direction so that he would not need to use a match to know when he'd reached either end of the meat locker. Every few times, when he came to the door, he would stop and hammer his fist on the heavy steel. Eventually one of his sons, upstairs in the ballroom, would miss him and remember where he had gone. He *had* told one of them, hadn't he? For a moment, Georgi explored the question. Yes. Very definitely. He had told his second son, Eugenios. Eugenios was a good boy. Eugenios would notice, Eugenios would come.

So far, Georgi could not say the cold was painful; he was too full of resinata. But he knew the pain would come. Giving the door another whack as he passed, Georgi forgot to count off the distance and ran head-long into a split lamb on the far side. It was an unpleasant sensation, a little frightening, like being in a fun house where the ghosts that fly up at you, instead of being made of cardboard and gauze, suddenly turn out to be real. Georgi shuddered; in the old country, thinking of the dead at a moment like this would be considered the worst of bad omens.

He swung around, startled and a little frightened by an answering series of thumps on the outside of the freezer door. Eugenios—God bless his second son—had remembered. Happily, Georgi pounded back on the door and started pacing faster, flapping his arms so he could laughingly show them, when they got the door open, how little the cold had affected him. Goddamn, he could tell them one thing: nothing like this had happened in '71.

If Georgi could have been standing outside the meat locker, he would have realized the pounding from the outside was done not so much in answer as in sheer frustration. Eugenios, along with his brothers, Orien and Christophorus, stood in the pale circle cast by a heavy flashlight and stared at the door. Like those on all meat lockers, it opened out. But crossing the door at an angle—and blocking it completely—lay one of the six-inch steel beams that had reinforced the flooring of the bandstand directly above. During the quake, the whole thing had come down into the cellar. The floor in front of the door was covered with a rubble of fallen brick, plaster, and wood, along with seats, music stands, and part of the small upright piano.

The three brothers looked at each other helplessly. Clearing away the lighter debris could be done, they supposed—it *had* to be done—but that heavy steel beam was going to be impossibly tough without help from the fire department.

With a shrug, Orien stepped forward and methodically began clearing away the lighter wreckage; the steel beam was a problem they would face later. Christophorus headed for the remains of the stairway to round up help from the partyers in lifting the beam. Only Eugenios, the second oldest stared and did nothing. He wasn't as sure as they were that they had that much time. The problem wasn't a supply of air—the freezer was vented. What bothered him was a dim recollection.

Like his father, he could remember the '71 quake.

Unlike his father, Eugenios could also remember that the Van Norman Dams had almost gone then, and could only wonder—and worry—if they would hold this time.

When Orien started to whistle as he tugged at the fallen bricks, he was startled to receive a sudden, disapproving shove from his younger brother, Eugenios.

Maybe, Orien thought, Eugenios was as drunk as some of the guests upstairs.

Chapter Fourteen

The psychological post-shock period that follows any natural disaster is rich in life-objective changes; it is a time of frank introspection and re-examination of values. There is a sudden awareness that life is finite, and people tend to move out of ruts of their own devising.

Were it not for the loss of life, the injuries, and the economic unheaval entailed, an occasional natural disaster would probably be a healthy thing for all of us to experience.

—Dr. Alan Robbin
Behavioral Dynamics and Nature

At the Penthouse Terrace of the Park Plaza, Violet arrived too early for dinner, but just in time for cocktails. The maître d' stood with one foot on the upper tier where Adam and Dorothy were seated and one foot on the steps that led down to the main dining level, his face a nodding, somber mask. He wrote down Adam's order for hors d'oeuvres: tiny fried whitebait for madame (Dorothy Grimes had thrown more than one restaurant kitchen into disarray with her unusual but inevitable order); antipasto for monsieur.

The annoyed expression on the maître d's face was replaced by one of surprise, but neither Adam nor Dorothy Grimes got much chance to study it. One moment the man was there, the next he was gone. Without even an outcry, just a look of confused disbelief, he dropped silently and swiftly out of sight as the floor beneath him tore itself loose from the outer tier and plunged downward. The whole dining area—the recessed portion slightly below and inside the outer tier—had done this; first it buckled, then it dropped down inside the outer shell of the building, the first element in a series of falling dominoes that roared downward, taking all the floors below with it. People sitting on the outer tier, like Adam Mosely and Dorothy Grimes, were on flooring structurally attached to the outer shell of the building and, therefore, temporarily safe—although perched on the edge of a thirty-two-story hole.

Wrenched by the collapse of the inner floor, with which it shared some structural elements, even the outer tier buckled somewhat and took on a frightening downward tilt toward the void. Forcing himself to move, Adam grabbed Dorothy's arm and pulled her back with him, pressing hard up against the outer glass window-wall of the room. For a moment neither could say anything, but leaned limply against the window-wall and stared at the vast hole a few feet in front of them. Adam, unable to grapple with the situation taken in its entirety, concentrated on a single facet of the catastrophe. "The waiter," he said with awe. "That poor damned headwaiter. Gone. Just like that."

Dorothy Grimes was just as stunned as Adam. Typically, though, her reaction took a completely different shape. "They always hate it when I order whitebait."

Automatically, Adam started to say something unpleasant, but stopped; he knew Dorothy Grimes well enough to realize that her crude attempt at black humor was no more than her way of insulating herself against something she felt too deeply to let show. His eyes traveled the narrow ledge that still clung to the outer shell, carefully avoiding the gaping center hole from which a column of dust and oily black smoke rolled upward. Slowly, his mind began reconstructing the diagrams used in the *Trib* story of four years earlier; even with his near total recall, he could disinter only fragments of them at the moment, but he remembered how the article had pointed out that, given the proposed structural shortcuts, everything that had just happened was entirely predictable. The thought didn't provide much satisfaction.

Farther along the same tier, Anna and Sporades, still seated at their table, stared at the hole in numb disbelief. Beneath their feet, they could feel the sagging as their narrow strip of tier began to cant downward. Seeing Dorothy Grimes and Adam flattened against the outer glass window-wall, Sporades grabbed Anna and imitated their positions. He was surprised to see that Anna was crying and wondered if she was on the edge of hysteria, something that would seem very much out of character for her. (Actually, Anna wasn't crying about their own predicament; she was thinking of her family and friends back at Georgi's.) Sensing Sporades' confusion at her tears, she gave him a weak smile of reassurance. "I'm all right. Don't worry." Sporades sighed with relief. The only cure he knew for hysterics was a hard slap across the face; it would have been a very unfortunate start to a marriage.

Catty-cornered across the tier, on the other side of the room, Digit Vorhees and the psych major were having a slightly more complicated set of problems. As with the rest of the guests seated on the tier, they had watched horrified as the center of the room collapsed and dropped out of sight, diners and all. From below, they could hear the sickening crashes as each floor, one by one, crumbled under the weight of the floors falling on it from above. Like everyone else, they had moved as far away from the edge of the hole as they could get and flattened themselves against the outer window-wall of the building. Digit was for once even thoughtful enough to manage a few words of reassurance for the psych major. However, the psych major, an intensely practical person, ignored the palliation; she had assessed their situation and decided a brilliant career plumbing the depths of children's psyches had just been lost to the world.

"Whatever you do, don't look down," cautioned Digit. "Close your eyes, press hard against the window, and you'll be all right. That's it—right against the window." This was where the complication arose. Digit and the psych major were pressing no harder against their window than the rest of the survivors on the upper tier, but their section of the glass wall had somehow been weakened. With a sudden wobbling motion at its left end, the great picture window—each section was about twelve feet long—fell out the other side of the building and sailed gracefully down toward the street. "Down!" Digit shouted. And like soldiers suddenly hearing the whine of an approaching shell, both of them fell flat on the narrow strip of floor that remained, hugging the nubby carpet for their lives.

Adam Mosely watched, his mind seeing this and the rest of the room as if from a great distance. To look at him, one could have almost thought him disinterested, but his brain was totally occupied reconstructing the building plans of the Park Plaza. Slowly, floor by floor, he was putting them together in his head; the neat white lines with their elaborately lettered architectural script and precisely indicated measurements marched methodically across the structure's blueprints as he traced an imaginary route down a fire stair here, across an internal hallway there, taking note of the gaps where they would have to improvise. His eyes lifted a second and appraised Dorothy Grimes; she was not young, she was not in shape, and worst of all, she had a left leg weakened by a childhood riding accident, an impairment she managed to hide from just about everyone. The trip down would be difficult at best; Dorothy Grimes would make it infinitely harder.

Staring into her face intently, Adam placed a hand against the glass wall on either side of her head and smiled reassuringly. "I think I know a way to get us down from here."

To his surprise, Dorothy Grimes merely shook her head in a firm no.

"Look, Dorothy. I can't pretend it will be easy. But I think we—all of the people left here in this room—can make it. There's a fire stair along the outer building shell part of the way, but, in some places, well—we'll just have to improvise."

192

Her head shook again. "Not my style, Adam. I'll wait. Later on, after they get things under control out there"—with a nod, she indicated the blacked-out city beyond the window—"you can have the fire department send a helicopter for me."

Adam was just as firm. "You can't wait. These quakes usually have aftershocks. The building shell took the first one; it probably won't take another. And I swear to God, Dolly"— it was a name only her closest friends called her, and one which he had never used with her before—"I can and I *will* get you down."

Dorothy Grimes found a sudden rush of thoughts, emotions, and ideas sailing through her mind like a flight of archers' arrows. She certainly didn't want to die, but the picture Adam was drawing was an impossible one. And she would be the principal obstacle to any faint possibility of success Adam's escape route might hold for the rest of them. With the speed of decision that had put her where she was, her mind reached it conclusion, firmly, unalterably, and without looking back. "No," she said. "No, Adam. I'm an old lady. And I'm an old lady with one game leg, something you didn't even know about, did you? All I'd be is dead weight. Besides, I don't particularly care to begin my climb toward heaven crawling and scrambling down doubtful fire stairs and worse. You go. Take the rest of these people"—she let her eyes drift around the room—"they could use a leader just now—take them, organize them, and get *them* down. I'm staying here. Period." She studied his face for a second, saw doubt, and added, "It's not a grandstand play, Adam. I'm no hero. I'm just tired. Much too tired to even bother trying."

If Dorothy Grimes usually knew how to handle Adam, Adam almost as frequently knew how to handle Dorothy Grimes. He leaned back against the glass wall, crossed his right foot over his left, and, borrowing one of Dorothy's cigarettes, lit up—looking about as much in a hurry as a man watching an oak tree grow.

For a moment Dorothy Grimes stared at him. Then: "What in God's name are you up to, Adam?"

"If you're not going, I'm not going. We'll sit here—as you suggested—and hope there's no aftershock or that the building shell doesn't collapse of its own weight or that this tier doesn't tear itself free and follow the rest of the floor down the hole and maybe—I suppose there's an outside possibility we might get lucky—and maybe eventually a helicopter will happen to fly over and we'll get picked up." Adam let his eyes move slowly to their overturned table. "Too bad you didn't order your whitebait earlier. This could be a long wait."

"You're being unfair, and you know you are." She reached down and felt her bad leg. "You didn't know I had a game leg until I told you; I took great pains nobody did. But can you imagine me hiking down thirty floors?"

With a shake of his head, Adam gave a small sigh of wonder at the human capacity for self-deception. "I've known about your leg for years. Everybody did. Riding accident when you were twelve, if I remember. But bad leg or not, I said I would get you down, and I will."

Turning toward him, Dorothy Grimes almost forgot she didn't have the luxury of much movement on their narrow strip of floor and had to flatten herself against the window-wall again. "Adam, you're still being unfair. I'd be deadweight. A drag. There's no reason on earth for you to stay here with me. So cut out the act."

"Unfair? Totally. But necessarily." Adam turned just enough to rest his hand on the glass beside her head again. He smiled at her. "Call it—well, call it highly justified means to a very worthwhile end."

"I call it a lousy trick."

A small lingering rumble shook the building, followed, as if in an afterthought, by the stuttering crashes of more furniture and glassware sliding over the edge into the hole.

"Damn you, Adam." Dorothy shook her head again, but this

time it was a signal both of defeat and resignation. Helplessly, she threw up her hands. "Do what you have to."

Adam was as startled as Dorothy Grimes was when he leaned forward and touched her forehead with a light kiss, as fleeting and shy as a schoolboy's. "OK. We're in business." He straightened up and looked around. The kid and his girl, over there where the window-wall had collapsed behind them, were crawling slowly toward the safety of the next tier; that strip, at least, had one glass side as protection, but they still seemed in the most immediate danger of all. The other young couple—they looked like newlyweds somehow—seemed temporarily all right, although the girl's recent display of tears worried Adam. Both the young men, Adam noticed, looked strong and athletic, which was good; some way of carrying Dorothy Grimes was going to have to be figured out.

But first, Adam knew, command had to be established. Nobody was going to be very reassured by the scheme he had in mind; the plan would appear dangerous, tough, hair-raising, and impossible—but he hoped it would also appear essential to their survival. Some of these people would, of course, harbor resentment at the burden of having to cope with Dorothy Grimes' disability, even if the umbrage was never expressed.

As confidently as he could, he walked as close as he dared to the edge of the tier and cupped his hands. "Attention! Attention, please." The sound of his strong voice caused the others' heads to turn toward him, even in the case of the young couple who were crawling along the narrow strip of tier. "I am Adam Mosely," he announced firmly. "I think I know a way to get us down from here. If we all keep our cool, I think we can make it."

The faces stared at him blankly, the bodies attached to them appeared frozen in motion, like a still taken during a disaster at sea. Adam wasn't sure what sort of reaction he had expected, but the utter silence of this one threw him. He cleared his throat.

Dorothy Grimes decided his statement needed added authority. Like Adam, she cupped her hands and shouted across the empty space. "Mr. Mosely is editor-in-chief of the Los Angeles *Trib*."

Nobody applauded.

At St. Bridget's, on Wilshire Avenue, the unthinkable had happened. Violet, in what can only be viewed as a capricious moment, had put Father Reed, SJ, and Derek Usher, communicant, in the unlikely position of either surviving together or perishing alone.

The entire area near St. Bridget's was particularly devastated, partly because Violet, in her erratic course through Los Angeles, had chosen this part of the city for an agonizing series of shocks, but also because, like Watts, the neighborhood had substandard housing. Just before the impact, Father Reed, still followed by Derek, had excused himself for a moment and disappeared into his tiny office at the rear of the church. From here, he planned to talk with a friend of his who was a clinical psychologist and suggest Derek as a potential patient. To ensure privacy for the call, the Jesuit had noiselessly locked the door behind him.

When Father Reed heard the first shattering crash inside the building, his immediate reaction was that Derek was breaking down the door that separated them; it was only when he felt the ground shake and saw pieces of plaster fall out of the ancient ceiling that Father Reed realized what was happening. Quickly, he began unlocking the door so that he could get back into the church proper. The priest could have saved himself the effort; with a roaring crunch, the thin walls on either side of the door collapsed, and a moment or two later the door fell slowly and gracefully to the floor like a giant leaf settling to the ground.

Derek and Father Reed stared at each other unbelievably across the newly created open space; then both of them fell to the floor, as flat as they could make themselves, hugging the

196

ground to avoid the sudden assault of flying bricks, falling plaster, and splintered lathwork.

From Derek, his hands over his head, came an eerie moaning, his cries alternating with uncontrollable sobs and gaspings for air. Part of this was pure terror at being victim of what he, unlike many people, immediately recognized as an earthquake; part of it sprang from an awesome and terrible certainty that he was being punished by God—for both his blasphemy and the murder of his mother. It was not a hard conclusion for a once-devout Catholic like Derek to reach: he had sinned mortally; he had mocked God; he had used his Church as an alibi to avoid prosecution for his high crimes. An offended God had personally sent the earthquake to punish him, to make clear both to Derek and to the world how swift was His vengeance and how mighty His hand. Staging the event in a church whose priest must have distressed God as deeply as Derek was nothing more than an act of divine irony, but one, Derek, thought, that was a beautiful example of how intricate a pattern God could weave to make His point.

"Forgive me, Father, for I have sinned," cried Derek, although this time his confession was entirely genuine. Grabbing Father Reed by the arm, a torrent of guilt began pouring from Derek's mouth. "I had to do it, Father Reed—as God is my witness, I had to. I'm thirty-five and she treated me like I was ten and she wouldn't let go. Mother wasn't going to let go—ever. So I had to kill her. Tell me God will forgive me, Father, tell me—"

Father Reed didn't know whether to believe any of what Derek was saying or not. He *did* know this wasn't the time to weigh the matter because as Derek was pleading with him, a heavy supporting beam, one of several set into the ceiling, tore itself loose and fell diagonally across the room, the lower end just missing them.

To Derek, this became another sign from God, and he began chanting the litany in Latin, the way he'd said it as a

197

child, before people like Father Reed came along and turned everything into English.

The priest paused in crawling out from under the beam long enough to stare with desperation at Derek. They had to get out of this place quickly, and Latin would not do that for them. An earthquake was problem enough; having to share one with a madman was more than should be asked of anyone. Tugging hard, he pulled at Derek, trying to get him moving. Derek only shook his head vigorously and continued his chanting.

"Oh, shit," Father Reed groaned.

KBDT's guy in the sky was having his own troubles. From his year in the traffic chopper, Corbit had become used to seeing LA as a simple network of roads and freeways, almost like the grid on a map, with occasional easily recognizable buildings and spaces as reference points. As he looked down now, the familiar grid had all but disappeared—or was so drastically altered it was useless to him. Many of the reference points were even more unreliable; some of the buildings were still there, while others had simply dissolved into disordered piles of masonry. Only natural reference points—the Pacific, the wide green sweep of Griffith Park, the oil fields on the way to LAX, the foothills of the mountains and Mount Baldy itself—could be counted on, and most of these were far apart. If the city had boasted a river running through its center, the job would have been easier, but the Los Angeles River is so small and ordinarily short of water that it is little more than a cement culvert. And the day had not been kind to anything made of cement.

Corbit was a good pilot and had been an expert at finding his bearings over destroyed hamlets in Vietnam, but what he was seeing of the city through the bubble of his chopper was something no amount of combat training could have prepared him for.

The headset began buzzing again; the voice was Kraypool's.

198

"Corbit. Corbit, in the KBDT chopper. Can you hear me, Corbit?"

"I read you." Hearing Kraypool was not as easy as Corbit made it sound. The air was filled with strange calls and signals, emergency services and ham operators wandering off their assigned frequencies, trying to establish contact. Over this, Kraypool's voice sounded thin and distant, like a foreign station picked up on a shortwave radio, fading in and out, and oddly cluttered with snatches of music. Who the hell, Corbit wondered, was playing canned Mantovani at a moment like this? Powerful signals drifting in from someplace else was the best answer he could provide himself.

"Can you give me an overview yet, Corbit? This is Kraypool, this is Kraypool." Kraypool seemed to keep repeating his own name like this at regular intervals as if in a ritual invocation to prove he was still alive.

With an uncomfortable switching of his body in the seat, Corbit propped the clipboard with his notes on his knees and got ready to give what he could. The picture would not be complete in any sense, he warned Kraypool, or even terribly accurate. Corbit started to explain about the difficulties of demarking areas when the reference points were so far apart but gave up.

"I understand," Kraypool answered. "Go ahead, Corbit."

Grimly, Corbit gave the clearest picture he could. He started along the ocean and then worked his way inland. First of all, Malibu was a mess. Most of the houses along the cliffs were in the water or about to be. Yes, there were people there in trouble; rescue teams should be working the whole length of the coast road. Santa Monica, perhaps because of its flatter shoreline, was in better shape. Down at Long Beach, however, the principal trouble was the result of a small tidal wave stirred up by the quake. The *Queen Mary*, he reported, was loose from its permanent mooring at Pier J and drifting out to sea on a final voyage. Yes, sightseers were aboard her. Corbit, without much hope, suggested contacting the Coast Guard.

Through his headset, he could hear Kraypool sigh. The sound startled him; up until now, Kraypool's reactions had been remote and disembodied, quick little one-line questions without any apparent emotion attached. The sigh must also have surprised Kraypool. "I see," his voice commented so flatly it was as if he were denying the humanness of the sigh. "What about the airports?"

"The airports," Corbit repeated, leafing through his notes to find the right section. LAX was—and would be for some time to come—totally out of operation. The runways, like most of the freeways, were piles of broken and shattered concrete. The main control building was hard even to find. Aircraft—both those on the runways and those in hangers and staging areas—were splashed across the field, broken and forever unusable. Fuel tanks north of the airport had ruptured and were on fire. Listening to himself, Corbit began to loathe the sound of his own voice, reporting one dismal fact after another. With a definite attempt at brightness, he added that at least the airport, with its own firefighting equipment and broad expanses of open land, appeared to be getting things under control.

"Are there *any* runways that could operate?" asked Kraypool suddenly. "I'm thinking of something big enough to handle cargo planes from the Army. Hauling emergency equipment in, taking casualties out."

Corbit looked down, but he already knew the answer. "None there; it's a total wipeout. Maybe the secondary field at Lawford—I didn't go near enough it to notice."

There was another sigh from Kraypool. "I wasn't able to raise them on the OCD network, so I guess they're out of commission, too." There was a pause, then: "My home's not far from there."

Corbit didn't know how to respond. This was the first time Kraypool had become fully human, and the metamorphosis shook him. It was also the first time he'd had any contact with someone whose personal life was involved in the panoply of destruction he could see spread out below him. Corbit was a bachelor, from out of town, and only casual friends were somewhere down in that shattered mess; Kraypool sounded older, probably married, and from the tone of worry in his voice clearly concerned about his family.

A moment or two of crackling silence came over the headset; then Corbit rearranged the notes on his lap and returned to his grim recital. Watts in flames, with a full-scale riot also in progress. The city downtown untouched in some places, severely damaged in others. In the Valley, irregular patterns of destruction. Most importantly, the Van Norman Dams seemed to be holding, although Corbit reported he could see enormous cracks running across them "like a kid had been drawing on the concrete with a crayon."

While giving his report, Corbit was letting the chopper travel in a medium circle, and the aimless flight pattern was beginning to annoy him. He reshuffled the clipboard full of papers on his lap and decided the feeling came from his having to play a messenger of doom while knowing, at the same time, there was absolutely nothing he could do to help. An idea had been growing in his head but would have to wait until later, if ever. For the moment, he turned back to what Kraypool called his "overview," finishing up with a summary that was the ultimate in gloom.

The city, he noted, was isolated, with both roads and airports completely knocked out. Panic, flood, and fire in different areas, with people trapped inside—and on top of—many of the taller buildings. Downtown was pretty much the same; some of the high rises were intact, others were either totally collapsed or in various stages of falling apart. Lower Wilshire was particularly hard hit; a strange pattern of gorges had cut off whole areas into islands of land surrounded by crevices from which gas-fed flames and towering bursts of water were spouting into the air.

There were no lights anywhere, which was bad enough, but Corbit pointed out that the real hell would come in about an hour—after the sun had set and it began to grow dark. Anything that was going to be done on an individual basis would have to be accomplished before then.

"I know," said Kraypool miserably. "I also know I'm just about helpless to do anything about it."

In the chopper, Corbit grunted and went through the ritual of signing off. He banked the helicopter steeply and headed back toward the heart of the city.

It wouldn't be much, but there were a couple of things *he* could do.

At Goldstone, Dr. Feiner's lab was beginning to look and sound like a network newsroom on election night. With one big difference: *everybody* was losing.

The room, which ordinarily was amply large, was now jammed with men in shirt sleeves, each hurrying from one place in the lab to another, sheafs of paper waving in his hands. A constant shuffling noise and the subdued sound of exigent voices filled the room.

All their regular programmers—at least, all that they could reach at home—had been called in; they sat crouched over their machines, feeding in data being handed to them on long typed sheets of data paper. In addition, a complement of extra programmers, some lent to the lab by corporations in nearby towns, others by the Army Databank in Culver, added to the confusion. What Feiner had given them to do seemed impossible in the time they had been given to do it: construct a complete program of aftershock predictions for Violet, starting from scratch.

Before today, none of the data had been programmed because there had been no base point for the predictions—until Violet. All the information on aftershock activity from earlier quakes was available; the programmers were now trying to devise a program that would use the same predictive elements that had given advance warning of Violet to do the same for her possible aftershocks.

202

"The assignment's impossible," Nick Rivers, the head programmer told Feiner flatly. "What you're asking for is a couple of weeks' concentrated program work in a couple of hours. We can't do it."

Feiner, his self-assurance riding high since the computer's prediction of Violet, stared at the man and shook his head vigorously. "I'm not asking for it, dammit. I'm demanding it. The people in that beat-up city have to know. Their lives are on the line."

For a second, Nick Rivers stared at Feiner in silence, his lack of response accentuated by the constant ringing of phones in the background, the clatter of teleprinters, the whispered conferences of men huddled over tables piled high with paper. "It'll mean taking a lot of shortcuts, Mike," he said, already knowing what Feiner's answer was going to be. "And I don't have to tell you that shortcuts are dangerous."

"So are aftershocks."

With a shrug, the head programmer walked wearily back to reorganize the procedures for the programming model; he mistrusted speed, he mistrusted corner cutting, and most of all, he mistrusted any departure from the meticulous but time-consuming procedures he'd set up to avoid mistakes. Halfway across the room, Rivers stopped and turned back toward Feiner. "I can't take any responsibility for read-out reliability, Mike. This kind of speed just isn't sound programming practice."

"Nobody's asking you to."

From his small desk to one side, Ridgeway looked at Feiner and sighed. Feiner's zeal had run away with him, and Ridgeway wasn't sure what to do about it. Mike was acting cocky and the cockiness spelled trouble. His handling of Nick Rivers, the head programmer, had been unfortunate, his overemotional reference to the people of Los Angeles just short of outrageous, his attitude toward the men in the room impatient and irritable. Ridgeway didn't for a second doubt the value of what Feiner was trying to do; his concern was that Mike might be going too fast and, in the process, damage not only what he was trying to accomplish but himself as well.

"Michael," he said gently. "Michael, are you sure these shortcuts aren't a mistake? We could do a tremendous disservice with a faulty prediction at this point."

"We don't have any choice."

"We always have a choice." Ridgeway reached out and offered Feiner a match for the unlit cigarette hanging from one corner of his mouth; Feiner was about to begin chewing it like a cigar. "What I mean is—and I know I sound like a broken record of myself from before the tremor—a false prediction of aftershock could be worse than no prediction at all. As you just pointed out, a lot of lives are on the line."

At first, Feiner looked as if he hadn't heard him. He was staring at the programming teams, his lips moving in a silent litany to get the men moving faster. Abruptly, his face turned toward Ridgeway. "Look," he said firmly. "The Army is about to fly in cargo planes with rescue teams and hospital crews. They're looking for a place where they can land their cargo planes now. Helicopter squadrons are about to go in, too. But if there's going to be a big aftershock, they could lose all those people and supplies and the city would wind up farther behind the eight ball than it already is. Also, so far the Van Norman Dams seem to be holding—just. But if the Army puts rescue personnel in that Valley and then there's an aftershock, hell, they'd probably lose all their men and supplies there as well. They have to know. And as fast as we can let them know. The shortcuts are risky, but there's nothing else we can do. We *don't* have a choice."

To Ridgeway, it was clear Feiner was missing his point. But trying to bring Mike around to his way of thinking was, at this moment, impossible. He would get Rivers, the head programmer, aside later and see precisely how reliable the prediction would be after the shortcuts. For the moment, the best he could do was nod wearily at Feiner.

"OK, Michael. This is one of those awful paradoxes without a real answer."

But the plate theory of global tectonics, courtesy of Earth Tremor Violet, already had an answer ready and waiting for them.

Part III

Chapter Fifteen

The magic of Beverly Hills is locked in the secret of that bustling business activity, miraculously accomplished without ruffling the serene beauty of its lovely streets, homes, and gardens, or the orderly and relaxed routine of its inhabitants.

> —Beverly Hills City (Telephone)
> Directory published by the Beverly
> Hills Chamber of Commerce and Civic
> Association

AT first, Laura Vorhees was unable to make out the sound that reawoke her. Her sleep had been short but deep and had left her feeling groggy; the covers were pulled tightly up around her face, and for some reason not immediately clear to her, she was resisting a natural inclination to open her eyes and pinpoint the origin of the noise. Still, the sound persisted, a plaintive, mournful ululation, each time followed by a series of sharp clicks. Laura had lived too long close to the sea not to recognize, finally, even with her eyes closed, the source of the lonely wail: it was the cry of a gull. And with this realization, she understood why she was trying to keep her eyes shut. The gull was part of the nightmare of being suspended uncertainly over the Pacific; keeping her eyes closed helped her to deny the fact.

Reluctantly, she raised her eyelids. Nothing had changed: no miracle had restored her to safety; she was still on her Venetian bed, cantilevered out over the Pacific in a fashion no architect could have imagined. The only difference was in the gull. On its earlier visits, the seabird had merely flown around her, screaming reproachfully; now it was balancing itself precariously on the footboard of the bed, staring at her, its curious pink eyes glaring to indicate the gull considered Laura as unwelcome as Laura considered the gull.

Halfheartedly, Laura threw one of her pillows at the footboard to scare the bird, which teetered for a second, then, with a great flapping of its long, drooping wings, took off in a wide sweeping arc, screaming back in outrage. Exhausted from even this slight effort, Laura sank back against the headboard. She would have liked to close her eyes and again shut out the awful reality of where she was, but her eyelids refused to cooperate; they would allow Laura to close them partway but then take advantage of any slight sound to fly fully open once more. Given the circumstances, Laura knew that the eyelids were right and she was wrong; the realization automatically made her feel guilty.

And because of the familiar, numbing sense of guilt, her reaction to the next event was equally automatic. "Laura, what the hell are you doing down there?" a sudden, irritated voice bellowed at her. Her first reaction—that the voice belonged to her father—made no sense: his Pickwickian twinkle never included profanity (except in the privacy of his bathroom, where he could occasionally be heard swearing softly at elusive razor blades, inefficiently placed soap dishes, and, particularly as he grew older, the unfair rebelliousness of his digestive system). Besides, her father had been dead for more than twenty years. Her second impression—that the voice was that of her husband, George—was equally illogical; George was in Obispo, and even if George did happen, by some quirk, to be in the Los Angeles area, he would have been in the city proper, and not, of all places, near her house in Malibu.

"Laura! Can you hear me, Laura? *Laura?*" The voice persisted.

Laura's head swiveled toward the remains of the bed-wall behind her and saw that, however illogical, however

210

preposterous, however absurd the thought might be, the voice did indeed belong to George. He was leaning around the end of the shattered wall, his hands clutching the rough stones for support, his head and neck stuck out at an awkward angle to look at her, but his legs and body pulled far back to keep himself from getting too close to the cliff's edge.

Laura was stunned. Like the gull, he had no business being here. However, unlike the gull, he could not be dismissed with a hurled pillow. Involuntarily, one hand fastened itself onto the package of videotapes; simultaneously, she saw George's eyes follow her hand. Nothing more was required to explain what George had been doing in Malibu when the earthquake struck. Controlling herself firmly, Laura ignored George's eyes as they stared at the parcel. And when she finally spoke, her voice was strong, although tinged both with petulance and demand. "Don't just stand there, George. Get me out of here. God knows how long this bed is going to stay put."

After a moment's hesitation, George became all reassurance. "Stay still, Laura. Very still. If you don't move, there's nothing to be afraid of. I'll get you off of there. Somehow. Just hang on."

For Laura, her answer was so atypical the words surprised even *her*. "Oh, I'll hang on all right, George. If only because you're a bastard and I want to get these tapes to the district attorney so they can put you where you belong. Now stop staring and get moving."

Her answer was, in fact, so completely out of character that George obeyed, but after a few minutes of energetic searching, his knee-jerk reflex to Laura's command began wearing off. A host of worries, contingent disasters, and doubts were crowding his brain. Leaning against the still-standing chimney of the house—a chimney complete with mantel and fireplace, if lacking a wall—George tried to sort out the conflicting ideas. He had, he finally concluded, three options. For one, he could continue searching and probably find something that would help him get Laura to safety. The problem was that the "new" Laura had sounded very definite in her

211

plans for the tapes. With them in hand, the district attorney had a very solid case. Trying to wrestle the package from her once he got her off the bed and onto the cliff was unfeasible. Firmly, George dismissed that course of action as self-destructive.

Another possibility would simply be to wait. All around him, he could hear continuing rock slides as other pieces of the cliff fell into the sea. Given time enough, Laura, the house, and the tapes might eventually slide into the Pacific. This alternative was not exactly committing murder, he supposed. It was murder by noncommission.

The final option George rejected almost as quickly as it formed in his head. Clearly, not much would be required to "help" the total collapse of the wall supporting Laura—a little fussing around at the wall's base, a rock or two rolled over the edge to start a final crumbling of the cliff below. The operation would be both simple and discovery-proof, and George found it curious that he could envision this solution to his problems so easily, yet so quickly repudiate the means of accomplishing it.

As he pondered this phenomenon, a new plan began to take shape, a plan built on one of Laura's more obvious weaknesses: when she wasn't obsessed with guilt, she was consumed by paranoia. Because of this, George doubted that Laura would assume he had dismissed violence as a possibility. (The fact was, George was a bit startled by his out-of-hand rejection of violence.) Laura would, then, still be expecting extreme, possibly even lethal, measures from him. Capitalizing on this fear, he might be able to strike a bargain with her—her life, for instance, against the tapes and a promise of everlasting silence. If she were frightened enough, it might work, although even as he considered the plan, he could sense a flimsy, desperate quality about it. Still, the concept was worth exploring.

Repeated cries from Laura prodded him into action. Lying flat on his stomach, George inched his head well around the wall so that he could bargain with her face to face. As a natural-born salesman, George Vorhees knew that hard sales are more effectively made through eye-to-eye contact. "Laura," he called, leaning out as far as he dared, "now I want you to stay calm. I think I know a way to get you out of there, but, well, you understand, what I mean is, there's just this one small thing. . . ."

As so often had happened in George Vorhees' life, salesmanship became academic in the face of chance events that rendered the talent superfluous. From behind him —perhaps less than half a dozen feet behind him—came a strong, sympathetic voice.

"Jesus," said the voice urgently, as George turned his head to stare into the face of a young, tallish man in some sort of uniform. "What a mess, fella. But don't panic. I got a ladder on my truck. With that, we can get her up easy. I'll be right back with it. My truck went off the road just short of the drive back there."

George had seen the man for only an instant, but the writing on his workman's coveralls—right above the pocket, stitched in bold, red-woven script—burned as brightly as a neon beer sign in a darkened bar. "A-1 Exterminators. Death on Ants."

At the Griffith Park Zoo, Isaac Rosholman's private plan to keep the animals behind the moats was about to get its first test. Rosholman stood, one hand holding the unwanted shotgun, the other clutching one of the flare pistols taken from the admin building. He watched as a young lion moved closer to the remains of the moat, sniffing cautiously and curiously. With nothing more to go on than his own instincts, Rosholman was convinced that a flare, terrifying in its brightness, shot close to such an animal, would cause the creature to slink back into safer and more familiar territory. It was a far cry from the official contingency plan, but if his initial effort worked, Rosholman would return to the admin building, collect the rest of the guards, issue the flare pistols and give out the new instructions. Harmless animals—the

213

bonteboks, the giraffes, the wildebeests—would be allowed to cross and wander loose; the iron picket fence around the zoo's perimeter would keep them from getting themselves into any trouble.

The lion was pacing back and forth now on his own side of the moat, his gray-green eyes moving from Rosholman to the crushed concrete and back, uncertain of what this new situation held for him. Rosholman placed the shotgun under his arm and cocked the first barrel of the flare pistol; he knew from the movements that the animal was close to charging. As he saw the lion's rear leg muscles tighten and bunch in preparation for the leap, Rosholman raised the flare pistol and fired close to the lion's head.

Exactly what happened was never clear to Rosholman. Possibly, his aim was bad or the pistol inaccurate or the flare itself was defective. But instead of bursting *near* the lion, the burning flare virtually exploded in the beast's face. With a howl of pain and rage, the great animal leaped across the ruined moat directly at Rosholman. Then the searing flame from the flare reached the lion's eyes, and he began running in tight circles trying to shake loose the pain, finally rolling his muzzle in the dirt, his one undamaged eye staring straight at Rosholman.

Quickly, Rosholman began backing away. His plan was not reliable: if lions on the wrong side of the moat were dangerous, *wounded* lions on the wrong side were doubly so. The drafters of the zoo's contingency plan had perhaps foreseen this. Rosholman realized he would have to return to the admin building and see if there was anything else he could work out.

But the burned animal had plans of his own. Still shaking his head fitfully from the pain of the flare, he rose from the dirt and began circling Rosholman. From somewhere behind him, Rosholman heard another growl and could guess more lions had already crossed the moat and were also wandering loose. For a moment, the lion stopped circling and listened, then gave an answering growl. They were, Rosholman knew, getting the pride into hunting formation—lions rarely track game in anything but groups—and he, Rosholman, was the quarry. Never taking his eyes from them for a second Rosholman kept backing away slowly, taking great care so that no sudden movement would trigger the animal into a leap. As he watched, he saw another lion appear to the right of the first; almost immediately, after some sort of mysterious communication with the initial one, the second lion joined him in the circling. Rosholman continued to back away, although he had no idea of what he was retreating toward; he could recall no shelter in this part of the zoo.

Up until now Rosholman still was not overly scared. He had another flare in the pistol, which would at least slow down any attack, and, if worse came to worst, there was always the shotgun itself. The thought of using the gun, however, was unthinkable to him; even if his life were on the line, he wasn't sure he could. Rosholman hoped that something would distract them, that some sight or sound would draw their attention away from him. With a sinking sensation, he realized he was not sure the gun was loaded, and although the shells were in his pocket, he knew the sharp clicks of the gun's being breached would probably bring on the attack.

To his right, he saw a third member of the pride join the circling group, and as imperceptibly as possible, allowed his backing up to accelerate. Although probably necessary, the decision was unfortunate. With his eyes fixed on the animals, Rosholman never saw the branch he tripped over, falling backward and hitting the ground heavily and noisily. The lions charged. Desperately, Rosholman scrambled to his feet, trying to find the shotgun as he did. Unable to, he fired the remaining barrel of the flare gun at the lions. The bright light caused the animals to pause, but only for a second. Rosholman began running. The attempt to outrun them would be useless, but he had no choice.

From his left, a sudden voice made Rosholman turn his

head. "Haul ass over here, Ike—and for Christ's sake bring that shotgun with you," yelled Battock, his voice as unpleasant and strident as always.

What Rosholman saw, under any other circumstances, would have made him break into uncontrolled laughter, but this was a time for escaping, not laughing. Battock was in one of the retaining cages used by the zoo's vets—animals were tricked into them for shots, examinations and treatment—both the man's hands holding onto the cage's bars like a parody of a prison movie. As Rosholman ran, he could see Battock cranking up the chutelike opening at one end through which the animals, under normal conditions, were driven into the cage. With about ten feet to spare between him and the pride, Rosholman shot through the opening and heard Battock trigger the gate so that it roared down its greased tracks and slammed shut behind him.

Panting, Rosholman lay on the floor of the cage and tried to find breath enough to say thank you to his old enemy. Battock didn't wait for any words; he just looked at the collapsed Rosholman and groaned in disgust. "Where the hell's the shotgun, Rosholman? You had one—I saw it."

Wordlessly, Rosholman pointed into the underbrush. There was another agonized grunt from Battock. "We'll be here for the rest of our damned lives, you stupid Yid. Why wasn't them guns handed out like they was supposed to be anyway?"

Rosholman ignored both the insult and the question. "We'll be out in a few minutes," he gasped. "Look." A small herd of bubal hartebeests were dashing through the thicket, and the lions almost immediately abandoned the cage to slink into the underbrush, taking up stalking positions on the stragglers. With that much natural food within easy reach, Rosholman knew he and Battock were—at least temporarily—safe. "Come on," he told Battock. "Help me get this gate open." He reached through the bars and began cranking the handle on the winch which raised the gate.

"Hold it." Battock's voice was urgent and unpleasant. "I

216

damned near ought to let you go get yourself chewed up, Rosholman, for losing that shotgun. But I gotta tell you. There's another big cat out there. A real old one. He's how come I've been caged up in this contraption for the last fifteen minutes."

It was then that Rosholman, for the first time, saw Three Toes. The great ancient lion had withdrawn into the bushes when the rest of the pride had been near, but now that they were gone, he had once again taken up his position, lying flat on the ground directly in front of the cage; he stared hungrily at Rosholman and Battock, his once-proud but now-scraggly tail swinging back and forth.

"See?" asked Battock. "That makes twice already today I saved your ass."

Rosholman's reaction, when it finally came, stunned Battock. He stared at Rosholman unbelievingly as the man began to laugh, softly at first, then helplessly, holding onto the bars of the cage like some playful chimpanzee, shaking, rocking, gasping with almost hysterical laughter.

With a harsh explosion of disgust, Battock turned away. "You're crazy, Rosholman. Plain nuts."

Rosholman waved the remark aside with a helpless gesture and sank slowly to the floor of the cage, still unable to speak.

He was not crazy, Rosholman thought; the world was. The animals wandered through the zoo like sightseers, while the keepers were locked up in their cages.

At the moment, their only visitor was an old and hungry lion who had them figured as his first good meal in months.

And that should be enough to make any man laugh.

The search for Georgia Mosely was not going anywhere. Addie and Mishi had poked into all the closets, unused rooms, and attic space and found nothing. Outside the house, calling her name repeatedly, they had peered into pool house, garden shed, the damp recesses of the garage, even inside the heavy metal shelter where the garbage cans were kept, but without success.

217

Yet Addie knew she had to be somewhere near; a lady filled with that much vodka can go so far and no farther. He couldn't describe himself as deeply stricken by her disappearance—his life had been too frequently seared by embarrassing scenes in which he wished she *would* just disappear—but the dark shadows of shame were creeping over him. His father had put him in charge of her (or, more exactly, Mrs. Herkimer had), and he had failed.

With Mishi, things were even worse. She was torn between love and guilt. "Addie," she said, coming up to him as he sat on the back steps trying to think of other places his mother might be hiding, "Addie, my family—indeed, I must go see they are all right—it is so difficult—leaving you like this—your mother—I know you must find her—I should help—but my family—my family. . . ."

Addie threw up his hands. The child inside him wanted to protest this treachery, to say something to Mishi that would let her know how unfair it was to desert him, even while the almost-adult in him knew Mishi's logic about her family was impeccable. Instead of speaking the bitter words trembling on his tongue, he struggled to remain silent: then, seeing from her expression that this was not enough, he rose to his feet and put on a brave face. "Of course, you've got to go. For one thing, they'll be very worried about you. I'm sure they're all right, but they'll be wondering if you are."

With a hurried smile, Mishi nodded and looked away. The brave face could not fool someone who knew Addie as well as she did. Her love for her family, her guilt at not being with them were compounded now by her love for Addie and her guilt at leaving *him*. It was one of those complex questions to which she knew there was no possible right answer. Quickly, pasting on her own version of a brave face, she turned again to Addie. "I'll be back as soon as I know everything is OK." She paused for a moment, then: "No one must look sad in Mrs. Miniver's garden." The sudden flatness of their old game, recalling better times, only made her feel sadder. "I'm sorry," Mishi added.

218

Addie started to say something but was stopped by a sudden crashing sound from the tangled undergrowth that climbed up the hill beyond the pool. A man emerged, his hair and clothes disheveled, a pair of small, unfashionably round glasses perched on his nose at a disordered angle. Mishi, who had turned at the same time as Addie, gasped. "It is my father," she whispered, a strangely conspiratorial tone in her voice. "He looks hurt," she added, speaking louder. Letting go of Addie's arm she raced across the short stretch of flagstone to embrace him.

Addie watched, feeling curiously rejected as Mishi and her father exchanged a torrent of Japanese, Mishi laughing and smoothing back her father's hair and putting the glasses back on his nose correctly. The conspiratorial tenor of Mishi's voice when she first saw her father had confused Addie; now, watching her point across the flagstone at him, he could see small traces of worry gathering on her face. She appeared almost reluctant as she led her father toward him.

"And, Father, this is Addie."

Mr. Yoshura executed a stiff little bow while shaking Addie's hand, but a troubled expression had come over his face. He looked from Addie to Mishi, and spoke to her quickly—in Japanese. Mishi answered him, but Addie could tell from the gestures of her hands and the look on her face that she was, for some reason, very much on the defensive. Possibly, he thought, she was being scolded for not having come home as soon as the earthquake was over.

As if suddenly remembering Addie was there, Mr. Yoshura silenced Mishi and turned with a weak smile to him. "You must forgive us, Mr. Mosely," he said, "I am, of course, very pleased to meet you and must thank you for sheltering my daughter during this"—his hands gestured helplessly for a moment—"event." Mr. Yoshura frowned slightly before smiling at Addie again; his English was so like Mishi's Addie half expected him to unearth an old movie phrase for the end of his sentences. There was another brief exchange of Japanese between Mishi and him, which, to Addie's ear, sounded quite

219

heated, before Mr. Yoshura continued. "Mishi, needless to say, has talked much of you. She has spent so much time here with you, I hope it has not been too great a bother." Mr. Yoshura paused again, this time silencing Mishi as she began to say something to him. "You will have to pardon me if I appear confused. My daughter, you see, had told us"—Mishi's restraining hand was brushed away ignored—"had told us that you were a woman. A girl, I should say. Because only with a girl could she spend so much time. In Japan, you understand, we are very strict about such matters."

Mishi turned away, unable to face Addie. To Addie, the shock of Mishi's lie to her father—easily understandable—was far less difficult to accept than the hurt of Mishi's never having told him about it. In Addie's mind, they knew everything about each other, every facet of their lives a shared secret. He sought out Mishi's eyes and saw the suffering in them, the silent appeal to be forgiven. From what seemed very far away he heard Mr. Yoshura clear his throat and realized he was expected to show some reaction, although what he could say eluded him.

Mr. Yoshura looked as uncomfortable as Addie felt. "I hope her little deception does not upset you. I shall assume, of course, that you knew nothing of it."

"Of course not. What I mean is, of course, it doesn't upset me." Listening to his own voice, Addie realized how two-faced his response must have seemed; the way the words came out sounded as if he were siding with Mr. Yoshura, and Mishi was looking as betrayed as Addie had felt earlier. Quickly, Addie changed course. "Actually, sir, the idea of the deception was mine," he lied. "I'm sorry. I can only apologize for suggesting it."

The expression on Mr. Yoshura's face was plain. Clearly, he found Addie's effort at being noble transparent and juvenile, so much so that Addie could swear he saw traces of a patronizing smile forming at the corners of Mr. Yoshura's mouth. But Mr. Yoshura only bowed again—a little more stiffly this time, Addie thought—and looked up the hill behind Addie. "Of course. Well, it is a matter for me and my daughter to settle in private. Unpleasantly, I fear. For the moment, we had better be going home. Or Mrs. Yoshura will be convinced I have fallen into"—another pause and a groping in the air for a difficult word—"a chasm myself." Only his protruding upper teeth made Mr. Yoshura's effort at a smile even a little convincing.

"No."

The word was said softly, but the effect was as explosive as if Mishi had fired a pistol. Her father turned to stare at her, and even Addie found himself stunned. "We cannot go yet," she said, staring directly at her father not so much in defiance as in resolution. "First, we must find Addie's mother. She is here somewhere, but she is lost."

"*Lost?*"

"We cannot find her. Therefore, she is lost."

"I do not understand. She is here, but she is lost?"

Their conversation slipped quickly into Japanese, while Addie stood staring at Mishi and her father, lost in an agony of embarrassment at what Mishi must be explaining about his mother. Sympathy would be offered, the search would be joined, and a little of Addie would die because of it.

But Part IV of the Superior Court, County of Los Angeles, provided an unexpected alteration of Addie's worst fears. From around the corner of the pool house—off to one side where they had been unnoticed by anyone—Simon Pokress and Oskie Davenport had emerged. Pokress raised the sawed-off shotgun, and before any of the other three was aware that someone else was even there, he crashed the gun's butt as hard as he could into the base of Mr. Yoshura's neck. Mr. Yoshura fell forward silently and stiffly, as if one of his formal, diplomatic bows had gone out of control. Mishi screamed, and Addie spun around, one arm half raised as if he might attack either Pokress or Oskie but couldn't decide which.

The movement of Addie's arm, uncertain as it was, had not escaped notice; the gun in Pokress' hands swung around so that it was aimed directly at Addie's middle. "Take it easy, my friend," Pokress wheezed. "You'd look extremely funny with no insides."

The gun moved but remained silent, as Mishi fell to her knees and began cradling her father's head in her lap. Addie studied them for a moment and then let his eyes move to the intruders. They made a curious pair: the white one with the grossly oversized head not only looked mean, but was; the black, who had so far said nothing, was staring at Mr. Yoshura anxiously, as if he felt as unsettled by what his partner had done as Addie did.

"You live here?" the man with the gun asked Addie in his strange, whispering voice. Numbly, Addie nodded his head. "Anybody else in the house?"

"No one." Addie wondered if he should explain that his mother might come wandering out of any door but that no one knew where she was just now; if this happened, the gunman might decide Addie had been lying and shoot him. But the story was too long and complicated, and the white looked too tense and ugly to understand.

"Cars? You have cars?" demanded the white urgently. When Addie again nodded, the man seemed relieved. "Good. We'll need them later. When they get the roads cleared." The gun remained pointing at Addie as Pokress turned his enormous head halfway around and growled thickly at Oskie, "We'll hole up here for the time being. First, we drag the old man into the house so nobody can spot him. There must be rope or something inside. Truss him up—if he's still breathing." At this last statement, Oskie started to protest, but Pokress' glare stilled him. "Try and find enough rope so's we can tie up these other two too." Pokress smiled and sighed contentedly. "And cheer up, Mr. Gloom. We're very much home-free."

Things were moving too quickly for Oskie. He hadn't liked the idea of escape, he hadn't liked the escape itself, he didn't think Pokress should have even belted the old Jap like that, and now Pokress and his shotgun seemed to be heading them for even more trouble.

222

He wanted to say something, but with a man like Pokress, he wasn't sure even where to begin. Instead, he fastened on a detail. "Tie *them* up, too? Hell, Pokress. They're just kids."

Pokress let his huge eyes travel appraisingly over Mishi's slim body, tight inside what had been a trim white bathing suit, but now bloodied by her father's wound. "You be surprised how grown-up kids are these days," he said, and smiled slightly.

At 5:51:02 (PCT) the 600 XE spat out its first prediction on the aftershock probabilities for Violet. For the first time since the advent of Violet at 5:17:08 the room at Goldstone went quiet. The seismologists and programmers alike huddled around the single sheet of paper emerging from the teleprinter, staring at it with a mixture of awe and disbelief. In light of what the prediction promised the already-battered city of Los Angeles, their reaction, in fact, could almost have been considered understated.

ON BASIS OF PRESENT INPUT, FIRST AFTERSHOCK FOR TREMOR SAF (34N-108 W) #1176 [CODE VIOLET] ESTIMATED TO BE OF RICHTER SCALE MAGNITUDE PLUS 9, OR EQUAL TO ORIGINAL TREMOR. TIME PROJECTION SUBJECT LOWER RELIABILITY BUT AS OF PRESENT INPUT FIXED AT APPROX TWENTY HUNDRED HOURS PLUS OR MINUS ONE TODAY. SECOND AFTERSHOCK FOR TREMOR SAF (34N-108 W) #1176 [CODE VIOLET] ESTIMATED RICHTER SCALE MAGNITUDE 7. TIME FRAME NOT FIXED PENDING INPUT FROM FIRST AFTERSHOCK RELIABILITY EXCELLENT END.

What no one had expected was a prediction of *two* aftershocks, both virtually of the same intensity as Violet herself. And while the computer refused to commit itself on a time frame for the second, the 600 firmly fixed the first as due in roughly one hour and ten minutes, or, after adjusting for the time difference between Goldstone and LA, seven o'clock Los Angeles time—plus or minus the usual hour's tolerance.

The first person to move was Ridgeway. He had studied Feiner's face and realized his associate was so stunned by the printout that he was incapable of any action except an endless rereading of the torn-off sheet of paper. Somehow, Ridgeway suspected, Feiner was beginning to hold himself responsible for what the computer was predicting, as if the bearer of bad news were responsible for the ill tidings he carried (and for which, in other times, the messengers were put to death).

It was a potentially dangerous symptom, and one requiring immediate handling. Ridgeway reached over the shoulders of the others and plucked the printout away from the man pulling it out of the machine. With a nod to the head programmer, Nick Rivers, Ridgeway and he guided Feiner away from the crowd over to a table at the deserted end of the lab. His hope was to reach a calm decision on what to do with the prediction while Feiner was still semistunned and before his fervor steered him into any more dangerous and untried areas.

He could have saved himself the effort. Feiner, staring dolefully, first at the head programmer, then at Ridgeway, suddenly came out of his daze. "I'd better try and get Kraypool on the radio," he said, shaking his head as if to clear it.

A premature radio call to Kraypool—intermittent contact had been established through nearby La Costa Air Force Base, under a setup in which Goldstone's phone could be patched through the base's transmitter—was the sort of thing Ridgeway most wanted to avoid. Too many facts, Ridgeway felt, were still not clear; too many wrong decisions could be made on the basis of them, in both Washington and LA. Once again, Ridgeway seized Feiner by the arm. "Hold it, Michael. Let's talk a little first."

"What's to talk? You saw the printout."

"Yes, I saw the printout." Ridgeway sighed. "And, Michael,

224

I hate to keep sounding as if I were dragging my feet all the time—you were right and I was wrong on the prediction of the quake itself—but this, *this*"—he waved the printout mournfully in the air—"I think we owe it to everybody to talk about it a little first."

With a sullen expression he probably wasn't even aware of, Feiner shrugged. He reached over and took the printout and reread it, as if enough rereading might somehow change what was there. Feiner's hand, Ridgeway noticed, shook slightly when he lit his cigarette, a process eventually requiring three matches and a lot of subdued swearing. "Nick," Ridgeway said, taking the printout out of Feiner's hands and directing himself to Rivers, "the reliability factor on this. How good?"

"I don't know. Those shortcuts. . . ." The head programmer pursed his lips and studied the ceiling unhappily. "Well, hell, I don't think anybody could tell you for sure. If we'd had a little more time to build the usual fail-safe factors into the programming—you know, the kind that warn you when something's way off—I could be more definite. As it is, I plain just don't know."

"The computer itself says 'Reliability good.' What more do you need?" snapped Feiner, the head of steam that Ridgeway feared beginning to build up in him.

"No computer's better than what you put into it, you know that, Mike," the programmer noted, and shook his head in professional distress. "What the computer's saying there is that given what input it had, the reliability is within normal limits. It's what's *not* there that worries me."

"Computer double-talk."

"I told you I couldn't guarantee reliability before we started, dammit. Now you're bitching because I won't stand behind it."

Their voices had risen, and as the argument continued, they rose even farther; across the room, heads started to turn. Ridgeway, who felt his own nerves beginning to rub raw under the strain, finally stopped the discussion by pushing both Rivers and Feiner down into chairs beside the table. "Look," he said flatly, "the last thing this operation needs right now is a couple of loose tempers. Nick is right in what he says. With the shortcuts, he can't know whether the computer is predicting or guessing. And Michael is right in what's boiling away inside him—the urgency of telling LA, telling the Air Force and the rescue task force about what they may have to expect. What we have to figure out is the best way to use what information we've got, reliable or not, while working to improve it."

Both Rivers and Feiner started to object, but Ridgeway, strangely calm and forceful in this new set of circumstances, cut them off. "What I suggest, it seems to me, is the only objective option we have: to tell LA, to tell the task force, of the prediction, but also to tell them that we're not ready to stand behind it yet."

With an exasperated shake of his head, Feiner stood up; to him, all this seemed like a terrifying replay of the first prediction on Violet. "When *do* we stand behind a prediction then? Only after it's happened?"

Ridgeway was a calm man, an almost gentle man. His professional life had been lived by a set of rules as strict as church dogma; a hypothesis was something you did not act upon until validated by repetition, and then, only then, was the hypothesis grudgingly allowed to become theory. Something on which one could act. The whole process was as neat and orderly as the progression of the seasons and allowed little room for flashes of intuitive brilliance. So far he had managed to restrain himself with Michael Feiner; now the reservoir of patience was empty. Ridgeway allowed himself a rare show of temper. "Oh, shut up. You're acting like a spoiled child. What this lab does and doesn't do is, in the end, my responsibility. I ask you to remember that. Now, if you will, get on the phone and have the Air Force put the message out the way I outlined it: the prediction of the aftershocks, magnitude, timing, etc., but, only a reliability factor of"—he turned to the programmer—"of what, Nick? How much faith do you have in the readout?"

Matt Rivers shrugged and let one hand travel down his face. This kind of question was the kind he hated most; there was no mathematically sound way to compute odds such as these. "Fifty-fifty. Best I can do."

Ridgeway turned back to Feiner. "A reliability factor of only fifty percent. That ought to be emphasized. OK, Michael?"

Feiner said nothing. Ridgeway had never pulled rank on him before; it had been years since anybody had. Inside himself, he suspected Ridgeway felt badly about using rank —something rarely resorted to in the scientific community—and found himself hoping so. What he could not accept was that Ridgeway had resorted to it only because his own brashness was as unscientific as Ridgeway's use of rank was unusual. Still saying nothing, Feiner walked over to the phone. The word would go out as Ridgeway had ordered. The prediction would be fully hedged.

What neither he nor Ridgeway nor anyone in the room could realize was that, in the general rush to believe in this amazing new predictive tool, the authorities would completely ignore the hedging. And would act upon it as Gospel. Feiner's predictions would be taken at full face value as surely as if they had been engraved on stone tablets and handed down from the Mountain.

Chapter Sixteen

Good fortune will elevate even petty minds and give them the appearance of a certain greatness . . . but the truly noble and resolved spirit raises itself and becomes more conspicuous in times of disaster and ill fortune.

—PLUTARCH, *Lives, Eumenes*

DIGIT VORHEES gave another hard look and wished he'd never suggested it. Flat on his stomach, he lay staring down the glass-enclosed elevator shaft with wonder; the shaft was glued to the outside of the Park Plaza's northwest wall like an afterthought and, although a favorite attraction for tourists, was rapidly becoming a nightmare to Digit. Appraisingly, he continued his study of it. Most of the shaft's glass panels were gone, which was good; the lack of glass would make hand-holds easier to come by. The few large sheets of glass remaining on different floors would simply have to be avoided. Although you could barely make it out, the elevator itself lay in a shattered heap twenty-nine floors below. That was good, too, as it meant one less obstacle in the glass shaft to get around. With a sigh, Digit collapsed his growing sense of enthusiasm; the descent was going to be anything but easy—murderous was a better description—and Digit fervently wished he'd kept his mountain-climbing experience a secret and his mouth shut about the whole idea.

But when Adam's own scheme—to thread the group's way down via an intricate system of fire stairs attached to the outer shell—had proved unworkable (just one floor below, they found the stairs hopelessly blocked with rubble), Adam seized on Digit's offhand suggestion of rappelling down the external elevator shaft, and now Digit was stuck with proving that the thing could be done. Using his eye to measure the distance, Digit estimated the piece of rope they had found in the dumbwaiter shaft was long enough to reach about three floors, even when crisscrossed between the building-side landing and the outside of the shaft. A second piece of rope and a pulley—also discovered in the dumbwaiter shaft that ran between the restaurant and the kitchen two stories below—would be used to lower Mrs. Grimes, who was too old and too damaged, Digit had been told, to lower herself hand over hand as the rest of the party would; for her, Digit and Adam had improvised a variation on the breeches buoy, a rope and canvas sling she could sit on while being let down the three-story limit of the rope.

Digit squirmed so that his trunk extended farther out over the shaft, trying to pick out places on both the landing side and the service sides of the glass shaft to anchor the rope firmly; the rope also had to be fixed in such a way that it could be easily loosened and retrieved for the next three-story leg of the descent. Pressing hard against the floor to balance himself produced a curious effect; Digit first felt a warm stirring, then a sudden hard swelling grow beneath his thighs. If he hadn't been staring down thirty stories of glass abyss, Digit probably would have laughed; his prick, so uncooperative earlier this afternoon with the psych major, had chosen a highly peculiar moment to prove itself.

From behind him, came Adam Mosely's voice, sudden and urgent. "Do you think we can do it?"

Pulling himself around and up, Digit nodded without enthusiasm. As he looked at the small circle of anxious faces gathered around him, his proposal suddenly appeared both improbable and impossible. The thought of these people—without a day's worth of climbing experience among them—lowering themselves hand over hand down a swaying rope suspended over a thirty-story drop, completely terrified, exposed to unexpected situations even an experienced climber might have had difficulty coping with, made Digit shudder. Alone, he would have had no doubts about the descent, but this covey of amateurs might not only get themselves killed, but him as well. The persistent streak of compulsive loner in Digit found new justification; his first plan, in fact, had been to grab the psych major—he'd brought her out to dinner, after all, and at least owed her the opportunity to get home in one piece—and make the climb down without involving the others. But for reasons Digit could not explain, even to himself, the idea of leaving the rest of them behind had disturbed him sufficiently so that he ended by proposing his plan for all of them.

"Anything we can get you? Anything we can do?" Adam's voice was insistent.

"No. Just be sure everybody stays calm and doesn't look down any more than they have to. And be certain that when you get the bosun's chair with"—Digit indicated Dorothy Grimes with his head, unable or unwilling to remember her name—"the lady in it down to my floor, be sure that you throw the rope down *across* the shaft, so I can catch it. If we ever lose that rope, we're dead." Tactfully, he didn't point out that they wouldn't be as dead as Dorothy Grimes would be.

It was Adam's turn to nod. Then: "All right, sport. If you can pull this off, you're one tremendous guy." For Digit, so long unused to compliments or encouragement from anyone but transient girls, the initial pleasure he felt was vitiated when Adam followed the remark with a dazzling smile, of the same kind he had used on the secretaries outside his office earlier in the day. The smile, Digit recognized, belonged to a salesman and thus reminded him of his father's. But any comparison between Adam Mosely and George Vorhees was so outrageous that the warm feeling Digit had first felt quickly returned.

Digit picked up the ropes, neatly wound into coils he could sling over his shoulder, hooked the pulley from the dumbwaiter onto a small loop fastened to his belt, and looked at Adam with a shy grin. "Keep them calm. Calm as you can, anyway. And be ready to start down as soon as I finish the first leg." Adam nodded. He and Digit had already agreed on the order in which the party would descend. First, of course, would be Digit. Sporades would follow, both because they felt he was strong enough to negotiate the climb easily and because that fact would give the rest confidence. Anna Kristaboulos would come directly after her husband—partly because Sporades would have it no other way and partly because Anna too looked athletic enough to manage the hand-over-hand climb without difficulty. Next in order—and something of a question mark—was the psych major. She claimed a deathly fear of heights, and although Digit didn't know how seriously to take her, he felt if anyone were going to panic, it would probably be she; putting her near the end, therefore, seemed to make the most sense. Next to last was Dorothy Grimes in the carry chair. Once she was safely down each leg of the climb and the rope from the carry chair retrieved, Adam would descend the rope hand over hand as the rest had. When everyone else was down, Digit then would climb *up* the rope, unfastening it at the top, and scramble monkeylike down the steel frame of the shaft itself, carrying the newly recoiled rope over his shoulder.

With a purposeful frown, Digit securely tied the rope's end to a piece of broken pipe that rose out of the floor beside the elevator landing, fed it around his waist and through a rope loop to his hand; the remaining coil he slung over his shoulder. Confident enough of this part of the descent, he automatically tested the feel of the line in his hands. Then, with a lightly spoken "Well, here goes nothing," he quickly payed out a length of rope and disappeared over the edge.

Adam turned the smile on the waiting people behind him. "He makes it look easy," he said breezily, and then·pretended to become very busy organizing the rest of them for the first leg of their journey down.

For Digit, the first part *was* easy. Forcing himself to watch, Adam saw him rappelling down the shaft; he would bounce

231

against the inside wall until he developed enough of a swing-ing motion to land on the outside service landing of the elevator, attach the rope, and let gravity swing him back toward the building—attaching the rope there, too—before starting over again. This arrangement made the rope crisscross back on itself between floors, something which Digit and Adam figured would be easier for the rest of them to negotiate than a rope that hung straight down. As he watched, Adam was filled with admiration; not only was Digit a good climber, but he was an expert. Excellence at anything always moved Adam, and he found himself making a wistful com-parison with Addie, who seemed to drift only with what came easily, with what life offered him gratuitously. Adam pondered how much of his son's attitude was his fault and how much was Georgia's before sharply reminding himself that his only concern at the moment should be that Addie was safe.

A shout from below forced Adam to lean far out and look down the glass elevator shaft; Digit Vorhees had completed the first leg of the journey, the rope was anchored, and he was calling for Sporades to start down.

After giving Anna a quick kiss, Sporades said something in Greek to her and lowered himself over the edge. In less than five minutes he had reached Addie's level, where he joined him on the outer landing, both of them pulling hard on the rope to steady it against the wind. Earlier—when Digit first made his proposal—the wind had been so light as to pose little problem. Now it was rising, and when the gusts swept across the top of the Park Plaza at a certain angle, the wind would cause the elevator shaft to act as a giant flute, giving forth a hollow, empty shriek.

At the last minute, Adam had agreed to switch the descent order, with the psych major going ahead of Anna. This change was made at Anna's insistence. In spite of what Sporades had made her promise—that she would follow directly after him—Anna could see the other girl's fragile nerves beginning to shatter. This, combined with the rising wind, prompted her to whisper to Adam that if they didn't get the girl down now, they never would. She would deal with Sporades, Anna told Adam firmly.

When her turn came, the psych major negotiated the rope with surprising ease, although she occasionally stumbled on the outer landings when turning herself around to begin the next climb down.

"Next!" Digit was enjoying himself. Early in life he had learned not to depend on anyone else, so others had soon come not to depend on him. An operation of which he was in charge, an undertaking in which he was the expert and leader, was a new and gratifying experience to him.

Anna turned to Dorothy Grimes. "Are you sure you don't want me to wait until after you've gone down? Maybe I should stay and help you; that carry chair doesn't look like the easiest thing in the world."

Dorothy Grimes squeezed Anna's hand in a rare gesture of affection. Almost immediately, as if embarrassed, she laughed her throaty laugh. "No, dear. The longer I *don't* go, the better I like it. Besides, that nice husband of yours is probably having fits by now."

Anna leaned over and kissed her, then turned and walked toward the downward-slanting rope. Her hand fluttering at her mouth nervously, Dorothy Grimes watched her. "Adam, they all go at it backwards," she whispered to him. "They don't like looking down, so they lower themselves over the edge with their faces toward the building. Actually, that sort of hand-over-hand business is much easier if you can see where your hands are going, not where they've been."

Adam was unwilling to tamper with what had so far been successful; Dorothy Grimes was probably right, but she didn't have to do the climbing. "She'll be all right," he reassured her with a nod toward Anna. "She's strong and athletic-looking. I think she knows exactly what she's doing."

But Dorothy Grimes could not accept this. "Anna," she called suddenly, just as the girl reached up to grasp the rope stretched above her, "Anna, dear, I think you'll find it easier if you turn around and look forward, not back."

233

It was never clear to Adam precisely what happened next because he could not separate the parts in his mind. Anna, in reaching up, had turned her head around to judge the effects of the wind on the rope; she stood on the narrow landing platform that led from the glass elevator into the Penthouse Restaurant, a landing designed to be used only when the elevator was stopped at the level and its floor flush with the landing. Dorothy Grimes' shouted instructions came at a ticklish moment, with Anna straining upward to get a firm grip on the rope; off-balance and taken by surprise, she turned her head toward Dorothy to hear her better. At the same time, one of the peculiar gusts of wind played its eerie flute note on the glass shaft and Anna, as if by reflex, swiveled sharply toward the source of this unexpected sound. All these movements happened too quickly for someone as critically balanced as Anna, and she swung heavily against one of the cracked glass panels of the shaft. The lower half of the panel fell out of its frame from the sudden pressure, while the upper half, suddenly left with nothing below to support the panel in place, began to collapse inward and fell toward Anna.

Both of Anna's hands automatically let go of the rope and tried to fend off the approaching guillotine edge. But the reaction came too late. A strong gust of wind sailed the lower edge of the glass panel across Anna's neck like a knife, slicing her head cleanly from her shoulders. For a second her body stood there, the hands still raised to fend off the glass, groping the emptiness above her shoulders as if desperately trying to locate the missing head. At first almost gracefully, then with a convulsive shuddering, the torso, pumping blood, sagged to the landing; a second later it slipped off the thin strip and fell down the glass shaft without a sound.

Since he had heard only the breaking glass, Digit Vorhees was stunned to see the body go hurtling by, trailing blood like the tail of a comet. He glanced at Sporades. The entire accident had happened so quickly that for a second it didn't even occur to Sporades that the torso was his wife's; he simply stood where he was and watched the body fall past him. The realization was not long in coming. Slowly, he looked down at his shirt, covered now, as were his hands and face, with blood. Absently, Sporades released his grip on the rope and stared at his hands in disbelief, as if they belonged to someone else, some other person in some other place, who had used them to commit murder. Swaying dangerously, Sporades sank to his knees, rocking back and forth so far that Digit had to reach forward to steady him. His own mind was still shaken by the picture of Anna's head falling down the outside of the shaft, bouncing high off the building abutments like a soccer ball with long blond hair. It was a sight fortunately spared Sporades.

Above, on the Penthouse Restaurant landing, Dorothy Grimes collapsed against Adam. "Oh, Adam. That nice girl. That poor, nice girl." A troubled expression clouded Adam's face. He could feel that Dorothy Grimes was shuddering but could not tell if this was because she was crying or because she was trying so hard not to. In the sixteen years he had spent with her, this was the first time he had ever thought of her as even near tears. Certainly there had been times he knew she must have felt like crying—as there had been times when he felt like crying himself. He patted her back, like a father consoling a disappointed child.

She looked up at him, the tears under control, but still visible. "And it was my fault, Adam. If I hadn't called to her, hadn't made her turn around, if I'd just let her do it her own way. . . . Oh, Adam! Why do I always have to try to tell people what to do?"

Adam said nothing but held Dorothy closer to him, trying to give her the forgiveness no one ever could. For Dorothy Grimes, he knew, was only being Dorothy Grimes. The same conviction that she—and only she—had all the answers was what had destroyed the *Trib*'s principles. And the objectivity of its writers and reporters. And had come very near to destroying him.

Now it had cost Anna Kristaboulos her life.

Henry Kraypool was disgusted. In spite of all the carefully filed contingency plans, his Office of Emergency Preparedness had not been prepared for the scope and suddenness of Violet's arrival. For this, Kraypool blamed the local Civil Defense authorities, who in turn blamed it on the mayor's office, which, for its part, accused Burt Aptner of not giving them all the facts.

At this point, fixing the precise responsibility was of little importance; the situation in Los Angeles was too critical to afford bureaucratic finger pointing. Kraypool, who had been talking on the radiophone to the San Diego Naval Base, had just learned that the promised men and equipment supposedly being flown up as part of the rescue task force were now being held off. The reason: a prediction of two aftershocks, magnitude 7 and plus 9, to strike the area within the hour. The source: Dr. Michael Feiner in Goldstone, Colorado. In view of the prediction, Washington felt it was wiser to hold the entire rescue force outside LA until the aftershocks had taken place.

Washington's decision left Kraypool stunned and resentful; he was particularly incensed that the source of the prediction should be Goldstone. Earlier the seismologists there had insisted on hedging their prediction on the earthquake; now that these had come true, they apparently were making no attempt to hedge their prediction on the aftershocks. To Kraypool, it was a heads-I-win, tails-you-lose performance. He had thought better of Feiner than that.

Speaking rapidly into the radiophone to Tracey Air Base outside Denver, he tried to get through to Feiner. Perversely, the radioman in Denver was unable to; the lines at the Goldstone lab were all tied up, the man reported, but he would keep trying. Kraypool hung up, defeated. The sensation was ridiculous—and Kraypool knew it—but a tinge of paranoia had begun to color his thinking. Feiner was against him, the mayor was against him, Burt Aptner had been against him, Washington was against him, and now even the telephone system in Colorado had it in for him.

He picked up the radiophone again and had himself put through to Mayor Ortiz. How do you explain to the mayor of the country's third largest city that what's happening to his town is the result of a conspiracy of fate?

Up in the slowly deepening skies over the San Fernando Valley, Ken Corbit, KBDT's guy in the sky, had just looped southward and was banking his chopper to head directly over the city and on toward Arcadia. On the radiophone—before it became tied up trying to reach Goldstone—Kraypool had discovered that the Arcadia area's Civil Defense man could still be reached. The zone was almost totally unaffected, the man reported. More important—both to Kraypool and Corbit—Arcadia was where Santa Anita Racetrack was located, and the track, some years earlier, had built a helicopter pad for the convenience of its more affluent visitors. That pad, untouched by Violet, was where Corbit's chopper would refuel. Corbit had told Kraypool he had to gas up soon or set down, and since for the moment he was Kraypool's eyes, the man had gone to considerable efforts to find a refueling spot for him.

For this, Kraypool would receive no thanks from Corbit. Corbit could not explain to him how frustrated he had become by his "overview" assignment—although he could have told him why. During the war in 'Nam, he could remember how much he pitied the aerial observers, restricted to merely watching, surveying, and reporting, while he was in the thick of things, ferrying troops, firing his rockets in seek-and-destroy missions against enemy outposts, evacuating the wounded. The observers, he had thought then, were a breed detached, trying to win a war with aerial photographs, overlays, and three-dimensional relief maps. "Dirty old men," Corbit could remember having called them—more interested in pornography than intercourse.

To his disgust, he was now like them. Below him, people were being rescued, people were dying and—people were dying because they were not being rescued. As he flew across

237

the city, not far above the low, flat roofs of the lower Wilshire Boulevard area, he could see them signaling frantically to him for help; the entire section was now crisscrossed by a network of awesome gorges, the earth torn apart into little islands of land separated by space, as on a drought-stricken mud flat. From the gorges, broken gas mains and water lines were shooting columns of flame and water toward the sky; in the places where these met, eerie clouds of steam drifted upward in a Dante-esque vision of hell. The people—most of them old, from what Corbit could make out—had gathered on the flat rooftops to get themselves as far away as they could from the terrible open crevices that surrounded them. This was, Corbit could see, only an illusion of safety. Many of the buildings were already on fire from the gas mains; others were simply collapsing as their foundations gave way. Desperately, they waved as Corbit flew close over their heads; he rocked the chopper to show that he saw them. In his ear, he could hear the radioman in Kraypool's office trying to reach him for information on his present status. Corbit first ignored the voice, then switched his radio to "off."

He refused to be like the dirty old men of 'Nam. As soon as he was gassed up, he would return to lower Wilshire, set his helicopter down on any reliable-looking rooftop, and taking on as many people as he dared, fly them to a safe place. Kraypool might not approve, but he and Kraypool were no longer in communication. Sorry, sir—radio failure.

As he set down at Santa Anita, Corbit tried to figure where he should evacuate the people to. Arcadia itself appeared in good shape, but was too great a distance for the number of rescue flights he would have to make.

Up in the air again, Corbit headed the chopper toward Alhambra (from there, he would veer southwest to start his lower Wilshire rescue mission), still pondering the best place to disembark those he plucked off the rooftops. As he rose, a great green patch caught his eye, almost due west. Corbit snapped his fingers, simultaneously berating himself for not having thought of it earlier. The land there was relatively flat, rolling terrain—open, smooth, and free of any buildings that could collapse on his refugees. If he remembered correctly, the place had public toilets and a natural supply of water. There his rescued passengers would be safe, secure, and possibly even comfortable—the safest, securest, most comfortable people in the entire city.

It was perfect. After all, what could happen to anybody in Griffith Park?

Mayor Manuel Ortiz received word that the Army task force was holding up its entrance into Los Angeles with a strange calm. Burt Aptner had let him down; Henry Kraypool had let him down; the contractors who had assured him that their shortcuts in the buildings codes were harmless had let him down, so why not the federal government?

He went about organizing what forces he could inside the city, but within himself he was a defeated man. The idea that this earthquake had been sent as his own personal punishment was occupying his mind more and more, a morbid, compulsive line of reasoning he knew was as unsound as it was overpowering. If he were to be punished, surely even the most inefficient God could have found a way that didn't involve dislocating, injuring, and killing as many innocent bystanders as Violet entailed. To think of the earthquake in so personal a frame of reference was an almost blasphemous act of conceit. Still, the aberrant idea persisted, unshakable and all-pervasive, like a child's fear of darkness.

The radioman signaled to indicate that Kraypool was on his radiophone. Automatonlike, Ortiz picked up the receiver. "Without any outside help coming," he asked grimly, "what's our hospital situation like?"

"Lousy."

"*How* lousy?"

Kraypool glanced at the cluster of red (nonoperational) disks pasted over the hospitals on the emergency control map. By now the map looked like the stomach of a kid with measles. "Well, both San Martinez General and Isidro Receiving are

239

totally knocked out. The buildings collapsed." Kraypool paused. "Both of them were built directly over the fault."

"Directly *over* it?"

"So was Olive View in the Valley. After seventy-one, you'd have thought they'd have learned. As for West Central Emergency and Carteret, there isn't much left. Both of them can *use* help, not give it. They're several miles from the fault itself, but somebody built them to their own set of specs, not the city's."

On his end of the line, Ortiz squirmed uncomfortably. Both were new buildings. Both had been built under relaxed building codes—part of his minority-hiring arrangement with the contractors—and therefore, by Kraypool's specifications, were substandard. Both were now back to haunt him. He wondered if Kraypool knew about the deal and was making his point for effect or if he had just volunteered the observation in frustration. Paranoia again, Ortiz decided.

Kraypool continued: "From what I've got so far, Alameda Central is completely out, ditto Burbank Special Surgery and Pasadena Memorial. Some of the outlying ones are in pretty good shape—Westlake Cedars, for instance—but without those Air Force choppers, we can't get any of the injured *to* them."

"The governor," said Ortiz helplessly, "has called in the National Guard. When they get here, they're supposed to be for riot and looting control; however, I guess we can bend their orders a little. But the helicopters are all federal, and the Guard's Air Auxiliary is under strict orders not to release them into the area without Washington's explicit OK. Which, as you know, they won't give until the aftershocks are through. We're nowhere."

The pause on Kraypool's end of the radiophone was so long Ortiz first thought they'd lost contact. But his radioman, monitoring the same pause, shook his head; the channel was still good. When Kraypool's voice came back on the receiver, it seemed uncertain what to say, how to say it, or even if it should say anything. Finally: "Ham operator just called in. The Van

Norman Dams. They went. The whole goddamned reservoir is in the Valley."

"I see." Ortiz knew his response was ridiculously out of proportion. He should have yelled or screamed or wept or cursed or choked. But his ability to react verbally had become numbed. His mind raced, putting together a picture of billions of gallons of water tearing through the Valley below the Van Normans and of what was happening to the eighty thousand people who lived in the housing developments there.

Telling the radioman to get him Sacramento again, he picked up the receiver to wait for contact with the governor to be made.

Weeping was for later.

To anyone coming upon them suddenly, they would have presented a curious picture. Father Reed, SJ, and Derek Usher were kneeling together on the flat tar-surface roof of St. Bridget's, heads bowed. No one would have found the sight more curious than Father Reed. He felt uncomfortably hypocritical about this performance, but the praying was at Derek's insistence, and Father Reed had given in, not because he believed anything would come of it, but because he feared that Derek, growing more wild-eyed and less coherent by the moment, might kill either him or himself if the prayer weren't offered.

Earlier the two of them, Derek still muttering darkly about murdering his mother, had finally forced open the front door of the storefront church, only to discover St. Bridget's now stood on an island of land, surrounded by a jagged series of yawning cracks in the earth's surface. There was one in front of the church, where the Wilshire sidewalk used to be, one on either side, where Al's Yoga Parlor and Madame Aubad's Astrology Center had formerly stood, and a fourth directly behind St. Bridget's. Oddly, Father Reed found he could not remember what used to be there. Each of the crevices—giant fissures torn in the earth—were ten to fifteen feet wide. They

241

appeared bottomless and were belching great clouds of flame and smoke. Looking around, they could see other people on Wilshire faced the same problem: cut off from escape, they could only watch the buildings, one after the other, slowly join the rest in catching fire.

Most of the survivors had struggled to the rooftops, not because the roofs offered any safety, but because there was no place else to go. After he had studied the narrow apron of ground around them, Father Reed decided they would be better off staying on the strip of overgrown grass, perhaps ten by twenty feet square, behind St. Bridget's. There, provided they could keep clear of falling debris, they at least stood a chance. Derek disagreed. With a herdlike instinct unusual for him, he wanted to be on the rooftop like the others. But the Jesuit had remained firm, insisting they were better off huddled on their narrow strip of backyard.

And it was from that same strip that Derek Usher and Father Reed had watched helplessly as the helicopter lowered itself suddenly from the heavens to pluck a remaining handful of survivors off the building next to theirs. As soon as they'd seen the chopper, Reed and Usher had rushed frantically to gain their own roof; but the stairs were blocked by fallen debris, and it had taken some time before they finally could climb free of the building proper and get out on top of it. By then the helicopter was no longer visible.

"I told you," whined Derek. "I told you, but you wouldn't listen. I told you we should be up on the roof like the rest of the people, but you wouldn't pay any attention. And now the helicopter's gone for good." Father Reed eyed him nervously; Derek's voice was becoming higher and shriller, and he sounded as if he might burst into tears momentarily. "You wouldn't listen to me, would you? You're just like my mother!" Derek screamed, and then suddenly remembering his mother—and that all this was punishment for what he had done to her—fell silent.

"The chopper will probably come back," Father Reed said reassuringly, although, in looking around, he could now see no other people still left on any of the nearby rooftops and doubted very much that the helicopter pilot would think there was anyone in the area left to save.

"You're lying, Father," sniveled Derek, his lip trembling visibly.

As a parish priest, even if an unconventional one, Father Reed had been trained to respond to despair. His automatic reaction was to offer any parishioner both solace and hope, to extend palliative thoughts and comforting words. But his experiences with Usher up to now had been so thoroughly unpleasant that Father Reed had great difficulty with the words. And when they finally came, the phrases sounded strangely hollow and fatuous—almost condescending—like the mouthings of a well-fed Anglican vicar to the starving inhabitants of an Indian village. "Mr. Usher," he said gently, "such things as these must always be faced with belief in the sureness of our ultimate salvation. And never without a sense of hope for a future we cannot always understand." Reed paused, aghast at his own pomposity. "Is there anything I can do to make things easier for you?"

Derek Usher raised his tearstained, sweat-streaked face. "A prayer, Father. The Lord's Prayer. I've always liked that one. Ever since I was a little boy."

"Of course." To Derek Usher, he nodded agreeably. To himself, he groaned. The Lord's Prayer had been giving him increasing problems, a sort of litmus paper of his faith. Until recently he had viewed the prayer as more of a social contract than a religious incantation, a symbolically expressed code for living; as such, it tied in well with the priest's view of religion as an instrument of social change. Because of this—and because of years of training that had begun in parochial school in Brooklyn and had extended through the Jesuit seminary—he had continued to say the Lord's Prayer daily, alone to himself, the one prayer of any sort he willingly offered. But in the past few months, as Father Reed began more and more to question formal religion even as an effective means to an end, he had had increasing difficulty in keeping his mind from wandering

243

as he prayed. Extraneous thoughts and concepts would be triggered by words in the prayer, and he sometimes found an entirely unrelated chain of thoughts developing in his head. Sometimes he had even forgotten which part of the prayer he was saying and had to begin all over again. Recently, the only way he could get through the Lord's Prayer at all was to imagine a giant white spotlight moving rapidly toward his eyes, like that of a locomotive roaring at him; the onrushing disc of brilliant light was something on which he could fix his mind while forcing the gentle cadences of the prayer out of himself.

Father Reed lowered his head, preparing to face the hypnotic locomotive headlight in his eyes for the spiritual comfort of a man he didn't even like.

"It always means more when you kneel," Derek said, wiping his chronically runny nose on his sleeve. The thought of what his mother would have said had she seen this movement caused him to shudder, but then, any thought of his mother was extremely unsettling at this point.

"Of course," said Father Reed again, and knelt obediently. "Our Father," he began, focusing his mind on the blinding white light racing toward him. "Who art in Heaven"—the light was, as usual, initially effective, but his ears began allowing outside sounds to intrude; Father Reed added the sound of the unrushing locomotive to blot out these extraneous noises—"Thy will be done"—the noise appeared to be growing louder and far out of proportion to the distance of the locomotive—"on earth as it is in Heaven. . . ."

He was no longer able to justify the sound. Father Reed's eyes snapped open. And when he looked up and saw the helicopter lowering itself noisily toward them, Father Reed, in spite of himself, for just an infinitesimal fraction of a second could almost believe in God.

With a mixture of thankfulness and trepidation, Laura Vorhees watched the ladder poking itself toward the bed. If a *deus ex machina* was to be lowered out of the heavens to save her, the last conceivable *deus* she would have chosen was her husband, George. She didn't trust him, nor had she any reason to. The man in the coverall-type uniform, she supposed, was insurance of a sort, but she feared the slightest pressure on the bed might send it sailing down into the Pacific, the sort of "accident" George could engineer easily, uniformed witness or not.

From the bed she had watched them carefully. The man in coveralls had raced off and returned lugging an aluminum extension ladder. After a lot of measuring, some pacing off of distances, and several disagreements with George, the ladder was finally extended along the ground to a length both of them figured would reach Laura. As she watched them, she could guess from their gestures that the plan was to weight one end of the ladder with stones and the uniformed man's body, while George lay flat on the end sticking out over the cliff. The ladder would then be extended and George could reach down and pull Laura up onto the ladder without anything's disturbing the precariously balanced bed. For a moment, Laura considered demanding that the man in coveralls be the one who came out on the ladder to perform the actual rescue—it would be very easy for George to drop her or to bounce her hard enough on the bed so that it would collapse into the sea—but the reasons for demanding this switch sounded so paranoid she decided not to raise the issue. If George tried anything funny, she would make sure he went into the sea with her. She must remember to impress that point on him.

"Now, lady," called the man, "you gotta stay very quiet. Understand? Everything's going to be OK, just don't start getting panicky and shake that bed. Your husband is coming out on the end of the ladder. When he holds out his hands, take 'em—but without making any sudden movements, OK? And pull yourself up onto the ladder gently, hear? Stay cool, lady, just stay cool."

Stay cool! What did this stranger in coveralls know about her, or George, or the tapes she was clutching? He had no way of guessing that the tapes would put George in jail or that George would easily commit murder to get his hands on them. How could the man even suspect that just an hour or so earlier, she herself had considered death a definite relief, the tapes her vengeance, her suicide George's punishment? He was a faceless, disinterested uniform, anonymity in coveralls, salvation in pale-blue denim. And he was acting out of the disembodied interest one might proffer a lost child or hurt animal, not because he knew her and liked her or even because he really cared very much whether she lived or died. *Machismo* with an aluminum ladder and red script writing on his pocket.

George's voice startled her. "The man is right, Laura. Don't make any sudden movements, just reach up slowly and take my hands when I get there." There was a significant pause. "About that package. I'm afraid, well, you'll just have to let the package stay where it is."

Laura half raised herself to stare at George, and the bed groaned alarmingly beneath her. "The package comes with me." She made her statement so flatly and with such vigor she could see the man in overalls, even at this distance, blink in surprise. She also saw his hands, palms down, gesture to her urgently, signaling her not to make any more such sudden movements. She lowered herself gently back onto the bed. George and the man held some sort of conference, whispering and pointing. The man turned back toward her, visibly baffled.

"Look, lady, the package is none of my business. But you only got two hands, see? And this is going to be tough enough as it is without complicating things. Do like your husband says: forget the package. Nothing could be worth that much."

Laura roared with laughter; the man stared; George shrugged his shoulders helplessly. "Lady," the man began again.

"The package. All the jewelry I own in the world is in it," lied Laura. "Either it comes with me or I stay here." There was another conference, this one somewhat exasperated, between

246

the man and George. While they were talking, Laura slipped the belt off her evening dress—it was a thin one, of some sort of gold link chain—ran a length of the belt through the string tying the parcel, then fastened the ends of the belt back together and hung it loosely around her neck. The evening dress might flap embarrassingly open in the wind, but the package of tapes would go with her—either back to the safety of the cliff or into the abyss of the Pacific, whichever way George planned to take her.

"It's all settled," Laura called. "See, tied around my neck. And both hands are still free." She said this not without a certain smugness. The man in coveralls appeared relieved that the impasse was resolved without the wasting of more time. On George's face there appeared a growingly worried look; unless he could think of something to say or do, the tapes were getting dangerously close to winding up in the district attorney's hands.

"Ready, mister?" Laura heard the man ask George. Grimly, George nodded, looking nervously at the heavy stones counterbalancing the cliff end of the ladder. The man caught the look. "Don't worry. Between my weight and them stones, that ladder couldn't tip over the edge if it wanted." Lying down on the ladder, the man ostentatiously bounced on the far part to reassure George, then pulled the rope hauling the extension of the ladder out over the cliff and toward the bed beyond.

George crawled gingerly out onto the extension, for the first time looking down and seeing nothing between him and the ocean but air. One rung at a time, he inched farther out, trying to keep his eyes fixed on the dully gleaming aluminum rungs and side pieces of the ladder so that the blue void below him remained out of focus and blurred. The effort was not entirely successful. Through his mind sailed a stream of thoughts: the package and how to get his hands on it; the tapes and what would happen to him if Laura carried through her threat. He decided to use intimidation, but did not know how far he dared to carry it when he got out to Laura. Beneath him, the wind moaned through the rungs, an aluminum Greek chorus singing of his fatal flaw: the capacity to be evil without the will to carry it through.

A sudden movement of the ladder made both his hands freeze around one of the rungs. Slowly, carefully, he turned his head around to look behind him and see if something was wrong at the other end of the ladder. The whole extension part now seemed to respond to his every movement, rising and falling like a delicately balanced, deadly seesaw.

On the cliff, he saw the man in coveralls, scrunched down on the inland end of the ladder, motioning him forward. "Nothing to worry about, mister," the man called. "Everything's solid here. That up-and-down wobble is because you're getting further out, that's all. As you get near the end, you'll feel the pitching even more, so watch yourself."

George resumed his painful edging ahead, muttering under his breath. "Nothing to worry about" was easy enough to say squatting on a ladder over solid ground; it was something else bouncing up and down over a sheer drop into the ocean.

Gripping the next rung, George felt his hands slip slightly and realized it was because they were sweating. In spite of the cold, damp wind blowing across him, he was drenched in sweat for the entire length of his body. He had taken off his jacket back on the cliff because it seemed warm; now the realization that he was soaking wet made him feel suddenly icy cold, and he shivered.

The man on the cliff was shouting something at him —encouragement, George figured—but he ignored him. Inch by inch, agonizingly, slowly, he moved forward. Almost without realizing it, he reached the end and suddenly found himself face to face with Laura.

George looked down at her. Their heads were probably not more than two or three feet apart, their eyes boring into each other's, seeking the answer to who would win. Laura's hand instinctively reached for the gold chain belt around her neck that supported the package of tapes, like an old lady clutching her pearls. The means for winning were all within George's grasp: a push, a missed handclasp, a bounce of the bed, and Laura and the tapes would cease to exist. A terrible tragedy, they would say, while commending the husband for his brave but futile attempt. The look in Laura's eyes told George that she was as aware of his winning hand as he was, but her eyes remained fixed on his, as if unable to tear themselves away.

"Well," said George softly. "Well, Laura. This is it, isn't it?"

Laura's father had provided her with no suitable response to the question.

Chapter Seventeen

All prejudices may be traced back to the intestine.

—NIETZSCHE,
Ecce Homo

ISAAC ROSHOLMAN'S laughter didn't last very long. Battock saw to that. At first, baffled, Battock had merely watched as the man's laughter grew to a series of dry, convulsive heavings, the tears rolling down his weathered Jewish features. And the more Rosholman laughed, the more irritated Battock became, finally exploding into what seemed a perfectly logical question. "What the hell's so funny?" he demanded, striding across the cage to stand threateningly over Rosholman where he lay curled up against the bars.

Instead of an answer, his question called forth new torrents. of laughter, Rosholman pointing helplessly off into the distance, his hand shaking from the effort of trying to restrain the exploding mirth, his breath coming only in short, air-starved gasps.

This new burst of laughter was too much for Battock. He had been stalked by lions, stunned by Rosholman's loss of the shotgun, forced to run for his life, and was now being made fun of by a man he not only disliked but resented. A year's accumulation of suppressed rancor and exasperation caused him to grab Rosholman by the jacket and haul him to his feet. Pulling Rosholman's face as close to his own as he could manage, he screamed at him, "You stupid fucking sheeny. You been bugging me ever since the day you got here. You swiped my job—or the job I shoulda had, anyway—on account the director's a Jew-boy, too. I know the score. Don't tell me that wasn't the reason." He began shaking Rosholman back and forth so hard his head was banging against the bars. "And if you ever laugh at me again, I'll give you a nose job the hard way. Understand? Hear me? You hear me, Ike?" Suddenly the fury drained out of Battock. Blinking, he let his hands drop from Rosholman's jacket and walked away, muttering to himself.

Slack-jawed, Rosholman stared at him. Battock turned his head to avoid Rosholman's eyes. What he had said were things inside him he'd wanted to say for a long, long time, but they were also the things you never said out loud. Even his most partisan beer-drinking buddies would have recoiled in shock if they'd heard him. There was little compassion in what Battock felt, only embarrassment. He shrugged, trying to sneak a look at Rosholman's face and judge his reaction, but he was still unable to look him in the eye. Falteringly, he tried to reverse his field. "I didn't mean that. I'm sorry." As from a great distance, Battock heard his own words and could sense their feebleness. Nonetheless, he was unable to force anything stronger from himself.

Rosholman turned away from Battock. He tried to find pity but could muster only contempt; he tried to find forgiveness but could marshal only a thin wedge of fear. The memories of *Kristallnacht*—the Night of Broken Glass—were still too vivid in his mind.

Battock tested the water. "You know, Rosh, if we tried real hard I bet we could get to the shotgun. That old lion's pretty beat-up-looking."

Rosholman had not missed the sudden, unsubtle change in the name Battock was using to address him, nor did the mention of the shotgun in the same breath with Three Toes do anything but compound his growing sense of disgust with Battock.

"What I mean, see," continued Battock, coming halfway over to him, "is that one of us can set up a ruckus at the far end of the cage, while the other one kind of sneaks out the chute and grabs the gun." Battock studied Rosholman's blank look and began pressing. "Christ, when you see that pitiful cat, you wonder how come the vet didn't put him outa his misery years ago. Two bits he can't hardly run anymore." The lack of any response from Rosholman began to rattle Battock, and he wondered if Rosholman was so terrified of him he was afraid of letting him get his hands on the shotgun. "I tell you what," he volunteered. "You can rattle, while I get the gun, or I'll rattle while *you* pick up the shotgun. Either way you want it, Rosh. And then, bang! bang! we're outa here and home-free."

For the first time since Battock's outburst, Rosholman turned his head and looked directly into Battock's eyes. Little eyes, he thought, like those of the peccaries in Section Six. Still staring at Battock, Rosholman spoke softly but with indelible firmness. "No one shoots that lion. Understand me? No one. For any reason. And anyone who tries has to shoot me first. I swear it."

"You're crazy, plain crazy." Battock's exasperation began to surface again. "We're supposed to stay locked up in this contraption because you say so? Balls. If you won't help me, then I'll go get the goddamned shotgun myself. I can beat that tired old heap of hair to it anytime."

The wedge of fear inside Rosholman suddenly seized him once more and the firmness dissolved before it. "Please, the lion . . . *that* lion . . . he's my friend." In spite of himself, Rosholman pleaded—already knowing what kind of response to expect from Battock.

"Shit," grunted Battock. "All you Jews are nuts." With a sudden movement, he reached out through the bars of the vet's cage and started to crank open the gate to the chute.

"No, please no." Rosholman put out a restraining arm.

Battock shook himself free and began crawling out the chute. For a second Rosholman stood motionless, then ducked down and started after him. Three Toes cocked his head to watch the men come out of the cage, then tensed his muscles, the sinews tightening beneath his thin layer of ancient skin. Once out of the chute, the two men got to their feet and began running desperately toward the gun, a pushing, shoving, frantic race for possession.

Soundlessly, Old Three Toes leaped.

The shotgun roared.

The noise shattered the air, and a great flame-colored cockatoo, freed from its cage by Violet, flapped its closely clipped wings in a desperate, futile struggle to fly.

Awkwardly, it crashed to the ground, screaming.

Beth Czemki, Isaac Rosholman's niece, was about to have some troubles of her own with the *goyim*. Once he'd heard Beth had left Gregory and Sarah alone in the house without a sitter, Matt, tight-lipped and furious, had dragged Beth through the rubble of the streets toward home. Although not very long, the trip was not easy. The first sight of their street in Westwood Village caused them both to stop dead; Matt, particularly, had trouble believing so little real damage could have been done. Ignoring the friends and neighbors who jammed the street—most of them clustered around a transistor radio listening to reports of the havoc in other parts of LA—Matt paused only briefly. Then, grabbing Beth by the hand again, he shoved his way through the crowd and up to their own front door. The door itself was jammed; Violet had caused just enough earth movement to throw it out of plumb. With a heave of his shoulder, Matt forced it open and charged inside, yelling the children's names loudly.

He was greeted by a silence broken only by the dripping of a fractured water pipe somewhere beyond the kitchen. It was a lonely, empty sound, menacing and unrelenting, and Beth could feel a sudden coldness grow in her stomach listening to its hostile drip, drip. "Gregory! Sarah!" she called, thinking

253

for a second that perhaps the children had been frightened by the thunderous sound of the door crashing open and then Matt's stern calls.

Drip. Drip.

Matt groaned and pushed past her into the living room. In front of him, Beth could see the plate of uncooked french fries on the floor and the general disorder Gregory always left behind him wherever he had been. Matt came back to the doorway and sagged against it. "Nowhere," he said.

"Maybe they're hiding. You know those two," Beth suggested, as if somehow denying the reality would cause the dread in her to disappear. "Come on, kids," she called. "Gregory! Sarah! Come on, you two, we know you're there."

Drip. Drip.

Beth tried to ignore the sound, straining to hear the stifled giggle or clumsy shuffle of feet that would herald the children's bursting out from behind some curtain, couch, or chair, beside themselves with pleasure. Beth's heart leaped as she saw one gauze curtain stir, but the movement came only from an acrid-smelling breeze flowing through the broken window. "Sarah? Gregory?" she asked anyway.

Drip. Drip.

"Oh, shut up, Beth." Matt avoided looking at her, turning away from the expression of hurt on her face. "Stop kidding yourself. They're not down here, and I can't believe they're upstairs either."

Still avoiding her eyes, he went up the stairs, two at a time, and checked the second floor regardless, shouting their names, banging doors open and shut, alternating threats of punishment if they were hiding somewhere with cajoleries, logic, and child-tempting promises. He came back down the stairs and sat dejectedly on the bottom tread, racking his brain for what to do next. Twice he looked toward Beth, but she could see his eyes were looking through, rather than at, her.

"Maybe," she tried again, "maybe, Matt, they are out-side—you know, watching all the excitement with one of the neighbors." The suggestion didn't sound very convincing, even to her, although she rationalized by telling herself that to expect two children to sit inside alone while all that excitement went on outside was not realistic. Matt should understand this. "Maybe," Beth began again.

Matt's eyes looked directly at her. His face wore an expression Beth never remembered seeing before, an ugly, self-righteous, accusing look devoid either of sympathy or understanding. "*Maybe!*" He spat the words out like the cracking of some dreadful whip. "*Maybe* they're hiding. *Maybe* they're upstairs. *Maybe* they're outside. All you know is 'Maybe.' " Almost as if he were shocked himself, Matt paused in his outburst. Then, the final twist of the knife. "*Maybe* if you'd waited until the sitter got here. . . ."

Beth dissolved. She tried to fling herself into Matt's arms, crying uncontrollably, but the solace she could usually find there was denied her. Matt stood as cold and uncomforting as a marble cenotaph. With an impatient, irritated little shove of his hands, he untangled himself from her and started for the door.

"I'm going outside and find out if anybody's seen them. Maybe one of the neighbors"—Matt caught himself using the forbidden word and, flushing slightly, rephrased himself—"if they're out there, somebody might have seen them."

As he started toward the front door, Beth automatically followed; Matt stopped and swung himself around to face her. "No, dammit. You stay here." The hurt on her face finally reached him, and his expression softened, not much, but a little. "Somebody's *got* to stay in the house—in case the kids come back on their own." He turned on his heel and walked out through the front door.

From outside, she could hear him calling the children's names; sometimes his voice would drop, and she knew he was talking to someone, asking, explaining, begging information. Finally, his voice disappeared completely. The constant murmur of excited talk outside contrasted starkly with the dead silence inside. Beth sat down on the stairs and leaned her head against the newel post, listening.

Drip. Drip.

Oskie Davenport was becoming increasingly uncomfortable. From the beginning he'd wanted no part of the mayhem that seemed to be escalating around him. First, the escape. Oskie hadn't even wanted that—with Gilla's story, he figured, the knife job at Lefrak's Soul Palace would be impossible to prove, and he'd be home free. Pokress—and Violet—had killed that possibility. Then, knocking that old Jap on the head with the shotgun; if he died, Murder One. And plenty of witnesses, none of them as cooperative as Gilla. Already, he suspected, they were chargeable with kidnapping. By grabbing those kids at gunpoint, by tying up the old Jap, he was becoming an accessory to things he didn't even like to think about. And worst of all, with a man like Pokress, you could never be sure what he might pull next. Arson? Rape? Mass murder? Oskie shivered, and looked around the living room of the house on Tutweiler.

The Jap, still bleeding, was lying, half-propped up on the couch. From an occasional moan, he knew the man was still alive, but how long he would keep breathing was another question. The young boy and girl, still in their bathing suits, were huddled against one wall of the room, held there by Pokress' shotgun. (That they hadn't been tied up too they owed to him, Oskie Davenport. He had taunted Pokress into leaving them unfettered by suggesting perhaps Pokress was scared of them—"just a couple of kids, and you're so afraid of them you want to truss 'em up like turkeys?")

The mess he was in, then, was all Pokress' fault. But would a jury believe that?

From the couch, a sudden, much louder moan indicated Mr. Yoshura was slowly coming around. Pokress flinched, and Oskie could see his finger tighten on the shotgun's trigger as Mishi, staring coldly into the muzzle, walked over and

256

began rubbing her father's neck. Pokress frowned but did nothing. Oskie breathed again, and Addie slumped back against the wall in relief. Pokress must have sensed that letting Mishi get away with something, even something as harmless as this, could undermine his authority. For although the moment for taking action was past, he struggled to regain control by pretending to "allow" Mishi's going to her father. "That's OK," Pokress breathed in his raspy voice. "Sure. You can help the old man if you want to. Please just don't do anything stupid or try to pull a fast one."

Mishi paid no attention to Pokress, not even allowing him so much as a nod of her head. She calmly continued rubbing her father's neck and reassuring him gently in Japanese. Mr. Yoshura looked at her gratefully; then his eyes swept past her to take in the rest of the people in the room. When he saw Simon Pokress holding the shotgun, turning it back and forth between Addie and his daughter, and realized his own hands and feet were tied, his face, pale and drained until now, flushed in outrage and a torrent of Japanese came spilling forth.

"Tell him," hissed Pokress, convinced they were up to something, "tell him, little girl, either to speak English or be quiet."

Mishi patted her father and tried to shush him, but the high-pitched, strange-sounding words kept tumbling out of him; at the same time, he strained against the ropes trying to struggle free.

"Hold it!" Pokress rasped, and aimed the gun directly at Mr. Yoshura. Mr. Yoshura stopped his squirming but stared at Pokress defiantly. "That's better," Pokress said. "Now, as I said, tell him to stay put and since he can't speak English, to shut up. Otherwise, instead of a sore neck, he's going to have a no neck." With a gesture of the gun for emphasis, Pokress smiled at his own sense of humor.

For the first time, Mr. Yoshura addressed Pokress. "I speak English every bit as well as you do, possibly better. And certainly louder. However, since you are in possession of the firearms, I shall pay heed to your instructions. In other words, I shall remain as motionless as I can and say the absolute minimum. And that in English."

"I ought to blow you open." From Pokress' expression it was hard to decide how seriously to take his threat, but one thing emerged quite clearly: Pokress was no man to put down.

"If you do, you do. In the meantime," suggested Mr. Yoshura, "I believe that you should release these children."

"*Children?*" asked Pokress, and laughed thickly, turning toward Mishi. "She doesn't look like any child to me. Nice little pair on her."

Fortunately, Mr. Yoshura didn't understand Pokress' slang. But Mishi did and blushed beneath her golden skin. Against the wall, Addie squirmed. This was the second such remark about Mishi Pokress had made, and some vague, undefinable fear mushroomed inside him, a dim sense of apprehension mixed with an illogical feeling of excitement he could neither understand nor tolerate. Suddenly ashamed, he found words coming out of his mouth that could only make matters worse "Don't talk about her like that. You're a goddam bastard."

Pokress sneered at Addie. "Pretty boy speaks." The thick, dry laugh again. "I'm scared. Terrified. Quaking."

From the far side of the room, Oskie intervened. It was no gesture of gallantry; he was afraid the ballooning confrontation with Addie would lead to more bloodshed, and they were in enough trouble as it was.

"Oh, lay off the kid, Pokress. We've gotta make plans. You know?"

"Plans, plans, plans," Pokress sighed. Whether he was relieved or disappointed by the opportunity to escape a showdown with Addie remained unclear, but there was enough logic in what Oskie suggested to demand action. "You have a radio—a transistor radio—in the house?" he asked Mishi. Apparently, in his mind, the house belonged to her family, not Addie's.

Mishi nodded toward the wall unit that held the television set and the stereo equipment. On the end of one of the shelves

258

beside some records was the small transistor radio she sometimes took to the pool.

After listening to it a little while, Pokress whistled, then turned it off and slammed it on the table behind the couch. "Plans? We aren't going anywhere for a while." He walked to the bar and grabbed a bottle of blended rye before striding back to Oskie with two glasses, the shotgun crooked under his elbow, his fingers still tracing the trigger guard.

Straddling a side chair, turned around so its back was in front of him to rest the shotgun on, Pokress sat down with his drink. The gun moved restlessly back and forth between Mr. Yoshura on the couch and Addie and Mishi against the wall. As Pokress pulled at the rye, it dawned on him that such an arrangement of his prisoners involved splitting his field of fire, and he ordered Addie and Mishi to sit at the foot of the couch, their backs against it and facing him; this put all his possible targets in one easily controlled, compact area.

Oskie pulled up a chair not too far from Pokress and sat down. "Cheer up, friend," Pokress muttered at him. "Cheer up and enjoy the amenities of the rich."

The glass in Pokress' hand halted midway toward his mouth. "You too, little girl," he said in a mock toast to Mishi. "We're stuck here for quite a while and we're your guests. Guests ought to be treated well. *Really* well." He drained his glass with a smirk, never letting his eyes stray from her.

Inside Addie, again the wave of fear and excitement.

He squeezed his legs together in shame.

The trip in Ken Corbit's traffic helicopter, he told them, would not be a very long one. In the front seat beside him sat Father Reed and Derek Usher; in the seat behind was an aged lady, who talked constantly, and her husband, who said nothing (he had been, the old lady explained, the victim of a stroke years earlier and had not spoken a word since; she appeared determined to make up for his silence). These two had already been aboard the helicopter when it picked up Usher and Reed; the chopper, by then carrying its capacity, swung away from the Wilshire area to deliver its load to safety.

"Don't you think, Father," asked the lady, "that we should offer a prayer of thanks?"

Father Reed, in keeping with the image of the storefront church, wore no clerical collar, but the old lady had spotted the heavy gold cross bouncing on the front of his black turtleneck shirt and cross-examined him until she discovered he was a priest. The lady's question bothered him, but he turned and smiled at her. "Perhaps when we get there would be more appropriate," he suggested with a warm, reassuring smile.

The old lady was not so easily put off. "I've never been in one of these things before, Father. Maybe we should have a prayer that we *do* get there."

"Just like my mother," hissed Derek to Father Reed. "Always correcting people."

To cut off both conversations, Father Reed asked Corbit, "What *is* our touchdown point?"

"Griffith Park. Flat, no tall buildings, and all the trees that are going to come down, already have."

The priest was mystified. "*Where* in Griffith Park?"

"Near the zoo. I left the other people on a flat place just below." He banked the chopper and turned to Reed, feeling proud of himself. "I've taken about forty or fifty people out of the lower Wilshire area so far, most of them older—well, that is, senior citizens." He nodded his head to indicate the old couple.

Father Reed had caught the note of pride and responded as expected. "That's a great job you're doing. Anybody who stayed back there—myself included—couldn't have lasted much longer."

A soft moan came from one of the rear seats, and the lady leaned forward and tapped Corbit on the shoulder. "Will it be much longer? My husband, you see. I think he has to move his bowels."

"Just getting ready to come down now, in fact," answered

Corbit, bringing the helicopter in for a much faster landing than usual.

But when they started to get out of the helicopter, they discovered the old man was no longer in a position to move anything. His face was the color of dried putty, drained of blood, and when Corbit touched the skin of his face, he withdrew his hand quickly from the unnatural coldness of it. The moan had been the last of the old man's breath leaving him. Corbit, in a shaken voice, pronounced him dead. Probably, he said, the victim of a terminal stroke brought on by excitement and tension.

The lady, leaning heavily now on Father Reed for support, stared in disbelief as Corbit and Derek Usher removed her husband's body from the plane; in the storage compartment, Corbit found a tattered gray blanket and decorously covered the man with it. (Secretly, he suspected that as the night grew cold, someone would remember that blanket and remove it from the body to wrap around himself.)

The tear-streaked face of the old lady searched Father Reed's. Through her soft sobbing, making out exactly what she was saying became difficult, but a repeated, although muffled reference to last rites was inescapable.

The priest shifted uncomfortably. The adherence to nonrelevant rituals like Hail Marys, stations of the cross, and the other various sacraments were a part of what he considered wrong with the modern church, a semianimistic hangover from other times; yet, studying this shaken widow, fingering her rosary for comfort and asking so little of a God who had just robbed her of her home, her husband, and almost her life, he found it impossible to ignore the request.

Kneeling, he slipped the golden cross off the black turtleneck and up over his head, holding it in front of himself in place of the purple silk *stolum* he had never had. "May the Lord forgive you," he began with effort, "by this holy anointing and His most loving mercy. . . ."

The old lady, kneeling beside him, was crying. But Father

Reed could see her shake her head vigorously and hear her soft pleading: "In Latin, Father. Please, in Latin."

Father Reed nodded, searching his brain for the long-forgotten words of childhood. Oddly, from his other side, he suddenly heard Derek Usher in a whispered prompting. Reed listened a moment, then began again. *"Per istam sanctam unctionum et suam piisimam misericordia indulgeat tibi . . ."*

For a priest, Father Reed's Latin was absolutely terrible.

Chapter Eighteen

Honesta turpitudo est pro causa bona.

—PUBLICUS SYRUS

WORKING in the operations room, lit dimly by the emergency system, Henry Kraypool was on the Civil Defense radiophone with Mayor Ortiz. Earlier, when he'd finally reached Feiner at Goldstone, the call had produced no new information, just reaffirmation of when the first aftershock was supposed to strike. Now that they were well into the projected time period without any signs of tremor activity, Kraypool was back trying to get Ortiz to pressure the authorities into releasing the emergency task force into the area.

"Look, Mr. Mayor, Goldstone's prediction was for seven P.M. Los Angeles time. They've got the usual plus or minus one hour built in, of course, but it's now seven twenty-five. We could sit here all night waiting for something that isn't going to happen."

From the other end of the phone, over the static and jumble, Ortiz sounded unreal and very tired. "I know. But so far only by minutes. How much of a case can we make with that?"

"The first time around, when no one wanted to take the prediction seriously, they made quite a case with it. Now, when *we* don't want to take it at face value, the prediction is considered foolproof." Kraypool paused, studying the blank wall ahead of him, giving Ortiz time to absorb the unfairness of how they were being treated. "Can't you get to the governor and ask him to pressure Washington?"

"I have. I will again. They *are* letting a few choppers in to take people off high ground and rooftops in the Valley, but they say any mass evacuations will have to wait." The pause that came from Ortiz's end was filled with particularly loud static. "Have your men heard anything from there?"

Kraypool sighed. The area was an almost total wipeout. He knew it; Ortiz knew it. "Only scattered reports—from the high ground, above the Valley. And what I am getting sounds very bad."

Ortiz's voice had sunk to a whisper. "Eighty thousand people lived there. . . ." He didn't finish the sentence; he didn't need to. Kraypool's radioman turned to him to note that the radio contact had been broken.

The interior emergency phone on Kraypool's desk was ringing. Someone, somewhere in the building, with some new disaster to report.

He stared at the phone for a long time before he picked it up.

Still trapped in the meat locker, Georgi was listening with satisfaction to the noises outside the door. It sounded as if his sons had rounded up the entire male contingent of the wedding party to rescue him; a colossal series of bangs and crashes came from outside the freezer as beams, stones, and crushed masonry were pulled away. They were trying, he supposed, to release the door lock as well as clear away enough space so that the door could be manhandled open a crack.

Georgi was no longer worried—either about getting out or of becoming too cold. The banging and heaving outside the door had removed the first concern; Georgi's own inventiveness combined with an unusual run of good luck had removed the second. In searching the meat locker for a coat or a jacket, *anything* to wrap himself in, Georgi had almost fallen over the cases of Fix that were stacked in one corner to be chilled. Exploring them expertly, his fingers detected one case that didn't belong with the rest, and using one of his few remaining matches, Georgi discovered it was a case of ouzu, the powerful Greek version of pernod. Someone would be taken to task later for such unforgivably sloppy storekeeping, but for the moment, the fiery ouzu was keeping Georgi comfortably warm inside. He had not neglected his outer self either. In front of him burned a small, smoky fire, fueled by strips of lamb fat wrapped in the old newspapers he'd discovered at the bottom of the ouzu case. The combination of the fire, the ouzu, and the expectation of early release had put Georgi in unusually high spirits, and he was singing loudly of his warm and sunny land seven thousand miles to the east when a sound suddenly disturbed him.

No, not a sound exactly, but the absence of *any* sound. The banging and knocking outside the door had stopped. Possibly, he thought, they were getting ready to yank open the door, which would be followed by huggings and the kissing of both cheeks by many men, and laughter and singing and even, he suspected, some crying.

The sudden silence began to make him nervous, and Georgi got up from the fire and, groping his way through the dim light, pressed his ear tight against the door. What little he could hear through the heavy metal struck him now as being very far away—and strangely muffled. With a growing apprehension that something he didn't understand had gone wrong, Georgi banged heavily on the door and waited for an answering thump. None came. As he banged again, he was disturbed by the curiously flat, dull sound his fists made; where there had been a booming echo before, there was only a heavy, dull thump, as if he were not hammering on a steel door but on a thick brick wall behind which stood several feet of well-packed earth. For a moment, panic seized him. Then he remembered: his sons, Eugenios, Orien, and Christophorus, were out there, and if the sound beyond the door had changed, it had changed for a good reason. *Their* **reason.**

265

Escape was only a matter of time, Georgios reminded himself, ashamed of his lack of faith. Calmly, he walked back to
the small fire and sat down. He drank a small private toast to
the goodness of his sons. And softly, perhaps not as convinc-
ingly as before, he began singing again of the sun-drenched
beauty of his homeland.

Georgi would not have been singing at all had he been able
to see outside the meat locker's door. The curious dullness his
banging produced was the result of the cellar's sudden flood-
ing with water when the Van Norman Dams went, releasing
billions of gallons into the low-lying San Fernando Valley. For
a time, Orien and Christophorus had been able to cling to the
remains of Georgi's roof, their hands locked around roof
timbers that looked strong enough to resist the rushing
waters. But little by little, the roof itself disintegrated, and the
two brothers, one after the other, had been sucked into the
roaring current and drowned.

Eugenios hadn't survived even that long. When the water
started pouring down the stairs into the cellar, Eugenios was
the first to realize what had happened and yelled at his two
brothers to get out while they could. Yet he didn't follow his
own advice. Instead, he raced over to the meat locker and,
straining as hard as possible, managed to close the valve controlling the flow of outside air into the freezer. With the valve
shut, at least no water could get into the meat locker. Any
estimate of how long the air inside would last was grim, but
closing the valve was the only chance his father had. Then
Eugenios, neck-high in the water by now, turned to swim
toward the stairs. But a desperate hammering on the meat-
locker door made him stop; he wanted to return and bang
back in reassurance, but the water was rising too fast. So fast,
in fact, that when he tried to swim toward the cellar door, he
found his head was being pressed against the ceiling.

He took a deep breath and dived down toward the staircase
but was unable to locate it, and when he resurfaced only a
couple of inches remained between his upturned face and the
ceiling. After another deep breath, he dived for the cellar

door once more, but the water was too dark and filled with hidden obstructions for him to find it. His lungs almost bursting, Eugenios surfaced again. There was now so little space that he had to press his face flat up against the ceiling to breathe at all; he found himself screaming, the sound of his cries returning to him almost immediately, dully, without any resonance or echo.

He tried one final plunge in an effort to find the door in the dark water, but the breath he had taken was too small. His lungs felt as if they were pushing through his ribs. He wanted to cry out, to scream, to pray, but could not.

The next time he came to the surface, there *was* no air space. For a second, Eugenios thrashed futilely, but after a moment or two, the struggling lessened, then ceased, and he floated face up, bumping gently against the rough wood ceiling of Georgi's Restaurant and Meeting Hall, his arms and legs dangling loosely around him, an underwater marionette whose strings had been cut by an evil puppeteer named Violet.

On the fourteenth-floor level, the glass cage surrounding the Park Plaza's external elevator became larger by half. This was not entirely designed for the benefit of the customers, but so that the metal frame supporting the shaft could make use of heavier beams. (Obviously, the elevator itself could be no larger than the smallest part of the shaft it traveled through, but the widening of the glass shaft gave people the illusion that the elevator suddenly grew larger as it shot past the fourteenth floor.)

To Digit Vorhees, studying this unexpected structural twist, the widening of the shaft presented a new problem: since the rope would now have to travel farther to reach from one side to the other in following its zigzag course downward, descent from here on would have to be maneuvered two, rather than three, floors at a time. He grimaced. The change would probably be welcomed by the others; but for him the wider shaft and shortened number of floors negotiable in each leg meant more trips up and down, more fastening and unfastening of the rope, and more scalings of the framework to retrieve the end of the line and bring it down to the next climbing level.

And Digit was tired. For every floor the rest climbed down, he had to make two additional trips, one up the rope, one scrambling down the always slightly frightening steel skeleton. He was young, he was strong, he was a good climber, but Digit could feel the ache in his arms and shoulders growing. The fourteenth floor was a logical halfway point, and possibly, he thought, given a few minutes' time, he could jimmy open the elevator doors into the building and get some water for everybody; his own thirst was becoming all-consuming, and he could imagine the rest must be suffering too.

Originally, his plan was to get everyone on the same floor before calling the break, but after shepherding the psych major and Sporades down, he was too exhausted to face straining on the pulley arrangement for Mrs. Grimes without a rest. Lowering her in the rope carry chair had always been difficult, but now, shattered by the loss of Anna, Sporades, although saying nothing, had become less and less of a help.

Swinging out from one of the supporting beams so that he could look up the shaft, Digit called up loudly to Adam Mosely. "Hello! Hello! Can you hear me, Mr. Mosely?"

Adam's head appeared over the edge of the landing, three floors above, looking anxious. "I'm here. Is everybody all right?" Adam was worried by Sporades' behavior. If the man had wept, or yelled, or kicked something, he would have understood. But Sporades had remained silent, staring vacantly off into space when not actually busy with the rope, occasionally talking softly to himself in Greek.

"I think we'd better take a breather." Digit's voice sounded distant and strained.

"Is something wrong?"

"No, I just think everybody's getting pretty beat. We're at

about the halfway point, Mr. Mosely." (Adam had tried to get Digit to call him by his first name, but Digit, after trying it a couple of times, found the first name awkward and had abandoned the effort.)

"All right," Adam called back. "Probably a good idea." He didn't understand why the break had been called when Dorothy Grimes and he were separated from the rest by three floors, and the fact bothered him. Digit seemed to guess what he was thinking.

"We could get you and Mrs. Grimes down here first, of course," he volunteered, "but I'd rather take the break right now. I'm going to try to scare up some water for us all."

The unspoken plea in Digit's voice was clear. "Fine," Adam agreed. "Just holler when you're ready to start again." Adam started to pull himself back from the edge, then stopped, looking straight down the shaft into Digit's upturned eyes. "And let me tell you, my friend, I for one think you're doing one hell of a job." Even at this distance Adam could see Digit's face redden with embarrassment; he was a boy not good at handling compliments from older people, and Adam wondered why. Possibly, Adam thought, Digit was the product of a distant, undemonstrative family. But whatever the reason, he was a good, solid youth; he only hoped his own boy, Addie, was acquitting himself half as well. Adam pondered. Addie, too, was the product of a distant, undemonstrative family, although undoubtedly of a completely different kind: a father who deliberately stayed out of sight and a mother who had castrated his father into inaction, stolen his self-assuredness, cheated him into indecisiveness, and left him easy prey to a Dorothy Grimes. Adam was startled. He had never thought of Georgia's drinking as affecting him that much, yet the changes that ended his true effectiveness with the *Trib* had begun at almost exactly the same time as Georgia's covered-up accident. The realization surprised him, but not as much as his blindness up until now to the reasons behind the change. "What's up?" Dorothy

Grimes interrupted his chain of thought. She was sitting in the doorway of the landing, leaning against one of the beams for support.

"That kid wants to take a break, and I don't blame him; he sounds beat. While he's at it, he's going to look around to see if he can get his hands on some water. I guess they're all as thirsty as we are."

From the look on her face, Adam could tell she was going to make one of her brittle responses. "Damned thirsty. If I'd known it was going to be like this, I'd have brought along my drink."

Adam shrugged, not caring whether he smiled as expected. He nodded to indicate he'd heard and sat down, leaning against the beam opposite hers. Beyond, through some shattered glass still left in the framework of the shaft, he could see the city of Los Angeles, the lowering sun gleaming redly off an occasional window and competing for attention with the glowing spots of flame that seemed to be everywhere.

His mind, in spite of his efforts to avoid the subject, returned to what he considered Georgia's role in his undoing. Two totally contrary thoughts crossed his mind at the same time. On the one hand, he could see how the completely illogical process of dealing with an alcoholic could sap a man's self-confidence. The rules, after all, were insane. But it was still difficult to understand how this phenomenon could alter his professional outlook or undermine his decisiveness in completely unrelated areas. Yet the changes in himself that bothered him had no other explanation. And the timing was, if anything, too perfect.

On the other hand, Adam couldn't help wondering if this conclusion wasn't a neat way to remove the blame from himself and shift it to Georgia. Wonder if he wasn't using her problem as an excuse for some innate weakness of his own. Adam suddenly snorted. It was an odd time to pick for soul-searching—perched precariously seventeen floors up a none-too-solid building shell in the wake of an earthquake.

The disease, however, appeared to be catching. "Adam,"

Dorothy Grimes said from her corner. "Adam, I've been thinking. And I've reached a decision."

Adam turned to look at her. She appeared, as always, completely in command. Her face might be streaked and dirty, her hair windblown, her dress smudged, but the ivory cigarette holder held its usual cigarette, and her face wore its constant expression of utter self-confidence. Grudgingly, Adam had to admit it: Dorothy Grimes was an incredible woman.

Dorothy leaned back against the beam and absently ran her fingers across the nubby carpet of the landing. "When we get down, Adam—without you and that remarkable boy I would have said, 'if we get down,' but I'm thoroughly convinced now that we shall—when we get down, I'm making some changes. In my life, in the *Trib*." Biting her lip, as if unsure quite how to put what she was going to say, she studied the intricate carving of the ivory cigarette holder for a moment, then: "The paper—that damned paper—I'm assuming it will go on, although after this, it's going to take time to start things up again. You know what I mean: finding a new building, getting new presses, putting a staff together again. But once that's done, I'm withdrawing from the paper. Completely. Label it retirement, separation, old age, I don't really care. But I'm out—completely out." She paused, not looking at Adam but into space, and laughed. "Oh, I don't mean I'll stop taking profits out of it; this experience has been a shock, but it hasn't left me totally unhinged." The smile that had accompanied her brief laughter faded, and Dorothy looked directly at him. "What I mean is, well, withdrawing from operational control. I'm tired, Adam, very tired. Tired of telling the world what to do, then having to live with my conscience; I'm bored telling myself I'm smarter than everybody else and then discovering sometimes I'm not; I'm weary of forcing my gospel of change on people who may not want to change and who possibly could even be right not wanting to. In the last analysis, who, after all, gave me the right to decide what's right and what's wrong? I wasn't elected to the job by anyone; I just took it.

271

And then used all the power of the *Trib* to pound my conclusions into the country's consciousness. Well, no more."

A troubled look crossed her face. "I know this is a crazy
place to decide something like this, and an even crazier one to
choose for making the announcement, but I wanted to—had
to—get it off my chest. Anyway, Adam, to come back to the
point—about the operational control of the paper. That goes
to you. With no strings. Not a single one. You can continue the
Trib in the direction it's always gone or reverse it. You can
come out for George Wallace, if you think that's right. You
can print anything and everything you want, including rude
political cartoons of me, if you think I deserve them. You're
on your own. On your own to direct, decide, defend, to take
the credit and the blame, the bows and the boos, the glow
inside when you're right and the hurt inside when you're
wrong—I give it to you *in toto*—all the power *and* all the
responsibility."

Adam opened his mouth to speak, but Dorothy Grimes held
up her hand to stop him. "I know, I know. I said something a
little like this once before. But I swear to God I will neither
interfere nor try to influence you—and I plan to put that in
writing. Irrevocably. For working purposes, at least as far as
the *Trib* is concerned, I cease to exist."

Adam's response was both remarkable and unkind. "Oh,
shit." He looked quickly up at Dorothy, in part because he was
afraid she would take the remark as a judgment on her
speech, in part because his answer had surprised him as much
as it had probably surprised her, and he wanted to let her
know this.

For a moment, she stared at him in bewilderment. Then she
threw back her head and roared her particular laugh, the
deep throaty laugh that always captivated him. "Oh, Adam!
Adam, Adam, Adam. I don't know whether that's supposed to
be an acceptance or a refusal of my offer, but it's wonderful
anyway."

Adam had just gone through a thought process too close to
hers not to see what lay behind her "offer." "I'm not sure,

272

Dorothy, whether it's as much of a proposal as it is a copout, an excuse, an attempt at expiation."

For the first time Adam could remember, Dorothy Grimes looked shaken. Straightening herself up, she leaned forward and stuffed another cigarette into the holder with unusual viciousness. "What the hell is *that* supposed to mean?"

"The girl"—Adam struggled for Anna Kristaboulos' name but was unable to come close, even in his head, to anything that sounded at all right—"you know, the one on her honeymoon. This whole thing started with that poor girl. Exactly how you got from her to bailing out of the *Trib* is a bit mysterious, but to me it smacks of—well, a kind of self-crucifixion"—Adam's eyes traveled to Dorothy's ornately carved cigarette holder—"with the first scrimshaw nails since *Moby Dick.* 'Oh, shit' may be a little crude, but it's precisely how I feel about your running away. And that's about what all this self-pity adds up to, Dorothy: a running away from responsibility. . . ."

The just-lit cigarette in Dorothy Grimes' holder was crushed violently against the steel beam, a small shower of sparks flying from the ground-out end. Her eyes bored through Adam. She had been hurt, and when Dorothy Grimes was struck, the instinct to strike back was automatic. "If I were you, Adam Mosely, I don't believe I'd dare use the words 'run away' or 'self-pity.' You practically own them."

Adam shrugged; he didn't want the discussion to go further, and any rejoinder would only be a new challenge to Dorothy. He was not to be let off the hook so easily.

"Look at yourself, Adam, before you dare accuse me of 'running from responsibility.' Your wife had a problem—a real one—but where were you? Never home, that's where. Instead of working with her, forcing her, making her see the doctors or go to the places that might help her, you ran. Beautiful. If it had come right down to it, you could have had her committed until she got better. But no. You surrounded her with doctors, nurses, keepers, so you could tell yourself you were doing the right thing. Well, you weren't, and you

273

never were. You abandoned her. Ran away. Ducked the responsibility." Shoving in the knife, she put down the cigarette holder long enough to raise both hands toward Adam and applaud. "Bravo, Adam! Such a responsible, noble, self-sacrificing figure of a man!"

Adam could hear the wind moaning through the beamwork of the building far above them but what he was listening for was some sound from below indicating their descent was about to start again, thereby releasing him from Dorothy Grimes' venomous—but frighteningly accurate—tongue. The woman would not stop. "And another thing: you dare talk to me of being a copout. What about your copping out on Addie? He's only your son. Do you realize, Adam, that well as I know you, I've seen him only a handful of times? You leave him out there, in that crystal cage you built for Georgia, with no one to talk to but Georgia's jailers. Oh, I know, you take him out to dinner once a week, you bring him to the paper once in a while, you make little fatherlike noises now and then, but that's it." Dorothy Grimes was now enough in control of her fury to stuff another cigarette into her holder; Adam wondered how endless a supply could come from so small a purse. He tried to think of any irrelevancy to fend off Dorothy's hurtful words. She studied him through the smoke for a second, then concluded her attack. "What's the matter, Adam? When you tried to give to Georgia—and failed—did it hurt so much you don't dare risk trying to give yourself again to *anyone?*"

Pretending to hear sounds from below, Adam stood up and leaned out over the edge to look down. This should halt Dorothy's outburst, and it was one that had to be stopped. The argument was useless; they were both wrong, Dorothy and he, they *both* were running, both hiding from themselves. To belabor the point, to try to make Dorothy see that in her own way she was as wrong as he was—if she didn't already know it—would be useless.

When he'd first looked down onto the landing three floors below, he'd been able to detect little activity. The Greek was

274

staring off into space, not speaking, silently mourning his wife; the psych major had apparently tried conversation but given up, she was sitting beside Sporades, studying the smoldering skyline of the city; the remarkable Digit was nowhere to be seen.

Abruptly, Digit's head appeared, looking anxiously up. "Everything all right?"

Adam almost laughed. "Oh, yes. Everything's fine. How about down there?"

Digit looked discouraged. "No water. I got into the hall all right, but the drinking fountains aren't working, of course. I had a container, but no water. Dumb stunt. I'm sorry, but I guess we'll just have to go on being thirsty."

"Don't worry about the water," answered Adam almost too quickly; looking at the boy, he once again thought of Addie. Dorothy was right, painfully right. He had failed him. Too hurt by Georgia even to give himself to his own son. Damn Dorothy. He grinned down at Digit. "You're doing great. And don't worry about whether we're thirsty or not. We'll survive." The boy grinned back and disappeared, again revealing his strange shyness with adults.

"Well," Adam announced, turning for the first time since the argument to face Dorothy, "we're about to start down another leg. No water, though."

Dorothy struggled to her feet, leaning against the shaft's framework to take the weight off her left knee. "Another leg." She smiled at him faintly, trying in her own way to clear the air. "That's what I could really use—another leg."

It was not a very good joke; but the cement of even feeble humor can bond, and she accepted Adam's hand when he offered it, letting him help her adjust the rope carry chair beneath her. On shouted orders from below, Dorothy pushed herself over the edge and waved cheerfully to Adam as the pulley, squeaking painfully as it turned, slowly began to lower her.

Adam was not entirely sure in which order things happened next. He remembered hearing a woman's scream from below, short and urgent; then a shout—probably from Digit; glass breaking; and what might or might not have been the thud of a body falling against the sides of the shaft. Ordinarily, with a mind as trained for detail as his was, Adam would have been able to reconstruct the order of these sounds. But he was too frantically busy. For simultaneously with the woman's scream, the rope supporting Dorothy's carry chair went slack at one end; the line raced through the pulley, changing the pulley's pitch from a squeak to an agonizing whine; Dorothy Grimes appeared to pause, unsupported, in midair for a second, then began to drop precipitously.

Adam lunged for her, almost losing his balance and tumbling over the edge himself. At the same time, the supporting rope snapped taut, stopping her descent with a violent jerk. Adam, who had her halfway onto the platform by the time the rope stopped playing out, heard a painful *thud* as the lower half of her body in the carry chair crashed against the landing. To his amazement, Dorothy didn't even cry out, but merely put her arms around his neck and allowed herself to be half lifted, half dragged onto the landing.

Once there, she sank down onto the floor, blinking in bewilderment, rubbing her right leg tenderly where it had crashed into the landing. "One good knee, and I have to go smash it into a cement wall. That hurts." Smiling, she looked up at Adam. "And what's going to hurt worse, I suppose, is saying thanks. It's always embarrassing to have to show gratitude to someone you've just disemboweled."

"Are you all right? What the hell happened?"

"The rope slipped. Or someone let go. I don't know. Everything happened so fast."

Adam inched to the outside of the landing and peered over. Digit was on his stomach, also looking down the shaft, and the psych major was huddled in one corner, absently clinging to the slackened rope. Digit was shouting something down to someone, but the distance was too great for Adam to make out what he was saying. Pushing himself even farther over the edge, so far out that Adam experienced the unsettling feeling that at any minute his upper half might topple him forward, he could see that the boy was calling to Sporades. The Greek lay sprawled two or possibly three floor levels below, unmoving, one leg hanging loose over the edge of the landing. Digit was beginning to scramble down the shaft's framework to get to him; if the man was hurt or unconscious, the boy would need help. After a curt explanation to Dorothy, Adam slid down the still-secured climbing rope to where the girl was.

"What happened?" he asked the psych major.

"I don't know. He—Sporades—he was just standing there, hauling on the rope when he started crying. Digit said something to him, you know, trying to make him get with it, but he just shook his head like he really didn't care what happened. The next thing I knew he'd let go of the rope and stumbled backward over the edge. He was busted up over his wife, I guess, and it all came pouring out at once."

With a sad shake of his head, Adam put one foot on the outer framework of the shaft and swung himself outward to start down toward Digit and Sporades. But a new shout from below stopped him.

Digit was standing up, yelling through his cupped hands. Beside Digit on the landing, lay Sporades, still unmoving, although his leg had been retrieved from the edge. "Mr. Mosely! Don't try it, please. There's nothing you can do here anyway. He isn't breathing."

Adam was aghast. "Are you sure?"

"No pulse or heartbeat. And no signs of breathing." Digit paused, then, because he was still barely older than a child, couldn't resist adding proudly, "I used the back of my watch like a mirror. When I held it to his mouth, no fogging. It's something I learned when I was into climbing."

"Good work." The words didn't sound right, and Adam tried again. "Sad work, but good work. You did everything you could."

"Is the lady on top all right?"

"Bruised, dignity scarred, but otherwise fine. I don't know how you stopped that rope, but it was a great piece of thinking."

Adam had only time to see Digit blush again before he swung back onto the landing himself. Slowly, Adam started the climb up the rope toward Dorothy, battered both by what had happened and by his conscience. He was shaken to realize how quickly one becomes inured to death, how easily you begin to accept the fact of disaster for others. In the last half hour, a woman guillotined by a sheet of glass, her husband of only a few hours now dead from a broken neck. Yet, in the midst of all this, he and Dorothy Grimes arguing their faults and weaknesses. Digit's pride in his watch-case breath test. And now, just now, his own cavalier use of a phrase like "dignity scarred."

Insensitivity, he decided, was not the special province of the extreme right.

Chapter Nineteen

For that which befalleth the sons of men befalleth beasts; even one thing befalleth them: as the one dieth, so dieth the other; yea, they have all one breath; so that a man hath no preeminence above a beast. . . .

—Ecclesiastes 3:19

THE scene had a weird quality. The sky had darkened, and was shot through with scudding clouds of a pink too intense to be real; the ruins of Laura Vorhees' house stood etched against this background, every stone and piece of plaster thrown in high relief by the lengthening shadows. The lone wall now cast even longer shadows from the rapidly setting sun across the ravaged lawn, the fireplace mantel and chimney looking totally out of place unsurrounded by a house. To add to the unreal quality of the scene, George had rescued two small chairs from the rubble and set them in front of the fireplace. A brisk fire, fed by scraps of wood and clapboarding from the service ell, was burning beneath the mantel to ward off the chilly night air.

Laura sat shivering in one chair, wrapped in a blanket; George leaned tenuously on the mantel, not sure whether his weight would send the entire wall crumbling into the ocean. (The man from the exterminators, after helping rescue Laura, had disappeared into the night on foot to try to make it home and check on his family; his truck was left abandoned farther up the road.)

Laura, knowing the scene was staged, watched George carefully as she clutched the package of tapes under her blanket. She had sensed George's struggle with himself as he stared down at her from the swaying ladder above the bed; she had known, when he had relented and finally pulled her up onto the ladder to safety, he was rescuing her only because the exterminator man was there and he could do nothing else; she suspected that left to his own devices, George would have felt far better with both her and the tapes resting on the ocean floor. Now she braced herself, watching him carefully as he drank bourbon out of a cracked glass and leaned on the mantel, making small talk about the earthquake until he faced her with some new, unacceptable proposition.

She didn't have long to wait.

"Those tapes," George began.

"Are going to the district attorney," she finished.

George cleared his throat and stared at her; he was unused to a Laura who knew her own mind, a Laura who talked back, a Laura who didn't always assume herself to be wrong. But, he decided, it was still a Laura who could be threatened and terrified into doing what he wanted. "You realize," he noted, "that with all the confusion about the quake, with the house mostly gone, with houses all along Malibu disappeared into the sea, I could just take the tapes and push you over the edge. Who would know?" The threat had an empty sound, and George realized it; he was counting on Laura's usual pliability to provide the conviction he lacked. This was an error.

Laura howled with laughter. "Who would know, George? The man from the exterminators' would know, that's who. He might find it very odd that I tumbled into the ocean *after* he and you had already rescued me."

Without warning, George felt his elbow slip off the mantel, spilling some of the drink in his hand. This little accident, he thought, was symbolic of his crumbling façade. Fighting hard against the nonproductive rage growing inside him, he struggled to maintain the upper hand. "You have a point." George stared at her, trying to understand what was happening. Whatever the explanation, the bullying approach, historically effective, would no longer work. He came at Laura from a new angle, allowing just an edge of desperation to creep into his voice. "Those tapes—I mean I understand how you must feel—but I can't see what you stand to gain by turning them over to the police."

"Nothing. Except that you stand to lose a lot."

In desperation, George invented a new scenario. He would gain sympathy from Laura. "Do you want so badly to destroy me?"

"Yes."

George shook his head. Vengeance was a new emotion for Laura, part of a whole new frightening picture of herself she was presenting to him. His sudden inability to control her infuriated him so much he momentarily dropped his self-discipline. "Goddamn it, Laura . . ." he yelled, and then, remembering, turned his head away as if humbled. "I'm sorry. The whole thing is so awful . . . it has me climbing the walls . . .you don't realize, Laura. . . ."

"Any wall you climb, George, is probably poked full of camera holes. Those pictures! That little boy, those awful men with the scissors and buttons. How long have you been doing those filthy things?"

Even to Laura, the word "filthy" had a painfully antique sound to it, a word her father would have—had, in fact—delighted in using. "Filthy!" he had roared. "They're filthy!" (although, as Laura remembered, in that case he was not talking about any immoral act, but of her unconscionable use of a public toilet at the New York World's Fair, a depravity that sprang not from choice but necessity). She tried to recover her stance by using her limited grasp of vernacular. "You're a creep, George. Sick."

George was aware there are times to advance and times to retreat, as any good salesman, business executive, or politician must know. "I know, I know. I've been to see a doctor," he lied, expanding on the subject as he went. "He's been doing a lot for me, changing me. If we could make some sort of a deal, if you could see your way clear to. . . ."

281

George left the sentence hanging in the darkening sky above the naked mantelpiece, staring into the fire, waiting for some sort of reaction. When it came, the reaction stunned him. Laura had not really changed after all.

"Yes, George. I'll make a deal with you."

Something leaped inside him; he fought not to appear overanxious.

"I won't turn the tapes over to the police *if*. *If* you'll swear to God," Laura paused, and then elaborated, trying to overcome the obvious uselessness of any oath given by George. "No, with you there isn't any oath that would mean anything. All right, then. *If* you'll acknowledge *in writing* all the terrible things you've been doing—the cameras, the motel, the perversions, that boy, the whole setup. A witnessed document. And *if* you'll commit yourself—in writing again—to go on seeing that psychiatrist—five days a week, every week—until he can face me and say that you're cured of whatever sickness is inside you. Then, George—and I'd be letting you off easy, I think—then I'll give you the package of tapes, and you can take them to the edge of that cliff over there—and jump."

For a second, there was dead silence. George successfully suppressed the automatic howl of rage that came barreling up from inside him. The changes in Laura—could he blame the earthquake for them?—were too profound to respond to lung power. With a faint smile, she was watching him, waiting for him to respond to her little sortie into sadistic humor. The sight of Laura's smile released inside George an anger deeper than any he had ever felt. His hand on the mantel brushed the stones of the wall behind it; then he caught sight of an identical stone that was lying half on, half off the mantelshelf. Without changing his position, he let his eyes study the loose stone. Then let them travel toward Laura.

Laura's smile disappeared abruptly.

For a long time Isaac Rosholman could not speak. Battock, lying on the ground a few paces in front of Rosholman and slightly to the left, had half risen. A few feet to one side of him lay Three Toes, his great head lying in a pool of his own blood, his one visible eye staring at Rosholman as if puzzled. Just below the head, from the throat down to the upper chest, the shotgun had torn a gaping hole; immediately following the shotgun charge, air had whistled from his torn trachea and esophagus, in a sad, bubbling sigh. Three Toes had struggled to get to his feet, then, with a final wheeze had collapsed.

More than Three Toes died. Rosholman, standing now with the shotgun under one arm, looked at his old friend and wondered how he had had the courage to shoot him. For he could sense that Three Toes *was* himself, the old, the unwanted, the persecuted, and that Battock had been the enemy, the anti-Semitic ghost of a Germany that had pursued him ever since the Night of Broken Glass in Munich. He had escaped into nature because man seemed so cruel; now he had discovered that nature was as cruel as the cruelest man. This great earthquake was cruel; Three Toes was cruel; Battock was cruel. Yet in the end Rosholman had chosen to shoot Three Toes rather than have the animal destroy his enemy.

Without a word, he helped Battock to his feet. Battock, for once, had the sense to stay quiet, torn between wanting to thank Rosholman and wanting to yell at him for not issuing the shotguns in the first place. His silence was not entirely an act of intelligence or perception, but one of necessity; his brush with death, the physical exertion of his escape, the image burned into his brain of Three Toes' huge weight hurtling straight at him had left Battock with neither composure nor breath enough to speak.

Rosholman stood eyeing him for a moment, waiting for Battock to recover. Then he turned and, reloading the shotgun before retucking it under his arm, walked slowly toward the admin building. "Come on," he called over his shoulder to Battock. "I think we should perhaps issue the shotguns now. Yes?"

For Isaac Rosholman, the long flight from the Nazis was over.

For Isaac Rosholman's niece, Beth Czemki, the battle was not yet over, but some of the agony, at least, had been removed. Only a few minutes after Matt had stormed out of the house, leaving Beth shattered and almost collapsing under the weight of her sense of guilt, the front door burst open. Beth leaped to her feet; it was someone with the children. But it was not. Matt stood frozen in the doorway for a moment, then rushed across the room to her, to take her in his arms and whisper softly, over and over again, "It's not your fault, Beth. Whatever's happened, it's not your fault."

And although Beth was still seared in her very soul to think of Gregory and Sarah somewhere out there alone—lost probably, terrified certainly—at least Matt had come back to make her whole again.

"Leave a note—a great big note tacked right on the front door—and tell them to stay here if they come back while we're out looking," commanded Matt and began riffling through the desk for a Magic Marker to write with. Beth opened a small drawer and withdrew the one she had to keep hiding from Gregory.

"It's red, but it's *big*." Burrowing deeper to find some scotch tape, she handed the Magic Marker's pointed plastic container to Matt.

"STAY.... HERE...UNTIL...WE...GET...BACK ...MOMMY AND DADDY." Matt read each word out loud as he lettered it, groaning loudly when he forgot the E in "GET" and had to start over. When it was finally finished, Beth stuck three pieces of the tape to the top of the note and pressed them tight against the outer side of the front door, then added two more pieces at the bottom and one at each side so that the wind could not tear it loose.

"Well," Matt said, "to miss that, they'd have to be trying." A thought crossed his mind, a thought that under the circumstances he suspected he shouldn't be having. "Of course, the note's also an open invitation to come in and loot the place, but I don't see what else we can do."

284

"Oh, Matt." Her face told him his suspicion had been right. "I'm just afraid that the kids will see the note, but go out again anyway." She paused on the path from the front door and looked at him. "Maybe you were right before. Maybe I *should* stay here."

Matt shook his head. "With that crowd out there, two of us can cover twice as much ground as one. Look, you take the right-hand side—clear out to the middle of the street—I'll take the left. Ask everybody. Maybe you can find somebody to keep a lookout for them near the house." He waved her to the right side and surveyed the crowd on the street before plunging across. Then he turned back, a funny look on his face. "If they're not out here somewhere, Beth, I don't know what we do next." And with a worried shake of his head, he dived into the sea of people and disappeared.

As Beth moved slowly down the street, pushing her way, being jostled and shoved in return by strangers and near acquaintances, all of them wearing the apologetic, forced smiles of shared danger recently survived, she spotted a neighbor she felt particularly close to.

If there was a wrong thing that could have been said, the neighbor managed to say it. "Oh, you poor child!" she exclaimed, and pressed Beth's arm in sympathy, shaking her head. The effect was too much for Beth, who burst into tears and found herself being hugged to the neighbor's ample self. "Gregory and Sarah," whispered the neighbor meaningfully to another woman, less well known to Beth, but who she thought lived farther down the street. Yes, said the woman, she knew Gregory and Sarah and would keep a lookout for them, but . . . and she too shook her head in compassion. Then, distracted by someone's pointing to a man on a nearby roof and using a power saw on a tree branch, the woman disappeared into the chattering mass of people, dragging Beth's neighbor with her.

Feeling incredibly alone and totally miserable, Beth started down the street again, peering over shoulders and hedges, calling out, questioning utter strangers as she searched through the crowd for her two shamefully abandoned children.

The note taped to the front door rustled in the wind but remained fast—bold, eloquent, and unread.

Dr. Michael Feiner stared at the printout that Ridgeway had handed him and reread the 600 XE's latest announcement for the third time. A cold knot of dread was writhing inside his stomach, his tongue would not move when he bade it speak, and he could feel a clammy tingle of sweat breaking out on his chest, on his back, and beneath his arms. With a pained expression, he raised his head and let his eyes bore into Ridgeway's. Ridgeway said nothing; he could guess the mixture of contrary emotions sweeping through Feiner.

Nick Rivers could not. Clapping Feiner on the shoulder, he beamed at him in relief. "See, Mike, sometimes when you take time to do the programming right, the computer comes through with *good* news instead of bad. There was nothing wrong with your predictive model, only the under-the-gun way we had to run the first aftershock readings through." For the first time, the programmer seemed to realize the about-face Feiner would be required to do in light of the third running of the program. "I'm sorry, Mike, if the first run put you out on a limb, but, well, goddamn, I, uh, warned everybody about those shortcuts." His statement wasn't exactly an "I told you so," but it came as close as was decently possible.

Dr. Ridgeway looked at Feiner, waiting for him to say something and finally, when it became obvious nothing was forthcoming, spoke for him, as you might for a child gone suddenly shy. "I'm sure, Nick," he told Rivers "that Mike—all of us, in fact—understand that the findings of the first aftershock prediction were accepted only over your objections. We'll make that a matter of record. You've done an absolutely remarkable job under extremely difficult conditions, and we can only thank God you were able to complete the second and third computer reruns so quickly."

The head programmer realized that he stood squarely in the middle of an agonizing moment between the two scientists. Distantly, Feiner nodded a faint agreement with Ridgeway's statement, but without ever looking directly at Rivers. The latter busied himself with a sheaf of papers, and after a series of inconclusive "wells" backed away and disappeared toward his console.

Only when he was gone did Feiner trust himself to speak. "I blew it." He waved the printout at Ridgeway and stared off into space. "My God, all those rescue teams held out of LA because I didn't have the good sense to wait. People dead, I suppose, because Michael Irving Feiner had too much pride to listen when he was told he was going off half-cocked." His eyes came back to Ridgeway's face, as if searching there for some answer to give himself.

Ridgeway provided it. "This is a whole new business we're involved in. So stop feeling sorry for yourself, Michael. And start feeling happy for the people in LA, who won't have to take a beating from the aftershocks." He paused, as if not sure this was the right moment for a lecture, then continued: "Science—any science—can sometimes start being an end in itself instead of just a highly sophisticated human tool. OK, so your prediction of severe aftershocks turned out to be a lemon. If you separate out scientific ego, what possible better news could there be? Good God, what better news! My advice is to swallow hard, then get onto the radiophone and talk to your Civil Defense contact in LA—immediately. I'll call Washington and get the rescue task force back on its way in."

Feiner slumped into his chair. Inside himself, he was troubled that his defeat at the hands of the computer had rankled when it should have produced exultation, if only because of what was promised for Los Angeles. He should have been happy to lose; instead, he was torn. Given the circumstances, Ridgeway's reproof had been gentle, probably too gentle. A long time ago he could remember wondering how other scientists and doctors—after spending years of their lives working dedicatedly but futilely on the problem—must have felt when Jonas Salk burst upon the scene with his answer to polio. Those men would not have been human had they not felt a twinge of disappointment and anger mixed in with their relief that a cure, even if not theirs, had finally been found. Feiner recalled the medical infighting and controversy that initially surrounded Salk's discovery; other men with other ideas had struggled to demean and discredit Salk's vaccine by declaring it unsafe. His reaction, then, was not atypical; advanced medicine could be just as competitive and vicious as big business, and Ridgeway's observation that science can sometimes become an end in itself was entirely justified. The logic of his soul-searching was impeccable. But the most flawless logic has never been famous as an antidote to conscience, and Feiner could not shake his sense of all-pervasive guilt.

Feiner folded the printout and placed it in the center of his desk. For a long time he stared at the phone that connected the lab to the Air Force radiophone at Tracey Field. Then, as if realizing that even the briefest delay in telling Kraypool of the new information could only compound his guilt, Dr. Michael Feiner yanked the receiver off its cradle and told the operator to connect him immediately with the OEP in Los Angeles.

Yes, priority. Priority Urgent.

As the party of survivors neared the tenth-floor level of the Park Plaza, Digit Vorhees was the first to recognize an unexpected complication. Like all of them, Digit had assumed the elevator was on the bottom level of the glass shaft. He remembered considering it an almost suspicious stroke of good luck that the elevator had been at the lobby floor when the earthquake hit, or, if it had been on a higher floor, that the elevator had fallen all the way to the bottom without jamming. As they climbed downward, however, it became clear that the fortunate positioning of the elevator at ground level was an optical illusion; looking straight down the glass shaft onto the elevator's ceiling allowed no perspective to judge the

288

elevator's true relationship to the ground. The farther down the glass shaft Digit went, the more obvious it became that the elevator cage was permanently stuck at approximately the seventh floor.

"Hold everything," Digit shouted up the shaft to Adam. "It's nothing to worry about. Just a little problem in logistics."

Adam's head appeared over the edge of the landing three flights above. "Can I help? I'm pretty good at logistics." Digit grinned and shook his head, pleased that Adam had picked up and was using his word, even though both of them knew it was an inappropriate one. "Okay," Adam called. "You're the man in charge. But if you need anything, just holler." The head withdrew.

For a moment, before turning back to the problem at hand, Digit basked in the glow of Adam's words. In a world peopled, up until now, with faceless adults—adults who either ignored, overruled, or treated him with solicitous contempt—Adam Mosely was the first grown-up Digit had ever respected. It was difficult for Digit to separate how much of this respect sprang from Adam's obvious respect for *him* and how much came from the fact that the man was so different from other adults. Oh, there'd been some teachers at prep school who pretended to respect him, but Digit had always detected a smugness lying just beneath the surface of their pose.

Certainly, as he had grown older, his mother, too, pretended to respect him, but she interminged her deference with reminders to be sure he changed his socks every day, warnings about eating the right kinds of food, and awkwardly phrased suggestions that he not get mixed up with "the wrong kind of people, especially now that you're living by yourself." And always, implicit in anything she said to Digit, was the unspoken hurt that he was no longer living with her, the unvoiced pleading to be loved, the silent demand that he pay attention to her. Digit's father, he barely bothered to count. Their mutual disesteem, even dislike for each other, was patent.

Once again studying the problem below him, Digit realized

the only way to attack the situation was to make the painful climb down the glass shaft's steel skeleton and examine the elevator at first hand. As he maneuvered himself onto the frame for the exhausting climb down, Digit tried to force out of his head one upsetting question. Adam had a son—he'd mentioned him sometime during one of their pauses—but the boy had barely been more than referred to in passing. This bothered Digit. The son had sounded as if he were close to Digit's own age, and to Digit, Adam's curious detachment toward his son was out of character. Possibly, Digit told himself, the son was no good. Perhaps he was a mainliner or had run away or, for other good, if unknown, reasons was hated by his father. But Digit could not push the question completely aside, and starting down the steel skeleton, he almost slipped twice because his mind insisted on returning to the matter.

Although it was not yet dark, the sun was now low enough so that its shadows were long. The steel framework of the shaft was becoming increasingly difficult to make out. The shaft itself was on the side of the building away from the sun, which made seeing even more difficult.

When Digit, in the increasing gloom, reached the elevator, one thing became immediately obvious; getting around the elevator was going to be a good deal easier than he had originally imagined. And while the thought of the glass cage suspended over their heads for the rest of the climb down was not a pleasant one, one corner of the elevator was well jammed into the side of the shaft. If it hadn't worked itself loose by now, the possibility of its doing so in the period they would be in the shaft beneath it was small. To make sure, though, Digit kicked the elevator several times and even jumped up and down on its roof; the cage didn't so much as tremble. Leaning as far out from the landing as he dared, Digit shouted up the shaft, pleased with himself how readily the name fell from his lips. "Adam! Hey, Adam!" Adam's head appeared once more. "No logistics problem after all," Digit assured him with a smile. "I'll be right back up and we can start down as soon as I catch my breath."

290

Adam shouted something, but the wind carried the words away. Digit nodded, pretending he had heard. What he had just realized was that he had examined only the elevator's roof and never gone down far enough to see inside. This, Digit decided, was something to be corrected; he wanted no surprises as his dwindling group of survivors climbed past the elevator's shattered glass shell.

He worked himself down the skeleton until he could grab the roof with both hands, then swung himself halfway in. The sight inside stunned him. Apparently, the elevator had had three occupants—two passengers and the operator—when the earthquake tore it loose from the cables and sent it plunging down the shaft. From their condition, the cage must have been almost at the Penthouse level when the cables snapped; the swaying of the building had probably caused the safety braking ratchets beneath the cage not to catch at first, allowing the elevator to plunge nearly twenty stories. And when the safety devices *had* caught, the process must have been both brutally efficient and murderously sudden; two of the three people inside had gone partway through the floor before snapping bones and compressed flesh had overcome their downward momentum and finally stopped them. All three were still upright, the operator and a middle-aged woman passenger rammed through the floor up to their waists and supported by it. But unlike the others, the third passenger—he appeared to be the woman's son—had not gone through the elevator floor; in fact, his feet didn't even touch it. He was suspended tall and upright, his body deeply impaled on one of the upright posts that had supported the rail running around the three outer walls of the elevator. His mouth was open and his eyes bulged out. Skewered by the upright post and with the floor torn away from beneath him, he looked like a frozen popsicle or a blood-red Good Humor.

Fighting dizziness, Digit struggled to support himself. The boy was not much younger than he was, and for an absurd moment he wondered if the teen-ager could be Adam's son.

To keep his mind off the picture of the elevator's interior

while he readied himself for the upward climb, Digit speculated what kind of person he might have been had he had a father like Adam. What would it feel like to be the son of someone whom you could trust (and be trusted by), someone you could talk to, explain yourself to, be guided and respected and loved by?

Digit Vorhees was halfway in and halfway out of the elevator, both hands reaching out for the landing to pull himself up, when he discovered the question was one to which he would never know the answer.

At Goldstone, Feiner might have experienced a momentary surge of scientific self-justification as the 600XE delivered its printout:

TREMOR SAF (34N-108 W) #1177 IS INDICATED AS AFTERSHOCK FROM TREMOR SAF (34N-108 W) #1176 [CODE VIOLET]. TIME REPORTED: 8:02 CENTRAL ZONE, CORRECT TO 7:02 FOR PACIFIC COAST TIME. MAGNITUDE 1.3 RICHTER. MAGNITUDE VARIANCE FROM PREDICTION OF AFTERSHOCK STRENGTH (PRINTOUT CZB 6007) RECONCILED BY CORRECTED INPUT AS OF 5:48 CENTRAL ZONE. PREDICTION OF SECOND AFTERSHOCK CANCELED AS OF SAME INPUT. RELIABILITY EXCELLENT. END.

Violet's aftershock had arrived virtually on schedule, but of such mildness as to be almost imperceptible; the accelerated programming, then, had affected only the predicted Richter reading. Feiner, however, was too busy trying to explain to Kraypool about the faulty prediction to more than glance at the printout; Kraypool was being understandably difficult.

And no words or explanations could ever have satisfied Digit Vorhees. While the aftershock was very small, the height of the Park Plaza amplified its effects enormously. As with all such tall buildings, the upper floors swayed back and forth far out of proportion to the movement of the ground. For a

second, Digit could hear a terrible crashing sound as additional fragments of the building fell down its hollow center. Instinctively, he began scrambling to pull himself completely out
of the elevator and up onto the landing. But the same safety
braking mechanism that had failed the elevator when the
building swayed before—back during Violet—now failed
again from the new movement.

From his position three floors above, Adam saw Digit grab
frantically at the landing a few feet above him and start
pulling himself up; then the elevator plummeted downward.
Adam heard no scream and later was to wonder if his mind
had not deliberately blocked one out. Unable to make any
sound himself, Adam watched helplessly as Digit Vorhees was
sliced cleanly in half by the roof of the plunging elevator.

The news over the transistor radio—the nearest station still
able to broadcast was KWWB in Palm Springs, but the station
was in radio contact with the LA police department and could
therefore issue fairly reliable bulletins, emergency orders,
and requests for calm—was so discouraging that Oskie
Davenport, standing off to one side in the living room, wanted
to throw the machine to the floor. Anxiously, he studied
Simon Pokress, afraid of how Pokress would react to being
told all roads out of LA were blocked by either ruptured
concrete or rock slides. Ever since he had found the bar,
Pokress had been drinking steadily. Even when Pokress was
sober, Oskie had been afraid of him; now, as he became visibly
and progressively drunker, Oskie found him terrifying. The
deterioration—and its implications—was not going unnoticed
by the others. The hostages, he could see, were becoming
more servile and silent, even the old Jap.

"What's the word on the roads, Oskie?" Pokress demanded
in his whisper, still resting the shotgun on the back of the chair
he was straddling. "It's time we got going."

For a moment, Oskie wasn't sure how to answer. If he lied
and told him the roads were almost clear, he would only have
to face Pokress with the facts later; if he told the truth, Pokress

was apt to shoot someone out of rage or frustration. Possibly, Oskie suspected, Pokress would even enjoy the excuse to indulge his meanness.

"I said, what did you hear, *boy?*"

The word stung Oskie, but Pokress was no one to challenge on the issue. "The station in Palm's gotten loused up or something. I don't get anything," Oskie lied, turning the selector dial slightly past KWWB and then turning up the volume.

Pokress hooked the shotgun under the crook of his arm and went over to the bar to refill his glass. From the couch where Mr. Yoshura lay came a sudden, soft voice.

"Could you bring my father back a glass of water?" asked Mishi. "He has lost much blood."

Pokress, his too-large head swinging back and forth on his slight frame, studied Mishi through his steel-rimmed glasses. "I'm no waiter. Come get it yourself, little girl." He leaned back against the bar casually, the shotgun aimed directly at her as Mishi rose to her feet uncertainly, rubbed the calf muscles of her right leg to get the circulation flowing again, and walked over toward the bar. "Not you, there," rasped Pokress, when Addie rose to his feet too.

Addie sank back down, his heart beating so loudly he wondered if Mr. Yoshura, stretched out on the couch behind him, could hear it. The earlier uncontrollable excitement that so shamed him had disappeared now, overwhelmed by fear of what a drunken Pokress might do with his shotgun if Mishi, suddenly that close to him, said anything slightly disrespectful.

With a low sweeping bow and a mirthless smirk, Pokress presented an empty glass to Mishi, indicating with a nod of his head the water pitcher on the bartop. "Oh, allow me, little girl," he breathed with mock unctuousness, and, keeping the shotgun crooked under his arm so that it was still aimed straight at her, solemnly filled the water glass in her hand.

For a second Addie held his breath. He could see the hesitation in Mishi's face, the almost imperceptible movement of her eyes from water pitcher to Pokress to shotgun, and could guess she was calculating her chance of being able to heave the water into his eyes and grab the weapon before he recovered.

Pokress could guess it, too. The thin smile widened and the shotgun came up as he calmly put the pitcher back on the bar. Clucking, he shook his head in reproach. "No way to treat a guest, little girl. Thoughts such as you were having only make a man nervous, you know?" The smile translated itself into a look of infinite sadness, an expression of having taken the measure of youth and found it wanting. For a tense moment, Pokress stood rooted to the floor.

But as Mishi turned to walk back toward her father, he suddenly reached forward and knocked the glass from her hand, simultaneously spinning Mishi around and pinning her to the bar with the sawed-off shotgun. With the gun pressed against her throat, he jammed it forward so hard that Mishi's head and body had to arch backward. She was able to support herself only by stretching her hands behind her and resting them on the Formica bartop. The sound of Addie getting to his feet made Pokress turn his head, but the gun remained pressed against Mishi's neck. "Sit down, pretty boy," Pokress said, in his soft, whispering voice. Addie sank back onto the floor, defeated and shamed, trying to separate how much of his defeat grew out of fear for Mishi and how much came from cowardice in himself. "You, too, old man," ordered Pokress, and Mr. Yoshura, suddenly half sitting up on the couch, lowered himself back down, his eyes staring at Pokress in an agony of disbelief. Pokress laughed, "Good. Everybody gets the message. Try anything, and it's good-bye, little girl."

"Hey, Pokress, Pokress, listen." It was Oskie, holding out the transistor radio, shaking it excitedly, trying anything he could think of to cool off Pokress before he got them deeper into trouble. "The radio. I think they're saying something now."

Pokress didn't even bother to look toward Oskie, his grotesquely large eyes riveted on Mishi. He gave his dry, rattling laugh. "Somehow, I doubt if they rebuilt the roads since you heard that station last time. Bug off, boy." Pokress wet his lips nervously, as if searching for saliva. Leaning farther forward—so far that Mishi, curved back over the bar by his gun, knocked the pitcher off the counter with one of her backward stretched arms—Pokress wet his lips again and reached around her for something. "But *you* don't want to say 'goodbye,' do you, little girl?" Although his voice never raised itself above a whisper, each word he spoke seemed shouted into her ear; Mishi shook her head, blinking hard at him. She tried to avoid looking at the hand which had reached around behind her; in it, Pokress now held a stainless steel paring knife, the kind used to slice razor-thin sections of lemon peel to float on a martini. The whisper never changed pitch. "No, you don't want to say 'good-bye,' you want to say 'hello.' A nice, big friendly 'hello.' "

Mute with fear, Mishi shook her head vigorously at Pokress, who seemed not even to notice the movement. She started as the bright knife flashed past her eyes and cut the shoulder strap holding up the top of her bathing suit. Instinctively, one of her supporting hands struggled to raise itself off the bartop to cover herself, but Pokress pressed the gun harder against her neck. Again, the knife passing by her face made Mishi blink; then she felt the other shoulder strap cut and the entire top slid slowly down her arched stomach onto the floor.

From somewhere, she saw Oskie's giant shape loom forward. He reached toward Pokress but carefully stopped short of touching him. "Pokress, Pokress," he whined. "You don' wanna do that. Listen, man, it's crazy-like, you know?"

Without turning his head, Pokress laughed. "You're jealous, Oskie. Nothing more. Go on back and take pretty boy." For an instant, he let his eyes leave Mishi to stare first at Addie, then at Oskie.

Oskie tried to laugh. "You been in prison too long, Pokress. Come on. Fuck the highways. We can make it overland. On foot. Okay?"

There was a small click, meaningless to Addie or Mishi, but

of great significance to Oskie. He backed away hurriedly, his eyes on the gun, suddenly aware that his crack about being in prison too long hadn't set well.

Addie at first found himself frozen into immobility. But the fear, he decided with relief, was fear not for himself, but for Mishi, because any effort to rush to Mishi's defense, terrible as her situation was, would only result in Pokress' pulling the trigger and killing her. Pokress knew that and was counting on Addie and her father's knowing it too. Twice, though, Addie had to stop Mr. Yoshura—who apparently could see the matter only as a choice of his own life against Mishi's —from rushing across the room. "No, please, no," Addie had whispered. "No matter what he does, you have to stay where you are. Anything is better than having him kill her." Mr. Yoshura gave Addie a glance that told him he wasn't entirely sure he agreed. To keep him occupied, Addie, in the lowest voice he could manage, outlined a plan he already knew wouldn't work. If nothing else, even an impractical plan that would never be executed might keep the old man from doing something desperate.

The paring knife glinted again in the late-afternoon sun. From the angle at which the gun kept her head, Mishi could not see what Pokress was doing, but she could feel the knife carefully slicing the fasteners one by one off the side of her bathing suit bottom. By now her skin was damp with fear and sticky so the suit did not immediately slip to the floor, but flapped slowly open; then she felt Pokress' free hand yank it down roughly and knew the suit was all the way off only when she felt the cloth land on her feet. From what sounded like a great distance, she heard a low moan from Pokress as his free hand began traveling—lightly at first, then more aggressively—across the front of her body.

Abruptly, the hand stopped, and Mishi heard him swear, grumbling in frustration that he had only one hand with which to operate. She saw his eyes spot something on the bar behind her, saw the hand take it, then saw him unscrew the

297

cap of her sun-cream tube by holding the cap between his teeth and turning the tube with his hand. The gun was removed from her neck, and bewildered, she watched him smearing the twin muzzles with the cream. A few seconds later, the gun disappeared and she felt an excruciating pain as the barrel was roughly thrust deep inside her, then withdrawn slightly, then thrust deep again, in, out, slowly and rhythmically, more or less in time with Pokress' rapidly accelerating breathing.

Mishi was not stupid. She knew any sound of pain from her would force either Addie or her father into some sort of action. With a desperate effort, she managed to control the scream that rose inside her, biting her lip so hard it bled. She found odd questions racing through her mind and concentrated on them to keep control of herself; her body was moving back and forth, not because she wanted it to, but because of the in-and-out movements of the shotgun. Would this be construed by Addie to mean she was somehow enjoying herself? The accelerating tempo of the shotgun's movements was keeping time with Pokress' breathing; was the logical conclusion of this, when he reached orgasm, the explosive firing of the gun inside her?

When the gun fired, would she feel anything before eternity overcame her? Was all this happening because she had lied about Addie and then made love with him? If some miracle happened and she escaped, would Addie ever be able to think of her as the same person again? Would her father? Would *she?*

Dimly, Mishi was aware that Pokress was fumbling at his belt buckle with his one free hand; his breath now came in gasps. The free hand suddenly reached under and up behind her, two fingers penetrating her cruelly and at the same time forcing her forward further onto the gun. She struggled to stay soundless, allowing only a short sharp intake of breath to escape her. But when the gun, which up until now had had both of its twin barrels inserted vertically, was suddenly twisted to the horizontal at the same time as the hand behind her thrust her deeper onto the gun, the pain became unbearable, and the scream inside her, so long suppressed, tore at the room around her, ripping open the silence, renting wide the self-imposed inaction of Addie and her father.

Mishi was never entirely sure what happened. She was aware that Pokress was so lost in his orgiastic fantasy that he did not respond quickly enough. Addie pulled Pokress' head back, and the shotgun was yanked out of Mishi as Pokress spun it toward Addie. Oskie was knocked backward by the butt thrust, but the roar of the gun that left Pokress with no face, not much of a head, and a wide, slimy-red cavity in his neck, made no sense, because the unfired shotgun was still in his suddenly limp hands when he staggered backward and collapsed. The last thing Mishi remembered before losing contact with reality was the sight of Addie spinning around in amazement to look at something behind him, his mouth open, his face slightly cut by a sudden shower of broken glass.

Silently, Mishi escaped the imponderable and slipped unconscious to the floor.

Chapter Twenty

If the individual tries to equate a natural disaster with punishment for moral transgressions, either personal or communal, he begins a path that leads to dangerous blind alleys.

—JOHN J. FRIED, *Life Along the San Andreas Fault*

BATTOCK'S first reaction when he and Rosholman entered the admin building was to swear, loudly and feelingly. The gun rack was empty. The heavy iron bar that kept the guns in place—with the locking device that had so frustrated him earlier—had somehow been neatly removed from the wall.

Battock shook his head in wonder, running his fingers over the empty hinges. "I don't know how, but one of the guards must have figured a way to get it off. Maybe Jerry. He's got a knack with stuff like that. But damned if I can figure how he did it. I tried myself and couldn't get anywhere." He made this last statement very softly; the confession was one he would not have made to Rosholman an hour earlier.

Rosholman knew better and shook his head. If one of the guards had taken the guns and issued them, they would have seen or heard the men on their way past the moats to the building. "No," Rosholman said. "The guards are gone. They probably tried the gun rack but, like you, got nowhere. And when they saw what was happening with the animals, they took off. Without guns, I can't blame them. The whole thing is my fault."

Battock did not disagree. "Okay, but who then? Who the hell could have gotten away with them?"

Rosholman shrugged and smiled faintly. "Perhaps the animals have armed themselves. Against *us*."

Ignoring him, Battock turned his head to an odd angle, as if listening. "Hold it. Hold it and listen: I swear to God I can hear people singing."

Rosholman listened. To his amazement, from the bottom of the hill, shrouded in a gathering darkness punctuated only by the flickering light of a small, distant fire, he could hear voices singing lustily in unison. The tune was familiar, but he could not place it, and besides, it made little difference; that people were singing at all was startling enough. A sudden burst of gunfire came in sharp contrast, but the song continued uninterrupted, as if the unseen singers around the fire were used to the sound.

"Perhaps," Rosholman said solemnly, "the animals have armed themselves *and* learned how to sing." An unamused Battock was straining to make out the words:

> Swift to its close
> Ebbs out life's little day;
> Earth's joys grow dim,
> It's glories fade away . . .

Down the hill, near the fire, the singers faltered when the next two gunshots followed very rapidly and too close by. But the pause was only momentary:

> Change and decay
> In all around I see

they continued, then fumbled badly, searching for the next set of words.

"Oh, you who changes not!" yelled a voice, giving them the next line loudly and clearly.

> Oh, you who changes not
> Abide with me.

301

The singers finished obediently.

"I need your presence!" shouted the voice again, prompting the group like the song leader at a camp meeting. The singers continued, the strong voices of the women sounding louder than the men's, possibly because of pitch, possibly because they threw themselves into the hymn singing with more enthusiasm.

The scene was a curious one. Father Reed stood in the center of a small circle of elderly people, waving his arms, shouting the words to each line before the group reached it, singing louder himself than any two of the people in the crowd. The singers had their arms locked behind them and swayed slightly as they sang, pale, aged ghosts of militants throwing themselves into "We Shall Overcome." In the center of the circle, a small fire, fueled by fallen branches from the nearby trees, blazed; additional fires were being built outside the perimeter of the group by Derek Usher.

To Derek could also be attributed the disappearance of the shotguns which had so mystified Rosholman and Battock. Shortly after the crudely performed last rites for their fellow passenger, Usher and Father Reed discovered that the "safest place in Los Angeles," as it had been glowingly described by Corbit, was anything but. The earlier arrivals, they later learned, seeing the helicopter come down again, had tried their best to reach the machine and tell its pilot that the area was filled with dangerous animals, but most of this survivor group from lower Wilshire were elderly and had not been able to get to the new spot where Corbit landed fast enough. By the time they did get there the chopper had taken off, leaving behind three additional survivors and a corpse. For a moment, the group had studied the new arrivals.

Because they found Father Reed in the middle of conducting a religious ceremony, they automatically made an authority figure out of him. They desperately needed a leader, and a priest would do as well as anyone else. These tired, elderly, and frightened souls, driven from their homes by earthquake and fire, flown here in a terrifying machine, and then set upon by wild and hostile animals, were drawn to him like a magnet. In their present circumstances, he combined the two things they need most: authority and blind faith.

Neither role came to Father Reed easily. But it was clear that unless something were done, these people, already on the verge of panic, would scatter and be picked off, one by one, by the marauding lions and leopards. The chewed remains —mauled, ugly, and partially eaten—of two of the group, were already grim evidence of this. Father Reed considered himself a gentle philosopher, not a leader of men, and felt faintly ridiculous shouting orders, yelling at stragglers, herding these people into some semblance of a compact circle; his quiet, beneficent nature was offended by having to order them to look for objects—sticks, clubs, stones, anything that would serve as a weapon—with which they could defend themselves. And the ridiculousness of his position, the sense of a world suddenly gone mad, was dramatized by an observation of Derek's: "The Christians in Rome, Father, I believe just prayed as the lions came into the circus."

In spite of an automatic bristling at Usher, Reed had to admit the parallel. The group assembled around the priest who was not quite a priest, the occasional growls from outside the circle as the lions drew closer in, the singing of hymns in the face of probably certain death, all combined to re-create in Reed's mind some misty, half-forgotten picture. Slowly, the picture took more definite shape: it was a drawing from a childhood book—one he thought his mother had given to him—*Lives of the Christian Saints and Martyrs.* Father Reed snorted. Derek Usher and his mother would have liked each other.

But annoyed as he might get at Usher's observations, Reed was forced to admit he kept delivering solid, workable ideas. The fire blazing in the center of the circle had been his suggestion; Usher thought he'd read somewhere that the animals would keep their distance longer if worried by their natural enemy, fire, and what Usher had read was right. The animals moved back several yards as soon as the flames were

303

going. Father Reed's only contribution had been to decide that as soon as he could, Usher should build fires *outside* the circle as well.

But by the time Reed got around to suggesting it, Derek was gone; Usher had seen the profile of the admin building on top of the hill and set off to look for help. To him, unlocking the shotguns was easy. Because of his lifelong fascination with electricity, he always carried a complete set of mini-sized insulated screwdrivers, drills, and bits in an inconspicuous leatherette case that hung from the back of his trouser belt, unnoticeable beneath his jacket. With these, unscrewing the hinges and drilling loose the dead bolts that held the iron lock bar in place was a simple matter. And when he returned to Father Reed, his arms weighted down with the weapons, the Jesuit stared at him for a long time before he dared speak.

"Derek," he said finally, clapping him on the shoulder, "you baffle me." As he spoke, Father Reed smiled, the smile as much a reaffirmation of his own faith in his fellowman as it was in appreciation of Derek. The strange look on Usher's face told Reed to lighten his statement a little; the man was embarrassed. "I mean"—the priest laughed—"you always baffled me, Derek. In fact, for a while I thought you were some kind of nut, if you really want to know. But what you've done here tonight—first, thinking of the fire, now this"—his hands indicated the pile of shotguns—"well, you've saved a lot of lives. No one can tell how many. I don't know what the civilian awards for heroism are. . . ."

Derek tore himself away from the priest and dumped the pile of guns on the ground, shoving one at Father Reed and keeping one for himself. The ammunition he placed on the ground near the weapons. "They're to kill animals with, not make speeches about," he snapped. "I'll take the outer perimeter myself; you can hand the rest out to anyone you think looks able to handle one. And cut out the hero crap. You know better than that."

Father Reed shrugged. Among his other peculiarities, the man, apparently, was acutely shy. Well, everyone had quirks.

Father Reed had forgotten, in his sudden warmth toward Derek, that these quirks of Derek's included an earlier confession to murdering his mother, a confession so convincing that, at the time, the priest had debated seriously whether to telephone a psychiatrist to help Derek or summon a policeman to arrest him.

Derek Usher had not forgotten. He might well become a hero—briefly. Pictures would be taken, articles written, a small footnote concerning him contemplated for the history of the great quake. But when the police searched the area of lower Wilshire and came upon his mother, the microwave oven, and the timer, his brief moment as a public hero would end. And he could see no way he could get back to hide the evidence before the search parties set out. The injustice of it was enough to make Derek want to cry. (Although, in his innermost self, Derek was forced to concede that the situation once again illustrated with what superb irony God meted out His punishments: the same earthquake that had created him a hero and proved him a man—therefore making the murder of his mother largely unnecessary—would simultaneously expose him to the world as a matricide, the most loathsome in the pecking order of psychotic crimes.)

From one side, the low growl of a lion warned Derek he was being stalked through the underbrush; instead of feeling fear, Usher was so mad at himself that he spun, and with great satisfaction killed the beast with the first blast of his 40-40 shotgun.

Mayor Manuel Ortiz had finally chased everyone out of his office. During the freeze on outside aid, precipitated by Goldstone's prediction of massive aftershocks, aides seemed to collect there, wanting to voice their indignation at both state and federal governments for their callousness. Their outrage was deeply shared by Ortiz, but he could see no point in dwelling on it, once the fury had been expressed. Initially, after the freeze was lifted, the aides and assistants all had been busy, communicating, coordinating, focusing the energies of

305

the various city departments on the overall plan provided by Kraypool. Now, with less to do—and more of the operation being directed from Kraypool's office—they had drifted back, huddling in the mayor's office to exchange reports from various districts and to vent their frustration.

Ortiz had no patience with them. There was a job to be done, and Kraypool seemed to be doing it well; to indulge at this point in the perennial infighting of the city's prerogatives vis-à-vis Sacramento or Washington was a luxury their beleaguered constituents could ill afford. Manuel Ortiz was famous for his ability to get along with just about anybody, for his even temper, for his sense of compromise, even in small things; with the exception of his earlier assault on Burt Aptner, no one could remember ever seeing him lose his temper. Ortiz prided himself on this quality, considering explosive Latin emotional displays as a part of the Chicano stereotype.

But today, under the combined pressure of Violet and Michael Irving Feiner's 600 XE, Ortiz exploded. With one wide sweep of his hand, he sent everything on his desk flying across his office. The astonished gathering of aides—a cross section of the minorities that formed his coalition: blacks, Irish Catholics, WASP liberals, and his own Mexican-American bloc—stared at him mutely as Ortiz went on to yank one of the yellow watered-silk draperies framing the window behind him off its valance and flourish the flowing material in front of him like a beleaguered matador facing the unpredictable whims of the *aficionados.*

"*Madre de dios!*" It was a rare use of expletive for him, rarer yet because it was in Spanish. Dramatically, he threw the torn heap of silk across his desk at them. "There it is, gentlemen. For all of you." The drapery was caught, more by accident than design, by his chief press secretary, Claude Lamont, who stared at it lying lumped in his hands, and tried to figure out what the cloth was supposed to mean. Lamont's face reflected his confusion. "Your crying towel," the mayor explained bitterly. "So you can all weep about your damaged prerogatives

306

while the city falls down around your ears." Ortiz spun around and faced his bodyguard, a burly, red-faced giant of a man. "Shawn, get these creeps out of here, keep everybody out, and stay out yourself."

The phlegmatic Shawn shrugged slightly, then raised his great arms and moved the stunned group backward. As the last of them was going through the door, the mayor spoke gently to the bodyguard, calling him back; Shawn was one of his favorites, one of the few he really trusted, a member of the original group of followers that had been drawn to Ortiz early in his climb and had stayed with him. "I'm sorry, Shawn," Ortiz said softly. "I didn't mean to include you in that outburst. But you must know how deeply I feel this thing."

"Indeed, I know, Manuel, indeed I know. It is a sad day for all of us, for the city, for the country. God himself must be weeping. But, Manuel. . . ." The Irishman hesitated; he had been with Ortiz through elections won and elections lost, through crises that had strengthened and crises that had almost destroyed, through despair and exultation, but he had never seen Ortiz look before as he did now. The fact worried him. Shawn suspected he knew the cause but wasn't sure he dared explore the area. Finally, the totally lost look in Ortiz's eyes forced him to gamble. "But, Manuel, no one, not one living breathing soul on God's green earth, can say you didn't do everything a man could do. The people who don't like you—the people who always hated you anyway—will bring out their sharpest knives and scream righteous screams about all the things you might have done before today—prevention programs, more rigid precautions, and the like—but they'll just be whistling into the wind, looking for a chink in your armor, making capital out of a great misfortune of nature. And surely, you're used to the likes of them by now. So all I'm saying—and it's a presumption for me to be saying anything, I know—is that you've got nothing to blame yourself for, Manuel, and that to start holding yourself responsible for anything that's happened today would be to presume upon God Himself."

307

Finished, the man shrugged again, embarrassed but relieved to have said what he had. Ortiz looked at Shawn for a long time, wanting to agree with him, wishing that the charges and accusations and finger pointing that were sure to follow the quake would be nothing more than political haymaking. Inside himself, the mayor knew better. "Thank you, Shawn. You're very kind. I appreciate it."

Awkwardly, Shawn backed out through the door. "I'll keep everybody out in the hall," he announced. "Your secretary's down in first aid—just a small cut over her eye, but it wanted looking after—so if you need anything—anything at all—I'm right there."

After he'd left, Ortiz stared into space. He wondered if people like Shawn would feel betrayed by him when the inevitable investigations turned up the facts—or if people like Shawn already knew about them anyway. Slumping into his chair, running his hand over the leather arms, touching it tenderly as if for the last time, he struggled to reconcile his conscience with his motives. He did not regret the deals that involved hiring practices because they had been right, philosophically and morally. But because of the deals, people today had died in improperly built buildings. And those people were just as dead as if he had taken money under the table instead of using the leverage the deals provided to ensure some vestige of racial equality.

And Shawn was right in principle, if not in fact. His enemies would not understand how a minority mayor could endanger the public safety to further his own people's cause. They would never understand because they did not want to understand and because, by not understanding, they had a powerful weapon with which to discredit him.

With a shake of his head, Ortiz tried to pull himself out of his depression; many things were still to be done. From somewhere he heard a distant sound, plaintive and piercing. At first, he thought it was a child crying, but as he listened, he suspected the sound was less human than animal. Ortiz tried to shake the crying out of his consciousness but was unable to.

As if propelled by some unrecognizable force, he moved out of his office and into his empty anteroom. There the crying was both louder and clearer. It seemed to be coming from behind the doorway to the fire stairs. For a second, he weighed opening the anteroom door and calling in Shawn, but then he realized that by removing him from guard duty outside the door, he would again subject his office to invasion by others. By pulling with all his strength, Ortiz was able to yank open the steel fire door, unused, if he remembered correctly, since the last fire drill almost a year ago. Grabbing a flashlight off his secretary's desk, he shone its pale yellow beam around the grimy metallic shaft of the stairwell. The place had never been clean, but the advent of Violet left it filled with rubble; plaster from not only the ceiling on this floor but from floors above had fallen down the open shaft and littered the metal treads and banisters; broken glass from the orblike ceiling lights was everywhere; a pipe someplace in the building had broken—early in Violet's shaking, before the water pressure disappeared for good—and a thin stream of water dripped mournfully down the stairs.

The crying came again, only this time sharper and more insistent, so that Ortiz's flashlight quickly located the source: a small dog—almost a puppy—was lying on the small shelf formed by the recessed window ledge, halfway between floors. Dimly, he recognized the animal; it belonged, he thought, to Addison Wade's young daughter, Pamela. (Animals were strictly forbidden in City Hall, but he remembered seeing the little girl earlier in the day, holding onto her father with one hand and onto the puppy with the other. He even remembered having smiled at the little girl and her father's embarrassed apology for breaking the rules and his own hearty laughter as he told Wade not to worry about it.) How the dog had become trapped there or why it had been abandoned were things he chose not to think about. The animal, terrified, wet, and dirty, tried to wag its tail at Ortiz, giving a strange little cry of hope at seeing man, its friend, coming to its rescue.

From outside the closed fire door behind him, Ortiz could hear voices: people looking for him. He should be there, not here, but suddenly, rescuing Pamela Wade's puppy had become the most important thing in Ortiz's life.

Ortiz could not have explained why. Neither could he have rationalized why he risked his life to climb precariously upon the railing, reaching far above him to pull the small wriggling animal to safety. Least of all, could he have found a reason for being so careless as to let one foot slip off the railing and send him plunging down the stairwell to the ground level five floors below.

"The sweetest revenge is forgiveness, for it robs the victim of his only real excuse to despise you." As always, the words had been delivered, with the twinkle, but in this case her father had barely bothered to conceal his basic cynicism.

To Laura Vorhees, watching George eyeing the rock on the mantel, her father's statement made sudden good sense. By clinging to her insistence on turning the tapes over to the district attorney, she was, for one thing, putting her life in jeopardy. For another, she would be delivering to George a beautifully constructed excuse to despise her, something that George would both relish and enjoy for the rest of his life. Frowning, Laura tried to think of her father; he had been dead so long his face, his appearance, his mannerisms all had vanished. Only his words remained.

Meanwhile, George was saying nothing, merely staring at the loose stone, occasionally turning to look at her, boring into her with his eyes and probably wondering if she knew what he was thinking. No further point would be served, Laura finally decided, by letting him wonder any longer.

"George," she said. "First of all, let me apologize for my cruel little joke—about jumping, I mean. Under the circumstances it was pretty unkind. But, you know, I've been thinking—about the tapes and you and sending you to jail. I suppose you ought to be punished for everything you've done over the years—not just to the strangers at your motel, but to all the other people I don't even know about. I suppose, too, that you should be taken out of circulation somehow and put away someplace where your sickness can't ever affect anyone else again. But, well, I don't know." A strange expression was growing on George's face, one of curiosity mixed with doubt and laced with a glimmer of hope.

Laura ignored the look and for the first time unclasped the package of tapes and placed it loosely on her lap. George stared at it, his eyes as fixed as a hypnotized snake's. "Because of these"—Laura waved the package at him—"because of these tapes, any or all of those things are within my discretion. Remember that." The eyes remained glued to the package as Laura leaned down from her chair, picked up a piece of broken glass, and neatly sawed through the heavy string with which the package was tied. "However personally satisfying it might be for me to send you to jail, though, I'm never sure imprisonment serves much useful purpose." Laura paused in her unwrapping and looked directly at George. "Did you know it was the early Quakers in Pennsylvania who invented the penitentiary? At that time, the idea was considered an almost immorally lenient treatment of criminals. Because up until then, a thief, for instance, would have had his hand cut off." Laura smiled at George. "Under that system, I'm not sure what they'd cut off you, George, but I could give them several suggestions."

Studying him, Laura was disappointed to see that George wasn't even pretending to be amused. His eyes were riveted on her hands as first the 3M box, then the two heavy reels of videotape were exposed.

"However, George, as I said, the penitentiary system is one tenet of the Quaker faith I've never particularly agreed with. So I'm left with no option except to forgive you. It's the one canon of the Quaker faith I *do* believe in."

Dramatically, Laura rose from her chair, took three long strides to the edge of the cliff, and, holding the end of each tape between her fingers, let the reels plummet down into the ocean, the whole length of the tapes unwinding and flapping like streamers at a bon voyage party. A second later Laura loosed the end of the tapes she held and watched them billow out. Laura turned to George, wearing a smile of almost treacly consistency. "I forgive you, George. The rest is up to God."

Blinking in disbelief, George walked toward the edge of the cliff and stared down into the water; there was no sign of the tapes, only the waves beating themselves futilely against the cliff base. He said nothing, but his face was a mask of suspicion; the most he had been hoping for from Laura was a complicated set of promises and commitments, some involved arrangement in which he was held permanent hostage by her possession of the tapes. He struggled to recover himself. "Well, Laura, I mean, I just don't quite know what to say. That is, I never expected—" His voice trailed away like the tapes in the wind, unable to think precisely what it was he had never expected.

"You never anticipated anything but the worst from anyone, George. I said I forgave you, and that's all there is to it." Laura watched George's face carefully; the thin, worried lines of suspicion were rapidly giving way to thicker, more blatant indications of disbelief. "I would hope you will continue seeing that psychiatrist you mentioned, of course, but I no longer have any way of forcing you to. I would also hope you'll never go back to being a sort of electronic Peeping Tom or any of the other disgusting activities you amused yourself with, but without the tapes, I can't assure myself of that either. I simply have to trust your sense of honor."

The terrible suspicion in George's mind could be contained no longer; the words escaped from his mouth as if they had lives of their own. "Those things you threw over the cliff. How do I know they really *were* the tapes? Maybe they were blanks. Maybe they were duplicates. They could have been anything. I have no way of knowing *what* they were." His doubts had been voiced accusingly, and George knew this wasn't wise under the circumstances. Quickly he held up both hands in a gesture of apology. On the verge of speaking, he was cut off by Laura.

"No, George. You have no way of knowing. And never will. That's why you'll have to trust me, trust in my forgiveness. The forgiveness is your punishment."

To George, who had never trusted anyone in his life and to whom "forgiveness" was a foreign word, the cold gray picture of his future appeared. Laura was right. Her forgiveness was punishment. He had to trust her, trust that the forgiveness was genuine, for if it wasn't and the real tapes—or more likely, duplicate tapes—were still available, the courts would do the punishing for her. At her whim. This added twist of the knife—setting the situation up so that he could never be certain, one way or the other—verged on the diabolic. He grudgingly conceded to himself her scheme was an exquisite torture, almost Chinese in its subtlety and of a kind never expected to originate with Laura. His thanks were not overly convincing. "I don't know what to say, Laura. Except thanks."

"Don't say anything, George. Just go. Back to what I trust will be an antiseptically pure Obispo. You may hear from me from time to time," she added with a smile of infinite sweetness, "and you can be sure I'll be hearing, not from, but about you. In fact, that's about the only thing you *can* be sure of."

George Vorhees, hesitated, wanting to protest violently but not daring to. The web of maddening uncertainty she had woven around him left him helpless. He had no choice but to smile bravely, doing his best to conceal his sense of total defeat, and begin walking slowly down the long road that led from her house.

For a moment, she watched him grow smaller as he walked away. Then, she smiled—this time genuinely. For the first time since she had married George some twenty years ago, she felt alive. Her father might not have been much of a parent, his constant aphorisms might have been a bore, but his pronouncement on revenge had been superbly accurate. Slowly, the realization of why her father would have chosen forgiveness as a way to punish George dawned on Laura; it was because he was so like George himself he could appre-

313

ciate how much the punishment would hurt. The corollary mystery of why she had replaced a disliked father by marrying a despicable George was too disquieting to consider, so she dismissed it.

With a deep sigh of contentment, Laura walked over to the fireplace and stirred the burning scrap lumber with a curtain rod. Beyond the fireplace, she could see the shimmering darkness of the sea, its surface empty of the usual reflections of shore lights. On either side, the coast was dark, the blackness broken only occasionally by the emergency floodlights of some rescue crew at work on the cliffs to the south. A pale fisherman's moon hung over the water, now and then hidden by racing ghost clouds, the night free of any sounds but the distant, infrequent blasts of Civil Defense sirens warning the residents of imminent danger. What, Laura wondered, was left to warn them about?

Slipping easily into the pervasively quiet mood of the night, Laura was surprised to find how calm and at peace she felt. She reached for the bottle of bourbon George had left behind and poured herself a stiff drink.

It was a moment to be celebrated.

Adam Mosely found his reaction to the death of Digit Vorhees upsetting; his feeling of loss because of a single casualty was, in light of all the others, philosophically indefensible. But while the death of Anna and Sporades Kristaboulos had jarred him and the fates of the hundreds of thousands of people in Los Angeles deeply concerned, grieved and horrified him, he could not relate to them personally.

Digit Vorhees, on the other hand, was someone with whom he had forged an inexplicable bond of affection, almost love; that his youth, his competence, his constant cheerfulness and intelligence could be so senselessly extinguished seemed a distillation and synthesis of the city's tragedy.

"What's going on down there?" Adam had been so wrapped up in his thoughts that the sudden voice from behind startled him. It was the psych major. She was standing beside Dorothy Grimes, urgently wanting to know what had happened, but unwilling, because of her feeling about heights, to come any closer than she already was to the elevator landing where Adam lay. "All that shaking and noise had to mean something," she added. Adam crawled back, stood up, and turned around to face her; the tie between the girl and Digit was, he suspected, not deep, but the explanation was going to be painful regardless.

"It's Digit," he explained. "There was an accident. That shaking—an aftershock, I guess—well, Digit is gone." Adam studied both of them carefully, wondering if he could get away with so inexplicit an explanation; they were far better spared the details. Neither the girl nor Dorothy said anything. They just stared back at him, apparently beyond reacting. The only movement Adam could see was Dorothy's reaching out to pat the girl's hand comfortingly, although the gesture seemed more automatic than felt.

For a long time, no one said anything, each reviewing this sudden, grim new situation. Finally, Dorothy spoke. "Adam, what I said earlier. About leaving me and going on down yourselves. I think we've reached the point where you have to accept that that is the only solution. This girl and you can't possibly handle the carry chair by yourselves; you'll have a tough enough time as it is without having to struggle with me. Use your head. It's the old 'eleven-people-in-the-ten-man-lifeboat' quandary. You know the question. Do you throw the feeble eleventh overboard to save the healthy ten or keep the eleventh on board and have the whole bunch die? Well, I'm the eleventh on this particular lifeboat, plenty feeble, and I don't see a damned thing to be gained, Adam, by you and this girl losing your lives trying to accomplish the impossible." Dorothy paused. "And you don't even have to go through the unpleasantness of throwing me overboard; just leave me where I am and make your own way down. To put your consciences at rest, I figure there's a more than even chance I still will be very much alive by the time you can get a rescue

315

team back up to me. No arguments, please. My mind's made up. This time for good."

Adam roared with laughter, causing Dorothy Grimes to look at him as if he might have cracked under the strain. "Very noble, Dorothy. But if you really believed your lifeboat analogy, by the same token we'd eliminate Social Security and welfare because the economy can't afford to support the marginal population, or let the Africans and Indians starve because there are already too many people in the world for the food supply to handle. I seem to remember your taking very firm stands on both those matters. And they didn't include throwing any sick and feeble overboard."

Dorothy Grimes snorted. "The analogy isn't meant to be perfect. Technology will eventually produce enough to take care of everybody, no matter what the world population is."

"And a steamship could always pop up on the horizon and save all eleven people on the lifeboat."

"Dammit, Adam. We're not talking about lifeboats or Africans or welfare. We're talking about you and me and"—like everyone else, she found it impossible to remember the girl's name—"and this poor, young girl here. Anyway, Adam, with that unfortunate young man gone, there's absolutely no way to handle me in the carry chair, and we might as well all face it."

The psych major looked at Dorothy Grimes and shook her head. "I have to agree with Mr. Mosely. Even in the lifeboat analogy, there's always the chance of something unexpected turning up to save everybody, not just the ten. For myself, I won't go without you."

"It's impossible."

The mention of Digit had started a series of wheels turning in Adam's head. A sudden recollection of Digit's pained expression when he returned to announce he had found the water fountain (but, no water) swam before Adam's eyes. Simultaneously, the architectural plans from the *Trib*'s long-ago exposé on the Park Plaza came briefly but graphically into focus. Triumphantly, he turned toward them. "No, it's not in the least impossible. That steamship just popped up on the horizon. Everybody into the lifeboats."

Whirling, he walked, almost ran, the short distance from the elevator landing to the inner platform.

About half an hour earlier, Georgia Mosely had awakened from her sleep in the garden shed, crawled out from under the tarp to stretch her muscles, and immediately began to pour more vodka into the jelly glass. She felt like hell. Her intention was to calm her nerves with the vodka and then slip back beneath the tarp until the enemy was safely past her house and advancing into inland California. But the day had been a bad one for Georgia Mosely, and apparently things weren't going to get any better. She had fallen asleep in bed and set the mattress on fire; she had been hauled from her blazing bed and dumped, none too gently, onto an outdoor chaise; the Japanese invasion forces had swarmed over Beverly Hills and forced her to hide in her own garden shed. Now, as she started to pour the vodka, the bottle slipped from her hands, dropped to the cement floor, and shattered. Her mouth open in stricken disbelief, she watched the precious, colorless fluid spread across the light-gray cement, darkening one patch with an irregularly shaped black stain, as eccentric and imponderable as an ink blot from a Rorschach.

For a long time, she stood there, helpless to move or think. Part of any alcoholic's deepest need is positive assurance of a continuing supply; the sheer terror of being caught without a reserve produces a panic a normal person has difficulty understanding and Georgia could feel remote ganglia in her body began to quiver in an insistent demand to be reassured, to be soothed—and to be resupplied.

Pressing her hands hard against a damp forehead, Georgia tried to think of how to accomplish this. The garden shed had nothing to offer; it had provided even a glass only grudgingly. She wondered if Harry kept anything in the garage, but besides the doubtfulness of this, getting there would involve crossing an open area. Looking down, she realized her hands

317

were beginning to shake, her lip to quiver, the small muscles in her face to tingle beneath her skin.

Georgia Mosely faced reality; she had a choice of staying where she was, safe from discovery by the invading forces and with some chance of slipping away unnoticed once they had passed—but without any way to replace her supply of vodka. Or she could leave her hiding place, cross the lawn between the garden shed and the main house—with all the dangers that implied—and slip into the back door. There, assuming the enemy wasn't in the house itself, she could gain access to the liquor supply closet off the pantry. For someone in Georgia's position, the decision was easy. Opening the garden shed door, she measured the distance between the shed and the house and sprinted across the lawn, her peignoir flapping around her as she ran.

Once in the deserted pantry, Georgia went directly to the liquor and found the vodka. With trembling hands, she poured herself a small fix to make the return trip possible. A single bottle, she decided, was not reassuring enough; two would be better. But since God alone knew how long she would have to stay hidden in the shed two bottles might not be enough either, Georgia pondered. What she really needed was at least half a case. But this raised the question of how to transport it to the shed; half a case—perhaps a whole case would be more sensible—was far too heavy for her to handle. Then she remembered seeing the gardener's carry cart—a high-sided, little plywood wagon with large bicyclelike wheels—parked outside the kitchen door. She'd watched Pepe use it once, and the carry cart had appeared both light and maneuverable. An entire case of vodka, along with any other provisions she might need, could easily be moved in it; moreover, when abandoned outside the garden shed, the gardener's wagon would arouse no curiosity.

Painfully she lugged a case of Smirnoff's—she'd been considering two cases, but this effort changed her mind—and put it into the cart. To this, she added a couple of packages of Triscuits, a six-pack of tonic, and a tall clean glass. One final item was brought along at the last moment. One never knew what those dreadful little Japs might do to a lady should they find her—she'd read of some pretty terrible things—and arming herself struck her as highly advisable.

While in the liquor supply closet, she'd seen the shotgun Adam had bought for Addie's birthday the year before, complete with an automatic skeet pull. Addie had never used either. The gun was stacked in the corner, while the ammunition lay piled on a shelf just behind the thin row of liqueurs—Kirsch, Drambuie, B&B, Cointreau, and Kahlúa. Georgia transferred the gun and the ammunition to the carry cart and began trundling her haul back toward the garden shed, marveling at how easily the little wagon glided across the smooth lawns. This time, to keep the exposed portion of her journey to a minimum, Georgia stayed very close to the house, slipping along the north wall, ducking her head and body to stay blow the sight lines of the windows, steering the cart carefully to avoid running into any outcroppings of the irregularly plotted foundation plantings. As she passed the living room, she could hear voices arguing. Addie was saying something she couldn't make out and was being answered by someone unknown to her; possibly, she conceded, her imagination was at work, but she also thought she heard words being spoken in what could have been Japanese. Because Addie was inside—and might be in trouble—Georgia let maternal instinct overcome prudence. Stepping over a pair of low spreading yews, she peered carefully in through the window. From her angle, all she could see clearly was Addie—he was still in his bathing suit—standing with his back toward her. A Japanese general lolled brazenly on her couch, occasionally passing his hand over his temples, either to smooth down his hair or because he had a headache. Dimly, over by the bar, she could see the Japanese girl Addie had been running around with leaning back provocatively against the bartop and talking to another Jap who seemed to be caressing her. She wouldn't swear to this; Georgia was aware her vision was a bit blurred.

319

A scream came from the room and she saw Addie start running toward the bar, followed by the Japanese general, who seemed to have difficulty walking. The other Jap in front of the bar was doing something very curious with a shotgun and appeared to be wrestling with Addie, while another Jap—very dark, almost black—was heading for Addie, too. Between them, they would probably kill him. Georgia could not allow this. She snatched the shotgun from the carry cart just as the blackish Jap was about to tackle Addie from behind, and fired blindly through the closed window.

Immediately, Georgia suffered a series of small shocks. The first was the roar of the shotgun. The sound, far louder than Georgia had expected, was followed by a cascading, almost musical tinkling as the window fell slowly out of its frame into the house. The second shock came from the recoil, a sudden painful blow against her right shoulder. The third shock lay in realizing how little she could make out of what happened in the room following the blast. For in the instant before the shotgun charge tore away his face, all Georgia Mosely could see was that the man at the bar struggling with Addie appeared to be white, not Japanese. Of course, she could not be positive about this because the image was blurred and had been only a very brief one; his face had dissolved so quickly into a mass of red pulp and there was so much blood everywhere that the man could just as easily have been black or green or yellow as white. The last impression she had of the room before she fell over backward was that everyone in it—Addie, the girl at the bar (who appeared to be wearing no clothes), the Japanese general, and the man with no face—all seemed to be staring straight at her in amazement.

With an ungraceful thud, Georgia landed on the lawn. The picture she retained of everyone staring at her rankled. Particularly in Addie's case. Had she done something wrong? Was he surprised? Reproachful? Furious? Where was his patriotism, his gratitude? Besides being unfair, his attitude made no sense, but in the last few years so little had that Georgia's life had become like one of those dreams you have when you're only half asleep, fleeting, incoherent, hard to pin down and even harder to make any sense of when you wake up. Her crazy sense of time again, she supposed. Shaking her head, Georgia struggled to reorient herself.

Suddenly, she felt hands beneath her arms and looked up to discover that the Japanese general was trying to help her to her feet. He was smiling, and in the dim, twilight memory that was all Georgia possessed, she realized that he wasn't a Japanese general at all, but an ordinary Oriental trying to be helpful. The war—Pearl Harbor—that was all a long time ago, wasn't it? A very long time ago. FDR dead. The atom bomb and Harry Truman. VJ-Day. Peace. Now was nineteen seventy-something.

Georgia shook her head again, and the Japanese man was dusting the mud and dirt from her peignoir and looking at her anxiously. "Are you all right, Mrs. Mosely?" he asked. "I am Mishi's father. Are you *sure* you're all right? We owe so much to you, such a debt for what you did. . . ."

Georgia allowed herself to be helped to her feet and blinked at the man, filled with sudden misery that she could so easily slip in and out of a world thirty years misplaced. Once on her feet, she staggered, and Mr. Yoshura's hands shot out to steady her, his eyes troubled by what he was just beginning to understand, but filled with warmth and an honest desire to be kind. "Is there anything I can do to help you?" he asked softly.

And without entirely being sure why, Georgia Mosely suddenly found herself crying.

It was such a sad question.

Chapter Twenty-one

N O one was crying at the lab in Goldstone, Colorado; they were too tired. Since their job was basically done, the hastily gathered programmers from Army Databank and the men borrowed from nearby corporations were now sitting around, waiting only for official word their mission was completed and that they could be released. Ridgeway had had the good sense to have several cases of beer sent in, and some of the men were talking among themselves, comparing professional notes, but most were gathered around a portable television set in one corner, watching the news coverage of Violet. What little there was came from an Army helicopter hovering over the city, its television camera manned by a network pool setup; another helicopter, this one private, was operating out of San Diego, its camera also part of the network pool. The scenes were awesome. In the fast-fading light, the camera picked up the collapsed network of highways and bridges; occasionally, one of the choppers would move in closer to show individual buildings in the city itself.

No estimate of dead and injured had yet been given, but property damage was easier to calculate: somewhere in the billions, one anchorman said. A rescue task force made up of Army and Navy choppers was on its way, another anchorman announced; at the same time, cargo aircraft were going to try to land at Lawford Field to evacuate the injured and bring in emergency supplies of sulfa, whole blood, plasma, and thousands of units of desperately needed typhoid vaccine.

With the announcement about the task force, Dr. Feiner turned away from the receiver and walked back toward the back of the lab; the subject of this task force—it could easily have gone in an hour earlier—was too painful to think about. He sat down at his desk, looking at his phone and wondering if he should call Rachel, but not sure he could even face *her*. From behind, a voice startled him.

"I thought you might like something," Ridgeway said, and put two paper cups and a bottle of cheap blend down on the desktop. "Not very good stuff, I'm afraid, but better than beer."

Right now the last thing Feiner wanted was a long, philosophical conversation with Ridgeway, who, in his mind, had somehow become identified with—almost responsible for—his own failure. Feiner realized this was ridiculous; today's fiasco was his own fault, no one else's, and, in fact, Ridgeway had done his utmost to save him from it. Pushing his chair back, Feiner nodded. "Right now," he noted, "raw turpentine would taste good."

For a moment they sipped in silence, neither of them unable to keep their eyes away from the television screen for very long. At the moment, the picture showed the San Fernando Valley, the houses and litter racing along the flow below the Van Norman Dams. In a closeup, the churning water and its tattered jetsam looked small and unimportant, as if the

323

picture were of stocked brook trout pouring through a water lock in the Adirondacks or a photograph of some badly polluted stream in Connecticut.

To get Feiner's attention from the set—and to help relieve the agony his eyes clearly showed—Dr. Ridgeway made a face as he pulled on the rough-tasting blend and spoke almost conversationally. "Well, Michael, what I'm going to say will probably sound heartless, but in spite of everything else, the predictability theory is now proved fact. And in the end, lives will be saved because of it. I know—you feel responsible for the errors in predicting the aftershocks, but the only intelligent way to handle that is to write it off to extraordinary conditions, to being forced to come up with all the answers too fast. Before you—before any of us—were ready."

"I'm not sure the people who died because the predictions held the task force out of the city would be quite so philosophical," Feiner said bitterly, "but thanks for trying to make me feel better. I can't absolve myself that easily; the fault is mine."

"New areas, new errors. Part of the learning process."

"If I were sure we'd learned the right lesson, I'd settle for that. But I still have problems—possibly it's a way of hiding from my own failure, I don't know—problems with the miscalling of those aftershocks. The first one arrived right on schedule; only the Richter mag was off. The second one—possibly, we shouldn't have dismissed it so easily. Hell, I don't know."

Ridgeway studied him. His own feeling was that Feiner was still trying to crawl out from under the aftershock predictions, possibly even without realizing it. Rationalizing. Finding excuses. This was so unlike Michael Feiner that Ridgeway found himself floundering; the only cure he could think of for a man in Feiner's state was hope for the future—a cliché even in geophysics. "Nobody does," said Ridgeway. "But I do know one thing, Michael; you have to find a way, now that the predictive theory has been proved, to advance the time frame. Not predictions that can only be measured in terms of hours or days, but in weeks."

"Agreed. But that's just a partial answer—a stopgap." Feiner was doodling on a small pad and spoke without looking up. "No amount of lead time will ever made any predictive system the real answer. Because people won't act on what they don't want to believe. Certainly, the predictive technique has to be perfected—but for another reason entirely."

"I'm afraid you lose me, Michael."

Disconsolately, Feiner crumpled the top sheet of paper and tossed it across the room. His eyes rose to meet Ridgeway's. "Prevention. Instead of just prediction, *prevention*. A couple of months ago I started talking to Earl Unger in Berkeley. He's working on the water-injection theory. I know it sounds like science fiction, but he postulates—more than that, he can prove—that massive water injections into a fault zone, over a period of time, can prevent the major tremor which would inevitably occur along the area's fault line. His verifying figures are extremely impressive—and with reason.

"We all know it's the sudden movement of the two sides of a fault that causes the major damage, the wrenching and tearing of the earth's crust as the two plates on either side of the fault try to catch up with each other's movement. Well, Unger would pump millions of gallons of water into the most vulnerable areas of the fault; this would trigger a series of small tremors, small movements between the sides of the fault, a string of minor earthquakes under controlled conditions rather than one big one like Violet. Result: no disaster. His plans will require a massive investment of federal money, of course, but after an event like today's, the investment will probably seem cheap."

Dr. Ridgeway, reasonably familiar with Unger's hypothesis, tried to keep any expression of skepticism out of his voice. "I've read about Unger's work, of course. But where would you fit in?"

"Outside of money, Unger's biggest problem is predicting

325

where, when, and how big his small, controlled tremors will be. People along the fault line have an understandable reluctance to being part of even a small artificially induced quake. The fact that the series of small, slow 'sliders' might eventually save them—or someone else—from a really mammoth tremor is an advantage hard to convince them of."

Ridgeway smiled. "I can see why. Particularly, if he thought the major quake might miss his house entirely and get somebody else's."

"The worst part is simple fear. The uncertainness of where and how big the small quakes will be. Once we get our predictive system's accuracy factor increased, I hope to be able to provide Unger with the means of overcoming that uncertainty."

Ridgeway poured himself another paper cupful and sipped at it, putting his feet up on the desk and leaning back in his chair. He had accomplished what he had set out to do—to get Feiner's mind off brooding about his own guilt and thinking, talking, growing enthusiastic about the future. "People's fear of the unknown is the strongest kind of fear there is," Ridgeway agreed. "And of course the idea of an induced quake—no matter how accurately pinpointed and even if predicted within limits that would please a brain surgeon—will panic people. Some highly localized damage will inevitably take place, and everybody in the affected area will want to know why the program was undertaken at all. It's like surgery: people are frequently more afraid of curative cutting than the malignancy itself."

"The predicting would have to be incredibly accurate. One slip, one minor error, and the program would be shot down forever. If the process is going to hurt, nobody wants to be the means of saving someone else's neck."

Ridgeway laughed. "I don't suppose it would do any good to point out that any major quake is in itself a means of avoiding a larger catastrophe. What I mean is, if the pressure along a fault weren't released through tremors—either one large one such as Violet or a series of smaller ones over a period of time—if those pressures along a fault line weren't relieved, the earth's crust would rupture completely. The planet would—well, explode. In other words, an earthquake is a natural means of preserving the planet's structural integrity."

It was Feiner's turn to laugh. "Not only would it do no good, I think they'd come and take you away in wet sheets. Right now, for instance, call Kraypool in LA and tell him that things may seem bad, but his town's just been the means of preserving the planet's structural integrity. His response should be colorful." With the mention of Los Angeles and Kraypool, Feiner's eyes traveled toward the television set. The only operative cameras were still those in the helicopters—more and more of them were appearing over the city as the networks geared themselves up—and the pictures on the screen now were a series of close-ups taken at Disneyland. The park itself had escaped serious damage, but a panic had overtaken the visitors, who had stampeded in a useless rush toward their immobilized cars in the parking lots. The camera's zoom lens suddenly brought into focus the auto-animated figure of Abraham Lincoln, the wax dummy knocked flat on its back, its mechanically driven mouth opening and closing in sync to a recording that kept repeating the Gettysburg Address over and over again.

The cameras then cut to another shot of the parking lots; enough space had now been cleared by two Army bulldozers—they simply shoved rows of cars off to one side in a heap—so that the Army choppers could begin landing to evacuate the injured.

Feiner sagged at the small table where he and Ridgeway were sitting. Ridgeway studied him, filled with sympathy. He let one hand reach out to touch Feiner's. "Don't let it get to you, Michael. You did what you thought was right; that's all any man can do."

Without even looking at him, Feiner stood up. "I'm going home." And he walked out the door, not even stopping to pick up his raincoat.

Ridgeway moved over to where the programmers were

327

finishing the last of the beer. He should, he knew, have brought out another case—some of them had come a considerable distance to help out—but Ridgeway couldn't bring himself to; any offer of more would seem too close to making it a celebration.

Feeling almost drugged by defeat, Beth Czemki struggled through the crowd and made her way back to her own front door; the makeshift paper sign, neatly lettered by Matt, was still forlornly taped to the door. Beth had been the length of the street in both directions—as well as up and down some of the smaller side streets—canvassing every neighbor she knew (and some she didn't), but no one could remember seeing either Gregory or Sarah. Other children Gregory and Sarah sometimes played with were equally unhelpful. Prodded by their mothers, they would try to answer Beth's questions, but they were too excited and too anxious to recite their own experiences with Violet to concern themselves for long with anything as prosaic as the whereabouts of a sometimes playmate.

As she walked up the steps, Beth's heart leaped; the front door was opening, and a woman she'd never seen before stood in the doorway. "Mrs. Czemki?" the woman asked. Beth could not make out what the woman was wearing, but it was all white, somehow official-looking, possibly the uniform of someone from a hospital—or worse. "I'm Mrs. Oliver," the woman began.

"Mommy! Mommy! Mommy!" Gregory and Sarah hurled themselves through the doorway at Beth, almost knocking her over. At first she found she couldn't speak and then realized it wouldn't have made any difference if she could; Gregory and Sarah both were talking at once, as fast as it is possible for a human mouth to open and close, the words all running together and not making too much sense, but having something to do with Gregory having got sick from the uncooked french fries and the nice lady trying to take him to the doctor, only the earthquake came and she brought them to her home instead and their stomachs were fine now and wasn't the earthquake exciting and where was Daddy and where had she been when they needed her anyway?

All Beth could do was shake her head, squeezing them both so hard that they yelped with delight. The tears ran down her face and she could barely see.

And later, after Gregory and Sarah had calmed down enough so that Beth could hear, Mrs. Oliver told her that she was an optometrist and had been waiting for the light to change so she could go home from her office when Sarah came running out of her house, crying and sobbing about Gregory dying from eating bad potatoes and thinking Mrs. Oliver must be a trained nurse because of her white coat. No one else was around, so Mrs. Oliver had gone in and discovered that Gregory was indeed sick—but definitely not dying—although she didn't think he ought to be left alone, sick like that, and because none of the neighbors seemed to be around, she'd bundled them into her car and driven them to her own home, which was about two blocks west of here, planning to keep calling Beth's house until someone there answered the phone and came to pick up the children. Then, of course, Violet hit, and after a while she knew the children's parents would be frantic, so she'd walked them back —uncooked french fries don't do much lasting damage—and she'd just left a note inside the house when Beth came home.

Beth was too relieved to ask why Mrs. Oliver hadn't left a note *before* she took the children with her, and anyway, the lady had just been being kind and trying to do the right thing.

While she and Mrs. Oliver were talking about the effects of the french fries on Gregory, Beth felt her own stomach do a sudden flop. "Are you all right?" asked Mrs. Oliver, wondering if the whole family might not be a little fragile.

The baby, thought Beth, my God, I'd forgotten all about the baby, and sat down in the nearest chair. Out in the hall, she heard Matt coming back and heard him attacked by Gregory and Sarah, the laughter and the shouting making the whole house shake happily.

"Oh, yes," she assured Mrs. Oliver. "Everything's fine, absolutely fine." And then, almost hysterically; "Oh, my God, everything's absolutely *great!*"

And without any word of explanation to Mrs. Oliver, Beth rushed into the hall and threw herself at Matt as hard as the children had, covering him with kisses and tears and laughter and making easily just as little sense as the children were.

> Oh you can't get to heaven
> On roller skates,
> For they won't let you roll
> Through them Pearly Gates. . . .

The caliber of the songs being performed near the Griffith Park Zoo had taken a decidedly upbeat, if less ecclesiastical, turn. In the center of the circle, the fire that had earlier burned for protection now blazed in celebration; beyond the perimeter, the other fires had been stoked with fallen branches to the point of becoming a hazard, and Father Reed, in between songs, had twice cautioned against adding any more fuel to them.

Standing slightly to one side of the circle's center, the priest was no longer leading the singing. Earlier, he had spotted an elderly man who was able to come up with the lyrics to the songs everybody knew but no one could quite remember the words for. With relief, the priest turned over the reins over to him and, after standing awhile and watching, settled himself down on the bare ground to think. These people had been remarkable, all things considered. Without complaint, old as many of them were, they had climbed off rooftops and window ledges, out of mind-boggling ruptures in the ground and from beneath collapsed and smoldering buildings, leaving behind them everything they valued and probably nearly everything they owned to climb up a fragile rope ladder into an unfamiliar and frightening machine: the chopper. Yet not one of them had panicked, then or later. But in spite of how proud he was of them, Father Reed was also mystified by them.

Disgorged from the helicopter, they had prayed—for the safety of others. Faced with circling wild animals, they had sung—hymns. An elderly woman, in accepting the loss of her husband, had requested not words of comfort for herself but last rites for her husband—in Latin. An unstable man who was convinced the Church was being taken over by Communists had prompted the priest in the forgotten litany, then vanished—to return laden down with guns so that Father Reed's curious flock could be protected from the rampaging animals.

Their reactions represented a challenge to the priest's carefully structured, highly pragmatic assessment of religion. Because the chain of events demonstrated that for some people at least—and in extraordinary circumstances—faith apparently could be an end in itself. Father Reed silently repeated "for some people" and "in extraordinary circumstances"; the phrases were necessary to battle a growing uncertainty inside him.

From the distance, quite far outside the perimeter, came another shotgun blast. Those two men from the zoo —Rosholman and Battock, wasn't it?—were still on protective patrol, shooting any of the animals they could track down, but staying close enough to make sure no wandering marauder attacked the group. The sound was reassuring to the priest because it helped reaffirm how truly extraordinary their circumstances were.

From behind him, a soft voice startled the priest. "I'm going now, Father," said Derek Usher. "But I wanted to thank you for all you've done and to beg forgiveness for trying to use your confessional as an alibi. You understand, of course, that I have to go before the police catch on to me."

Blinking, Father Reed stared with perplexity at Usher. Derek Usher's earlier insistence that he had murdered his mother and was being punished for it had become lost in the

331

frenzy of the chopper flight, the attacking animals, and the emergence of Usher as a minor hero. Thinking back, Father Reed put the pieces together again and decided Usher must be suffering a throwback to a childhood guilt of some sort; he found it remarkable that the man could be so rational about some things and so unstable about others. Violet, he decided, was shaking loose all sorts of complexes; Usher would have to be handled carefully.

"Well, Derek"—Father Reed laughed—"of course, if you feel you have to leave, that's your business. But I don't know what I'll do without you. Why don't you stick around for a bit, and when things get back to normal, we can sit down and talk the whole thing out? It's a lousy moment to be making major decisions."

"I've got to go *now*, Father." Derek's voice was so insistent, tinged with either desperation or fear, that Father Reed decided not to argue. Usher would doubtless calm down after he got over the normal guilt feelings of having escaped death in a disaster that killed many others; they would talk then, and perhaps he could help him.

Father Reed stood up and shook Derek's hand warmly. "OK, Derek. Good luck, and get in touch with me. Poor St. Bridget's is gone, but the diocese will always know how to reach me. Promise?"

Derek nodded, shaking his head as if to rid it of some lingering temptation to stay, and slowly walked through the perimeter of people. Outside, Father Reed saw him pause, then spin around and walk away until swallowed up by the darkness. A very curious man, the priest decided.

Derek Usher would have found the reason for his departure less supportable if he could have seen, on the far left side of the crowd, a frowzy-looking woman clad only in her bathrobe, standing with the last group of people Ken Corbit had evacuated to the area. Because of the animals, the group had been put down farther away from the fire. Derek—and possibly Father Reed—would have been fascinated by the lady's story; the woman was Derek Usher's

332

mother. She had, Mrs. Usher was telling anyone who would listen, been spared death because of a minor electrical failure. The way it happened was that she had been sitting in the tub listening to her favorite radio program when the electricity had suddenly gone off. Climbing out and going into the kitchen, she discovered her son—he was always messing around with electrical junk—had been playing with the microwave oven again and blown a fuse. While she was searching for another, Violet struck. The bathroom she had just left dropped right into the street, tub and all—could they believe it? If the fuse hadn't blown, well, she would have been in that gorge, along with the rest of the bathroom. And oh, yes, by any chance had anyone seen her son? About thirty-five, although he was really still a child. . . .

People listened for a while, but soon ignored her; stories of close brushes with death were too common to hold anybody's interest for long. Besides, the singing made conversation difficult.

I have seen him in the watchfires of a hundred circling
    camps,
He has builded me an altar in the evening dews and
    damps.
I can read His righteous sentence by the dim and
    flaring lamps,
His Truth goes marching on. . . .

Father Reed could not explain it, but he'd felt a slight shiver as the wavering voices hit the high notes; the man leading the group was well versed in his Julia Ward Howe, and the supply of lyrics appeared endless. Very soon, without his realizing it, the priest's voice was rising louder and stronger than anyone else's, a clear tenor that rolled across the gentle slopes of Griffith Park and soared upward into a sky alive with a million stars.

The last leg of the descent from the Park Plaza was so easy it

333

came almost as an anticlimax. Adam Mosely, piecing together his recollection of the building plans, went inside and discovered that all that now lay between them and street level was seven flights of fire stairs. Although relieved for Dorothy Grimes, Adam was furious with himself. His original scheme of using the fire stairs had been abandoned back when they were at the Penthouse level and found the stairs totally blocked with debris. But they had been far below that level for a long time now, and he had never once thought to check the stairs again. Like most modern buildings, the Park Plaza grew progressively larger as it got closer to the ground, and the fire stairs, attached to the outer shell, necessarily began over again with each succeeding enlargement. Looking at the stairs, here on the seventh floor, he could see they were clear both up and down. Stupid, stupid, stupid, he muttered. The long, killing climb down the glass elevator shaft had been unnecessary. So, therefore, had been the death of Sporades Kristaboulos--and certainly Digit's. (Anna Kristaboulos had died at the top level where the fire stairs *were* blocked, so he could not reproach himself for what happened to her, at least.)

Summoning up his strength to return to the landing and tell Dorothy Grimes and the psych major the good news, Adam was unable to stop torturing himself for his role in the loss of Digit. He had killed him. Not through malice, not through cowardice, but through blindness and inaction. Possibly, he thought, the same combination of blindness and inaction was what had destroyed Georgia and would eventually demolish Addie. Painful as the admission was, Adam could see how right Dorothy Grimes had been. He had run from them. "Copped out" was the way either Digit or Addie might have put it. With a small shiver, Adam left the hallway and went back to Dorothy Grimes and the girl.

In all, the final seven flights took slightly less than fifteen minutes. And the only reason they took that long was that Adam and the psych major had to carry Dorothy down six of them. For the last flight, though, Dorothy brushed them both aside.

"I'll make the final one under my own steam, thank you. Nobody's going to see me carried anywhere, unless it's into the family crypt." And wrapping the torn and smudged remains of her long gown around her, clutching the dusty iron railing of the fire stairs for support, Dorothy Grimes painfully made her way down. In spite of what the wind, the dirt, and the climb had done to her face and clothes, she managed to appear elegant—a determined, regal figure emerging from the ruins of a hotel with the poor taste to collapse beneath her.

In the Park Plaza's parking oval, they were stunned to find not only Dorothy's Bentley, but her driver, still standing loyally by for her to come back out of the building. For a second, Dorothy was touched. But after looking around, she wondered if the driver's loyalty might not have been more to the car than to her. Even had he wanted to, the driver could not have moved the Bentley more than ten feet in either direction. Both the oval and the city streets beyond were blocked by ruptured concrete and impassable piles of fallen rubble.

If the Bentley couldn't go anywhere, the car at least provided a clean, comfortable place for Dorothy Grimes to sit down. And the bar, built into the back of the driver's seat, was still stocked with the rarest item in town: clean water. "Not a bad year," quipped Dorothy, settling comfortably back into the seat cushions. In her familiar surroundings, the ivory cigarette holder held at high port, a lap robe around her knees against the chill night air, she made it difficult to believe that an entire city had fallen down around her.

Adam, after slumping into the dark comfort of the car, took a deep breath and put his hand on the muted chromium brilliance of the door handle. His decision was made. "I'm going now, Dorothy. Between the driver and"—he looked at the psych major and, like everyone else, found her name impossible to remember—"this girl to look after you, you'll be fine. Other people will be along, and, if worse comes to worst, you can always curl up right where you are and get some sleep."

"What do you mean, Adam, 'You're *going*'? Going where? And how?"

"Beverly Hills. To see what's happened and do what I can—for Georgia and Addie."

"With the roads blocked? My God, Adam, only a tank or a bulldozer could make it."

"On foot."

"On foot, Beverly Hills is a long, long way. Miles."

"For me, Beverly Hills will be a long way no matter how I get there. But Beverly Hills is where I'm going."

A glimpse of panic crossed Dorothy Grimes' face. "The paper, Adam. The paper. There'll be a million things to do starting it up again." She studied his face and watched, with growing uneasiness, as he slowly shook his head. Finally: "What I said up there. The paper. The whole thing is yours. With no strings. I meant every word I said."

"I know you did. But you also meant what you said about my running away, my hiding from what I owe Georgia and Addie. And you were right." Adam reached over and squeezed her hand, then leaned forward and gave her a schoolboy's kiss. "You'll be fine, Dorothy. So will the paper." He started out the door but found Dorothy pulling on his arm.

"I'll put it all in writing, Adam. As soon as things get back to some semblance of normal, I'll call in the lawyers and—" Her voice trailed off; the expression on Adam's face told her what she was trying was useless. In a small gesture of defeat, she threw up her hands and smiled.

"Thank you, Dorothy. For a moment, I was afraid you were going to plead, and that wouldn't become you."

Dorothy Grimes loosed her throatiest laugh. "For a moment I was afraid you were going to give in, Adam. But you're back to being yourself—the old Adam, the Adam I first knew, the Adam who didn't give a damn about anything except doing what was right. Welcome home." She took both his hands in hers and squeezed so hard it almost hurt. "Good luck," she said, and waved him away. Through the door

336

window, she watched as he turned and began threading his way across the littered pavement, waking slowly and carefully and permanently out of her life.

Traveling in the opposite direction, but also on foot, Oskie Davenport was stumbling and falling as he fought his way through the underbrush of Beverly Hills. No one inside the house had even tried to stop his escape. Perhaps they already knew what, down inside him, Oskie was coming to realize: that real escape was impossible. He would be running for the rest of his life—at least, until he was caught. The police would check their records to find who was in the sheriff's car with Simon Pokress, and the terrible things done at the house would be blamed on him, Oskie, because Pokress was dead and he was not.

For no good reason, Oskie was heading toward Watts. Of all the places he could have chosen, Watts was the least logical because Watts was the first place the police would check and Oskie knew it. But he had to find Gilla. Gilla would know what to do. Gilla always knew what to do. Perhaps they could run away someplace together. She was good at figuring things like that out. He came to the top of a small hill and looked down on the city; so much of it was burning that old landmarks were hard to find. Finally, he spotted what he thought was the dim outline of Watts and began scrambling down through the scrub growth toward the perimeter of the city and Gilla.

Gilla was in no position to help anybody. Half an hour earlier she had been scurrying through the crowd on James Street (wrapped, in spite of the heat, in the new black coat with the little fur collar) when she'd felt a small, sharp pain in the left side of her back. So many people were rushing up and down the street, some carrying things they'd salvaged from their homes, others with items looted from nearby stores, that Gilla at first thought the sharp ache came from an accidental collision with one of these objects. But the pain was insistent and grew suddenly overwhelming, and, as Gilla tried to spin her body to see what was causing it, she realized she had been stabbed. The sharp thing stuck in her back was holding her, skewering her, and now began to move up and down inside her. Gilla screamed, but no one paid any attention.

Only when she fell—forward at first, then turning in midair as the knife was withdrawn—could she see whoever it had been behind her. Lying on the pavement, through the suddenly blood-red filter of her vision, Gilla looked up into the grinning, satisifed face of Coverdale Kelly. No phony witness would be in court to frame *him* for the knife job at Lefrak's Soul Palace.

Old scores have a way of being settled in Watts. The methods are brutal, but rarely has anyone been known to complain.

Laura Vorhees sat huddled in front of her wall-less fireplace, drawing something in pencil on a scrap of paper she'd found. To support the paper, she used the empty 3M carton that had contained the reels of videotape. The drawings were only rough plans, of course, but they were something she could use as a talking point when discussing her new house with the architect. Squinting, Laura held the paper up to the light from the fire and studied the sketch. Much better than the old house, she told herself. More glass, more room, even a separate guest cottage for Digit. Perhaps that would lure him back.

After another glance at the drawing, she put it down on the 3M carton to make some changes. This time, she decided, the house should be considerably farther back from the cliff; you couldn't always expect the exterminator to show up when you needed him. With a final, satisfied sigh, Laura opened the empty carton to slip the paper inside and pulled the blanket tighter around her against the night chill. Her eyelids fluttered slowly downward.

Immediately, they flew open again. Her feeling of contentment was both unreasonable and baffling. Only a few hours earlier she had been concentrating on suicide; now she

338

was sketching plans for a new house. Nothing had changed, yet everything had changed. Laura struggled, trying to pin down what had made such a difference in her outlook.

Somehow, escaping the earthquake had allowed her to escape from George, and in escaping George, she had escaped from her father, and in escaping from her father, she had completely escaped from her past. The catharsis was massive.

Still, Laura had a streak of realist in her and knew that she could never really be happy. What the day's events *had* provided her was a way to start over, a point from which she could begin again.

Some place, like her new house, a few feet farther back from the precipice.

Preceded only by a curt radioed message from Washington—received in LA a scant four minutes before the event occurred—a giant, gleaming United States Air Force helicopter descended from the sky and landed gently on Henry Kraypool's roof. From the plane, almost before the blades had stopped rotating, climbed a brisk, efficient-looking team of men. Two of them immediately sought out Kraypool. The first was Albert Black, Kraypool's superior at the OES (and its regional director), who had flown from his headquarters in San Francisco to Bakersfield by jet, then the rest of the way by chopper. Black took very little time making it clear to Kraypool that as of now he was personally taking charge.

With him was an Army major general who spoke in a highly private language. Pacing the floor of Kraypool's office, he kept shaking his head disapprovingly at the wall maps, glancing derisively at the situation reports, and making urgent pronouncements about "minimum sustenance put-through," "communications integrity," and "echelon mobility shortfall." Woven in among these phrases—about three times to the sentence, Kraypool estimated—was the word "Washington," spoken in a tone somewhere between reverence and awe.

In short, along with the helicopter, the full weight of federal bureaucracy had landed on Kraypool's roof.

Both the new arrivals appeared shocked at Kraypool's inability to provide them with any clear picture of the overall situation. Kraypool had explained the difficulties, adding that he had been getting at least a partial perspective from the pilot of a traffic chopper, but that radio contact had been lost and the man must be presumed to have crashed.

"I'll handle that in a hurry," said the general; he picked up the radiophone, barked some unintelligible orders to persons unknown, and then looked up, addressing himself to Black: "We'll have a complete AirRec SitRep in less than half an hour."

Asked by Black if he could yet give any estimate of the dead and injured, Kraypool could only reply that he had no way of knowing. Besides, he added, it was far too early; people, both the dead and the living, would continue to be discovered for days. At that, Black and the general went into a huddle.

Nothing official had been said, of course, but Kraypool was already feeling both unneeded and unwanted. And a little later, when he surrendered his office to them, moving into a smaller one down the hall, neither Black nor the major general even seemed to notice. If he had had a way of getting there, Kraypool would have gone home.

He doubted if the two of them would have noticed that either.

Kraypool had been wrong: Corbit was not dead. Once he'd turned his radio receiver off, he'd never bothered to turn it back on. And as soon as he had seen the Air Force choppers of the task force dotting the sky, he had followed them to their marshaling point at Lawford Field. His rescue mission on lower Wilshire he considered over; he now planned to volunteer himself and his helicopter for duty with his old branch of service.

It came as something of a shock to discover, in talking to the pilots—some of them barely old enough, Corbit thought, to drive a car—that a flier from the Vietnam War was thought of as a figure from the past, an "old-timer," much in the same

340

way Corbit himself had once thought of pilots from the Korean era. He was treated respectfully, but condescendingly. When he presented his credentials and explained that he knew the city well because he flew over it twice a day in a traffic chopper, the young lions stared at him as if he were an aging racing driver who'd taken to driving a taxi. And when he volunteered himself and his chopper for service, they rejected him—but commandeered his plane.

About the only thing these breathlessly young men seemed to have in common with pilots Corbit had known during the war was a hastily erected tent that soon sported a thriving bar.

If Kraypool had been wrong in assuming Corbit's demise, he had been right in suggesting that people, both dead and alive, would continue to be discovered for days to come. Georgi, for instance, was not found for a full seventy-two hours, still trapped in his meat locker. At that, he could count himself lucky. When he had seen his lamb-fat fires smoking heavily and then going out, he had checked the inside controls of the air vent and finding them closed, had opened them. Fortunately the water level in the cellar had receded sufficiently by then to let in air, not water. Still, the door was tightly jammed, and Georgi could hear no sound from beyond it. In spite of this, he pounded regularly on the door, positive that one of his sons—where they had gone was a question to which he had no answer—would come back and rescue him.

This regular banging on the door was what saved him. After three days, a patrolling crew from the fire department heard it while routinely scouring the ruins of the building in search of bodies. With an acetylene torch, they cut through the door and hauled him out. To them, Georgi presented a spectacular sight. He was wrapped in a foul-smelling lambskin, recently stripped from the body of a partially thawed ewe, his eyes reddened to incandescence by the smoke of his fire, unshaved, and incredibly drunk.

Georgi's half-glassed over, swollen eyes held little curiosity

341

about his rescuers; he blinked uncertainly at them for a moment before making his only recorded statement. "More ice for table twelve," he commanded, and then passed out. He was the sole survivor of the wedding party.

Addie sat by the edge of the wrecked pool. He was fully dressed now and had come out here after Mishi and her father had left. To help him see, Addie lit a pair of the kerosene-filled Hawaiian torches that outlined the terrace. The effect created by the tall, blazing flames was eerie and unreal, yet Addie was unable to stay away from the pool—an old friend, a fellow conspirator, something that he could share his misery with.

Mishi's leave-taking had been hectic and shattering, filled with the officiousness of grown-ups and leaving the two of them with no chance to exchange anything but the briefest of conversations. The doctor—Addie had run farther up Tutweiler, found old Dr. Wilson, and practically dragged the doctor back with him—had pronounced Mishi physically unharmed, but understandably exhausted, shaken, and terribly upset. He advised strong sedation and ordered Mishi put to bed immediately, here in the Mosely house, without any attempt being made to take her home.

Listening to her fate being decided, Mishi lay stretched out on the couch—the same couch where Mr. Yoshura had lain an hour earlier—and tossed restlessly. Addie was crouched beside her, holding her hand beneath the blanket covering her. When the doctor gave his opinion, Addie squeezed the hand lightly; the doctor's instructions would give them a chance to talk, to try to put their shattered world back together.

But on hearing the doctor's pronouncement, Mr. Yoshura became intractable. With all due deference to the doctor, he said, he would go to his home—he only lived up the road, he pointed out—and come back with the houseboy; between them, they would carry Mishi back. Then, as the doctor suggested, strong sedation.

Dr. W..son was an old man, weary and semiretired, and to him, nothing in this house had ever quite made sense. But Mr. Yoshura was now endangering his patient, and that was something the doctor still responded to. Quietly but firmly, he insisted that Mishi stay where she was. And the more he insisted, the more intransigent Mr. Yoshura became, politely reminding the doctor that Mishi, after all, was his daughter and finally leaving to go get the houseboy.

Meanwhile, Mrs. Mosely's brief spell of lucidity had vanished beneath an additional wave of vodka, and she was upstairs in a small, rarely used guest room, complaining bitterly because no one else in the house believed in Peter Pan. From somewhere, she had dragged out her childhood dolls and lined them up on the narrow daybed, lecturing them, between crying spells, on the difficulties of being ten years old in Wichita, Kansas.

The few moments when the doctor went to tend her were the only ones Mishi and Addie had in which they were really able to talk. At the beginning, Addie was all reassurance. "Don't worry, Mishi, even if your father does make you go home. He's worried and upset. I'll come see you first thing in the morning—or, anyway, whenever the knockout pills wear off—and we'll just sit and talk and laugh about everything." A shadow crossed his face as he added, "Well, *almost* everything."

Addie was startled when Mishi shook her head firmly and turned away to avoid his eyes. "You don't understand, do you? You don't understand."

"What happened—that man, Mishi—it doesn't change a thing. Honest."

"Oh, my Addie, but it does, indeed, it does. That's what I mean you don't understand." She fumbled with the blanket, withdrawing her hand from Addie's, still keeping her eyes turned away. "You don't understand that for us, there will be no tomorrow. It is all over. Completely and terribly over. The wish is not mine, but merely the way things must be. You don't understand—how could you?—how different things are in

Japan. My father knows now that I lied to him about you. That was bad enough; at home, for a girl to lie to her father in such a matter means only one thing. We would have difficulty seeing each other again just because of that. But then, there is what happened with that awful man. My father—his self-esteem—his sense of family—even his feeling for me—all those things are changed because of that. He will probably ask to be sent some other place immediately, and the Foreign Office, when they hear why, will agree with him completely. Even at that his career is probably over. The whispers. . . ."

Mishi moved her head and finally looked directly at Addie; she searched his eyes for understanding and could find only confusion. "I love you, my Addie. Indeed, I love you. But everything is different now. Even with *me*, it is different." For a second she let her hand touch his face, then quickly withdrew it as if the hand were contaminated. "Please don't hate me." She raised her head slightly, hearing Dr. Wilson just outside the room. Quickly, she spoke. "Addie, tell me now you understand."

But Addie could not because he did not. Mishi left a few minutes later.

Sitting by the pool, staring at the inky water and the grotesque reflections of the flickering Hawaiian torches, Addie struggled to put the pieces together. He and Mishi, he supposed, had been living in a dreamworld, an enchanted one, but illusory, like children playing grown-up. At fifteen, what had he really expected? That he and Mishi would hang forever suspended in time? Even if nothing had happened, when the summer was over and they both had to go back to school, wouldn't their dreamworld have dissolved anyway?

Wearily, Addie lay down on his stomach, reached over, and pulled the white rubber birthday swan, floating forlornly in the shallow water, out of the pool. For no reason, he let the air out of the valve and watched as the swan deflated and collapsed onto the coping.

"And the Lord told me, 'Thee must kill the white whale, Ahab!' " roared Gregory Peck, and Mishi had laughed, and so

344

had he, Captain Addie, punching the swan as it bobbed along on top of the sun-dappled, sparkling water of the pool.

But that had been another day that summer, some much earlier time, a time before Violet.

At precisely four minutes after three that morning, the teleprinter at the Western Seismological Institute, Goldstone, Colorado, began to chatter, flashing its small blue light to indicate the 600 XE had something of importance to predict.

What the 600 had to say was awesome. The cancellation of the second aftershock warning should be ignored, it stated, and the shock expected as originally predicted, at approximately 4 A.M., Los Angeles time. The magnitude was estimated at from 7 to 9 on the Richter Scale.

No one was in the lab when the computer spoke; the last of the programmers, scientists, and newsmen had left around midnight, exhausted. And because no one was there to read the printout, no one was there to evaluate whether this new prediction—or rather, this return to an earlier one—was based on yet more faulty programming or was the result of additional new input. (As always, information was being fed to the computer in Goldstone automatically from all stations of the World-Wide Standardized Seismologic Network.)

Dr. Michael Feiner had already stated he felt the original predictions of the aftershocks were being dismissed too lightly, but Dr. Ridgeway had considered his protest as a sad, flailing effort to justify his earlier error. "Science is only a highly sophisticated human tool," Ridgeway had noted, trying to help Feiner with his conscience.

As for the people in Los Angeles, it would be another hour before they would know whether this new piece of information was true. At the moment, most of them were still in shock from the effects of Violet's original strike at 5:17 that afternoon. Some were loudly mourning the loss of their homes, their families, their whole world. Others were too numbed to mourn and had fallen into the deep sleep of exhaustion. A very few had even begun to laugh at the

345

nearness of their own escapes, the way people in the back seat of a car sometimes give a nervous giggle when another car just misses sideswiping theirs.

Slowly, an uneasy calm settled over the city.

How long the calm would last was a question whose answer was known to only one source.

Violet.